D0293050

BEYOND THE THRESHOLD

FIC Mille

Miller, L.
Beyond the threshold.

PRICE: $9.89 (3710/af/ch)

Also available from MIRA Books and
LINDA LAEL MILLER

USED-TO-BE LOVERS
JUST KATE
WILD ABOUT HARRY
PART OF THE BARGAIN
ESCAPE FROM CABRIZ
RAGGED RAINBOWS
SNOWFLAKES ON THE SEA
GLORY, GLORY
MIXED MESSAGES
DARING MOVES
STATE SECRETS

48

LINDA LAEL MILLER

BEYOND THE THRESHOLD

INNISFIL PUBLIC LIBRARY
P.O. BOX 7049
INNISFIL, ON L9S 1A8

MIRA®

If you purchased this book without a cover you should be aware
that this book is stolen property. It was reported as "unsold and
destroyed" to the publisher, and neither the author nor the
publisher has received any payment for this "stripped book."

ISBN 1-55166-911-0

BEYOND THE THRESHOLD
Copyright © 2002 by MIRA Books.

THERE AND NOW
Copyright © 1992 by Linda Lael Miller.

HERE AND THEN
Copyright © 1992 by Linda Lael Miller.

All rights reserved. Except for use in any review, the reproduction or
utilization of this work in whole or in part in any form by any electronic,
mechanical or other means, now known or hereafter invented, including
xerography, photocopying and recording, or in any information storage or
retrieval system, is forbidden without the written permission of the publisher,
MIRA Books, 225 Duncan Mill Road, Don Mills, Ontario, Canada M3B 3K9.

All characters in this book have no existence outside the imagination of the
author and have no relation whatsoever to anyone bearing the same name
or names. They are not even distantly inspired by any individual known or
unknown to the author, and all incidents are pure invention.

MIRA and the Star Colophon are trademarks used under license and registered
in Australia, New Zealand, Philippines, United States Patent and Trademark
Office and in other countries.

Visit us at www.mirabooks.com

Printed in U.S.A.

TABLE OF CONTENTS

THERE AND NOW   9

HERE AND THEN   219

STATS

PINE RIVER, WASHINGTON 1892

Population: 300

4 saloons

1 U.S. Marshal

One-room schoolhouse

1 doctor—
Jonathan Fortner, M.D.

2 churches

3 livery stables

172 horses
(within the city limits)

PINE RIVER, WASHINGTON 1992

Population: 5,500

1 tavern/pool hall

5 full-time police officers

1 elementary school, 1 high school
and 1 junior college

15 physicians
and 1 hospital

6 churches

4 full-service filling stations

53 horses
(outside the city limits)

THERE AND NOW

For Darlene Layman, the best darn secretary ever,
and her very nice husband, Lloyd

CHAPTER 1

Elisabeth McCartney's flagging spirits lifted a little as she turned past the battered rural mailbox and saw the house again.

The white Victorian structure stood at the end of a long gravel driveway, flanked by apple trees in riotous pink-white blossom. A veranda stretched around the front and along one side, and wild rose bushes, budding scarlet and yellow, clambered up a trellis on the western wall.

Stopping her small station wagon in front of the garage, Elisabeth sighed and let her tired aquamarine eyes wander over the porch, with its sagging floor and peeling paint. Less than two years before, Aunt Verity would have been standing on the step, waiting with smiles and hugs. And Elisabeth's favorite cousin, Rue, would have vaulted over the porch railing to greet her.

Elisabeth's eyes brimmed with involuntary tears. Aunt Verity was dead now, and Rue was God only knew where, probably risking life and limb for some red-hot news story. The divorce from Ian, final for just a month, was a trauma Elisabeth was going to have to get through on her own.

With a sniffle, she squared her shoulders and drew a deep breath to bolster her courage. She reached for her purse and got out of the car, pulling her suitcase after her. Elisabeth had gladly let Ian keep their ultramodern plastic-and-smoked-glass furniture. Her books, tapes and other personal belongings would be delivered later by a moving company.

She slung her purse strap over her shoulder and proceeded toward the porch, the high grass brushing against the knees of her white jeans as she passed. At the door, with its inset of colorful stained glass, Elisabeth put down the suitcase and fumbled through her purse for the set of keys the real-estate agent had given her when she stopped in Pine River.

The lock was old and recalcitrant, but it turned, and Elisabeth opened the door and walked into the familiar entryway, lugging her suitcase with her.

There were those who believed this house was haunted—it had been the stuff of legend in and around Pine River for a hundred years—but for Elisabeth, it was a friendly place. It had been her haven since the summer she was fifteen, when her mother had died suddenly and her grieving, overwhelmed father had sent her here to stay with his somewhat eccentric widowed sister-in-law, Verity.

Inside, she leaned back against the sturdy door, remembering. Rue's wealthy parents had been divorced that same year, and Elisabeth's cousin had joined the fold. Verity Claridge, who told fabulous stories of ghosts and magic and people traveling back and forth between one century and another, had taken both girls in and simply loved them.

Elisabeth bit her lower lip and hoisted her slender frame away from the door. It was too much to hope, she thought with a beleaguered smile, that Aunt Verity might still be wandering these spacious rooms.

With a sigh, she hung her shoulder bag over the newel post at the base of the stairway and hoisted the suitcase. At the top of the stairs were three bedrooms, all on the right-hand side of the hallway. Elisabeth paused, looking curiously at the single door on the left-hand side and touched the doorknob.

Beyond that panel of wood was a ten-foot drop to the sun-porch roof. The sealed door had always fascinated both her and Rue, perhaps because Verity had told them such convincing stories about the world that lay on the other side of it.

Elisabeth smiled and shook her head, making her chin-length blond curls bounce around her face. "You may be gone, Auntie," she said softly, "but your fanciful influence lives on."

With that, Elisabeth opened the door on the opposite side of the hallway and stepped into the master suite that had always been Verity's. Although the rest of the house was badly in need of cleaning, the real-estate agent had sent a cleaning crew over in anticipation of Elisabeth's arrival to prepare the kitchen and one bedroom.

The big four-poster had been uncovered and polished, made up with the familiar crocheted ecru spread and pillow shams, and the scent of lemon furniture polish filled the air. Elisabeth laid the suitcase on the blue-velvet upholstered bench at the foot of the bed and tucked her hands into the back pockets of her jeans as she looked around the room.

The giant mahogany armoire stood between two floor-to-ceiling windows covered by billowing curtains of Nottingham lace, waiting to receive the few clothes Elisabeth had brought with her. A pair of Queen Anne chairs, upholstered in rich blue velvet, sat facing the little brick fireplace, and a chaise longue covered in cream-colored brocade graced the opposite wall. There was also a desk—Verity had called it a secretary—and a vanity table with a seat needle-pointed with pale roses.

Pushing her tousled tresses back from her face with both hands, Elisabeth went to the vanity and perched on the bench. A lump filled her throat as she recalled sitting here while Verity styled her hair for a summer dance.

With a hand that trembled slightly, Elisabeth opened the ivory-inlaid jewel box. Verity's favorite antique necklace, given to her by a friend, lay within.

Elisabeth frowned. *Odd,* she reflected. She'd thought Rue had taken the delicate filigree necklace, since she was the one who loved jewelry. Verity's modest estate—the house, furnishings, a few bangles and a small trust fund—had been left to Elisabeth and Rue in equal shares, and then the cousins had made divisions of their own.

Carefully, Elisabeth opened the catch and draped the necklace around her neck. She smiled sadly, recalling Verity's assertions that the pendant possessed some magical power.

Just then, the telephone rang, startling her even though the agent at the real-estate office had told her service had been connected and had given her the new number.

"Hello?" she said into the receiver of the French phone sitting on the vanity table.

"So you made it in one piece." The voice belonged to Janet Finch, one of Elisabeth's closest friends. She and Janet had taught together at Hillsdale Elementary School in nearby Seattle.

Elisabeth sagged a little as she gazed into the mirror. The necklace looked incongruous with her Seahawks sweatshirt. "You make it sound like I crawled here through a barrage of bullets," she replied. "I'm all right, Janet. Really."

Janet sighed. "Divorce is painful, even if it was your own idea," she insisted quietly. "I just think it would have been better if you'd stayed in Seattle, where your friends are. I mean, who do you know in that town now that your aunt is gone and Rue is off in South Africa or Eastern Europe or wherever she is?"

Through the windows, Elisabeth could see the neighbor's orchard. It was only too true that most of her friends had long since moved away from Pine River and her life had been in Seattle from the moment she'd married Ian. "I know myself," she answered. "And the Buzbee sisters."

Despite her obvious concerns, Janet laughed. Like Elisabeth, she was barely thirty, but she could be a real curmudgeon at times. "The Buzbee sisters? I don't think you've told me about them."

Elisabeth smiled. "Of course, I have. They live across the road. They're spinsters, but they're also card-carrying adventurers. According to Aunt Verity, they've been all over the world—they even did a joint hitch in the Peace Corps."

"Fascinating," Janet said, but Elisabeth couldn't tell whether she meant it or not.

"When you come down to visit, I'll introduce you," Elisabeth promised, barely stifling a yawn. Lately, she'd tired easily; the emotional stresses and strains of the past year were catching up with her.

"If that's an invitation, I'm grabbing it," Janet said

quickly. "I'll be down on Friday night to spend the weekend helping you settle in."

Elisabeth smiled, looking around the perfectly furnished room. There wasn't going to be a tremendous amount of "settling in" to do. And although she wanted to see Janet, she would have preferred to spend that first weekend alone, sorting through her thoughts and absorbing the special ambiance of Aunt Verity's house. "I'll make spaghetti and meatballs," she said, resigned. "Call me when you get to Pine River and I'll give you directions."

"I don't need directions," Janet pointed out reasonably. "You were married in that house, in case you've forgotten, and I was there." Her voice took on a teasing note. "You remember. Rue and I and two of your friends from college were all dressed alike, in floaty pink dresses and picture hats, and your cousin said it was a shame we couldn't sing harmony."

Elisabeth chuckled and closed her eyes. How she missed Rue, with her quick, lethal wit. She drew a deep breath, let it out, and made an effort to sound cheerful so Janet wouldn't worry about her any more than she already did. "I'll be looking for you on Friday, in time for dinner," Elisabeth said. And then, after quick good-byes, she hung up.

With a sigh of relief, Elisabeth crossed the room to the enormous bed, kicked off her sneakers and stretched out, her hands cupped behind her head. Looking up at the intricately crocheted canopy, she felt a sense of warm well-being wash over her.

She would make a list and shop for groceries later, she promised herself. Right now she needed to rest her eyes for a few moments.

She must have drifted off, because when the music awakened her, the spill of sunlight across the hooked rug beside the bed had receded and there was a slight chill in the air.

Music.

Elisabeth's heart surged into her throat as she sat up and looked around. There was no radio or TV in the room, and yet the distant, fairylike notes of a piano still teased her ears, accompanied by a child's voice.

"Twinkle, twinkle, little star
how I wonder what you are...."

Awkwardly, Elisabeth scrambled off the bed to pursue the sound, but it ceased when she reached the hallway.

All the same, she hurried downstairs.

The small parlor, where Aunt Verity's spinet was kept, was empty, and the piano itself was hidden beneath a large canvas dust cover. Feeling a headache begin to pulse beneath her right temple, Elisabeth checked the big, old-fashioned radio in the large parlor and the portable TV set on the kitchen counter.

Neither was on.

She shoved her hands through her already-mussed hair. Maybe her friends were right to be concerned. Maybe the divorce was affecting her more deeply than she'd ever guessed.

The thing to do, she decided after a five-minute struggle to regain her composure, was to get her purse and drive into Pine River for groceries. Since she'd left her shoes behind, she started up the rear stairway.

An instant after Elisabeth reached the second floor, the piano music sounded clearly again, thunderous and discordant. She froze, her fingers closed around Aunt Verity's pendant.

"I don't want to practice anymore," a child's voice said petulantly. "It's sunny out, and Vera and I are having a picnic by the creek."

Elisabeth closed her eyes, battling to retain her equilibrium. The voice, like the music, was coming from the other side of the door Aunt Verity had told so many stories about.

As jarring as the experience was, Elisabeth had no sense of evil. It was her own mental state she feared, not the ghosts that supposedly populated this old house. Perhaps in her case, the result of a broken dream had been a broken mind.

She walked slowly along the highway, gripped the doorknob and rattled it fiercely. The effort to open the door was hopeless, since the passage had been sealed long ago, but Elisabeth didn't let up. "Who's there?" she cried.

She wasn't crazy. Someone, somewhere, was playing a cruel joke on her.

Finally exhausted, she released her desperate hold on the knob, and asked again plaintively, "Please. Who's there?"

"Just us, dear," said a sweet feminine voice from the top of the main stairway. The music had died away to an echo that Elisabeth thought probably existed only in her mind.

She turned, a wan smile on her face, to see the Buzbee sisters, Cecily and Roberta, standing nearby.

Roberta, the taller and more outgoing of the two, was holding a covered baking dish and frowning. "Are you quite all right, Elisabeth?" she asked.

Cecily was watching Elisabeth with enormous blue eyes. "That door led to the old part of the house," she said. "The section that was burned away in 1892."

Elisabeth felt foolish, having been caught trying to open a door to nowhere. She managed another smile and said, "Miss Cecily, Miss Roberta—it's so good to see you."

"We've brought Cecily's beef casserole," Roberta said, practical as ever. "Sister and I thought you wouldn't want to cook, this being your first night in the house."

"Thank you," Elisabeth said shakily. "Would you like some coffee? I think there might be a jar of instant in one of the cupboards...."

"We wouldn't *think* of intruding," said Miss Cecily.

Elisabeth led the way toward the rear stairway, hoping her gait seemed steady to the elderly women behind her. "You wouldn't be intruding," she insisted. "It's a delight to see you, and it was so thoughtful of you to bring the casserole."

From the size of the dish, Elisabeth figured she'd be able to live on the offering for a week. The prospective monotony of eating the same thing over and over didn't trouble her; her appetite was small these days, and what she ate didn't matter.

In the kitchen, Elisabeth found a jar of coffee, probably left behind by Rue, who liked to hole up in the house every once in a while when she was working on a big story. While water was heating in a copper kettle on the stove, Elisabeth sat at the old oak table in the breakfast nook, talking with the Buzbee sisters.

She neatly skirted the subject of her divorce, and the sisters were too well-mannered to pursue it. The conversation centered on the sisters' delight at seeing the old house occupied again. Through all of it, the child's voice and the music drifted in Elisabeth's mind, like wisps of a half-forgotten dream. *Twinkle, twinkle...*

Trista Fortner's small, slender fingers paused on the piano keys. Somewhere upstairs, a door rattled hard on its hinges. "Who's there?" a feminine voice called over the tremendous racket.

Trista got up from the piano bench, smoothed her freshly ironed poplin pinafore and scrambled up the front stairs and along the hallway.

The door of her bedroom was literally clattering in its frame, the knob twisting wildly, and Trista's brown eyes went wide. She was too scared to scream and too curious to run away, so she just stood there, staring.

The doorknob ceased its frantic gyrations, and the woman spoke again, "Please. Who's there?"

"Trista," the child said softly. She found the courage to touch the knob, to twist her wrist. Soon, she was peering around the edge.

There was nothing at all to see, except for her bed, her dollhouse, the doorway that led to her own private staircase leading into the kitchen and the big, wooden wardrobe that held her clothes.

At once disappointed and relieved, the eight-year-old closed the door again and trooped staunchly back downstairs to the piano.

She sighed as she settled down at the keyboard again. If she mentioned what she'd heard and seen to Papa, would he believe her? The answer was definitely no, since he was a man of science. He would set her down in his study and say,

"Now, Trista, we've discussed this before. I know you'd like to convince yourself that your mother could come back to us, but there are no such things as ghosts. I don't want to hear any more of this foolishness from you. Is that clear?"

She began to play again, dutifully. Forlornly.

A few minutes later, Trista glanced at the clock on the parlor mantel. Still half an hour left to practice, then she could go outside and play with Vera. She'd tell her best friend there was a ghost in her house, she supposed, but only after making her swear to keep quiet about it.

On the other hand, maybe it would be better if she didn't say anything at all to anybody. Even Vera would think Trista was hearing things just because she wanted her mama to come back.

"Twinkle, twinkle," she muttered, as her fingers moved awkwardly over the keys.

"My, yes," Roberta Buzbee went on, dusting nonexistent crumbs from the bosom of her colorful jersey print dress. "Mama was just a little girl when this house burned."

"She was nine," Miss Cecily put in solemnly. She shuddered. "It was a dreadful blaze. The doctor and his poor daughter perished in it, you know. And, of course, that part of the house was never rebuilt."

Elisabeth swallowed painfully, thinking of the perfectly ordinary music she'd heard—and the voice. "So there was a child," she mused.

"Certainly," Roberta volunteered. "Her name was Trista Anne Fortner, and she was Mama's very best friend. They were close in age, you know, Mama being a few months older." She paused to make a tsk-tsk sound. "It was positively tragic—Dr. Fortner expired trying to save his little girl. It was said the companion set the fire—she was tried for murder and hanged, wasn't she, Sister?"

Cecily nodded solemnly.

A chill moved through Elisabeth, despite the sunny warmth of that April afternoon, and she took a steadying sip from her coffee cup. *Get a grip, Elisabeth,* she thought, giving herself an inward shake. *Whatever you heard, it wasn't a dead child singing and playing the piano. Aunt Verity's stories about this house were exactly that—stories.*

"You look pale, my dear," Cecily piped up.

The last thing Elisabeth needed was another person to worry about her. Her friends in Seattle were doing enough of that. "I'll be teaching at the Pine River school this fall," she announced, mainly to change the subject.

"Roberta taught at the old Cold Creek schoolhouse," Cecily said proudly, pleased to find some common ground, "and I was the librarian in town. That was before we went traveling, of course."

Before Elisabeth could make a response, someone slammed a pair of fists down hard on the keys of a piano.

This time, there was no possibility that the sound was imaginary. It reverberated through the house, and both the Buzbee sisters flinched.

Very slowly, Elisabeth set her coffee cup on the counter. "Excuse me," she said when she was able to break the spell. The spinet in the parlor was still draped, and there was no sign of anyone.

"It's the ghost," said Cecily, who had followed Elisabeth from the kitchen, along with her sister. "After all this time, she's still here. Well, I shouldn't wonder."

Elisabeth thought again of the stories Aunt Verity had told her and Rue, beside the fire on rainy nights. They'd been strange tales of appearances and disappearances and odd sounds, and Rue and Elisabeth had never passed them on because they were afraid their various parents would refuse to let them go on spending their summers with Verity. The thought of staying in their boarding schools year round had been unbearable.

"Ghost?" Elisabeth croaked.

Cecily was nodding. "Trista has never rested properly, poor child. And they say the doctor looks for her still. Folks have seen his buggy along the road, too."

Elisabeth suppressed a shudder.

"Sister," Roberta interceded somewhat sharply. "You're upsetting Elisabeth."

"I'm fine," Elisabeth lied. "Just fine."

"Maybe we'd better be going," said Cecily, patting Elisabeth's arm. "And don't worry about poor little Trista. She's quite harmless, you know."

The moment the two women were gone, Elisabeth hurried to the old-fashioned black telephone on the entryway table and dialed Rue's number in Chicago.

An answering machine picked up on the third ring. "Hi, there, whoever you are," Rue's voice said energetically. "I'm away on a special project, and I'm not sure how long I'll be gone this time. If you're planning to rob my condo, please be sure to take the couch. If not, leave your name and number and I'll get in touch with you as soon as I can. Ciao, and don't forget to wait for the beep."

Elisabeth's throat was tight; even though she'd known Rue was probably away, she'd hoped, by some miraculous accident, to catch her cousin between assignments. "Hi, Rue," she said. "It's Beth. I've moved into the house and—well— I'd just like to talk, that's all. Could you call as soon as you get in?" Elisabeth recited the number and hung up.

She pushed up the sleeves of her shirt and started for the kitchen. Earlier, she'd seen cleaning supplies in the broom closet, and heaven knew, the place needed some attention.

Jonathan Fortner rubbed the aching muscles at his nape with one hand as he walked wearily through the darkness toward the lighted house. His medical bag seemed heavier than usual as he mounted the back steps and opened the door.

The spacious kitchen was empty, though a lantern glowed in the center of the red-and-white-checked tablecloth.

Jonathan set his bag on a shelf beside the door, hung up his hat, shrugged out of his suitcoat and loosened his string tie. Sheer loneliness ached in his middle as he crossed the room to the stove with its highly polished chrome.

His dinner was congealing in the warming oven, as usual. Jonathan unfastened his cuff links, dropped them into the

pocket of his trousers and rolled up his sleeves. Then, taking
a kettle from the stove, he poured hot water into a basin,
added two dippers of cold from the bucket beside the sink
and began scrubbing his hands with strong yellow soap.

"Papa?"

He turned with a weary smile to see Trista standing at the
bottom of the rear stairway, wearing her nightgown. "Hello,
Punkin," he said. A frown furrowed his brow. "Ellen's here,
isn't she? You haven't been home alone all this time?"

Trista resembled him instead of Barbara, with her dark hair
and gray eyes, and it was a mercy not to be reminded of his
wife every time he looked at his daughter.

"Ellen had to go home after supper," Trista said, drawing
back a chair and joining Jonathan at the table as he sat down
to eat. "Her brother Billy came to get her. Said the cows got
out."

Jonathan's jawline tightened momentarily. "I don't know
how many times I've told that girl..."

Trista laughed and reached out to cover his hand with her
own. "I'm big enough to be alone for a few hours, Papa,"
she said.

Jonathan dragged his fork through the lumpy mashed potatoes on his plate and sighed. "You're eight years old," he
reminded her.

"Maggie Simpkins is eight, too, and she cooks for her father and all her brothers."

"And she's more like an old woman than a child," Jonathan said quietly. It seemed he saw elderly children every day,
though God knew things were better here in Pine River than
in the cities. "You just leave the housekeeping to Ellen and
concentrate on being a little girl. You'll be a woman soon
enough."

Trista looked pointedly at the scorched, shriveled food on
her father's plate. "If you want to go on eating that awful
stuff, it's your choice." She sighed, set her elbows on the
table's edge and cupped her chin in her palms. "Maybe you
should get married again, Papa."

Jonathan gave up on his dinner and pushed the plate away.

Just the suggestion filled him with loneliness—and fear. "And maybe you should get back to bed," he said brusquely, avoiding Trista's eyes while he took his watch from his vest pocket and frowned at the time. "It's late."

His daughter sighed again, collected his plate and scraped the contents into the scrap pan for the neighbor's pigs. "Is it because you still love Mama that you don't want to get another wife?" Trista inquired.

Jonathan went to the stove for a mug of Ellen's coffee, which had all the pungency of paint solvent. There were a lot of things he hadn't told Trista about her mother, and one of them was that there had never really been any love between the two of them. Another was that Barbara hadn't died in a distant accident, she'd deliberately abandoned her husband and child. Jonathan had gone quietly to Olympia and petitioned the state legislature for a divorce. "Wives aren't like wheelbarrows and soap flakes, Trista," he said hoarsely. "You can't just go to the mercantile and buy one."

"There are plenty of ladies in Pine River who are sweet on you," Trista insisted. Maybe she was only eight, but at times she had the forceful nature of a dowager duchess. "Miss Jinnie Potts, for one."

Jonathan turned to face his daughter, his cup halfway to his lips, his gaze stern. "To bed, Trista," he said firmly.

She scampered across the kitchen in a flurry of dark hair and flannel and threw her arms around his middle. "Good night, Papa," she said, squeezing him, totally disarming him in that way that no other female could. "I love you."

He bent to kiss the top of her head. "I love you, too," he said, his voice gruff.

Trista gave him one last hug, then turned and hurried up the stairs. Without her, the kitchen was cold and empty again.

Jonathan poured his coffee into the iron sink and reached out to turn down the wick on the kerosene lantern standing in the center of the table. Instantly, the kitchen was black with gloom, but Jonathan's steps didn't falter as he crossed the room and started up the stairs.

He'd been finding his way in the dark for a long time.

Apple-blossom petals blew against the dark sky like snow as Elisabeth pulled into her driveway early that evening, after making a brief trip to Pine River. Her khaki skirt clung to her legs as she hurried to carry in four paper bags full of groceries.

She had just completed the second trip when a crash of thunder shook the windows in their sturdy sills and lightning lit the kitchen.

Methodically, Elisabeth put her food away in the cupboards and the refrigerator, trying to ignore the sounds of the storm. Although she wasn't exactly afraid of noisy weather, it always left her feeling unnerved.

She had just put a portion of the Buzbee sisters' casserole in the oven and was preparing to make a green salad when the telephone rang. "Hello," she said, balancing the receiver between her ear and shoulder so that she could go on with her work.

"Hello, darling," her father said in his deep and always slightly distracted voice. "How's my baby?"

Elisabeth smiled and scooped chopped tomatoes into the salad bowl. "I'm fine, Daddy. Where are you?"

He chuckled ruefully. "You know what they say—if it's Wednesday, this must be Cleveland. I'm on another business trip."

That was certainly nothing new. Marcus Claridge had been on the road ever since he had started his consulting business when Elisabeth was little. "How are Traci and the baby?" she asked. Just eighteen months before Marcus had married a woman three years younger than Elisabeth, and the couple had an infant son.

"They're terrific," Marcus answered awkwardly, then cleared his throat. "Listen, I know you're having a rough time right now, sweetheart, and Traci and I were thinking that... well...maybe you'd like to come to Lake Tahoe and spend the summer with us. I don't like to think of you burrowed down in that spooky old house...."

Elisabeth laughed, and the sound was tinged with hysteria. She didn't dislike Traci, who invariably dotted the *i* at the end of her name with a little heart, but she didn't want to spend so much as an hour trying to make small talk with the woman, either. "Daddy, this house isn't spooky. I love the place, you know that. Who told you I was here, anyway?"

Her father sighed. "Ian. He's very worried about you, darling. We all are. You don't have a job. You don't know a soul in that backwoods town. What do you intend to do with yourself?"

She smiled. Trust Ian to make it sound as if she were hiding out in a cave and licking her wounds. "I've been substitute teaching for the past year, Daddy, and I *do* have a job. I'll be in charge of the third grade at Pine River Elementary starting in early September. In the meantime, I plan to put in a garden, do some reading and sewing—"

"What you need is another man."

Elisabeth rolled her eyes. "Even better, I could just step in front of a speeding truck and break every bone in my body," she replied. "That would be quicker and not as messy."

"Very funny," Marcus said, but there was a grudging note of amused respect in his tone. "All right, baby, I'll leave you alone. Just promise me that you'll take care of yourself and that you'll call and leave word with Traci if you need anything."

"I promise," Elisabeth said.

"Good."

"I love you, Daddy—"

The line went dead before Elisabeth had completed the sentence. "Say hello to Traci and the baby for me," she finished aloud as she replaced the receiver.

After supper, Elisabeth washed her dishes. By then, the power was flickering on and off, and the wind was howling around the corners of the house. She decided to go to bed early so she could get a good start on the cleaning come morning.

Since she'd showered before going to town, Elisabeth simply exchanged her skirt and blouse for an oversize red football jersey, washed her face, scrubbed her teeth and went to bed. Her hand curved around the delicate pendant on Aunt Verity's necklace as she settled back against her pillows.

Lightning filled the room with an eerie light, but Elisabeth felt safe in the big four-poster. How many nights had she and Rue come squealing and giggling to this bed, squeezing in on either side of Aunt Verity to beg her for a story that would distract them from the thunder?

She snuggled down between crisp, clean sheets, closed her eyes and sighed. She'd been right to come back here; this was home, the place where she belonged.

The scream brought her eyes flying open again.

"Papa!"

Elisabeth bolted out of bed and ran into the hallway. Another shriek sounded, followed by choked sobs.

It wasn't the noise that paralyzed Elisabeth, however; it was the thin line of golden light glowing underneath the door across the hall. That door that opened onto empty space.

She leaned against the jamb, one trembling hand resting on the necklace, as though to conjure Aunt Verity for a rescuer. "Papa, Papa, where are you?" the child cried desperately from the other side.

Elisabeth pried herself away from the woodwork and took one step across the hallway, then another. She found the knob, and the sound of her own heartbeat thrumming in her ears all but drowned out the screams of the little girl as she turned it.

Even when the door actually opened, Elisabeth expected to be hit with a rush of rainy April wind. The soft warmth that greeted her instead came as a much keener shock.

"My God," she whispered as her eyes adjusted to a candle-lit room where there should have been nothing but open air.

She saw the child, curled up at the very top of a narrow bed. Then she saw what must be a dollhouse, another door and a big, old-fashioned wardrobe. As she stood there on the threshold of a world that couldn't possibly exist, the little girl moved, her form illuminated by the light that glowed from an elaborate china lamp on the bedside table.

"You're not Papa," the child said with a cautious sniffle, edging farther back against the intricately carved headboard.

Elisabeth swallowed. "N-no," she allowed, extending one toe to test the floor. Even now, with this image in front of her, complete in every detail, her five senses were telling her that if she stepped into the room, she would plummet onto the sunporch roof and break numerous bones.

The little girl dragged the flannel sleeve of her nightgown across her face and sniffled again. "Papa's probably in the barn. The animals get scared when there's a storm."

Elisabeth hugged herself, squeezed her eyes tightly shut and stepped over the threshold, fully prepared for a plunge. Instead, she felt a smooth wooden floor beneath her feet. It seemed to her that "Papa" might have been more concerned about a frightened daughter than frightened animals, but then, since she had to be dreaming the entire episode, that point was purely academic.

"You're the lady, aren't you?" the child asked, drawing her knees up under the covers and wrapping small arms around them. "The one who rattled the doorknob and called out."

This isn't happening, Elisabeth thought, running damp palms down her thighs. *I'm having an out-of-body experience or something.* "Y-yes," she stammered after a long pause. "I guess that was me."

"I'm Trista," the girl announced. Her hair was a dark, rich color, her eyes a stormy gray. She settled comfortably against her pillows, folding her arms.

Trista. The doctor's daughter, the child who died horribly in a raging house fire some seventy years before Elisabeth was even born. "Oh, my God," she whispered again.

"You keep saying that," Trista remarked, sounding a little critical. "It's not truly proper to take the Lord's name in vain, you know."

Elisabeth swallowed hard. "I k-know. I'm sorry."

"It would be perfectly all right to give me yours, however."

"What?"

"Your name, goose," Trista said good-naturedly.

"Elisabeth. Elisabeth McCartney—no relation to the Beatle." As she spoke, Elisabeth was taking in the frilly chintz curtains at the window, the tiny shingles on the roof of the dollhouse.

Trista wrinkled her nose. "Why would you be related to a bug?"

Elisabeth would have laughed if she hadn't been so busy questioning her sanity. *I refuse to have a breakdown over you, Ian McCartney,* she vowed silently. *I didn't love you that much.* "Never mind. It's just that there's somebody famous who has the same last name as I do."

Trista smoothed the colorful patchwork quilt that covered her. "Which are you?" she demanded bluntly. "My guardian angel, or just a regular ghost?"

Now Elisabeth did laugh. "Is there such a thing as a 'regular ghost'?" she asked, venturing farther into the room and sitting down on the end of Trista's bed. At the moment, she didn't trust her knees to hold her up. "I'm neither one of those things, Trista. You're looking at an ordinary, flesh-and-blood woman."

Trista assessed Elisabeth's football jersey with a puzzled expression. "Is that your nightdress? I've never seen one quite like it."

"Yes, this is my—nightdress." Elisabeth felt light-headed and wondered if she would wake up with her face in the rain gutter that lined the sun-porch roof. She ran one hand over the high-quality workmanship of the quilt. If this was an hallucination, she reflected, it was a remarkably vivid one. "Go to sleep now, Trista. I'm sure it's very late."

Thunder shook the room and Trista shivered visibly. "I won't be able to sleep unless I get some hot milk," she said, watching Elisabeth with wide, hopeful eyes.

Elisabeth fought an urge to enfold the child in her arms, to beg her to run away from this strange house and never, ever return. She stood, the fingers of her right hand fidgeting with the necklace. "I'll go and make some for you." She started back toward the door, but Trista stopped her.

"It's that way, Elisabeth," she said, pointing toward the inner door. "I have my own special stairway."

"This is getting weirder and weirder," Elisabeth muttered, careful not to stub her toe on the massive dollhouse as she crossed to the other door and opened it. "Let's see just how far this delusion goes," she added, finding herself at the top of a rear stairway. Her heart pounded so hard, she thought she'd faint as she made her way carefully down to the lower floor.

She wouldn't have recognized the kitchen, it was so much bigger than the one she knew. A single kerosene lantern burned in the center of the oak table, sending up a quivering trail of sooty smoke. There were built-in cabinets and bins along one wall, and the refrigerator and the stove were gone. In their places were an old-fashioned wooden icebox and an enormous iron-and-chrome monster designed to burn wood. The only thing that looked familiar was the back stairway leading into the main hallway upstairs.

Elisabeth stood in the middle of the floor, holding herself together by sheer force of will. "This is a dream, Beth," she told herself aloud, grasping the brass latch on the door of the icebox and giving it a cautious wrench. "Relax. This is *only a dream.*"

The door opened and she bent, squinting, to peer inside. Fortunately, the milk was at the front, in a heavy crockery pitcher.

Elisabeth took the pitcher out of the icebox, closed the door with a distracted motion of one heel and scanned the dimly lit room again. "Wait till you tell Rue about this," she chattered on, mostly in an effort to comfort herself. "She'll want to do a documentary about you. You'll make the cover of the *Enquirer,* and tabloid TV will have a heyday—"

"Who the hell are you?"

The question came from behind her, blown in on a wet-and-frigid wind. Elisabeth whirled, still clutching the pitcher of cream-streaked milk to her bosom, and stared into the furious gray eyes of a man she had never seen before.

A strange sensation of being wrenched toward him spiritually compounded Elisabeth's shock.

He was tall, close to six feet, with rain-dampened dark hair and shoulders that strained the fabric of his suitcoat. He wore a vest with a gold watch chain dangling from one pocket, and his odd, stiff collar was open.

For some confounding reason, Elisabeth found herself wanting to touch him—tenderly at first, and then with the sweet, dizzying fury of passion.

She gave herself an inward shake. "This is really authentic," Elisabeth said. "I hope I'll be able to remember it all."

The stranger approached and took the endangered pitcher from Elisabeth's hands, setting it aside on the table. His eyes raked her figure, taking in every fiber of the long football jersey that served as her favorite nightgown, leaving gentle fire in their wake.

"I asked you a question," he snapped. "Who the devil are you?"

Elisabeth gave an hysterical little burst of laughter. The guy was a spirit—or more likely a delusion—and she felt a staggering attraction to him. She *must* be 'round the bend. "Who I am isn't the question at all," she answered intractably. "The question is, are you a ghost or am *I* a ghost?" She paused and spread her hands, reasoning that there was no sense in fighting the dream. "I mean, who ya gonna call?"

The man standing before her—Elisabeth could only assume he was the "Papa" Trista had been screaming for—puckered his brow in consternation. Then he felt her forehead with the backs of four cool fingers.

His touch heated Elisabeth's skin and sent a new shock splintering through her, and Elisabeth fairly leapt backward. Hoping it would carry her home to the waking world, like some talisman, she brought the pendant from beneath her shirt and traced its outline with her fingers.

"What is your name?" the man repeated patiently, as though speaking to an imbecile.

Elisabeth resisted an impulse to make a suitable noise with a finger and her lower lip and smiled instead. She had a drunken feeling, but she assured herself that she was bound to wake up any minute now. "Elisabeth McCartney. What's yours?"

"Dr. Jonathan Fortner," was the pensive answer. His steely eyes dropped to the pendant she was fiddling with and went wide. In the next instant, before Elisabeth had had a chance even to brace herself, he'd gripped the necklace and ripped it from her throat. "Where did you get this?" he demanded, his voice a terrifying rasp.

Elisabeth stepped back again. Dream or no dream, she'd felt the pull of the chain against her nape, and she was afraid of the suppressed violence she sensed in this man. "It—it belonged to my aunt—and now it belongs to my cousin and me." She gathered every shred of courage she possessed just to keep from cowering before this man. "If you'll just give it back, please...."

"You're a liar," Dr. Fortner spat out, dropping the necklace into the pocket of his coat. "This pendant was my wife's—it's been in her family for generations."

Elisabeth wet her lips with the tip of her tongue. This whole experience, whatever it was, was getting totally out of hand. "Perhaps it belonged to your—your wife at one time," she managed nervously, "but it's mine now. Mine and my cousin's." She held out one palm. "I want it back."

He looked at her hand as though he might spit in it, then pressed her into a chair. Her knees were like jelly, and she couldn't be sure whether this was caused by her situation or the primitive, elemental tug she felt toward this man.

"Papa?" Trista called from upstairs.

Dr. Fortner's lethal glance followed the sound. He stood stock still for a long moment, then shrugged out of his coat and hung it from a peg beside the door. "Everything is all right," he called back. "Go to sleep."

Elisabeth swallowed the growing lump in her throat and started to rise from the chair. At one quelling glance from Dr. Fortner, however, she thought better of it and sank back to her seat. She watched with rounded eyes as her reluctant host sat down across from her.

"Who are you?" he asked sternly.

He was a remarkable man, ruggedly handsome and yet polished, in a Victorian sort of way. The sort Elisabeth had fantasized about since puberty.

She tried to keep her voice even and her manner calm. ''I told you. I'm Elisabeth McCartney.''

''All right, Elisabeth McCartney—what are you doing here, dressed in that crazy getup, and why were you wearing my wife's necklace?''

''I was—well, I don't know what I'm doing here, actually. Maybe I'm dreaming, maybe I'm a hologram or an astral projection....''

His dark eyebrows drew together for a moment. ''A what?''

She sighed. ''Either I'm dreaming or you are. Or maybe both of us. In any case, I think I need Aunt Verity's necklace to get back where I belong.''

''Then it looks like you won't be going anywhere for a while. And I, for one, am not dreaming.''

Elisabeth gazed into his hard, autocratic face. Doubtless, the pop-psychology gurus would have something disturbing to say about the irrefutable appeal this man held for her. ''You're probably right. I don't see how you could possibly have the sensitivity to dream. Alan Alda, you definitely aren't. It must be me.''

''Papa, is Elisabeth still here?''

The doctor's eyes scoured Elisabeth, then softened slightly. ''Yes, Punkin, she's still here.''

''She was going to bring me some warm milk,'' Trista persisted.

Jonathan glowered at Elisabeth for a moment, then gestured toward the pitcher. She stumbled out of her chair and proceeded to the wall of cupboards where, with some effort, she located a store of mugs and a small pan.

She poured milk into the kettle, shaking so hard, it was a wonder she didn't spill the stuff all over the floor, and set it on the stove to heat. She glanced toward the doctor's coat, hanging nearby on a peg, and gauged her chances of getting the necklace without his noticing.

They didn't seem good.

''If you want that milk to heat, you'll have to stoke up the fire,'' he said.

Elisabeth stiffened. The stove had all kinds of lids and doors, but she had no idea how to reach in and ''stoke'' the flames to life. And she really didn't want to bend over in her nightshirt. "Maybe you could do that," she said.

He took a chunk of wood from a crude box beside the stove, opened a little door in the front and shoved it inside. Then he reached for a poker that rested against the wall and jabbed at the embers and the wood until a snapping blaze flared up.

Elisabeth, feeling as stirred and warm as the coals at the base of the rejuvenated fire, lifted her chin to let him know she wasn't impressed and waited for the milk to heat.

Dr. Fortner regarded Elisabeth steadily. "I'm sure you're some kind of lunatic," he said reasonably, "though I'll be damned if I can figure out how you ended up in Pine River. In any case, you'll have to spend the night. I'll turn you over to the marshal in the morning."

Elisabeth was past wondering when this nightmare was going to end. "You'd actually keep me here all night? I'm a lunatic, remember? I could take an ax and chop you to bits while you sleep. Or put lye down your well."

By way of an answer, he strode across the room, snatched the pan from the stove and poured the milk into a mug. Then, after setting the kettle in the sink, he grasped Elisabeth's elbow in one hand and the cup in the other and started toward the stairs, stopping only to blow out the lamp.

The suitcoat, Elisabeth noticed, was left behind, on its peg next to the door.

He hustled Elisabeth through the darkness and up the steep, narrow, enclosed staircase ahead of him. Her knees trembled with a weird sort of excitement as she hustled along. "I'm not crazy, you know," she insisted, sounding a little breathless.

He opened the door to Trista's room and carried the milk inside, only to find his daughter sleeping soundly, a big, yellow-haired rag doll clutched in her arms.

A fond smile touched Jonathan Fortner's sensual mouth, and he bent to kiss the child lightly on the forehead. Then, after setting the unneeded milk on the bedstand, he motioned for Elisabeth to precede him into the hallway.

The fact that she'd originally entered the Twilight Zone from that door was not lost on Elisabeth. She rushed eagerly through it, certain she'd awaken on the other side in her own bed.

Instead, she found herself in a hallway that was familiar and yet startlingly different from the one she knew. There was a painted china lamp burning on a table, and grim photographs stuck out from the walls, their wire hangers visible. The patterned runner on the floor was one Elisabeth had never seen before.

"It must have been the beef casserole," she said.

Dr. Fortner gave her a look and propelled her down the hall to the room next to the one she was supposed to be sleeping in. "Get some rest, Miss McCartney. And remember—if you get up and start wandering around, I'll hear you."

"And do what?" Elisabeth said as she pushed open the door and stepped into a shadowy room. In the real world, it would be the one she and Rue had always shared during their visits.

"And lock you in the pantry for the rest of the night," he replied flatly.

Even though the room was almost totally dark, Elisabeth knew the doctor wasn't kidding. He *would* lock her in the pantry, like a prisoner. But then, all of this was only happening in her imagination anyway.

He pulled back some covers on a bed and guided her into it, and Elisabeth went without a struggle, pursued by odd and erotic thoughts of him joining her. None of this was like her at all; Ian had always complained that she wasn't passionate enough. She decided to simply close her eyes and put the whole crazy episode out of her mind. In the morning, she would wake up in her own bed.

"Good night," Dr. Fortner said. The timbre of his voice was rich and deep, and he smelled of rain and horses and pipe tobacco.

Elisabeth felt a deep physical stirring, but she knew nothing was going to come of it because, unfortunately, this wasn't that kind of dream. "Good night," she responded in a dutiful tone.

She lay wide awake for a long time, listening. Somewhere in the room, a clock was ticking, and rain pattered against the window. She heard a door open and close, and she imagined Dr. Fortner taking off his clothes. He'd do it methodically, with a certain rough, masculine grace.

Elisabeth closed her eyes firmly, but the intriguing images

remained and her body began to throb. "Good grief, woman," she muttered, "this is a *dream*. Do you realize what Rue will say when she hears about this—and I know you'll be fool enough to tell her, too—she'll say, 'Get a life Bethie. Better yet, get a shrink.'"

She waited for a long time, then crept out of bed, grimacing as she opened the door. Fortunately, it didn't squeak on its hinges nor did the floorboards creak. Holding her breath, Elisabeth groped her way down the hall in the direction of the main staircase.

So much for your threats, Dr. Fortner, she thought smugly as she hurried through the large parlor and the dining room.

In the kitchen, she stubbed her toe trying to find the matches on the table and cried out in pain before she could stop herself. The fire was out in the stove and the room was cold.

Elisabeth snatched the coat from the peg and pulled it on, cowering in the shadows by the cabinets as she waited for Jonathan Fortner to storm in and follow up on his threat to lock her in the pantry.

When an estimated ten minutes had ticked past and he still hadn't shown up, Elisabeth came out of hiding, her fingers curved around the broken necklace in the coat's pocket. Slowly, carefully, she crept up the smaller of the two stairways and into Trista's room.

There she stood beside the bed for a moment, seeing quite clearly now that her eyes had adjusted again, looking down at the sleeping child. Trista was beautiful and so very much alive. Tears lined Elisabeth's lashes as she thought of all this little girl would miss by dying young.

She bent and kissed Trista's pale forehead, then crossed the room to the other door, the one she'd unwittingly stumbled through hours before. Eyes closed tightly, fingers clutching the necklace, she turned the knob and stepped over the threshold.

For almost a full minute she just stood there in the hallway, trembling, afraid to open her eyes. It was the feel of plush carpeting under her bare feet that finally alerted her to the fact that the dream was over and she was back in the real world.

Elisabeth began to sob softly for joy and relief. And maybe because she missed a man who didn't exist. When she'd regained some of her composure, she opened the door of her own room, stepped inside and flipped the switch. Light flooded the chamber, revealing the four-poster, the fireplace, the vanity, the Queen Anne chairs.

Suddenly, Elisabeth was desperately tired. She switched off the lights, stumbled to the bed and fell onto it face first.

When she awakened, the room was flooded with sunlight and her nose itched. Elisabeth sat up, pushing back her hair with one hand and trying to focus her eyes.

The storm was over, and she smiled. Maybe she'd take a long walk after breakfast and clear her head. That crazy dream she'd had the night before had left her with a sort of emotional hangover, and she needed fresh air.

She was passing the vanity table on her way to the bathroom when her image in the mirror stopped her where she stood. Shock washed over her as she stared, her eyes enormous, her mouth wide open.

She was wearing a man's suitcoat.

Her knees began to quiver and for a moment, she thought she'd be sick right where she stood. She collapsed onto the vanity bench and covered her face with both hands, peeking through her fingers at her reflection.

"It wasn't a dream," she whispered, hardly able to believe the words. She ran one hand down the rough woolen sleeve of the old-fashioned coat. "I was really there."

For a moment, the room dipped and swayed, and Elisabeth was sure she was going to faint. She pushed the bench back from the table and bent to put her head between her knees. "Don't swoon, Beth," she lectured herself. "There's a perfectly logical explanation for this. Okay, it beats the hell out of me what it could be, but there *is* an answer!"

Once she was sure she wasn't going to pass out, Elisabeth sat up again and drew measured breaths until she had achieved a reasonable sense of calm. She stared at her pale face in the mirror and at her startled blue eyes. But mostly she stared at Dr. Jonathan Fortner's coat.

She put her hand into the right pocket and found the necklace. Slowly lifting it out, she spread it gently on the vanity table. The necklace was broken near the catch, but the pendant was unharmed.

Elisabeth pulled in a deep breath, let it out slowly. Then, calmly, she stood up, removed Dr. Fortner's coat and proceeded into the bathroom.

During her shower and shampoo, she almost succeeded in convincing herself that she'd imagined the suitcoat as well as the broken necklace. But when she came out, wrapped in a towel, they were where she'd left them, silent proof that something very strange had happened to her.

With a lift of her chin, Elisabeth dressed in gray corduroy slacks and a raspberry sweater, then carefully blew her hair dry and styled it. She took the necklace with her when she went out of the room, but left the suitcoat behind.

In the hallway, her eyes locked on the door across the hall. She tried the knob, but it was rusted in place, and the plastic seal that surrounded the passage was unbroken.

"Trista?" she whispered.

There was no answer.

Elisabeth went slowly down the back staircase, recalling that there had been two of them in her "dream." She ate cereal, coffee and fruit while staring at the kitchen table, fetched her purse, got into her car and drove slowly along the puddled driveway toward the main road.

The house still needed cleaning, but Elisabeth's priorities had been altered slightly. Before she did anything else, she meant to have the necklace repaired.

CHAPTER 3

"It should be ready by Friday morning," said the clerk in Pine River's one and only jewelry store, dropping Aunt Verity's necklace into a small brown envelope.

Elisabeth felt oddly deflated. She didn't know what was happening to her, but she suspected that the antique pendant was at the core of things, given Aunt Verity's stories, and she didn't want to let it out of her sight. "Thank you," she said with a sigh, and left the shop.

After doing a little more shopping at the supermarket, she drove staunchly back to the house, changed into old clothes, covered her hair with a bandanna and set to work dusting and sweeping and scrubbing.

She'd finished the large parlor and was starting on the dining room when the doorbell sounded. Elisabeth straightened her bandanna and smoothed her palms down the front of her frayed flannel shirt, then answered the rather peremptory summons.

Ian was standing on the porch, looking dapper in his three-piece business suit. His eyes assessed Elisabeth's work clothes with a patronizing expression that made her want to slap him.

Ironic as it was, he seemed to have no texture, no reality. It was as though *he* were the other-worldly being, not Jonathan.

"Hello, Bethie," he said.

She made no move to invite him in. "What do you want?" she asked bluntly. Her ex-husband was handsome, with his glossy chestnut hair and dark blue eyes, but Elisabeth had no illusions where he was concerned. To think she'd once believed he was an idealist!

He patted the expensive briefcase he carried under one arm. "Papers to sign," he said with a guileless lift of his eyebrows. "No big deal."

Reluctantly, Elisabeth stepped back out of the doorway. Since she didn't feel up to a sparring match with Ian, she didn't state the obvious: if Ian had left his very profitable seminars and taping sessions to deliver these papers personally, they were, indeed, a "big deal."

She saw his gaze sweep over the valuable antique furnishings as he stepped into the main parlor. Had his brain been an adding machine, it would have been spitting out paper tape.

"Your father called," he said, perching in a leather wing chair near the fireplace. "He's been worried about you."

Elisabeth kept her distance, standing with her arms folded. "I know. I talked to him."

Ian sighed and opened the briefcase on his lap, taking out a sheaf of papers. "I'm concerned about your inheritance, Bethie,—"

"I'll just bet you are," she interjected, holding her shoulders a little straighter.

He gave her a look of indulgent reprimand. "I have no intention of trying to take anything from you," he told her, shaking a verbal finger in her face. "It's just that I have questions about your ability to manage your share of the estate." He looked around again at the paintings, the substantial furniture and the costly knickknacks. "I don't think you realize what a bonanza you have here. You could easily be taken in."

"And your suggestion is…?" Elisabeth prompted dryly.

"That you allow my accountant to run an audit and give you some advice on how to manage—"

"Put the papers back in your briefcase, Ian. Neither Rue nor I want to sell this place or anything that's in it. Besides that, Rue's father had everything appraised soon after the will was read."

Ian's chiseled face was flushed. Clearly he was annoyed

that he'd taken time away from his motivational company to visit his hopelessly old-fashioned ex-wife. "Elisabeth, you can't be serious about keeping this cavernous, drafty old house. Why, you could live anywhere in the world on your share of the take...."

Elisabeth walked to the front door and opened it, and Ian followed, somewhat unwillingly. Not for one moment did she believe the man had ever had her best interests at heart—he'd been planning to file for changes in the divorce agreement and get a piece of what he called "the take."

"Goodbye," she said.

"I'm getting married next Saturday," he replied, almost smugly, as he swept through the doorway.

"Congratulations," Elisabeth answered. "You'll understand if I don't send a sterling-silver pickle dish?" With that, she shut the door firmly and leaned against it, her arms folded.

Her throat thickened as she remembered her own wedding, right here in this marvelous old house, nearly a decade before. There had been flowers, old-fashioned dresses and organ music. Somehow, she'd missed the glaring fact that Ian didn't fit into the picture, with his supersophistication and jet-set values.

In retrospect, she saw that Ian had always been emotionally unavailable, just like her father, and she'd seen his cool distance as a challenge, something to surmount with her love.

After a few years, she'd realized her mistake—Ian didn't want children or a real home the way she did, and he cared far more about money than the ideals he touted in his lectures and books. Furthermore, there would be no breaching the emotional wall he'd built around his soul.

Elisabeth had quietly returned to teaching school, biding her time and saving her money until she'd built up the courage to file for a divorce and move out of Ian's luxury condo in Seattle.

With a sigh, she thrust herself away from the door and went back to her cleaning. The road to emotional maturity had been a painful, rocky one for her, but she'd learned who she was and what she wanted. To her way of thinking, that put her way out in front of the crowd.

Carefully, she removed Dresden figurines and Haviland plates from the big china closet in the dining room. As she worked, Elisabeth cataloged the qualities she would look for in a second husband. She wanted a gentle man, but he had to be strong, too. Tall, maybe, with dark hair and broad shoulders—

Elisabeth realized she was describing Jonathan Fortner and put down the stack of dessert plates she'd been about to carry to the kitchen for washing. Her hands were trembling.

He's not real, she reminded herself firmly. But another part of her mind argued that he was. She had his suitcoat to prove it.

Didn't she?

What with all the things that had been happening to her since her return to Pine River, Elisabeth was beginning to wonder if she really knew what was real and what wasn't. She hurried up the back stairs and along the hallway to her bedroom, ignoring the sealed doorway in the outside wall, and marched straight to the armoire.

After opening one heavy door, she reached inside and pulled out the coat, pressing it to her face with both hands. It still smelled of Jonathan, and the mingled scents filled Elisabeth with a bittersweet yearning to be near him.

Which was downright silly, she decided, since the man obviously lived in some other time—or some other universe. She would probably never see him again.

Sadly, she put the jacket back on its hanger and returned it to the wardrobe.

By Friday morning, Elisabeth had almost convinced herself that she *had* dreamed up Dr. Fortner and his daughter. Probably, she reasoned, she'd felt some deep, subconscious sympathy for them, learning that they'd both died right there in Aunt Verity's house. Her ideal man had no doubt been woven from the dreams, hopes and desperate needs secreted deep inside her, where a man as shallow as Ian could never venture.

As for the suitcoat, well, that had probably belonged to Verity's long-dead husband. No doubt, she had walked in her sleep that night and found the jacket in one of the trunks in the attic. But if that was true, why was the garment clean and unfrayed? Why didn't it smell of mothballs or mildew?

Elisabeth shook off the disturbing questions as she parked her car in front of Carlton Jewelry, but another quandary immediately took its place. Why was she almost desperately anxious to have Aunt Verity's necklace back in her possession again? Granted, it was very old and probably valuable, but she had never been much for bangles and beads, and money hardly mattered to her at all.

She was inordinately relieved when the pendant was poured from its brown envelope into the palm of her hand, fully restored to its former glory. She closed her fingers around it and shut her eyes for a second, and immediately, Jonathan's face filled her mind.

"Ms. McCartney?" the clerk asked, sounding concerned.

Elisabeth remembered herself, opened her eyes and got out her wallet to pay the bill.

When she arrived home an hour later with the makings for spaghetti, garlic bread and green salad, the moving company was there with her belongings. The two men carried in her books, tape collection, stereo, microwave oven, TV sets and VCR and boxes of seasonal clothes and shoes.

Elisabeth paid the movers extra to connect her VCR and set up the stereo, and made them tuna sandwiches and vegetable soup for lunch. When they were gone, she put on a Mozart tape and let the music swirl around her while she did up the lunch dishes and put away some of her things.

Knowing it would probably take hours or even days to find places for everything, Elisabeth stored her seasonal clothes in the small parlor and set about making her special spaghetti sauce.

Seeing her practical friend Janet again would surely put to rest these crazy fancies she was having, once and for all.

As promised, Janet arrived just when the sauce was ready to be poured over the pasta and served. She had straight reddish-brown hair that just brushed her shoulders and large hazel eyes, and she was dressed in a fashionable gray-and-white, pin-striped suit.

Elisabeth met her friend on the porch with a hug. "It's so good to see you."

Janet's expression was troubled as she studied Elisabeth. "You're pale, and I swear you've lost weight," she fretted.

Elisabeth grinned. "I'm *fine*," she said pointedly, bending to grasp the handle of the small suitcase Janet had set down moments before. "I hope you're hungry, because the sauce is at its peak."

After putting Janet's things in an upstairs bedroom, the two women returned to the kitchen. There they consumed spaghetti and salad at the small table in the breakfast nook, while an April sunset settled over the landscape.

From the first, Elisabeth wanted to confide in her friend, to show her the suitcoat and tell her all about her strange experience a few nights before, but somehow, she couldn't find the courage. They talked about Janet's new boyfriend and Rue's possible whereabouts instead.

After the dishes were done, Janet brought a video tape from her room and popped it into the VCR, while Elisabeth built a fire on the parlor hearth, using seasoned apple wood she'd found in the shed out back. An avid collector of black-and-white classics, Janet didn't rent movies, she bought them.

"What's tonight's feature?" Elisabeth asked, curling up at one end of the settee, while Janet sat opposite her, a bowl of the salty chips they both loved between them.

Janet gave a little shudder and smiled. *"The Ghost and Mrs. Muir,"* she replied. "Fitting, huh? I mean, since this house is probably haunted."

Elisabeth practically choked on the chip she'd just swallowed. "Haunted? Janet, that is really silly." The FBI warning was flickering on the television screen, silently ominous.

Her friend shrugged. "Maybe so, but a funny feeling came over me when I walked in here. It happened before, too, when I came to your wedding."

"That was a sense of impending doom, not anything supernatural," Elisabeth said.

Janet laughed. "You're probably right."

As they watched the absorbing movie, Elisabeth fiddled with the necklace and wondered if she wouldn't just turn around one day, like Mrs. Muir with her ghostly captain, and see Jonathan Fortner standing behind her.

The idea gave her a delicious, shivery sensation, totally unrelated to fear.

After the show was over and the chips were gone, Elisabeth and Janet had herbal tea in the kitchen and gossiped. When Elisabeth mentioned Ian's visit and his plans to remarry, Janet's happy grin faded.

"The sleaseball. How do you feel about this, Beth? Are you sad?"

Elisabeth reached across the table to touch her friend's hand. "If I am, it's only because the marriage I thought I was going to have never materialized. Like so many women, I created a fantasy world out of my own needs and desires, and when it collapsed, I was hurt. But I'm okay now, Janet, and I want you to stop worrying about me."

Janet looked at Elisabeth for a long moment and then nodded. "All right, I'll try. But I'd feel better if you'd come back to Seattle."

Elisabeth pushed back her chair and carried her empty cup and Janet's to the sink. "I played a part for so many years," she said with a sigh. "Now I need solitude to sort things out." She turned to face her friend. "Do you understand?"

"Yes," Janet answered, albeit reluctantly, getting out of her chair.

Elisabeth turned off the downstairs lights and started up the rear stairway, which was illuminated by the glow of the moon flooding in from a fanlight on the second floor. The urge to tell Janet about Jonathan was nearly overwhelming, but she kept the story to herself. There was no way practical, ducks-in-a-row Janet was going to understand.

Reaching her room, Elisabeth called out a good-night to her friend and closed the door. Everything looked so normal and ordinary and *real*—the four-poster, the vanity, the Queen Anne chairs, the fireplace.

She went to the armoire, opened it and ferreted out the suitcoat that was at once her comfort and her torment. She held the garment tightly, her face pressed to the fabric. The scent of Jonathan filled her spirit as well as her nostrils.

If she told Janet the incredible story and then showed her the coat—

Elisabeth stopped in midthought and shook her head. Janet would never believe she'd brought the jacket back from another era. Most of the time, Elisabeth didn't believe that herself. And yet the coat was real and her memories were so vivid, so piquant.

After a long time, Elisabeth put the suitcoat back in its place and exchanged her blouse and black corduroy slacks for another football jersey. Her fingers strayed to the pendant she took off only to shower.

"Jonathan," she said softly, and just saying his name was a sweet relief, like taking a breath of fresh air after being closed up in a stuffy house.

Elisabeth performed the usual ablutions, then switched off her lamp and crawled into bed. Ever since that morning when she'd recovered the necklace, a current of excitement had coursed just beneath the surface of her thoughts and feelings. She ached for the magic to take her back to that dream place, even though she was afraid to go there.

It didn't happen.

Elisabeth awakened the next morning to the sound of her clock radio. She put the pendant on the dresser, stripped off her jersey and took a long, hot shower. When she'd dressed in pink slacks and a rose-colored sweater, she hurried downstairs to find Janet in the kitchen, sipping coffee.

Janet was wearing shorts, sneakers and a hooded sweatshirt, and it was clear that she'd already been out for her customary run. She smiled. "Good morning."

"Don't speak to me until I've had a jolt of caffeine," Elisabeth replied with pretended indignation.

Her friend laughed. "I saw a notice for a craft show at the

fairgrounds," she said as Elisabeth poured coffee. "Sounds like fun."

Elisabeth only shrugged. She was busy sipping.

"We could have lunch afterward."

"Fine," Elisabeth said. "Fine." She was almost her normal self by the time they'd had breakfast and set out for the fairgrounds in Elisabeth's car.

Blossom petals littered the road like pinkish-white snow, and Janet sighed. "I can see why you like the country," she said. "It has a certain serenity."

Elisabeth smiled, waving at Miss Cecily, who was standing at her mailbox. Miss Cecily waved back. "You wouldn't last a week," Elisabeth said with friendly contempt. "Not enough action."

Janet leaned her head back and closed her eyes. "I suppose you're right," she conceded dreamily. "But that doesn't mean I can't enjoy the moment."

They spent happy hours at the craft show, then dined on Vietnamese food from one of the many concession booths. It was when they paused in front of a quilting display that Elisabeth was forcibly reminded of the Jonathan episode.

The slender, dark-haired woman behind the plankboard counter stared at her necklace with rounded eyes and actually retreated a step, as though she thought it would zap her with an invisible ray. "Where did you get that?" she breathed.

Janet's brow crinkled as she frowned in bewilderment, but she just looked on in silence.

Elisabeth's heart was beating unaccountably fast, and she felt defensive, like a child caught stealing. "The necklace?" At the woman's nervous nod, she went on. "I inherited it from my aunt. Why?"

The woman was beginning to regain her composure. She smiled anxiously, but came no closer to the front of the booth. "Your aunt wouldn't be Verity Claridge?"

A finger of ice traced the length of Elisabeth's backbone. "Yes."

Expressive brown eyes linked with Elisabeth's blue-green ones. "Be careful," the dark-haired woman said.

Elisabeth had dozens of questions, but she sensed Janet's discomfort and didn't want to make the situation worse.

"What was that all about?" Janet asked when she and Elisabeth were in the car again, their various purchases loaded into the back. "I thought that woman was going to faint."

Chastity Pringle. Elisabeth hadn't made an effort to remember the name she'd read on the woman's laminated badge; she'd known it would still burn bright in her mind after nine minutes or nine decades. Whoever Ms. Pringle was, she knew Aunt Verity's necklace was no ordinary piece of jewelry, and Elisabeth meant to find out the whole truth about it.

"Elisabeth?"

She jumped slightly. "Hmm?"

"Didn't you think it was weird the way that woman acted?"

Elisabeth was navigating the early-afternoon traffic, which was never all that heavy in Pine River. "The world is full of weird people," she answered.

Having gotten the concession she wanted, Janet turned her mind to the afternoon's entertainment. She and Elisabeth rented a stack of movies at the convenience store, put in an order for a pizza to be delivered later and returned to the house.

By the time breakfast was over on Sunday morning, Janet was getting restless. When noon came, she loaded up her things, said goodbye and hastened back to the city, where her boyfriend and her job awaited.

The moment Janet's car turned onto the highway, Elisabeth dashed to the kitchen and began digging through drawers. Finding a battered phone book, she flipped to the *P*'s. There was a Paul Pringle listed, but no Chastity.

After taking a deep breath, Elisabeth called the man and asked if he had a relative by the name of Chastity. He barked that nobody in his family would be fool enough to give an innocent little girl a name like that and hung up.

Elisabeth got her purse and drove back to the fairgrounds. The quilting booth was manned by a chunky, gray-haired grandmother this time, and sunlight was reflected in the rhinestone-trimmed frames of her glasses as she smiled at Elisabeth.

"Chastity Pringle? Seems like a body couldn't forget a name like that one, but it appears as if I have, because it sure doesn't ring a bell with me. If you'll give me your phone number, I'll have Wynne Singleton call you. She coordinated all of us, and she'd know where to find this woman you're looking for."

"Thank you," Elisabeth said, scrawling the name and phone number on the back of a receipt from the cash machine at her Seattle bank.

Back at home, Elisabeth changed into old clothes again, but this time she tackled the yard, since the house was in good shape. She found an old lawn mower in the shed and fired it up, after making a run to the service station for gas, and spent a productive afternoon mowing the huge yard.

When that was done, she weeded the flower beds. At sunset, weariness and hunger overcame her and she went inside.

The little red light on the answering machine she'd hooked up to Aunt Verity's old phone in the hallway was blinking. She pushed the button and held her breath when she heard Rue's voice.

"Hi, Cousin, sorry I missed you. Unless you get back to me within the next ten minutes, I'll be gone again. Wish I could be there with you, but I've got another assignment. Talk to you soon. Bye."

Hastily, Elisabeth dialed Rue's number, but the prescribed ten minutes had apparently passed. Rue's machine picked up, and Elisabeth didn't bother to leave a message. She felt like crying as she went wearily up the stairs to strip off her dirty jeans and T-shirt and take a bath.

When she came downstairs again, she heated a piece of leftover pizza in the microwave and sat down for a solitary supper. Beyond the breakfast nook windows, the sky had a sullen, heavy look to it. Elisabeth hoped there wouldn't be another storm.

She ate, rinsed her dishes and went upstairs to bed, bringing along a candle and matches in case the power were to go out.

Stretched out in bed, her body aching with exhaustion from the afternoon's work, Elisabeth thoroughly expected to fall into a fathomless sleep.

Instead, she was wide awake. She tossed from her left side to her right, from her stomach to her back. Finally, she got up, shoved her feet into her slippers and reached for her bathrobe.

She made herself a cup her herbal tea downstairs, then settled at the desk in her room, reaching for a few sheets of Aunt Verity's vellum writing paper and a pen.

"Dear Rue," she wrote. And then she poured out the whole experience of meeting Jonathan and Trista, starting with the first time she'd heard Trista's piano. She put in every detail of the story, including the strange attraction she'd felt for Jonathan, ending with the fact that she'd awakened the next morning to find herself wearing his coat.

She spent several hours going over the letter, rewriting parts of it, making it as accurate an account of her experience as she possibly could. Then she folded the missive, tucked it into an envelope, scrawled Rue's name and address and applied a stamp.

In the morning, she would put it in the mailbox down by the road, pull up the little metal flag and let the chips fall where they may. Rue was the best friend Elisabeth had, but she was also a pragmatic newswoman. She was just as likely to suggest professional help as Elisabeth's father would be. Still, Elisabeth felt she had to tell somebody what was going on or she was going to burst.

She was just coming upstairs, having carried the letter down and set it in the middle of the kitchen table so she wouldn't forget to mail it the next morning, when she heard the giggles and saw the glow of light on the hallway floor.

Elisabeth stopped, her hand on the necklace, her heart racing with scary exhilaration. They were back, Jonathan and Trista—she had only to open that door and step over the threshold.

She went to the portal and put her ear against the wood, smiling as Trista's voice chimed, "And then I said to him,

Zeek Filbin, if you pull my hair again, I'll send my papa over to take your tonsils out!''

Elisabeth's hand froze on the doorknob when another little girl responded with a burst of laughter and, ''Zeek Filbin needed his wagon fixed, and you did it right and proper.'' Vera, she thought. Trista's best friend. How would the child explain it if Elisabeth simply walked into the room, appearing from out of nowhere?

She knew she couldn't do that, and yet she felt a longing for that world and for the presence of those people that went beyond curiosity or even nostalgia.

The low, rich sound of Jonathan's voice brought her eyes flying open. ''Trista, you and Vera should have been asleep hours ago. Now settle down.''

There was more giggling, but then the sound faded and the light gleaming beneath the door dimmed until the darkness had swallowed it completely. Elisabeth had missed her chance to step over the threshold into Jonathan's world, and the knowledge left her feeling oddly bereft. She went to bed and slept soundly, awakening to the jangle of the telephone early the next morning.

Since the device was sitting on the vanity table on the other side of the room, Elisabeth was forced to get out of bed and stumble across the rug to snatch up the receiver.

''Yes?'' she managed sleepily.

''Is this Elisabeth McCartney?''

Something about the female voice brought her fully awake. ''Yes.''

''My name is Wynne Singleton, and I'm president of the Pine River County Quilting Society. One of our members told me you were anxious to get in touch with Ms. Pringle.''

Elisabeth sat up very straight and waited silently.

''I can give you her address and telephone number, dear,'' Mrs. Singleton said pleasantly, ''but I'm afraid it won't do you much good. She and her husband left just this morning on an extended business trip.''

Disappointed, Elisabeth nonetheless wrote down the number and street address—Chastity Pringle apparently lived in the neighboring town of Cotton Creek—and thanked the caller for her help.

After she hung up, Elisabeth dressed in a cotton skirt and matching top, even though the sky was still threatening rain, and made herself a poached egg and a piece of wheat toast for breakfast.

When she'd eaten, she got into her car and drove to town. If Rue were here, she thought, she'd go to the newspaper office and to the library to see what facts she could gather pertaining to Aunt Verity's house in general and Jonathan and Trista Fortner in particular.

Only it was early and neither establishment was open yet. Undaunted, Elisabeth bought a bouquet of simple flowers at the supermarket and went on to the well-kept, fenced grave-yard at the edge of town.

She left the flowers on Aunt Verity's grave and then began reading the names carved into the tilting, discolored stones in the oldest part of the cemetery. Jonathan and Trista were buried side by side, their graves surrounded by a low iron fence.

Carefully, Elisabeth opened the gate and stepped through it, kneeling to push away the spring grass that nearly covered the aging stones. "Jonathan Stevens Fortner," read the chiseled words. "Born August 5, 1856. Perished June 1892."

"What day?" Elisabeth whispered, turning to Trista's grave. Like her father's, the little girl's headstone bore only her name, the date of her birth and the sad inscription, "Perished June 1892."

There were tears in Elisabeth's eyes as she got to her feet again and left the cemetery.

After leaving the Pine River graveyard, Elisabeth stopped by the post office to mail the letter she'd written to Rue the night before. Even though she loved and trusted her cousin, it was hard to drop the envelope through the scrolled brass slot, and the instant she had, she wanted to retrieve it.

All she'd need to do was ask the sullen-looking man behind the grilled window to fetch the letter for her, and no one would ever know she was having delusions.

Squaring her shoulders, Elisabeth made herself walk out of the post office with nothing more than a polite, "Good morning," to the clerk.

The library was open, but Elisabeth soon learned that there were virtually no records of the town's history. There was, however, a thin, self-published autobiography called, *My Life in Old Pine River,* written by a Mrs. Carolina Meavers.

While the librarian, a disinterested young lady with spiky blond hair and a mouthful of gum, issued a borrower's card and entered Elisabeth's name in the computer system, Elisabeth skimmed the book. Mrs. Meavers herself was surely dead, but it was possible she had family in the area.

"Do you know anyone named Meavers?" she asked, holding up the book.

The child librarian popped her gum and shrugged. "I don't pay a lot of attention to old people."

Elisabeth suppressed a sigh of exasperation, took the book and her plastic library card and left the small, musty building. She and Rue had visited the place often during their summer visits to Pine River, devouring books they secretly thought they should have been too sophisticated to like. Elisabeth had loved Cherry Ames, student nurse, and Rue had consumed every volume of the Tarzan series.

Feeling lonely again, Elisabeth crossed the wide street to the newspaper office, where the weekly *Pine River Bugle* was published.

This time she was greeted by a competent-looking middle-aged man with a bald spot, wire-rimmed glasses and a friendly smile. "How can I help you?" he asked.

Elisabeth returned his smile. "I'm doing research," she said, having rehearsed her story as she crossed the street. "How long has the *Bugle* been in publication?"

"One of the oldest newspapers in the state," the man replied proudly. "Goes back to 1876."

Elisabeth's eyes widened. "Do you have the old issues on microfilm?"

"Most of them. If you'll just step this way, Ms....?"

"McCartney," she answered. "Elisabeth McCartney."

"I'm Ben Robbins. Are you writing a book, Ms. McCartney?"

Elisabeth smiled, shook her head and followed him through a small but very noisy press room and down a steep set of stairs into a dimly lit cellar.

"They don't call these places morgues for nothing," Mr. Robbins said with a sigh. Then he gestured toward rows of file cases. "Help yourself," he said. "The microfilm machine is over there, behind those cabinets."

Elisabeth nodded, feeling a little overwhelmed, and found the long table where the machine waited. After putting down her purse and the library book, she went to work.

The four issues of the *Bugle* published in June of 1892 were on one spool of film, and once Elisabeth found that and figured out how to work the elaborate projection apparatus, the job didn't seem so difficult.

During the first week of that long-ago year, Elisabeth read, Anna Jean Maples, daughter of Albert and Hester Eustice Maples, had been married to Frank Peterson on the lawn of the

First Presbyterian church. Kelsey's Grocery had offered specials on canned salmon and "baseball goods."

The *Bugle* was not void of national news. It was rumored that Grover Cleveland would wrest the presidency back from Benjamin Harrison come November, and the people of Chicago were busy preparing for the World Columbian Exposition, to open in October.

Elisabeth skimmed the second week, then the third. A painful sense of expectation was building in the pit of her stomach when she finally came upon the headline she'd been searching for.

DR. FORTNER AND DAUGHTER PERISH IN HOUSE FIRE

She closed her eyes for a moment, feeling sick. Then she anxiously read the brief account of the incident.

No exact date was given—the article merely said, "This week, the people of Pine River suffered a tragic double loss." The reporter went on to state that no bodies or remains of any kind had been found, "so hot did the hellish blazes burn."

Practically holding her breath, Elisabeth read on, feeling just a flicker of hope. She'd watched enough reruns of *Quincy* to know just how stubbornly indestructible human bones could be. If Jonathan's and Trista's remains had not been found, they probably hadn't died in the fire.

She paused to sigh and rub her eyes. If that was true, where had they gone? And why were there two graves with headstones that bore their names?

Elisabeth went back to the article, hoping to find a specific date. Near the end she read, "Surviving the inferno is a young and apparently indigent relative of the Fortners, known only as Lizzie. Marshal Farley Haynes has detained her for questioning."

After scanning the rest of that issue and finding nothing but quilting-bee notices and offers to sell bulls, buggies and nursery furniture, Elisabeth went on to late July of that fateful year.

MYSTERIOUS LIZZIE TO BE TRIED FOR MURDER
OF PINE RIVER FAMILY

Pity twisted Elisabeth's insides. Her head was pounding, and she was badly in need of some fresh air. After finding several coins in the bottom of her purse, she made copies of the last newspaper of June 1892, to read later. Then she carefully put the microfilm reel back in its cabinet and turned off the machine.

Upstairs, she found Ben Robbins in a cubicle of an office, going over a stack of computer printouts.

"I want to thank you for being so helpful," Elisabeth said. Her mind was filled with dizzying thoughts. Had Trista and Jonathan died in that blasted fire or hadn't they? And who the heck was this Lizzie person?

Ben smiled and took off his glasses. "Find what you were looking for?"

"Yes and no," Elisabeth answered distractedly, frowning as she shuffled the stack of microfilm copies and the library book resting in the curve of her arm. "Did you know this woman—Carolina Meavers?"

"Died when I was a boy," Ben said with a shake of his head. "But she was good friends with the Buzbee sisters. If you have any questions about Carolina, they'd be the ones to ask."

The Buzbee sisters. Of course. She guessed this was a case of overlooking the obvious. Elisabeth thanked him again and went out.

Belying the glowering sky of the night before, the weather was sunny and scented with spring. Elisabeth got into her car and drove home.

By the time she arrived, it was well past noon and she was hungry. She made a chicken-salad sandwich, took a diet cola from the refrigerator, found an old blanket and set out through the orchard behind the house in search of a picnic spot.

She chose the grassy banks of Birch Creek, within sight of the old covered bridge that was now strictly off limits to any traffic. Elisabeth and Rue had come to this place often with

Aunt Verity to wade in the sparkling, icy stream and listen to those endless and singularly remarkable stories.

Elisabeth spread the blanket out on the ground and sat down to eat her sandwich and drink her soda. When she'd finished her lunch, she stretched out on her stomach to read about Lizzie's arrest. Unfortunately, the piece had been written by the same verbose and flowery reporter who had covered the fire, and beyond the obvious facts, there was no real information.

Glumly, Elisabeth set aside the photographs and flipped through the library book. There were pictures in the center, and she stopped to look at them. The author, with her family, posing on the porch—if those few rough planks of pine could be described as a porch—of a ramshackle shanty with a tarpaper roof. The author, standing on the steps of a country schoolhouse that had been gone long before Elisabeth's birth, clutching her slate and spelling primer to her flat little chest.

Elisabeth turned another page and her heart leapt up into her sinus passages to pound behind her cheeks. Practically the entire town must have been in that picture, and Elisabeth could see one side of the covered bridge. But it wasn't that structure that caught her eye and caused her insides to go crazy with a strange, sweet anxiety.

It was Jonathan's image, smiling back at her from the photograph. He was wearing trousers and a vest, and his dark hair was attractively rumpled. Trista stood beside him, a basket brimming with wildflowers in one hand, regarding the camera solemnly.

Elisabeth closed her eyes. She had to get a hold on her emotions. These people had been dead for a century. And whatever fantasies she might have woven around them, they could not be a part of her life.

She gathered the book and the photocopies and the debris of her lunch, then folded the blanket. Despite the self-lecture, Elisabeth knew she would cross that threshold into the past again if she could. She wanted to see Jonathan and warn him about the third week in June.

In fact, she just plain wanted to see Jonathan.

Back at the house, Elisabeth found she couldn't settle down to the needlework or reading she usually found so therapeutic. There were no messages on the answering machine.

Restless, she took the Buzbees' covered casserole dish, now empty and scrubbed clean, and set out for the house across the road.

An orchard blocked the graceful old brick place from plain view, and the driveway was strewn with fragrant velvety petals. Elisabeth smiled to herself, holding the casserole dish firmly, and wondered how she had ever been able to leave Pine River for the noise and concrete of Seattle.

Miss Cecily came out onto the porch and waved, looking pleased to have a visitor. "I *told* Sister you'd be dropping in by and by, but she said you'd rather spend your time with young folks."

Elisabeth chuckled. "I hope I'm not interrupting anything," she said. "I really should have called first."

"Nonsense." Cecily came down the walk to link Elisabeth's arm with hers. "Nobody calls in the country. They just stop by. Did you enjoy the casserole, dear?"

Elisabeth didn't have the heart to say she'd put most of it down the disposal because there had been so much more than she could eat. "Yes," she said. "Every bite was delicious."

They proceeded up fieldstone steps to the porch, where an old-fashioned swing swayed in the mid-afternoon breeze. The ponderous grandfather clock in the entryway sounded the Westminster chimes, three o'clock, and Elisabeth was surprised that it was so late.

"Sister!" Cecily called, leading Elisabeth past the staircase and down a hallway. There was a note of triumph in her voice, an unspoken "I told you she would come to visit!" "Oh, Sister! We have company!"

Roberta appeared, looking just a little put out. Obviously, she preferred being right to being visited. "Well," she huffed, in the tone of one conceding grudging defeat, "I'll get the lemonade and the molasses cookies."

Soon the three women were settled at the white iron ice-cream table on the stone-floored sun porch, glasses of the

Buzbee sisters' incomparable fresh-squeezed lemonade brimming before them.

"Elisabeth thought the casserole was delicious," Cecily announced with a touch of smugness, and Elisabeth resisted a smile, wondering what rivalries existed between these aging sisters.

"Wait until she tastes my vegetable lasagne," said Roberta, pursing her lips slightly as she reached for the sampler she was embroidering.

"I'd like to," Elisabeth said, to be polite. She took a molasses cookie, hoping that would balance things out somehow. "Mr. Robbins at the newspaper told me you probably knew Mrs. Carolina Meavers."

"My, yes," said Roberta. "She was our Sunday-school teacher."

"The old crow," muttered Cecily.

Elisabeth nibbled at her cookie. "She wrote a book about Pine River, you know. I checked it out of the library this morning."

Roberta narrowed her eyes at Elisabeth. "It's that crazy house. That's what's got you so interested in Pine River history, isn't it?"

"Yes," Elisabeth answered, feeling as though she'd been accused of something.

"There are some things in this world, young woman, that are better left alone. And the mysteries of that old house are among them."

"Don't be so fractious, Sister," Cecily scolded. "It's natural to be curious."

"It's also dangerous," replied Roberta.

Elisabeth could see that this visit was going to get her nowhere in unraveling a century of knotted truths, so she finished her cookie and her lemonade and made chitchat until she could politely leave. As Cecily was escorting her through the parlor, Elisabeth was jolted out of her reveries by a brown and hairy shrunken head proudly displayed on the back of the upright piano.

"Chief Zwilu of the Ubangis," Cecily confided, having followed Elisabeth's horrified gaze. "Since the dastardly deed had already been done, Sister and I could see no reason not to bring the poor fellow home as a souvenir."

Elisabeth shivered. "The customs people must have been thrilled."

Cecily shook her head and answered in a serious tone, "Oh, no, dear. They were quite upset. But Sister was uncommonly persuasive and they allowed us to bring the chief into the country."

Just before the two women parted at the Buzbee gate, Cecily patted Elisabeth's arm and muttered, "Don't mind Sister, now. She was just put out because she's always considered my beef casserole inferior to her vegetable lasagna."

"I won't give it another thought," Elisabeth promised. She didn't smile until she was facing away from Cecily, walking down the long driveway.

Reaching the downstairs hallway of her own house, Elisabeth found the light blinking on the answering machine and eagerly pushed the play button.

"Hello, Elisabeth." The voice belonged to Traci, her father's wife. "Marcus asked me to call and find out if you need any money and if there's anything we can do to convince you to come and spend the summer in Tahoe with us. If I don't hear from you, I'll assume you're all right. Bye-ee."

"Bye-ee," Elisabeth chimed sweetly, just as another message began to play.

"Elisabeth? It's Janet. Just wanted to say I had a great time visiting. How about coming to Seattle next weekend? Give me a call."

Elisabeth turned off the machine and went slowly up the stairs. On a whim, she continued up a second flight to the attic.

There was one way to find out if she'd walked in her sleep that night and found a man's coat to use as proof of the unprovable.

The attic door squeaked loudly on its hinges, and Elisabeth thought to herself that the shrill sound should have awakened the dead, let alone a sleepwalker. A flip of the switch located just inside the door illuminated the dust-covered trunks, bureaus, boxes and chairs.

Even from where she stood, Elisabeth could see that neither she nor anyone else had visited this chamber in a very long time. There were no tracks in the thick dust on the floor.

Taking the necklace out from under her sweater, Elisabeth returned to the second floor and stood opposite the sealed door. Her heart was beating painfully fast, and the pit of her stomach was jittery. "Be there," she whispered. "Please, Jonathan. Be there."

Elisabeth tried the knob, but even before she touched it, she knew it wasn't going to turn. Obviously, she could not enter the world on the other side of that door at will, even wearing the necklace. Other forces, all well beyond Elisabeth's comprehension, had to be present.

"I have to tell you about the fire," she said sadly, sliding down the wooden framework to sit on the hallway floor, her knees drawn up, her forehead resting on her folded arms. "Please, Jonathan. Let me in."

She must have dozed off right there on the floor. She came to herself with a start when she heard her name being whispered.

"Elisabeth! Elisabeth, come back! I *need* to talk to you!"

Elisabeth glanced wildly toward the fanlight at the end of the hall and saw that it was still light outside. Then she scrambled to her feet.

"Trista?" She reached for the doorknob, and it turned easily in her hand. On the other side of the door, she found the child who was a lifetime her senior.

Trista was sitting on the floor of her room, next to the big dollhouse, and her lower lip protruded. "I'm being punished," she said.

Elisabeth knelt beside the little girl and gave her a heartfelt hug, hoping she wouldn't feel the trembling. "What did you do?"

"Nothing." Jonathan's daughter handed Elisabeth a tiny

china doll as she sat beside her on the rag rug, and Elisabeth smiled at its little taffeta dress and painted hair.

"Come on, Trista," she said. "Your father wouldn't restrict you to your room for no reason."

"Well, it wasn't a very *good* reason."

Elisabeth raised her eyebrows, waiting, and Trista's little shoulders rose and fell in a heavy sigh.

"I couldn't help it," she said. "I told my friend Vera about you, and she told everybody in the county that Papa had a naked woman here. Now I have to come straight to my room after school every day for a solid month!"

Elisabeth touched the child's glossy dark pigtail. "I'm sorry, sweetheart. I didn't mean to get you in trouble. I do, however, feel duty bound to point out that I wasn't naked— I was wearing a football jersey."

"You didn't get me into trouble," Trista said. "Vera did. And what's a football jersey?"

"A very fancy undershirt. Is your papa at home, Trista?" Elisabeth couldn't help the little shiver of excitement that passed through her at the prospect of encountering Jonathan again, though God knew he probably wouldn't be thrilled to see *her*.

Glumly, Trista nodded. "He's out in the barn, I think. Maybe you could tell him that a month is too long to restrict a girl to her bedroom."

Elisabeth chuckled and kissed the child's forehead. "Sorry, short person. It isn't my place to tell your father how to raise his daughter."

With care, Elisabeth unclasped the necklace and put it in a little glass bowl on Trista's bureau. "You'll keep this safe for me, won't you?"

Trista nodded, watching Elisabeth with curious eyes. "I've never seen a lady wear pants before," she said. "And I'll bet you haven't got a corset on, neither."

Elisabeth grinned over one shoulder as she opened the door. "That's one bet you're bound to win," she said. And then she was moving down the hallway.

The pictures of glowering men in beards and steely eyed,

calico-clad women were back, and so was the ghastly rose-patterned runner on the floor. Elisabeth felt exhilarated as she hurried toward the back stairway, also different from the one she knew, and walked through the kitchen.

There was a washtub hanging on the wall outside the back door, and chickens clucked and scratched in the yard. A woman was standing nearby, hanging little calico pinafores and collarless white shirts on a clothesline. She didn't seem to notice Elisabeth.

Wife? Housekeeper? Elisabeth decided on the latter. When Jonathan had snatched the necklace from Elisabeth's neck during her first visit, he'd spoken of his spouse in the past tense.

When she stepped through the wide doorway of the sturdy, unpainted barn—which was a teetering ruin in her time—she saw golden hay wafting down from a loft. A masculine voice was singing a bawdy song that made Elisabeth smile.

"Jonathan?" she called, waiting for her eyes to adjust to the dimmer light. The singing instantly stopped.

Jonathan looked down at her from the hayloft, his chest shirtless and glistening with sweat, a pitchfork in one hand. His dark hair was filled with bits of straw. Something tightened inside Elisabeth at the sight of him.

"You." His tone was so ominous, Elisabeth took a step backward, ready to flee if she had to. "Stay right there!" he barked the moment she moved, shaking an index finger at her.

He tossed the pitchfork expertly into the hay and climbed down rough-hewn rungs affixed to the wall beside the loft. Standing within six feet of Elisabeth, he dragged his stormy-sky eyes over her in angry wonderment, then dragged a handkerchief from his hip pocket and dried his brow.

Elisabeth found the sight and scent of him inexplicably erotic, even though if she could have described her primary emotion, she would have said it was pure terror.

"Trousers?" he marveled, stuffing the handkerchief back into his pocket. "Who are you, and where the devil did you disappear to the other night?"

Elisabeth entwined her fingers behind her back, hiding the

crazy, nonsensical joy she felt at seeing him again. "Where I come from, lots of women wear—trousers," she said, stalling.

He went to a bucket on a bench beside the wall and raised a dipperful of water to his mouth. Elisabeth watched the muscles of his back work, sweaty and hard, as he swallowed and returned the dipper to its place.

"You don't look Chinese," he finally said, dryly and at length.

"Listen, if I tried to tell you where I really came from, you'd never believe me. But I—I know the future."

He chuckled and shook his head, and Elisabeth was reminded of his medical degree. The typical man of science. Jonathan probably believed only in things he could reduce to logical components. "No one knows the future," he replied.

"I do," Elisabeth insisted, "because I've been there. And I'm here to warn you." She swallowed hard as he regarded her with those lethally intelligent eyes. Somehow she couldn't get the words out; they'd sound too insane.

"About what?"

Elisabeth closed her eyes and forced herself to answer. "A fire. There's going to be a terrible fire, the third week of June. Part of the house will be destroyed, and you and Trista will—will disappear."

Jonathan's hand shot out and closed around her elbow, tight as a steel manacle. "Who are you, and what asylum did you escape from?" he snapped.

"I told you before—my name is Elisabeth McCartney. And I'm *not* insane!" She paused, biting her lip and futilely trying to pull out of his grasp. "At least, I don't think I am."

He dragged her into the dusty, fading sunlight that filled the barn's doorway and examined her as though she were a creature from another planet. "Your hair," he muttered. "No woman I've ever seen wears her hair sheared off at the chin like that. And your clothes."

Elisabeth sighed. "Jonathan, I'm from the future," she said bluntly. "Women dress like this in the 1990s."

He touched her forehead, just as he had once before. "No

fever,'' he murmured, as though she hadn't spoken at all. ''This is the damnedest thing I've ever seen.''

''I guess they didn't cover this in medical school, huh?'' Elisabeth said, getting testy because he seemed to see her as more of a white mouse in a laboratory than a flesh-and-blood woman. ''Well, here's another flash for you, Doc—they're not bleeding people with leeches anymore, but there's still no cure for psoriasis.''

Jonathan's grip on her arm didn't slacken. ''Who are you?'' he repeated, and it was clear to Elisabeth that her host was running out of patience. If he'd ever possessed any in the first place.

''Margaret Thatcher,'' she snapped. ''Damn it, Fortner, will you let go of my arm! You're about to squeeze it off at the elbow!''

He released her. ''You said your name was Elisabeth,'' he said in all seriousness.

''Then why did you have to ask who I am? It isn't as though I haven't told you more than once!''

He crossed the barn, snatched a shirt from a peg on the wall and slipped his arms into it. ''How did you manage to vanish from my house last week, Miss McCartney?''

Elisabeth waited for him in the doorway, knowing she'd never be able to outrun him. ''I told you. There's a passageway between your time and mine. You and I are roommates, in a manner of speaking.''

Jonathan placed a hand on the small of Elisabeth's back and propelled her toward the house. There was no sign of the woman who had been hanging clothes on the line. The set of his jaw told Elisabeth he was annoyed with her answers to his questions.

Which wasn't surprising, considering.

He steered her up the back steps and through the door into the kitchen. ''They must have cut your hair off while you were in the asylum,'' he said.

''I've never been in an asylum,'' Elisabeth informed him. ''Except in college, once. We visited a mental hospital as part of a psychology program.''

Jonathan's teeth were startlingly white against his dirty face. "Sit down," he said.

Elisabeth obeyed, watching as he took a kettle from the stove and poured hot water into a basin. He added cold from the pump over the sink and then began to wash himself with pungent yellow soap. She found she couldn't look away, even though there was something painfully intimate in the watching.

By the time he turned to her, drying himself with a damask towel, Elisabeth's entire body felt warm and achy, and she didn't trust herself to speak. The man was so uncompromisingly masculine, and his very presence made closed places open up inside her.

Jonathan took his medical bag from a shelf beside the door, set it on the table with a decisive thump and opened the catch. "The first order of business, Miss McCartney," he said, taking out a stethoscope and a tongue depressor, "is to examine you. Open your mouth and say awww."

"Oh, brother," Elisabeth said, but she opened her mouth.

"Are you satisfied?" Elisabeth demanded when Dr. Jonathan Fortner had finished the impromptu examination. "I'm perfectly healthy—physically *and* mentally."

There were freshly ironed shirts hanging from a hook on the wall behind a wooden ironing board, and Jonathan took one down and shrugged into it. Elisabeth tried to ignore the innately male grace in the movements of his muscles.

He didn't look convinced of her good health. "I suppose it's possible you really believe that," he speculated, frowning.

Elisabeth sighed. "If all doctors are as narrow-minded as you are, it's a real wonder they ever managed to wipe out diphtheria and polio."

She had Jonathan's undivided attention. "What did you say?"

"Diphtheria and polio," Elisabeth said seriously. But inside, she was enjoying having the upper hand for once. "They're gone. No one gets them anymore."

The desire to believe such a miracle could be accomplished was plain in Jonathan's face, but so was his skepticism and puzzlement. He dragged back a chair at the table and sat in it, staring at Elisabeth.

She was encouraged. "You were born in the wrong century, Doc," she said pleasantly. "They say more medical advances were made in the twentieth century than in all the rest of time put together."

He was watching her as if he expected her head to spin around on her shoulders.

Elisabeth was enjoying the rare sense of being privy to

startling information. "Not only that, but people actually walked on the moon in 1969, and—"

"Walked on the moon?" He shoved back his chair, strode across the room and brought back a dipperful of cold well water. "Drink this very slowly."

Disappointment swept over Elisabeth when she realized she wasn't convincing him after all. It was followed by a sense of hopelessness so profound, it threatened to crush her. If she didn't find some way to influence Jonathan, he and Trista might not survive the fire. And she would never be able to bear knowing they'd died so horribly, because they were real people to her and not just figures in an old lady's autobiography.

She tasted the water, mostly because she knew he wouldn't leave her alone until she had, and then turned her head away. "Jonathan, you must listen to me," she whispered, forgetting the formalities. "Your life depends on it, and so does Trista's."

He returned the dipper to the bucket, paying no attention to her words. "You need to lie down."

"I don't...."

"If you refuse, I can always give you a dose of laudanum," Jonathan interrupted.

Elisabeth's temper flared. "Now just a minute. *Nobody* is giving me laudanum. The stuff was—is—made from opium, and that's addictive!"

Jonathan sighed. "I know full well what it's made of, Miss McCartney. And I wasn't proposing to make you dependent and sell you into white slavery. It's just that you're obviously agitated—"

"I am *not* agitated!"

His slow, leisurely smile made something shift painfully inside her. "Of course, you're not," he said in a patronizing tone.

Now it was Elisabeth who sighed. She'd known Jonathan Fortner, M.D., for a very short time, but one thing she had learned right off was that he could be mule stubborn when he'd set his mind on a certain course of action. Arguing with him was useless. "All right," she said sweetly, even managing a little yawn. "I guess I would like to rest for a while. But you've got to promise not to send for the marshal and have me arrested."

She saw a flicker of amusement in his charcoal eyes. "You have my word, Elisabeth," he told her, and she loved the way he said her name. He took her arm and led her toward the back stairs, and she allowed that, thinking how different Dr. Fortner was from Ian, from *any* man she knew in her own time. There was a courtly strength about him that had evidently been lost to the male population as the decades progressed.

He deposited her in the same room she'd had during her last visit, settling her expertly on the narrow iron bed, slipping off her shoes, covering her with a colorful quilt. His gentle, callused hand smoothed her hair back from her forehead.

"Rest," he said hoarsely, and then he was gone, closing the door quietly behind him.

Elisabeth tensed, listening for the click of a key in the lock, but it never came. She relaxed, soaking up the atmosphere of this world that apparently ran parallel to her own. Everything was more substantial, somehow, more vivid and richly textured. The ordinary sound of an errant bee buzzing and bumping against the window, the support of the feather-filled mattress beneath her, the poignant blue of the patch of sky visible through the lace curtains at the window—all of it blended together to create an undeniable reality.

She was definitely not dreaming and, strangely, she was in no particular hurry to get back to her own century. There was no one there waiting for her, while here, she had Trista and Jonathan. She would stay a few days, if Jonathan would let her, and perhaps find some way to avert the disaster that lay ahead.

When the door of her room opened, she was only a little startled. Trista peered around the edge, her Jonathan-gray eyes wide with concerned curiosity. "Are you sick?" she asked.

Elisabeth sat up and patted the mattress. "No, but your father thinks I am. Come and sit here."

Shyly, Trista approached the bed and sat on the edge of the mattress, her small, plump hands folded in her lap.

"I've heard you practicing your piano lessons," Elisabeth said, settling back against her pillows and folding her arms.

Trista's eyes reflected wonder rather than the disbelief Elisabeth had seen in Jonathan's gaze. "You have?"

"I don't think you like it much," Elisabeth observed.

The child made a comical face. "I'd rather be outside. But Papa wants me to grow up to be a lady, and a lady plays piano."

"I see."

Trista smiled tentatively. "Do you like music?"

"Very much," Elisabeth answered. "I studied piano when I was about your age, and I can still play a little."

The eight-year-old's gapped smile faded to a look of somber resignation. "Miss Calderberry will be here soon to give me my lesson. I'm allowed to leave my room for that, of course."

"Of course," Elisabeth agreed seriously.

"Would you care to come down and listen?"

"I'd better not. Something tells me your father wouldn't want me to be quite so—visible. I'm something of a secret, I think."

Trista sighed, then nodded and rose to go downstairs and face her music teacher. She had the air of Anne Boleyn proceeding to the Tower. "Your necklace is in the dish on my bureau, just where you left it," she whispered confidentially, from the doorway. "You won't leave without saying goodbye, will you?"

Elisabeth felt her throat tighten slightly. "No, sweetheart. I promise I won't go without seeing you first."

"Good," Trista answered. And then she left the room.

After a few minutes, Elisabeth got out of bed and wandered into the hallway. At the front of the house was a large, arched window looking down on the yard, and she couldn't resist peering around the curtains to watch a slender woman dressed in brown sateen climb delicately down from the seat of a buggy.

Miss Calderberry wore a feathered hat that hid her face from Elisabeth, but when Jonathan approached from the direction of the barn, smiling slightly, delight seemed to radiate from the piano teacher's countenance. Her trilling voice reached Elisabeth's ears through the thick, bubbled glass.

"Dr. Fortner! What a pleasure to see you."

In the next instant, Jonathan's gaze rose and seemed to lock with Elisabeth's, and she remembered that she was supposed to be lying down, recovering from her odious malady.

She stepped back from the window, but only because she didn't want Miss Calderberry to see her and carry a lot of gossip back to the fine folks of Pine River. It wouldn't do to ruin whatever might be left of the good doctor's reputation following Vera's accounts of a naked lady in residence.

When Trista's discordant efforts at piano playing started to rise through the floorboards, Elisabeth grew restless and began to wander the upstairs, though she carefully avoided Jonathan's room.

She made sure the necklace was still in Trista's crystal dish, then peeked into each of the other bedrooms, where she saw brass beds, chamberpots, pitchers and basins resting on lovely hardwood washstands. From there, she proceeded to the attic.

The place gave her a quivery feeling in the pit of her stomach, being a mirror image of its counterpart in her own time. Of course, the contents were different.

She opened a trunk and immediately met with the scent of lavender. Setting aside layers of tissue paper, she found a delicate ivory dress, carefully folded, with ecru-lace trim on the cuffs and the high, round collar.

Normally, Elisabeth would not have done what she did next, but this was, in a way, her house. And besides, all her actions had a dreamlike quality to them, as though they would be only half-remembered in the morning.

She took the dress out of the trunk, held it against her and saw that it would probably fit, then she stripped off her slacks and sweater. Tiny buttons covered in watered silk graced the front of the gown, fastening through little loops of cloth.

When she had finished hooking each one, Elisabeth looked

around for a mirror, but there was none in sight. She dipped into the trunk again and found a large, elegantly shaped box, which contained a confection of a hat bursting with silk flowers—all the color of rich cream—and tied beneath the chin with a wide, ivory ribbon.

Elisabeth couldn't resist adding the hat to her costume.

Holding up her rustling skirts with one hand, she made her way cautiously down the attic steps and along the hallway to her room. She was inside, beaming with pleasure and turning this way and that in front of the standing mirror, when she sensed an ominous presence and turned to see Jonathan in the doorway.

He leaned against the jamb, the sleeves of his white shirt rolled up to reveal muscle-corded forearms folded across his chest.

"Make yourself right at home, Miss McCartney," he urged in an ill-tempered tone. An entirely different emotion was smoldering in his eyes, however.

Elisabeth had been like a child, playing dressup. Now her pleasure faded and her hands trembled as she reached up to untie the ribbon that held the hat in place. "I'm so sorry," she whispered, mortified, realizing that the clothes had surely belonged to his wife and that seeing someone else wearing them must be painful for him. "I don't know what came over me...."

Jonathan stepped into the room and closed the door against the distant tinkle of piano keys, probably not wanting their voices to carry to Trista and Miss Calderberry. His eyes were narrowed. "When I first met you, you were wearing my wife's necklace, and when it disappeared, so did you. Tell me, Elisabeth...do you know Barbara?"

Elisabeth shook her head. "H-how could I, Jonathan? She—I live in another century, remember?"

He arched one dark eyebrow and hooked his thumbs in the pockets of his black woolen vest. "Yet, somehow, my wife's necklace came to be here. Without Barbara. She never let it out of her sight, you know. She claimed it had powers."

A hard lump formed in Elisabeth's throat, and she swallowed. If Barbara Fortner had known about the necklace's special energy and had used it, she could have crossed the threshold into the modern world....

"This is all getting pretty farfetched," Elisabeth said, squaring her shoulders. "I didn't know your wife, Jonathan." She looked down at the lovely dress. "I truly am sorry for presuming on your hospitality this way, though."

"Keep the dress," he told her with a dismissive gesture of one hand. "It will raise a lot fewer questions than those trousers of yours."

Elisabeth felt as though she'd just been given a wonderful gift. "Thank you," she breathed softly, running her hands down the satiny skirt.

"You'd better hunt up some calico and sateen for everyday," he finished, moving toward the door. "Naturally, women don't cook and clean in such fancy getup."

"Jonathan?" Elisabeth approached him as he waited, his hand on the doorknob. She stood on tiptoe to kiss his now-stubbly cheek, and again she felt a powerful charge of some mystical electricity. "Thank you. But I won't need special clothes if I go back to my own time."

He rolled his eyes, but there was a look of tenderness in their depths. "Something tells me you're going to be here for a while," he said, and then his gaze moved slowly over Elisabeth, from her face to the incongruous toes of her sneakers and back again. His hands rested lightly on the sides of her waist, and she felt a spiritual jolt as he looked deeply into her eyes, as though to find her soul behind them.

It seemed natural when his lips descended toward hers and brushed lightly against them, soft and warm and moist. A moment later, however, he was kissing her in earnest.

With a whimper, Elisabeth put her arms around his neck and held on, afraid she would sink to the floor. The gentle assault on her senses continued; her mouth was open to his, and even through the dress and the bra beneath, her nipples hardened against the wall of his chest. A sweet, grinding ache twisted in the depths of her femininity, a wild need she had never felt with Ian, and if Jonathan had asked her, she would have surrendered then and there.

Instead, he set her roughly away from him and avoided her eyes. Trista's labored piano playing filled their ears.

"There's obviously no point in keeping you locked up in your room," he said hoarsely. "If you encounter Miss Calderberry, kindly introduce yourself as my wife's sister."

With that, he was gone. Elisabeth stood there in the center of her room, her cheeks flaring with color because he'd kissed her as no other man ever had—and because he was ashamed to have her under his roof. She wanted to laugh and cry, both at the same time, but in the end she did neither.

She crept down the back stairway and out the kitchen door and headed in the direction of the stream where she had picnicked by herself almost a hundred years in the future. The scent of apple blossoms filled her spirit as she walked through the recently planted orchard. Birds sang in the treetops, and in the near distance, she could hear the rustling song of the creek.

It occurred to her then that she could be blissfully happy in this era, for all its shortcomings. On some level, she had always yearned for a simpler, though certainly not easier, life and a man like Jonathan.

Elisabeth hurried along, the soft petals billowing around her like fog in a dream, and finally reached the grassy bank.

The place was different and yet the same, and she stood in exactly the spot where she'd spread her blanket to eat lunch and read. The covered bridge towered nearby, but its plank walls were new, and the smell of freshly sawed wood mingled with the aromas of spring grass and the fertile earth.

In order to protect her dress from green smudges, Elisabeth sat on a boulder overlooking the stream instead of on the ground. She removed the hat and set it beside her, then lifted her arms to her hair, winding it into a French knot at the back of her head even though she had no pins to hold it. Her reflection smiled back at her from the crystal-bright waters of the creek, looking delightfully Victorian.

A clatter on the road made her lift her head, her hands still

INNISFIL PUBLIC LIBRARY

cupped at her nape, and she watched wide-eyed as a large stagecoach, drawn by eight mismatched horses, rattled onto the bridge. The driver touched his hat brim in a friendly way when the coach reappeared, and Elisabeth waved, laughing. It was like playing a part in a movie.

And then the wind picked up suddenly, making the leaves of the birch and willow trees whisper and lifting Elisabeth's borrowed hat right off the rock. She made a lunge, and both she and the bonnet went straight into the creek.

With a howl of dismay, Elisabeth felt the slippery pebbles on the bottom of the icy stream give way beneath the soles of her sneakers. As the luscious hat floated merrily away, she tumbled forward and landed in the water with a splash.

Jonathan was standing on the bank when she floundered her way back to shore, her lovely dress clinging revealingly to her form, and though he offered his hand, Elisabeth ignored it.

"What are you doing?" she sputtered furiously, her teeth already chattering, her hair hanging in dripping tendrils around her face. "Following me?"

He grinned and shrugged. "I saw you walking this way, and I thought you might be planning to hitch a ride on the afternoon stage. It seems you've been swimming instead."

Elisabeth glared at him and crossed her arms over her breasts. Because of the unexpected dip in the creek, her nipples were plainly visible beneath the fabric. "It isn't funny," she retorted, near tears. "This is the prettiest dress I've ever had, and now it's ruined!"

He removed his suitcoat and laid it over her shoulders. "I suppose it is," he allowed. "But there are other dresses in the world."

"Not like this one," Elisabeth said despairingly.

Jonathan's arm tightened briefly around her before falling to his side. "That's what you think," he countered. "Go through the trunks again. If you don't find anything you like, I'll *buy* you another dress."

Elisabeth gave him a sidelong look, shivering inside his coat as they walked toward the orchard and the house beyond.

No one needed to tell her that nineteenth-century country doctors didn't make a lot of money; many of Jonathan's patients probably paid him in chickens and squash from the garden. "Did this dress belong to your wife?" she ventured to ask, already knowing the answer, never guessing how much she would regret the question until it was too late to call it back.

Jonathan's jawline tightened, then relaxed again. He did not look at her, but at the orchard burgeoning with flowers. "Yes," he finally replied.

"Doesn't it bother you to see another woman wearing her things?"

He rubbed his chin, then thrust both hands into the pockets of his plain, practical black trousers. "No," he answered flatly.

Elisabeth thought of the two graves inside the little fence, back in modern-day Pine River, and her heart ached with genuine grief to think of Jonathan and Trista lying there. At the same time, she wondered why Jonathan's mate wasn't buried in the family plot. "Did she die, Jonathan? Your wife?"

They had reached the grove of apple trees, and petals clung to the hem of Elisabeth's spoiled dress. Jonathan's hands knotted into fists in his trouser pockets. "As far as Trista and I are concerned," he replied some moments later, "yes."

Pressing him took all Elisabeth's courage, for she could sense the controlled rage inside him. And yet she had to know if she was feeling all these crazy emotions for another woman's husband. "She left you?"

"Yes."

"Then, technically, you're a married man."

Jonathan's eyes sliced to Elisabeth's face and the expression she saw in them brought color pulsing to her cheeks. "Technically?" He chuckled, but there wasn't a trace of humor in the sound. "An odd word. No, Elisabeth, I'm not the rogue you think I am. When it became clear that Barbara didn't plan to return, I went to Olympia and petitioned the legislature for a divorce. It was granted."

"All of this must have been very difficult for Trista," Elisabeth observed, wondering why Barbara Fortner hadn't taken her daughter along when she left. Perhaps Jonathan had prevented that by some legal means, or maybe the woman had doubted her own ability to support a child in such a predominantly male world.

The house was within sight now, and twilight was beginning to fall over the fragrant orchard. Elisabeth felt a tug in her heart as they walked toward the glow of lantern light in the kitchen windows. She knew she'd been homesick for this time, this place, this man at her side, all of her life.

He shocked her with his reply to her remark about the effect the divorce had had on Trista. "My daughter believes her mother died in an accident in Boston, while visiting her family, and I don't want anyone telling her differently. Since the Everses have disinherited their daughter, I don't think there's any danger that they'll betray the secret."

Elisabeth stopped to stare at him, even though it was chilly and her wet dress was clinging to her skin. "But it's a lie."

"Sometimes a lie is kinder than the truth." Having spoken these words, Jonathan picked up his stride and Elisabeth was forced to follow him into the kitchen or stand in the yard until she caught her death.

Inside, Jonathan turned the wicks up in the lamps so that the flames burned brightly, then he opened a door in the stove and began shoving in wood from the box beside it. Elisabeth huddled nearby, gratefully soaking up the warmth.

"A lie is never better than the truth," she said, having finally worked up the courage to contradict him so bluntly. He was bull stubborn in his opinions; Rue would have said he was surely a Republican.

He wrenched a blue enamel pot from the back of the stove, carried it to the sink and used the hand pump to fill it with water. Then he set the pot on to heat. "You'll be wanting tea," he remarked, completely ignoring her statement. "I'll go and find you a dressing gown."

Elisabeth drew closer to the stove, wanting the heat to reach the marrow of her bones. She had stopped shivering, at least, when Jonathan returned with a long flannel nightgown and a heavy blue corduroy robe to go over it.

"You can change in the pantry," he said, shoving the garments at Elisabeth without meeting her eyes.

She took them and went into the little room—where the washer and drier were kept in her time—and stripped in the darkness. The virginal nightgown felt blissfully warm against her clammy, goose-pimpled skin.

She was tying the belt on the robe when she came out of the pantry to find Jonathan pouring hot water into a squat, practical-looking brown teapot. "I'd be happy to cook supper," she said, wanting to be useful and, more than that, to belong in this kitchen, if only for an hour.

"Good," he said with a sigh, going to the wall of cupboards for mugs, which he carried back to the table. "Trista doesn't cook, and Ellen—that's our housekeeper—tends to be undependable on occasion. She was here earlier, but she wandered off and probably won't be back until tomorrow."

Elisabeth opened the icebox she'd discovered the first night and squatted to look inside it. Two large brook trout stared at her from a platter, and she carried them to the counter nearest the stove. "Did you catch these fish?" she asked, mostly because it gave her a soft, bittersweet sensation to be cooking and chatting idly with Jonathan.

He poured tea into the cups and went to the base of the back stairs to call Trista down. Evidently, she'd dutifully returned to her room after Miss Calderberry left.

"They were given to me," he answered presently, "in payment for a nerve tonic."

Elisabeth found a skillet in the pantry, along with jars of preserved vegetables and fruit. She selected a pint of sliced carrots and one of stewed pears, and carried them into the kitchen. By this time, Trista was setting the table with Blue Willow dishes, and Jonathan was nowhere in sight.

"He went out to the barn to feed the animals," Trista offered without being asked.

Elisabeth smiled. "Did you enjoy your piano lesson?"

"No," Trista answered. "How come your hair is all wet and straggly like that?"

Elisabeth put the trout into the skillet, minus their heads. "I fell into the creek," she replied. "Is there any bread?"

Trista went to a maple box on the far counter and removed a loaf wrapped in a checkered dish towel. She set it on a plate, then brought a bowl of butter from the icebox. "I fell in the creek once," she confided. "I was only two, and I think maybe I would have drowned if my mama hadn't pulled me right out."

Elisabeth felt a small pull in the tenderest part of her soul. "It's a good thing she was around," she said gently, remembering a small tombstone with Trista's name carved into it. She had to look away to hide sudden tears that burned hot along her lashes.

"Maybe you could play the piano for us, after supper," Trista said.

Subtly, Elisabeth dried her eyes with the soft sleeve of the wrapper Jonathan had brought to her. Like the spoiled dress, it smelled faintly of lavender. "I haven't touched a keyboard in weeks, so I'm probably out of practice," she said with a cheerful sniffle. She took her first sip of the tea Jonathan had made for her and found it strong and sweet.

Trista laughed. "You couldn't sound worse than I do, no matter how long it's been since you've practiced."

Elisabeth laughed, too, and hugged the little girl. Through the window, she saw Jonathan moving toward the house in the last dim light of day. In that moment, she was as warm as if the noontime sun had been shining unrestrained on her bare skin.

She dished up the fish and the preserved carrots while Jonathan washed at the sink, then they all sat down at the table.

Elisabeth was touched when Trista offered a short grace, asking God to take special care that her mama was happy in heaven. At this, Elisabeth opened her eyes for an accusing peek at Jonathan and found him staring defiantly back at her, his jawline set.

When the prayer was over, Jonathan immediately cut three perfect slices from the loaf of bread and moved one to his plate.

"Don't you have any cows?" Elisabeth asked. She'd noticed that Jonathan hadn't carried in a bucket of fresh milk, the way farmers did in books and movies.

He shook his head. "Don't need one," he replied. "I get all the butter and cream we can use from my patients."

"Do any of them give you money?" Elisabeth inquired, careful not to let so much as a trace of irony slip into her tone.

Still, Jonathan's look was quick and sharp. "We manage," he replied crisply.

After that, Trista carried the conversation, chattering cheerfully about the upcoming spelling bee at school and how she'd be sure to win it because she had so much time to practice her words. When supper was over, she and Elisabeth washed the dishes while Jonathan put on his suitcoat—it had been drying on the back of a chair near the stove—and reached for his medical bag.

"I won't be long," he said, addressing his words to Trista. "I want to check and see if Mrs. Taber is any closer to delivering that baby."

Trista nodded and hung up the dish towel neatly over the handle on the oven door, but Elisabeth followed Jonathan outside.

"You mean you're leaving your daughter all alone here, with a total stranger?" she demanded, her hands on her hips.

Jonathan took a lantern from the wall of the back porch and lit it after striking a wooden match. "You're not a stranger," he said. "You and I are old friends, though I admit I don't remember exactly where we met." He bent to kiss her lightly on the cheek. "In case I don't see you before morning, good night, Lizzie."

CHAPTER 6

Lizzie.

Being called by that name made Elisabeth sway on her feet. She grasped at the railing beside the porch steps to steady herself.

Jonathan didn't notice her reaction, which was probably just as well because Elisabeth was in no condition to offer more explanations. She watched, stricken, as he strode toward the barn, the lantern in one hand, his medical bag in the other.

The moment he disappeared from sight, Elisabeth sank to the steps and just sat there, trembling, her hands over her face. Dear God in heaven, why hadn't she guessed? Why hadn't she known that *she* was the woman accused of setting the fire that probably killed Jonathan and Trista?

"Elisabeth?" Trista's voice was small and full of concern. "Is something the matter?"

Elisabeth drew in a deep breath and made herself speak in a normal tone of voice. "No, sweetheart," she lied, "everything is just fine."

The child hovered in the doorway behind her. "Are you going to play for me?" she asked hopefully. "I'm still in trouble, but I know Papa wouldn't mind my staying downstairs for just one song."

Elisabeth rose from the step, feeling chilly even in the warm robe and nightgown Jonathan had brought her. What a scandal her state of dress would cause in Victorian Pine River, she thought in a wild effort to distract herself. But there was no forgetting—if she didn't do something to change history, two people she already cherished would die tragically and she would be blamed for their deaths.

"One song," she answered sadly, taking Trista's hand and holding it tightly in her own.

"Elisabeth played a boogie," Trista told her father the next morning as she ate the oatmeal Ellen had made for her. Jonathan frowned, and the housekeeper stiffened slightly in disapproval, her shoulders going rigid under her cambric dress.

"A what?" His head ached; deception did not come naturally to him. And he knew Ellen hadn't believed his story about his late wife's sister arriving suddenly for a visit.

"Land sakes," muttered Ellen, slamming the fire door after shoving another stick of wood into the stove.

"A boogie-woogie," Trista clarified, and it was clear from her shining face that she enjoyed just saying the word.

Just then, Elisabeth came somewhat shyly down the back stairs and Jonathan's sensible heart skittered over two full beats when he saw her. She'd pinned her hair up in back, but it still made soft, taffy-colored curls around her face, and she was wearing a blue-and-white-flowered dress he didn't remember seeing on Barbara.

She smiled as she advanced toward the kitchen table, where Trista had set a place for her. "Good morning."

Remembering his manners, Jonathan rose and stood until Elisabeth was seated. "Ellen," he said, "This is my—sister-in-law, Miss Elisabeth McCartney. Elisabeth, our housekeeper, Ellen Harwood."

Ellen, a plain girl with a freckled face and frizzy red-brown hair, nodded grudgingly but didn't return Elisabeth's soft hello.

Jonathan waited until Ellen had gone upstairs to clean to ask, "What in the devil is a boogie-woogie?"

Elisabeth and Trista looked at each other and laughed. "Just a lively song," Elisabeth answered.

"A *very* lively song," Trista confirmed.

Jonathan sighed, pushed back his plate and pulled his watch from his vest pocket to flip open the case. He should have been gone an hour already, but he'd waited for a glimpse of Elisabeth, needing the swelling warmth that filled his bruised, stubborn heart when he looked at her. He could admit that to himself, if not out loud to her. "If you're ready, Trista, I'll drop you off at the schoolhouse on my way into town."

His daughter cast a sidelong glance at their strange but undeniably lovely guest. "I thought I'd walk this morning, Papa," Trista answered. "Elisabeth wants to see where I go to school."

Jonathan narrowed his eyes as he regarded Elisabeth, silently issuing warnings he could not say in front of Trista. "I'm sure she wouldn't be foolish enough to wander too far afield and get herself lost."

"I'm sure she wouldn't," Elisabeth said wryly, watching him with those blue-green eyes of hers. Their beauty always startled him, caught him off guard.

Jonathan left the table, then, and took his suitcoat from the peg beside the back door. Trista was ready with his medical bag, looking up at him earnestly. "Don't worry, Papa," she confided in a stage whisper. "I'll take very good care of Elisabeth."

He bent to kiss the top of her head, then tugged lightly at one of her dark pigtails. "I'm sure you will," he replied. After one more lingering look at Elisabeth, he left the house to begin his rounds.

Elisabeth marveled as she walked along, Trista's hand in hers. In the twentieth century, this road was a paved highway, following a slightly different course and lined with telephone poles. It was so quiet that she could hear the whisper of the creek on the other side of the birch, cedar and Douglas fir trees that crowded its edges.

A wagon loaded with hay clattered by, drawn by two weary-looking horses, and Elisabeth stared after it. By then, she'd given up the idea that this experience was any kind of hallucination, but she still hadn't gotten used to the sights and sounds of a century she'd thought was gone forever.

Trista gazed up at her speculatively. "Where did you go when you went away before?"

"Back to my own house," Elisabeth replied after careful thought.

"Are you going to stay with Papa and me from now on?"

Elisabeth had to avert her eyes, thinking of the fire. She'd spent most of the night tossing and turning, trying to come up with some way to evade fate. For all she knew, it could not be changed.

Again, she took her time answering. "Not forever," she said softly.

Trista's strong little fingers tightened around Elisabeth's. "I don't want you to go."

In that moment, Elisabeth realized that she didn't want to leave...ever. For all its hard realities, she felt that she belonged in this time, with these people. Indeed, it was her other life, back in twentieth-century Washington state, that seemed like a dream now. "Let's just take things one day at a time, Trista," she told the child.

They rounded a wide bend in the road and there was the brick schoolhouse—nothing but a ruin in Elisabeth's day—with glistening windows and a sturdy shake roof. The bell rang in the tower while a slender woman with dark hair and bright blue eyes pulled exuberantly on the rope.

Elisabeth stood stock-still. "It's wonderful," she whispered.

Trista laughed. "It's only a schoolhouse," she said indulgently. "Do you want to meet my teacher, Miss Bishop?" The child gazed up at Elisabeth, gray eyes dancing, and dropped her voice to a confidential whisper. "She's sweet on the blacksmith, and Ellen says she probably won't last out the term!"

Elisabeth smiled and shook her head. "It's time for class to start, so I'll meet Miss Bishop later."

Trista nodded and hurried off to join the other children surging up the steps and through the open doorway of the schoolhouse. A few of them looked back over their shoulders at Elisabeth, freckled faces puzzled.

She stood outside, listening, until the laughter and noise faded away. Being a teacher herself, she relished the familiar sounds.

The weather was bright and sunny, and Elisabeth had no particular desire to go back to Jonathan's house and face that sullen housekeeper, so she continued on toward town. As she neared the outskirts, the metallic squeal of a steam-powered saw met her ears and her step quickened. Even though she was scared—her situation gave new meaning to the hackneyed term "a fish out of water"—she was driven by a crazy kind of curiosity that wouldn't allow her to turn back.

Her first glimpse of the town stunned her, even though she'd thought she was prepared. The main street seemed to be composed of equal measures of mud and manure, and the weathered buildings clustered alongside were like something out of a *Bonanza* rerun. Any minute now, Hoss and Little Joe were sure to come ambling out through the swinging doors of the Silver Lady Saloon....

There were horses and wagons everywhere, and the noisy machinery in the sawmill screeched as logs from the timber-choked countryside were fed through its blades. Elisabeth wandered past a forge worked by a man wearing a heavy black apron. and she sidestepped two lumberjacks who came out of the general store to stand in the middle of the sidewalk, leering.

When she saw Jonathan's shingle up ahead, jutting out from the wall of a small, unpainted building, she hurried toward it. There was a blackboard on the wall beside the door, with the word *In* scrawled on it in white chalk. Elisabeth smiled as she opened the door.

A giant man in oiled trousers and a bloody flannel shirt sat on the end of an old-fashioned examining table. Jonathan was winding a clean bandage around the patient's arm, but he paused, seeing Elisabeth, took off his gold-rimmed spectacles and tucked them into his shirt pocket.

A tender whirlwind spun in her heart and then her stomach.

"Is there a problem?" he asked.

Elisabeth was feeling a little queasy, due to the sight and

smell of blood. She groped for a chair and sank into the only seat available—the hard wooden one behind Jonathan's cluttered desk. "No," she answered. "I was just exploring Pine River."

The lumberjack smiled at her, revealing gaps between his crooked, tobacco-stained teeth. "This must be the lady you've been hidin' away out at your place, Doc," he said.

Jonathan gave his patient an annoyed glance and finished tying off the bandage. "I haven't been hiding anything," he replied. "And don't go telling the whole damn town I have, Ivan, or I'll sew your mouth shut, just like I did your arm."

Ivan stood and produced a coin from the pocket of his filthy trousers, but even as he paid Jonathan, he kept his eyes on Elisabeth. "Good day to you, ma'am," he said, and then he reluctantly left the office.

Jonathan began cleaning up the mess Ivan and his blood had made. "Coming here was probably not the most intelligent thing you ever did," he observed presently.

Elisabeth's attention had strayed to the calendar page on the wall. April 17, 1892. It was incredible. "I was curious," she said distractedly, thinking of a documentary she'd watched on public television recently. "In a few more months—August, if I remember correctly—a woman in Fall River, Massachusetts, will be accused of murdering her father and stepmother with an ax. Her name is Lizzie Borden. She'll be acquitted of the crime because of a lack of evidence."

His gaze held both pity and irritation. "Is that supposed to have some kind of significance—the fact that she has the same first name as you do?"

A chill went through Elisabeth; she hadn't thought of that. "No. Besides, nobody ever calls me Lizzie."

"I do," Jonathan answered flatly, pouring water into a clean basin and beginning to wash his hands.

"I'm glad to see that you're taking antisepsis seriously," Elisabeth said, as much to change the subject as anything. She still had that jittery feeling that being around Jonathan invariably gave her. "Most disease is caused by germs, you know."

Jonathan leaned forward slightly and rounded his eyes.
"No," he said, pretending to be surprised.

"I guess maybe you've figured that out already," Elisabeth
conceded, folding her hands in her lap.

"Thank you for that," he answered, drying his hands on a
thin, white towel and laying it aside.

Just then, the door opened and a tall man wearing a cowboy
hat and a battered, lightweight woolen coat strode in. He
needed a shave, and carried a rifle in his right hand, holding
it with such ease that it seemed a part of him. When he
glanced curiously at Elisabeth, she saw that his eyes were a
piercing turquoise blue. Pinned to his coat was a shiny nickel-
plated badge in the shape of a star.

Wow, Elisabeth thought. *A real, live lawman.*

"'Morning, Farley," Jonathan said. "That boil still bothering you?"

Farley actually flushed underneath that macho five-o'clock
shadow of his. "Now, Jon," he complained in his low drawl,
"there was no need to mention that in front of the lady. It's
personal-like."

Elisabeth averted her face for a moment so the marshal
wouldn't see that she was smiling.

"Sorry," Jonathan said, but Elisabeth heard the amusement
in his voice even if Farley didn't. He gave her a pointed look.
"The lady is just leaving. Let's get on with it."

Elisabeth nodded and bolted out of her chair. They
wouldn't have to tell her twice—the last thing she wanted to
do was watch Jonathan lance a boil on some private part of
the marshal's body. "Goodbye," she said from the doorway.
"And it was very nice to meet you, Mr. Farley."

"Just Farley," rumbled the marshal.

"Whatever," Elisabeth answered, ducking out and closing
the door. There was something summarial in the way Jonathan
pulled the shades on both windows.

Since her senses were strained from all the new things she
was trying to take in, Elisabeth was getting tired. She walked
back through town, nodding politely to the women who stared
at her from the wooden sidewalks and pointed, and she hoped

she hadn't ruined Jonathan's practice by marching so boldly into town and walking right into his office.

Reaching Jonathan's house, she found Ellen in the backyard. She'd hung a rug over the clothesline and was beating it with a broom.

Elisabeth smiled in a friendly way. "Hello," she called.

"If you want anything to eat," the housekeeper retorted, "you'll just have to fix it yourself!"

With a shrug, Elisabeth went inside and helped herself to a piece of bread, spreading it liberally with butter and strawberry jam. Then she found a blanket, helped herself to a book from Jonathan's collection in the parlor and set out for her favorite spot beside the creek.

She supposed Janet was probably getting worried, if she'd tried to call, and the Buzbee sisters would be concerned, too, if they went more than a few days without seeing her. She spread the blanket on the ground and sat down, tucking her skirts carefully around her.

A sigh escaped Elisabeth as she watched the sunlight making moving patterns on the waters of the creek. She was going to have to go back soon, back where she belonged. Her throat went tight. Before she could do that, she had to find some way to convince Jonathan that he and Trista were in very real danger.

The book forgotten at her side, Elisabeth curled up on the blanket and watched the water flow by, shimmering like a million liquid diamonds in the bright sunshine. And her sleepless night caught up with her.

When she awakened, it was to the sound of children's laughter echoing through the trees. Elisabeth rose, automatically smoothing her hair and skirts, and left the blanket and book behind to follow the path of the stream, walking beneath the covered bridge.

Presently, she could see the schoolhouse across the narrow ribbon of water. The children were all outside at recess. While the boys had divided up into teams for baseball, the girls pushed each other in the rustic swings and played hopscotch. She spotted Trista and wondered if the plain little girl at her side was Vera, who would eventually give birth to Cecily and Roberta Buzbee.

Deciding that her presence would just raise a lot of awkward questions for Trista, Elisabeth slipped away and, after fetching the blanket and Jonathan's book, went back to the house.

By this time, there was a nice stew simmering on the stove and fresh bread cooling on the counter under a spotless dishtowel. Ellen had apparently left for the day.

Relieved, Elisabeth opened the icebox and peered inside. There was a bowl of canned pears left over from breakfast, so she dished up a serving and went out onto the back step to eat them. She was enjoying the glorious spring afternoon when Jonathan pulled up alongside the barn, driving his horse and buggy. He sprang nimbly down from the seat and walked toward her, his medical bag in one hand.

Elisabeth felt a sweet tightening in the most feminine part of her as he approached. "Must have been an easy day," she said when he sat down beside her.

He chuckled ruefully. "'Easy' isn't the word I would use to describe it," he said. "I couldn't stop thinking about you, Elisabeth."

Elisabeth drew a deep breath, and suddenly her heart and her spirit and all of her body were full of springtime. She lifted one eyebrow and forced herself to speak in a normal tone. "I suppose you were wondering if I was chasing poor Ellen all over the farm with an ax."

Jonathan laughed and shook his head. "No, I've considered doing that myself." His expression turned solemn in the next moment, however, and his sure, callused hand closed over one of Elisabeth's. "Who are you?" he rasped out. "And what spell have you cast over me?"

Never before had Elisabeth guessed that tenderness toward another person could run so deep as to be painful. "I'm just a woman," she said softly. "And I wouldn't have the first idea how to cast a spell."

He stood slowly, drawing Elisabeth with him, discounting her words with a shake of his head. She knew where he meant to take her, but she couldn't protest because it seemed to her that she'd been moving toward this moment all of her life. Maybe even for all of eternity.

She closed her eyes as he held her hand to his mouth and placed featherlight kisses on her knuckles.

Once they were inside the house, he lifted her easily into his arms and started up the back stairs. Elisabeth buried her face in his muscular neck, loving the smell and the strength and the substance of him. She looked up when she heard the creak of a door and found herself in a version of her room back in the world she knew.

The bed, made of aged, intricately carved oak, stood between the windows facing the fireplace. The walls were unpapered, painted a plain white, and Elisabeth didn't recognize any of the furniture.

Jonathan set her on her feet and just as she would have found the wit to argue that what they were about to do was wrong, he kissed her. So great was his skill and his innate magnetism that Elisabeth forgot her objections and lost herself in his mastery.

He unpinned her hair, combing it through with his fingers, and then very slowly began unbuttoning the front of her dress. Uncovering the lacy bra beneath, he frowned, and Elisabeth reached up to unfasten the front catch, revealing her full breasts to him.

Jonathan drew in his breath, then lifted one hand to caress her lightly. The pad of his thumb moved over her nipple, turning it button hard and wrenching a little cry of pleasure and surrender from Elisabeth.

She tilted her head back in glorious submission as he bent his head to her breast, pushing the dress down over her hips as he suckled. Elisabeth entwined her fingers in his thick, dark hair, her breathing shallow and quick.

When both her nipples were wet from his tongue, Jonathan laid her gently on the bed, taking no notice of her sneakers as he pulled them off and tossed them away. She crooned and arched her back as he slipped her panties down over her legs and threw them aside, too. He caressed her until she was damp, her body twisting with readiness.

His clothes seemed to disappear as easily as hers had, and soon he was stretched out on the mattress beside her. The April breeze ruffled the curtains at the windows and passed over their nakedness, stirring their passion to even greater heights rather than cooling it.

Elisabeth moaned as Jonathan claimed her mouth in another consuming kiss, his tongue sparring with hers. Her fingers dug into the moist flesh on his back as he moved his lips down over her breasts and her belly. Then he gripped her ankles and pressed her heels to the firm flesh of her bottom. Boldly, he burrowed through the silken barrier and tasted her.

Elisabeth's head moved from side to side on the pillow. "Oh, Jonathan—please—it's too much—"

"I want you to be ready for me," he told her gruffly, and then he enjoyed her in earnest, as greedy as if she were covered in honey.

The exercise moistened Elisabeth's skin, making small tendrils of hair cling to her face, and her breath came hard as she rose and fell in time with the rhythm Jonathan set for her. A low, guttural cry escaped her when he set her legs over his shoulders and teased her into the last stages of response.

She called his name when a sweet volcano erupted within her, her body arched like a bow drawn tight to launch an arrow. He spoke gently as he laid her, quivering, upon the bed and poised himself over her. She was still floating when he began kissing her collarbone.

"Shall I make love to you, Elisabeth?" he asked quietly, and a new tenderness swept over her in that moment because she knew he would respect her decision, whatever it might be.

"Yes," she whispered, twisting one finger in a lock of his hair. "Oh, yes."

He touched her with his manhood, and Elisabeth trembled with anticipation and a touch of fear. After all, there had only been one other man in her life and her experience was limited.

"I promise I won't hurt you," Jonathan said, and she was

diffused with heat when he teased her by giving her just the tip of his shaft.

She clutched at his back. "Jonathan!"

He gave her a little more, and she marveled that he filled her so tightly. "What?"

"I want you—I need you—"

In a long, smooth glide, he gave her his length, and Elisabeth uttered a muffled shout of triumph. An instant later, she was in the throes of release, buckling helplessly beneath Jonathan, sobbing as her body worked out its sweet salvation.

She was embarrassed when she could finally lie still, and she would have turned her head away if Jonathan hadn't caught her chin in his hand and made her look at him.

"You were beautiful," he said. "So—beautiful."

Elisabeth's eyes brimmed with tears. Jonathan had given her a kind of pleasure she'd never dreamed existed, and she wanted to do the same for him. She cupped his face in her hands, moving her thumbs slowly over his jawbones, and she began to move beneath him.

He uttered a strangled moan and his powerful frame tensed, then he began to meet her thrusts with more and more force, until he finally exploded within her, filling her with his warmth. When it was over, he collapsed beside her, his head on her chest, one leg sprawled across her thighs, and Elisabeth held him.

After a long time, he asked quietly, "Who was he?"

Elisabeth braced herself, knowing men of Jonathan's generation expected women to come to their beds as virgins. "My husband," she said.

Instantly, Jonathan raised his head to stare into her eyes. "Your what?"

Her face felt hot. "Your honor is safe, Doctor," she assured him. "Ian and I were divorced a year ago."

He cleared his throat and sat up, reaching for his clothes. The distance in his manner wounded Elisabeth; she felt defensive. "Now I suppose I'm some kind of social pariah, just because my marriage didn't last," she said. "Well, things are different where I come from, Jonathan. Divorced women aren't branded as sinners for the rest of their lives.''

Jonathan didn't answer, he just kept dressing.

There was a black-and-blue-plaid lap robe folded across the foot of the bed. Elisabeth snatched it up to cover herself. ''Jonathan Fortner, if you walk out of here without speaking to me, I swear I'll never forgive you!''

He watched as she tried to dress without letting the lap robe slip. ''Why did he divorce you?''

Elisabeth was furious; her cheeks ached with color. ''He *didn't*—the choice was mine!''

Jonathan's shoulders slackened slightly, as though pressed under some great weight, and he sat down on the edge of the bed with a sigh. When he extended a hand to Elisabeth, she took it without thinking, and he settled her gently beside him, buttoning the front of her dress as he spoke.

''I'm sorry. I was judging what you did in terms of my own experience, and that's unreasonable.''

Elisabeth couldn't resist touching the dark, rumpled hair at his nape. ''Did she hurt you so badly, Jonathan?'' she whispered.

''Yes,'' he answered simply. And then he stood and started toward the door. ''Trista will be home soon,'' he said, without looking back. And he was gone.

Barely fifteen minutes later, when Elisabeth was in the kitchen brewing tea, Trista came in, carrying her slate and a spelling primer. The child set her school things down and went to the icebox for the crockery pitcher.

''How was school?'' Elisabeth asked.

Trista's gray eyes sparkled as she poured milk into a glass and then helped herself to cookies from a squat china jar. ''When Miss Bishop opened her lunch pail, there was a love letter inside—from Harvey Kates.''

''The blacksmith?'' Elisabeth took a cookie and joined Trista at the table.

The little girl nodded importantly, and there was now a milk mustache on her upper lip. ''His sister Phyllis is in the seventh grade, and he gave her a penny to put the note where Miss Bishop would be sure to find it.''

"And, of course, Phyllis told all of you exactly what her brother had written,'' Elisabeth guessed.

Trista nodded. ''He said he was crazy for her.''

Before Elisabeth could respond to that, Jonathan came into the kitchen. He gave Trista a distracted kiss on the top of her head, without so much as glancing at the houseguest he'd taken to bed only a short time before. ''You've paid your debt to society,'' he said to the child. ''You don't have to spend any more afternoons in your room.''

Trista's face glowed with delight and gratitude. ''Thank you, Papa.''

Elisabeth might have been invisible for all the attention Jonathan was paying her.

''I'll be on rounds. Would you like to go along?''

The child shook her head. ''I want to practice my piano lessons,'' she said virtuously.

Jonathan looked amused, but he made no comment. His gray eyes touched Elisabeth briefly, questioningly, and then he was gone. Sadness gripped her as she realized he now regretted what had happened between them.

While Trista trudged bravely through her music, Elisabeth made her way slowly up the back stairs and into the little girl's room. She was becoming too enmeshed in a way of life that could never be hers, and she had to put some space between herself and Jonathan before she fell hopelessly in love with him.

The decision was made. She would say goodbye to Trista, go back to her own time and try to make herself believe that all of this had been a dream.

CHAPTER 7

The necklace was gone.

Elisabeth dried her eyes with the back of one hand as relief and panic battled within her. After drawing a very deep breath and letting it out slowly, she made her way downstairs to the parlor, where Trista was struggling through *Ode to Joy* at the piano.

Elisabeth paused in the doorway, watching the little girl practice and marveling that she'd come to love this child so deeply in such a short time. "Trista?"

Innocent gray eyes linked with Elisabeth's and the notes reverberated into silence. "Yes?"

"I can't find my necklace. Have you seen it?"

Trista's gaze didn't waver, though her lower lip trembled slightly. "Papa has it. He said the pendant was valuable and might get lost if we left it lying around."

"I see," Elisabeth replied as righteous indignation welled up inside her. The fact that they'd been so gloriously intimate made Jonathan's action an even worse betrayal than it would ordinarily have been. "Do you know where he put it?"

Moisture brimmed along Trista's lower lashes; somehow, Trista had guessed that Elisabeth meant to leave and that the necklace had to go with her. She shook her head. "I don't," she sniffled. "Honest."

Elisabeth's heart ached, and she went to sit beside Trista on the piano bench, draping one arm around the little girl's shoulders. "There are people in another place who will be worrying about me," Elisabeth said gently. "I have to go and let them know I'm all right."

A tear trickled down Trista's plump cheek. "Will you be back?"

Elisabeth leaned over and lightly kissed the child's temple. "I don't know, sweetheart. Something very strange is happening to me, and I don't dare make a lot of promises, because I'm not sure I can keep them." She thought about the impending fire and a sense of hopelessness swept over her. "I'll tell you this, though—if I have any choice in the matter, I *will* see you again."

Trista nodded and rested her head against Elisabeth's shoulder. "Most times, when grown-up people go away, they don't come back."

Knowing the child was referring to her lost mother, Elisabeth hugged her again. "If I don't return, Trista, I want you to remember that it was only because I couldn't, and not because I didn't want to." She stood. "Now, you go and finish your practicing while I look for the necklace."

Elisabeth searched Jonathan's study, which was the small parlor in modern times, and found nothing except a lot of cryptic notes, medical books jammed with bits of paper and a cabinet full of vials and bottles and bandage gauze. From there, she progressed to the bedroom where he had made such thorough love to her only that afternoon.

She was still angry, but just being in that room again brought all the delicious, achy sensations rushing back, and she was almost overwhelmed with the need of him. She began with the top drawer of his bureau, finding nothing but starched handkerchiefs and stiff celluloid collars.

"Did you lose something?"

Jonathan's voice startled Elisabeth; like a hard fall, it left her breathless. She turned, her cheeks flaming, to face him.

"My necklace," she said, keeping her shoulders squared. "Where is it, Jonathan?"

He went to the night table beside his bed, opened the drawer and took out a small leather box. Lifting the lid, he looped the pendant over his fingers and extended it to Elisabeth.

"I'm going back," she said, unable to meet his eyes. For

the moment, it was all she could do to cope with the wild emotions this man had brought to life inside her. He had taught her one thing for certain: she had never truly loved Ian or any other man. Jonathan Fortner had first claim on both her body and her soul.

He kept his distance, perhaps sensing that she would fall apart if he touched her. "Why?"

"We made love, Jonathan," she whispered brokenly, her hands trembling as she opened the catch on the pendant and draped the chain around her neck. "That changed things between us. And I can't afford to care for you."

Jonathan sighed. "Elisabeth—"

"No," she said, interrupting, holding up one hand to silence him. "I know you think I'm eccentric or deluded or something, and maybe you're right. Maybe this is all some kind of elaborate fantasy and I'm wandering farther and farther from reality."

He came to her then and took her into his arms. She felt the hard strength of his thighs and midsection. "I'm real, Elisabeth," he told her with gentle wryness. "You're not imagining me, I promise you."

She pushed herself back from the warm solace of him. "Jonathan, I came here to warn you," she said urgently. "There was—will be—a fire. You've got to do something, if not for your own sake, then for Trista's."

He kissed her forehead. "I know you believe what you're saying," he replied, his tone gentle and a little hoarse. "But it's simply not possible for a human being to predict the future. Surely you understand that I cannot throw my daughter's life into an uproar on the basis of your...premonitions."

Elisabeth stiffened as a desperate idea struck her. "Suppose I could prove that I'm from the future, Jonathan—suppose I could show you the article that will be printed in the *Pine River Bugle?*"

Jonathan was frowning at her, as though he feared she'd gone mad. "That would be impossible."

She gave a brief, strangled laugh. "Impossible. You know, Jonathan, until just a short while ago, I would have said it was *impossible* to travel from my century to yours. I thought time was an orderly thing, rolling endlessly onward, like a river. Instead, it seems that the past, present and future are all of a piece, like some giant celestial tapestry.''

All the while she was talking, Jonathan was maneuvering her toward the bed, though this time it was for a very different reason. ''Just lie down for a little while,'' he said reasonably. His bag was close at hand, like always, and he snapped it open.

''Jonathan, I'm quite all right....''

He took out a syringe and began filling it from a vial.

Elisabeth's eyes went wide and she tried to bolt off the bed. ''Don't you dare give me a shot!'' she cried, but Jonathan put his free hand on her shoulder and pressed her easily back to the mattress. ''Ouch!'' she yelled when the needle punctured her upper arm. ''Damn you, Jonathan, I'm not sick!''

He withdrew the needle and reached for the plaid lab robe Elisabeth had tried to hide behind after their lovemaking that afternoon. ''Just rest. You'll feel better in a few hours,'' he urged, laying the blanket over her.

Elisabeth sat up again, only to find that all her muscles had turned to water. She sagged back against the pillows. ''Jonathan Fortner, what did you give me? Do you realize that there are laws against injecting things into people's veins?''

''Be quiet,'' he ordered sternly.

The door creaked open and Trista peered around the edge. ''What's wrong with Elisabeth?'' she asked in a thin, worried voice.

Jonathan sighed and closed his medical bag with a snap. ''She's overwrought, that's all,'' he answered. ''Run along and do your spelling lesson.''

''Pusher!'' Elisabeth spat out once the door had closed behind the little girl. The room was starting to undulate, and she felt incredibly weak. ''I should get that Farley person out here and have you arrested.''

''Don't you think you're being a little childish?'' Jonathan asked, bending over the bed. ''I admit I shouldn't have shoved you down that way, but you didn't give much choice, did you?''

Elisabeth rolled her eyes. "A pusher is... Oh, never mind! But you mark my words, *Doctor*—I'm filing a complaint against you!''

"And I'm sure Marshal Haynes will track me down and throw me in the hoosegow the minute his boil is healed and he can sit a horse again." In the next moment, Jonathan was gone.

Struggling to stay awake, Elisabeth wondered how she could ever expect to get through to this man if he was going hold her down and drug her every time she talked about her experience. She drifted off into a restless sleep, waking once to find Trista standing beside the bed, gently bathing her forehead with a cool cloth.

Elisabeth felt a surge of tenderness and, catching hold of Trista's hand, she gave it a little squeeze. Then she was floating again.

The house was dark when the medication finally wore off, and the realization that this was Jonathan's bed came to her instantly. She laid very still until she was sure he wasn't beside her.

Her hand rose to her throat, and she was relieved to find the necklace was still there. Another ten minutes passed before she had the wit to get out of bed and grope her way through the blackness to the door.

In the hallway, she carefully took the pendant off and tossed it over Trista's threshold. Only when she was on the other side did she put it on again.

There was pale moonlight shining in through the little girl's window, and Elisabeth went to her bedside and gently awakened her.

"You're leaving," Trista whispered, holding very tightly to her rag doll.

Elisabeth bent to kiss her forehead. "Yes, darling, I'm going to try. Remember my promise—if I can come back to you, I will."

Trista sighed. "All right," she said forlornly. "Goodbye, Elisabeth."

"Goodbye, sweetheart." Elisabeth put her arms around Trista and gave her a final hug. "No matter what happens, don't forget that I love you."

Trista's eyes were bright with tears as she sank her teeth into her lower lip and nodded.

Elisabeth drew a deep breath and went back to the door, closing her eyes as she reached for the knob, turned it and stepped through.

She was back in the twentieth century. Elisabeth opened her eyes to find herself in a carpeted hallway, then reached out for a switch and found one. Suddenly the electric wall sconces glared.

She opened the door to her room and peeked in. A poignant, bitter loneliness possessed her because there was no trace, no hint of Jonathan's presence. After lingering for a moment, she turned and went downstairs to the telephone table in the hallway.

Not surprisingly, the little red light on her answering machine was blinking.

There were three messages from Janet, each more anxious than the last, and several other friends had called from Seattle. Elisabeth shoved her fingers through her hair, sighed and padded into the kitchen, barefoot. She was still wearing the cambric dress Jonathan had given her, and she smiled, thinking what a sensation it would cause if she wore it to the supermarket.

Since she hadn't had dinner, Elisabeth heated a can of soup before finding the microfilm copies she'd made in the *Bugle* offices. It gave her a chill to think of showing Jonathan a newspaper account of his own death and that of his daughter.

While she huddled at the kitchen table, eating, Elisabeth read over the articles. It still troubled her that no bodies had been found, but then, such investigations hadn't been very thorough or scientific in the nineteenth century. Maybe the discovery had even been hushed up, out of some misguided Victorian sense of delicacy.

Flipping ahead in the sheaf of copies, Elisabeth came to her own trial for the murder of Jonathan and Trista Fortner. With a growing sense of unreality, she read that Lizzie McCartney, who ''claimed to be'' the sister of the late Barbara McCartney Fortner, had been found guilty of the crime of arson, and thus murder, and sentenced to hang.

Elisabeth pushed away the last of her soup, feeling nauseous. Destiny had apparently decreed her death, as well as Jonathan's and Trista's, and she had no way of knowing whether or not their singular fates could be circumvented.

She took her bowl to the sink and rinsed it, then went upstairs to take a long, hot shower. When that was finished Elisabeth brushed her teeth, put on a lightweight cotton nightgown and crawled into bed.

Unable to sleep, she lay staring up at the ceiling. It would be easy to avoid being tried and hanged—all she would have to do was drop the necklace down a well somewhere and never go back to Jonathan's time. But even as she considered this idea, Elisabeth knew she would discard it. She loved Trista and, God help her, Jonathan, too. And she could not let two human beings die without trying to save them.

Throughout the rest of the night, Elisabeth slept only in fits and starts. The telephone brought her summarily into a morning she wasn't prepared to face.

''Hello?'' she grumbled into the ornate receiver of the French telephone on the vanity table. Having stubbed her toe on a chest while crossing the room, Elisabeth made the decision to move the instrument closer to the bed.

''There you are!'' Janet cried, sounding both annoyed and relieved. ''Good heavens, Elisabeth—*where have you been?*''

Elisabeth sighed an sank down onto the vanity bench. ''Relax,'' she said. ''I was only gone for a couple of days.''

''A couple of days? Give me a break, Elisabeth, I've been trying to reach you for *two weeks!* You were supposed to come to Seattle and spend a weekend with me, remember?''

Two weeks? Elisabeth gripped the edge of the vanity table.

The question was out of her mouth before she could properly weigh the effect it would have. "Janet, what day is it?"

Her friend's response was a short, stunned silence, followed by, "It's the first of May. I'm on my way. Don't you set foot out of that house, Elisabeth McCartney, until I get there."

Elisabeth's mind was still reeling. If there was no logical correlation between her time and Jonathan's, she might return to find that the fire had already happened. The idea set her trembling, but she knew she had to keep Janet from coming to visit and get back to 1892.

She ran the tip of her tongue quickly over her dry lips. "Listen, Janet, I'm all right, really. It's just that I met this fascinating man." That much, at least, was true. Bullheaded though he might be, Jonathan *was* fascinating. "I guess I just got so caught up in the relationship that I wasn't paying attention to the calendar."

Janet sounded both intrigued and suspicious. "Who is this guy? You haven't mentioned any man to me."

"That's because I just met him." She thought quickly, desperately. "We were away for a while."

"Something about this doesn't ring true," Janet said, but she was weakening. Elisabeth could hear it in her voice.

"I—I really fell hard for him," she said.

"Who is he? What does he do?"

Elisabeth took a deep breath. "His name is Jonathan Fortner, and he's a doctor."

"I'd like to meet him."

Elisabeth stifled an hysterical giggle. "Yes—well, he and I are taking off for a vacation. But maybe I can arrange something after I—we get back."

"Where are you going?" Janet asked quickly, sounding worried again.

"San Francisco." It was the first place that came to mind.

"Oh. Well, I'll just come to the airport and see you off. That way, you could introduce Jonathan and me."

"Umm," Elisabeth stalled, biting her lower lip. "We're going by car," she finally answered. "I promise faithfully that I'll call you the instant I step through the doorway."

Janet sighed. "All right but, well, there isn't anything wrong with this guy, is there? I mean, it's almost like you're hiding something."

"You've pried it out of me," Elisabeth teased. "He's a vampire. Even as we speak, he's lying in a coffin in the basement, sleeping away the daylight hours."

The joke must have reassured Janet, because she laughed. A moment later, though, her tone was serious again. "You'd tell me if you weren't all right, wouldn't you?"

Elisabeth hesitated. As much as she loved Janet, Rue was the only person in the world she could have talked to about what was happening to her. "If I thought there was anything you could do to help, yes," she answered softly. "Please don't worry about me, Janet. I'll call you when I get back." *If I get back.* "And we'll make plans for my visit to Seattle."

Mollified at least for the moment, Janet accepted Elisabeth's promise, warned her to be careful and said goodbye.

She showered and put on white corduroy pants and a sea green tank top, along with a pair of plastic thongs. Then after a hasty trip to the mailbox—there were two postcards from Rue, one mailed from Istanbul, the other from Cairo, along with a forwarded bank statement and a sales flier addressed to "occupant"—Elisabeth made preparations to return to Jonathan and Trista.

As she looked at the copies of the June 1892 issue of the *Bugle,* however, she began to doubt that Jonathan would see them as proof of anything. He was bound to say that, while the printing admittedly looked strange, she could have had the articles made up.

Elisabeth laid the papers down on the kitchen table and went up the back stairs and along the hallway to her room. In the bathroom medicine cabinet, she found the half-filled bottle of penicillin tablets she'd taken for a throat infection a few months before.

The label bore a typewritten date, along with Elisabeth's name, but it was the medicine itself that would convince Jonathan. After all, he was a doctor. She dropped the bottle into the pocket of her slacks and went back out to the vanity.

Aunt Verity's necklace was lying there, where she'd left it before taking her shower that morning. Her fingers trembled with mingled resolution and fear as she put the chain around her neck and fastened the clasp.

Reaching the hallway, Elisabeth went directly to the sealed door and clasped the knob in her hand.

Nothing happened.

"Please," Elisabeth whispered, shutting her eyes. "Please."

Still, that other world was closed to her. Fighting down panic, she told herself she had only to wait for the "window" to open again. In the meantime, there was something else she wanted to do.

After riffling through a variety of scribbled notes beside the hallway phone, she found the name and number she wanted. She dialed immediately, to keep herself from having time to back out.

"Hello?" a woman's voice answered.

Elisabeth had a clear picture of Chastity Pringle in her mind, standing in that quilting booth at the craft show, looking at the necklace as though it was something that had slithered out of hell. "Ms. Pringle? This is Elisabeth McCartney. You probably don't remember me, but we met briefly at the craft fair, when you were showing your quilts—"

"You were wearing Verity's necklace," Chastity interrupted in a wooden tone.

"Yes," Elisabeth answered. "Ms. Pringle, I wonder if I could see you sometime today—it's important."

"I won't set foot in that house" was the instant response.

"All right," Elisabeth agreed quietly, "I'll be happy to come to you. If that's convenient, of course."

"I'll meet you at the Riverview Café," Chastity offered, though not eagerly.

"Twelve-thirty?"

"Twelve-thirty," the woman promised.

The Riverview Café was about halfway between Pine River and Cotton Creek, the even smaller town where Chastity lived. Elisabeth couldn't help wondering, as she stared blankly at a morning talk show to pass the time, why Ms. Pringle was being so cloak-and-dagger about the whole thing.

At twelve-fifteen, Elisabeth pulled into the restaurant parking lot, got out of her car and went inside. Chastity hadn't arrived yet, but Elisabeth allowed a waitress to escort her to a table with a magnificent view of the river and ordered herbal tea to sip while she waited.

Chastity appeared, looking anxious and rushed, at exactly twelve-thirty. She was trim and very tanned, and her long, dark hair was wound into a single, heavy braid that rested over one shoulder. She focused her gaze on Elisabeth's necklace and shuddered visibly.

Elisabeth waited until the waitress had taken their orders before bracing her forearms against the table edge and leaning forward to ask bluntly, "What was your connection with my Aunt Verity, and why are you afraid of this necklace?"

"Verity was my friend," Chastity answered, "at a time when I needed one very badly." The waitress brought their spinach and smoked salmon salads, then went away again. "As for the pendant..."

"It was yours once," Elisabeth ventured, operating purely on instinct. "Wasn't it...Barbara?"

The woman's dark eyes were suddenly enormous, and the color drained from her face. "You know? About the doorway, I mean?"

Elisabeth nodded.

Barbara Fortner reached for her water glass with an unsteady hand. "You've met Jonathan, then, I suppose, and Trista." She paused to search Elisabeth's face anxiously. "How is my little girl?"

"She believes you're dead," Elisabeth answered, not unkindly.

Barbara flinched. Misery was visible in every line of her body. "Jonathan would have told her something like that. He'd be too proud to admit to the truth, that he drove me away."

Elisabeth's hands tightened on the arms of her chair. Her entire universe had been upended, but here was a woman who understood. Whatever Elisabeth's personal feelings about Barbara might be, she was relieved to find a person who knew about the world beyond that threshold.

"Did he divorce me?" Barbara asked quietly, after a long moment.

Elisabeth hesitated. "Yes."

Jonathan's ex-wife took several sips of water and then shrugged, although Elisabeth could see that she was shaken. "How is Trista?"

Elisabeth opened her purse and took out the folded copies of the newspaper articles. "She's in a lot of danger, Barbara, and so is Jonathan. They need your help."

Barbara's face blanched as she scanned the newspaper accounts. "Oh, my God, my baby...I knew I should have found a way to bring her with me."

A quivering sensation in the pit of her stomach kept Elisabeth constantly on edge. She was aware of every tick of the clock, and the idea that it might already be too late to help Jonathan and Trista tormented her. "Sometimes I can make the trip back and sometimes I can't," she said in a low voice. "Do you know if there's some way to be sure of connecting?"

Tears glimmered in Barbara's eyes as she met Elisabeth's gaze. "I—I don't know—I only did it a couple of times—but I think there has to be some sort of strong emotion. Are you going back?"

Elisabeth nodded. "As soon as I can manage it, yes."

Barbara sat up very straight in her chair, her salad forgotten. "You're in love with Jonathan, aren't you?"

The answer came immediately; Elisabeth didn't even need to think about it. "Yes."

"Fine. Then the two of you will have each other." She leaned forward, her eyes pleading. "Elisabeth, I want you to send Trista over the threshold to me. It might be the only way to save her."

Barbara's statement was undeniable, but it caused Elisabeth tremendous pain. If she put the necklace on Trista and sent her through the doorway, she would disappear forever. Jonathan would be heartbroken, and he'd never believe the truth. No, he'd think Elisabeth had harmed the child, and he'd hate her for it.

And that wasn't all. Without the necklace, Elisabeth would be trapped in the nineteenth century, friendless and despised. Why, she might even be blamed for Trista's disappearance and hanged or sent to prison.

She swallowed hard. "Jonathan loves Trista, and he's a good father. Besides, your daughter believes you died in Boston, while visiting your family."

Barbara's perfectly manicured index finger stabbed at the stack of photocopies lying on the tabletop. "If you don't send her to me, she'll burn to death!"

Elisabeth looked away, toward the river flowing past. "I'll do what I can," she said. Presently, she met Barbara's eyes again, and she was calmer. "How could you have left her in the first place?" she asked, no longer able to hold the question back.

The other woman lowered her eyes for a moment. "I was desperately unhappy, and I'd had a glimpse of this world. I couldn't stop thinking about it. It was like a magnet." She sighed. "I wasn't cut out to live there, to be the wife of a country doctor. I had a lover, and Jonathan found out. He was furious, even though Matthew and I had broken off. I was afraid he was going to kill me, so I came here to stay. Verity took me in and helped me establish an identity, and I left the necklace with her because I knew I'd never want to go back."

"Not even to help your daughter?"

Color glowed in Barbara's cheeks. "I don't dare step over that threshold," she said, almost in a whisper. "I'm too afraid of Jonathan."

Although Elisabeth would never have denied that Jonathan was imposing, even arrogant and opinionated, she didn't believe for a moment that he would ever deliberately hurt another person. He was a doctor, after all, and an honorable man. She changed the subject.

"How long have you been here, in the twentieth century?"

Barbara dried her eyes carefully with a cloth napkin. "Fifteen years," she answered. "And I've been happy."

Elisabeth felt another chill. Fifteen years. And yet Trista was only eight—or she had been, when Elisabeth had seen her last. She gave up trying to figure out these strange wrinkles in time and concentrated on what was important: saving Trista and Jonathan.

"If I can find a way to protect Trista while still keeping her there, that's what I'm going to do," she warned, rising and reaching for her purse and the check. "Jonathan adores his daughter, and it would crush him to lose her."

Barbara lifted one eyebrow, but made no move to stand. "Are you really thinking of Jonathan, Elisabeth? Or is it yourself you're worried about?"

It was a question Elisabeth couldn't bear to answer. She paid for the lunches neither she nor Barbara had eaten and hurried out of the restaurant.

CHAPTER 8

By the time Elisabeth arrived at home, she was in a state of rising panic. She *had* to reach Jonathan and Trista, had to know that they were all right. She glanced fitfully at the telephone and answering machine on the hallway table, not pausing even though the message light was blinking.

Could you please connect me with someone in 1892? she imagined herself asking a bewildered operator.

Shaking her head, Elisabeth went on into the kitchen and tossed her purse onto the table. Then she crossed the room to switch the calendar page from April to May. She was still standing there staring, her teeth sunk into her lower lip, when a loud pounding at the back door startled her out of her wonderment.

Miss Cecily Buzbee peered at her through the frosted oval glass, and Elisabeth smiled as she went to admit her neighbor, who had apparently come calling alone.

"I don't mind telling you," the sweet-natured spinster commented after Elisabeth had let her in and offered a glass of ice tea, "that Sister and I have been concerned about you, since we don't see hide nor hair of you for days at a time."

Elisabeth busied herself with the tasks of running cold water into a pitcher and adding ice and powdery tea. "I'm sorry you were worried," she said quietly. She carried the pitcher to the table, along with two glasses. "I don't mean to be a recluse—I just need a lot of solitude right now."

Cecily smiled forgivingly. "I don't suppose there's any lemon, is there, dear?"

Elisabeth shook her head regretfully. Even if she'd remembered to buy lemons the last time she'd shopped, which she hadn't, that had been two weeks before and they would probably have spoiled by now. "Miss Cecily," she began, clasping her hands together on her lap so her visitor wouldn't see that they were trembling, "how well did you know my Aunt Verity?"

"Oh, very well," Cecily trilled. "Very well, indeed."

"Did she tell you stories about this house?"

Cecily averted her cornflower blue eyes for a moment, then forced herself to look at Elisabeth again. "You know how Verity liked to talk. And she *was* a rather fanciful sort."

Elisabeth smiled, remembering. "Yes, she was. She told Rue and me lots of things about this house, about people simply appearing, seemingly out of nowhere, and other things like that."

The neighbor nodded solemnly. "Sister and I believe that young Trista Fortner haunts this house, poor soul. Her spirit never rested because she died so horribly."

Unable to help herself, Elisabeth shuddered. If she did nothing else, she had to see that Trista wasn't trapped in that fire. "I can't buy the ghost theory," she said, sipping the tea and barely noticing that it tasted awful. "I mean, here are these souls, supposedly lost in the scheme of things, wandering about, unable to find their way into whatever comes after this life. Why would God permit that, when there is so much order in everything else, like the seasons and the courses of the planets?"

"My dear," Cecily debated politely, "reputable people have seen apparitions. They cannot all be dismissed as crackpots."

Elisabeth sighed, wondering which category she would fall into: crackpot or reputable person. "Isn't it just possible that the images were every bit as real as the people seeing them? Perhaps there are places where time wears thin and a person can see through it, into the past or the future, if only for a moment."

Miss Buzbee gave the idea due consideration. "Well, Elisabeth, as the bard said, there are more things in heaven and earth..."

Anxiety filled Elisabeth as her mind turned back to Jonathan and Trista. Would she return to 1892 only to find them gone—if she was able to reach them at all? "More tea?" she asked, even though she was desperate to be alone again so that she could make another attempt at crossing the threshold.

Trista's friend, Vera, had apparently trained her daughters not to overstay their welcome. "I really must be running along," Cecily said. "It's almost time for Sister and I to take our walk. Two miles, rain or shine," she said with resignation, frowning grimly as she looked out through the windows. Storm clouds were gathering on the horizon.

"I've enjoyed our visit," Elisabeth replied honestly, following Miss Cecily to the door. She wondered what Cecily would say if told Elisabeth had had a glimpse of Vera, the Buzbee sisters' mother, as a little girl playing on the school grounds.

A light rain started to fall after Cecily had gone, and Elisabeth stood at the back door for a long moment, her heart hammering as she gazed at the orchard. The beautiful petals of spring were all gone now, replaced by healthy green leaves—another reminder that two weeks of her life had passed without her knowing.

When thunder rolled down from the mountains and lightning splintered the sky, Elisabeth shuddered and closed the door. Then she hurried up the back stairs and along the hallway.

"Trista!" she shouted, pounding with both fists at the panel of wood that separated her from that other world. "Trista, can you hear me?"

There was no sound from the other side, except for the whistle of the wind, and Elisabeth sagged against the wood in frustrated despair. "Oh, God," she whispered, "don't let them be dead. *Please* don't let them be dead."

After a long time, she turned away and went back down the stairs to the kitchen. She put on a rain coat and dashed out to the shed for an armload of kindling and aged apple wood, which she carried to the hearth in the main parlor.

There, she built a fire to bring some warmth and cheer to that large, empty room. When the wood was crackling and popping in the grate, she put the screen in place and went to the piano, lifting the keyboard cover and idly striking middle C with her index finger.

"Hear me, Trista," she pleaded softly, flexing her fingers. "Hear and wish just as hard as you can for me to come back."

She began to play the energetic tune she'd described to Trista as a boogie-woogie, putting all her passion, all her hopes and fears into the crazy, racing, tinkling notes of the song. When she finally stopped, her fingers exhausted, the sound of another pianist attempting to play the song met her ears.

Elisabeth nearly overturned the piano bench in her eagerness to run upstairs to the door that barred her from the place where she truly belonged. She wrenched hard on the knob, and breathtaking exultation rushed into her when it turned.

Trista's awkward efforts at the piano tune grew louder and louder as Elisabeth raced through the little girl's bedroom and down the steps. When she burst into the parlor, Trista's face lit up.

She ran to Elisabeth and threw her arms around her.

Elisabeth embraced her, silently thanking God that she wasn't too late, that the fire hadn't already happened, then knelt to look into Trista's eyes. "Sweetheart, this is important. How long have I been gone?"

Trista bit her lip, seeming puzzled by the question. "Since last night, when you came in and kissed me goodbye. It's afternoon now—school let out about an hour ago."

"Good," Elisabeth whispered, relieved to learn that days or weeks hadn't raced by in her absence. "Was your father upset to find that I wasn't here?"

"He cussed," Trista replied with a solemn nod. "It reminded me of the day Mama went away to Boston. Papa got angry then, too, because she didn't say goodbye to us."

Elisabeth sat down on the piano bench and took Trista onto

her lap, recalling her talk with Barbara Fortner in the River-view Café. Sending Trista over the threshold to her mother might be the only way to save her, but Jonathan would never understand that. "Where is he now?"

Trista sighed. "In town. There was a fight at one of the saloons, and some people needed to be stitched up."

Elisabeth winced and said, "Ouch!" and Trista laughed.

"Papa's going to be happy when he sees you're back," the child said after an interval. "But he probably won't admit he's pleased."

"Probably not," Elisabeth agreed, giving Trista's pigtail a playful tug. She looked down at her slacks and tank top. "I guess I'd better change into something more fitting," she confided.

Trista nodded and took Elisabeth's hand. They went upstairs together, and the little girl's expression was thoughtful. "I wish Papa would let *me* wear trousers," she said. "It would be so much better for riding a horse. I hate sitting sideways in the saddle, like a priss."

"Do you have a horse?" Elisabeth asked as they reached the second floor, but continued on to the attic, where Barbara's clothes were stored.

"Yes," Trista answered, somewhat forlornly. "Her name is Estella, she's about a thousand years old, and she's a ninny."

Elisabeth laughed. "What a way to talk about the poor thing!" The attic door creaked a little as they went in, and the bright afternoon sunlight was flecked with a galaxy of tiny dust particles. "Most little girls love their horses, if they're lucky enough to have one."

Trista dusted off a short stool and sat down, smoothing the skirts of her flowered poplin pinafore as she did so. "Estella just wants to wander around the pasture and chew grass, and she won't come when I call because she doesn't like to be ridden. Do you have your own horse, Elisabeth?"

Opening the heavy doors of the cedar-lined armoire, Elisabeth ran her hand over colorful, still-crisp skirts of lawn and cambric and poplin and satin and even velvet. "I don't," she said distractedly, "but my Cousin Rue does. When her grand-father died, she inherited a ranch in Montana, and I understand there are lots of horses there." She took a frothy pink lawn gown from the wardrobe and held it against her, waltzing a little because it was so shamelessly frilly.

"Wasn't he your grandfather, too, if you and Rue are cousins?"

Elisabeth bent to kiss the child's forehead, while still enjoying the feel of the lovely dress under her hands. "Our fathers were brothers," she explained. "The ranch belonged to Rue's mother's family."

"Could we visit there sometime?" The hopeful note in Trista's voice tugged at Elisabeth's heart, and unexpected tears burned in her eyes.

She shook her head, turning her back so Trista wouldn't see that she was crying. "It's very faraway," she said after a long time had passed.

"Montana isn't so far," Jonathan's daughter argued politely. "We could be there in three days if we took the train."

But we wouldn't see Rue, Elisabeth thought sadly. *She hasn't even been born yet.* She stepped behind a dusty folding screen and slipped off her tank top and slacks, then pulled the pink dress on over her head. "I don't think your papa would want you to go traveling without him," she said, having finally found words, however inadequate, to answer Trista.

When Elisabeth came out from behind the screen, Trista drew in her breath. "Thunderation, Elisabeth—you look beautiful!"

Elisabeth laughed, put her hands on her hips and narrowed her eyes. "Thanks a heap, kid, but did you just swear?"

Trista giggled and scurried around behind Elisabeth to begin fastening the buttons and hooks that would hold the dress closed in back. "*Thunderation* isn't a swear word," she said indulgently. "But I don't suppose it's very ladylike, either."

The light was fading, receding across the dirty floor toward the windows like an ebbing tide, so the two went down the attic steps together, Elisabeth carrying her slacks and tank top over one arm. She felt a sense of excitement and anticipation, knowing she would see Jonathan again soon.

In her room, Elisabeth brushed her hair and pinned it up, while Trista sat on the edge of the bed, watching with her head tilted to one side and her small feet swinging back and forth.

Downstairs, Elisabeth checked the pot roast Ellen had left to cook in the oven. She found an apron to protect her gown, then set to work washing china from the cabinet in the dining room. In a drawer of the highboy, she found white tapers and silver candle sticks, and she set these on the formal table.

"We never eat in here," Trista said.

Outside, twilight was falling, and with it came a light spring rain. "We're going to tonight," Elisabeth replied.

"Why? It isn't Christmas or Easter, and it's not anybody's birthday."

Elisabeth smiled. "I want to celebrate being home," she said, and only when the words were out of her mouth did she realize how presumptuous they sounded. Jonathan had made love to her, but it wasn't as though he'd expressed a desire for a lifelong commitment or anything like that. This wasn't her home, it was Barbara's, as was the china she was setting out and the dress she was wearing.

As were the child and the man she loved so fiercely.

"Don't be sad," Trista said, coming to stand close to Elisabeth in a show of support.

Elisabeth gave her a distracted squeeze, and said brightly, "I think we'd better get some fires going, since it's so dreary out."

"I'll do it," Trista announced. "So you don't ruin your pretty dress." With that, she fetched wood from the shed out back and laid fires in the grates in the parlor and the dining room. Rain was pattering at the windows and blazes were burning cheerily on the hearths when Elisabeth saw Jonathan drive his buggy through the wide doorway of the barn.

It was all she could do not to run outside, ignoring the weather entirely, and fling herself into his arms. But she forced herself to remain in the kitchen, where she and Trista had been sipping tea and playing Go Fish while they waited for Jonathan.

When he came in, some twenty minutes later, he was wet to the skin. The look in his gray eyes was grim, and Elisabeth felt a wrench deep inside when she saw him.

"You," he said, tossing his medical bag onto the shelf beside the door and peeling off his coat. He wasn't wearing a hat, and his dark hair streamed with rain water. His shirt was so wet, it had turned transparent.

Elisabeth refused to be intimidated by his callous welcome. "Yes, Dr. Fortner," she said, "I'm back."

He glared at her once, then stormed up the stairs. When he came down again, he was wearing plain black trousers and an off white shirt, open at the throat to reveal a wealth of dark chest hair. But then, Elisabeth knew all about that wonderful chest...

"Go stand by the fire," she told him as she lifted the roasting pan from the oven. Inside was a succulent blend of choice beef, a thin but aromatic gravy and perfectly cooked potatoes and carrots. "You'll catch your death."

Trista was in the dining room, lighting the candles.

"Where were you?" Jonathan demanded in a furious undertone. "I searched every inch of this house and the barn and the woodshed...."

Elisabeth shrugged. "I've explained it all before, Jonathan, and you never seem to believe me. And, frankly, I'd rather not risk having you throw me down on a bed and inject some primitive sedative into my veins because you think I'm hysterical."

He rolled his wonderful gray eyes in exasperation. *"Where did you go?"*

"Believe it or not, most of the time I was right here in this house." She wanted to tell him about seeing Barbara, but the moment wasn't right, and she couldn't risk having Trista overhear what she said. "For now, Jonathan, I'm afraid you're going to have to be satisfied with that answer."

He glared at her, but there was a softening in his manner,

and Elisabeth knew he was glad she'd come back—a fact that made her exultant.

The three of them ate dinner in the dining room, then Trista volunteered to clear the table and wash the dishes. While she was doing that, Elisabeth sat at the piano, playing a medley of the Beatles ballads.

Jonathan stood beside the fireplace, one arm braced against the mantelpiece, listening with a frown. "I've never heard that before," he said.

Elisabeth smiled but made no comment.

He came to stand behind her, lightly resting his hands on her shoulders, which the dress left partially bare. "Lizzie," he said gruffly, "please tell me who you are. Tell me how you managed to vanish that way."

She stopped playing and turned slightly to look up at him. Her eyes were bright with tears because the name Lizzie had brought the full gravity of the situation down on her again, though she'd managed to put it out of her mind for a little while.

"There's something I want to show you," she said. "Something I brought back from—from where I live. We'll talk about it after Trista goes to bed."

He bent reluctantly and gave her a brief, soft kiss. He'd barely straightened up again when his daughter appeared, her round little cheeks flushed with pride.

"I did the dishes," she announced.

Jonathan smiled and patted her small shoulder. "You're a marvel," he said.

"Can we go to the Founder's Day picnic tomorrow, Papa?" she asked hopefully. "Since Elisabeth would be there to take me home, it wouldn't matter if you had to leave early to set a broken bone or deliver a baby."

Jonathan's gaze shifted uncertainly to Elisabeth, and she felt a pang, knowing he was probably concerned about the questions her presence would raise. "Would you like to go?" he asked.

Elisabeth thrived on this man's company, and his daughter's. She wanted to be wherever they were, be it heaven or hell. "Yes," she said in an oddly choked voice.

Pleasure lighted Jonathan's weary eyes for just a moment, but then the spell was broken. He announced that he had things to do in the barn and went out.

Elisabeth exchanged the pink gown for her slacks and tank top and began heating water on the stove for Trista's bath. Once the little girl had scrubbed from head to foot, dried herself and put on a warm flannel nightgown, she and Elisabeth sat near the stove, and Elisabeth gently combed the tangles from Trista's hair.

"I wish you were my mama," Trista confessed later, when Elisabeth was tucking her into bed, after reading her a chapter of *Huckleberry Finn.*

Touched, Elisabeth kissed the little girl's cheek. "I wish that, too," she admitted. "But I'm not, and it's no good pretending. However, we can be the very best of friends."

Trista beamed. "I'd like that," she said.

Elisabeth blew out Trista's lamp, then sat on the edge of the bed until the child's breathing was even with sleep. Her eyes adjusted now to the darkness, Elisabeth made her way to the inner door that led down to the kitchen.

Jonathan was seated at the table, drinking coffee. His expression and his bearing conveyed a weariness that made Elisabeth want to put her arms around him.

"What were you going to show me?"

Elisabeth put one hand into the pocket of her slacks and brought out the prescription bottle. "Nothing much," she said, setting it on the table in front of him. "Just your ordinary, everyday, garden-variety wonder drug."

He picked up the little vial and squinted at the print on the label. "Penicillin." His eyes widened, and Elisabeth thought he was probably reading the date. As she sat down next to him, he looked at her in skeptical curiosity.

"In proper doses," she said, "this stuff can cure some heavy hitters, like pneumonia. They call it an antibiotic."

Jonathan tried to remove the child-proof cap and failed, until Elisabeth showed him the trick. He poured the white tablets into his palm and sniffed them, then picked one up and touched it to his tongue.

Elisabeth watched with delight as he made a face and dropped all the pills back into the bottle. "Well? Are you convinced?"

Still scowling, the country doctor tapped the side of the bottle with his finger nail. "What is this made of?"

"Plastic," Elisabeth answered. "Another miracle. Take it from me, Jonathan, the twentieth century is full of them. I just wish I could show you everything."

He studied her for a moment, then shoved the bottle toward her. It was obvious that, while he didn't know what to think, he'd chosen not to believe Elisabeth. "The twentieth century," he scoffed.

"Almost the twenty-first," Elisabeth insisted implacably. No matter what this guy said or did, she wasn't going to let him rile her again. There was simply too much at stake. She let her eyes rest on the penicillin. "When you use that, do it judiciously. The drug causes violent reactions, even death, in some people."

Jonathan shook his head scornfully, but Elisabeth noticed that his gaze kept straying back to the little vial. It was obvious that he was itching to pick it up and examine it again.

She sighed, allowing herself a touch of exasperation. "All right, so you can dismiss the pills as some kind of trick. But what about the bottle? You admitted it yourself—you've never seen anything like it. And do you know why, Jonathan? Because it doesn't exist in your world. It hasn't been invented yet."

Clearly, he could resist no longer. He reached out and snatched up the penicillin as if he thought Elisabeth would try to beat him to it, dropping the bottle into the pocket of his shirt.

"Where did you go?" he demanded in an impatient whisper.

Elisabeth smiled. "Why on earth would I want to tell you that?" she asked. "You'll just think I'm having a fit and pump my veins full of dope."

"Full of what?"

"Never mind." She reached across the table and patted his hand in a deliberately patronizing fashion. "From here on out, just think of me as a...guardian angel. Actually, that should be no more difficult to absorb than the truth. I have the power to help you and Trista, even save your lives, if you'll only let me."

Jonathan surprised her with a slow smile. "A guardian angel? More likely, you're a witch. And I've got to admit, I'm under your spell."

Elisabeth glanced nervously toward the rear stairway, half expecting to find Trista there, listening. "Jonathan, while I was—er—where I was, I talked with Barbara."

The smile faded, as Elisabeth had known it would. "Where? Damn it, if that woman has come back here, meaning to upset my daughter—"

"She's a century away," Elisabeth said. "And Trista is her daughter, too."

"Are you telling me that Barbara..."

"Went to the future?" Elisabeth finished for him. "Yes. She was wearing my necklace at the time, though, of course, it was *her* necklace then."

Jonathan erupted from his chair with such force that it clattered to the floor. Elisabeth watched as he went to the stove to refill his coffee mug, and even through the fabric of his shirt, she could see that the muscles in his shoulders were rigid. "You're insane," he accused without facing Elisabeth.

"I saw her. She said she had a lover, and you'd found out about him. She was afraid of what you might do to her."

Jonathan went to the stairway and looked up to make sure his daughter wasn't listening. "Is that why you're here?" he snapped cruelly when he was certain they were alone. "Did Barbara send you to spy on me?"

It was getting harder and harder to keep her temper. Elisabeth managed, although her hands trembled slightly as she lifted her cup to her mouth and took a sip. "No. I stumbled onto this place quite by accident, I assure you—rather like

Alice tumbling into the rabbit hole. That story has been written, I presume?''

He gave her a look of scalding sarcasm. ''Every schoolchild knows it,'' he said. ''Where are those newspaper accounts you mentioned? The ones that cover my death?''

Elisabeth ran the tip of her tongue over dry lips. ''Well, I had them, but in the end I decided you would only say I'd had them printed up somewhere myself. What I can't understand is why you think I would want to pull such an elaborate hoax in the first place. Tell me exactly what you think I would have to gain by making up such a story.''

He took her cup, rather summarily, and refilled it. ''You probably believe what you're saying.''

She threw her hands out from her sides in a burst of annoyance. ''If you think I'm a raving lunatic, why do you allow me to stay here? Why do you trust me with your daughter?''

Jonathan smiled and sat down again. ''Because I think you're a *harmless* lunatic.''

Elisabeth shoved her fingers through her hair, completely ruining the modified Gibson Girl style. ''Thank you, Sigmund Freud.''

''Sigmund Who?''

''Forget it. It's too hard to explain.''

Her host rolled his eyes and then leaned forward ominously, in effect ordering her to try.

''Listen, you're bound to read about Dr. Freud soon, and all your questions will be answered. Though you shouldn't take his theories concerning mothers and sons too seriously.''

Jonathan rubbed his temples with a thumb and forefinger and sighed in a long-suffering way.

''How are you going to explain me to the good citizens of Pine River at that picnic tomorrow?'' Elisabeth asked, not only because she wanted to change the dead-end subject, but because she was curious. ''By telling them I'm your wife's sister?''

''I'm not about to change my story now,'' he said. ''Of course, Ellen's told half the county you're a witch, popping in and out whenever it strikes your fancy.''

Close, Elisabeth thought with grim humor, *but no cigar.* "Maybe it would be simpler if I just stayed here."

"We can't hide you away forever, especially after that visit you paid to my office."

Elisabeth fluttered her eyelashes. "I think I have an admirer in the big fella," she teased. "What was his name again? Moose? Svend?"

Jonathan laughed. "Ivan." He pushed back his chair and carried his cup and Elisabeth's to the sink, leaving them for Ellen to wash in the morning. Then he waited, in that courtly way of his, while Elisabeth stood. "Will you disappear again tonight?" he asked.

"You wouldn't tease if you knew how uncertain it is," she answered. "I could get stuck on the other side and never find my way back."

He escorted her to the door of the spare room and gave her a light, teasing kiss that left her wanting more. Much more. "Good night, Lizzie," he said. "I'll see you in the morning— I hope."

CHAPTER 9

Elisabeth was pleasantly surprised to learn that the Founder's Day picnic was to be held in one of her favorite places—the grassy area beside the creek, next to the covered bridge. All that sunny Saturday morning, while she and Trista were frying chicken and making a version of potato salad, wagons and buggies rattled past on the road.

When Jonathan returned from his morning rounds, the three of them walked through the orchard to the creek, Jonathan carrying the food in a big wicker basket. Elisabeth, wearing a demure blue-and-white checked gingham she'd found in one of the attic trunks, was at his side. Though her chin was at a slightly obstinate angle, there was no hiding her nervousness.

There were rigs lining the road on both sides of the bridge, and dozens of blankets had been spread out on the ground alongside the creek. Boys in caps and short pants chased each other, pursued in turn by little girls with huge bows in their hair. The ladies sat gracefully on their spreads, their skirts arranged in modest fashion. Some used ruffle-trimmed parasols to shelter their complexions from the sun, while others, clad in calico, seemed to relish the light as much as the children did.

Most of the men wore plain trousers and either flannel or cotton shirts, and Jonathan was the only one without a hat. They stood in clusters, talking among themselves and smoking, but when the Fortner household arrived, it seemed they all turned to look, as did the women.

Elisabeth was profoundly aware of the differences between herself and these people and, for one terrible moment, she had to struggle to keep from turning and running back to the shelter of the house.

Vera came over, a tiny emissary with flowing brown hair and freckles, and looked solemnly up into Elisabeth's face. "You don't look like a witch to me," she remarked forthrightly.

"Does this mean they won't burn me at the stake?" Elisabeth whispered to Jonathan, who chuckled.

"She's not a witch," Trista said, arms akimbo, her gray gaze sweeping the crowd and daring any detractor to step forward. Her youthful voice rang with conviction. "Elisabeth is my friend."

Jonathan set the picnic basket down and began unfolding the blanket he'd been carrying under one arm, while Elisabeth waited, staring tensely at the population of Pine River, her smile wobbling on her mouth.

Finally, one of the women in calico came forward, returning Elisabeth's smile and offering her hand. "I'm Clara Piedmont," she said. "Vera's mother."

"Lizzie McCartney," Jonathan said, making the false introduction smoothly, just a moment after Trista and Vera had run off to join the other kids, "my wife's sister."

"How do you do?" Clara asked as a shiver went down Elisabeth's back. As long as she lived, which might not be very long at all, she would never get used to being called Lizzie.

This show of acceptance reassured her, though, and her smile was firm on her lips, no longer threatening to come unpinned and fall off. She murmured a polite response.

"Will you be staying in Pine River?" Clara inquired.

Elisabeth glanced in Jonathan's direction, not certain how to respond. "I—haven't decided," she said lamely.

Although Clara was not a pretty woman, her smile was warm and open. She patted Elisabeth's upper arm in a friendly way. "Well, you come over for tea one day this week. Trista will show you where we live." She turned to Jonathan. "Would it be all right if Trista stayed at our house tonight? Vera's been plaguing me about it all day."

Jonathan didn't look at Elisabeth, which was a good thing, because even a glance from him would have brought the color rushing to her cheeks. With Trista away, the two of them would be alone in the house.

"That would be fine," he said.

Elisabeth felt a rush of anticipation so intense that it threatened to lift her off the ground and spin her around a few times, and she was mortified at herself. She didn't even want to think what modern self-help books had to say about women who wanted a particular man's lovemaking that much.

Over the course of the afternoon, she managed to blend in with the other women, and after eating, everyone posed for the town photographer, the wooden bridge looming in the background. Later, while the boys fished in the creek, girls waded in, deliberately scaring away the trout. The men puffed on their cigars and played horseshoes, and the ladies gossiped.

Toward sunset, when people were packing up their children, blankets and picnic baskets, the hooves of a single horse hammered over the plank floor of the bridge. The rider paused on the road above the creek bank and called, "Is Doc Fortner here? There's been a man cut up pretty bad, over at the mill."

Jonathan waved to the rider. "I'll get my bag and meet you there in ten minutes," he said. Then, after giving Elisabeth one unreadable look, he disappeared into the orchard, headed toward the house.

Elisabeth finished gathering the picnic things, feeling much less a part of the community now that Jonathan was gone. She was touched when Trista came to say goodbye before leaving with Vera's family. "I'll see you tomorrow, in church," she promised. "Could I have a kiss, please?"

With a smile, Elisabeth bent to kiss the child's smudged, sun-warmed cheek. "You certainly may." She was painfully conscious of how short her time with this child might be and of how precious it was. "I love you, Trista," she added.

Trista gave her a quicksilver, spontaneous hug, then raced off to scramble into the Piedmonts' wagon with Vera. Carrying the picnic basket, now considerably lighter, and the blanket, Elisabeth turned and started for home.

Although Jonathan had left a lamp burning in the kitchen, its glow pushing back the twilight, he had, of course, already left for the sawmill. Elisabeth shivered to think what horrors might be awaiting him in that noisy, filthy place.

Taking pitchy chunks of pine from the woodbox beside the stove, Elisabeth built up the fire and put a kettle on for tea. Then, because she knew Jonathan would be tired and shaken when he returned, she filled the hot-water reservoir on the stove and put more wood in to make the flames burn hotter.

His clothes were covered with blood when he came in, nearly two hours later, and his gray eyes were haunted. "I couldn't save him," Jonathan muttered as Elisabeth took his bag and set it aside, then began helping him out of his coat. "He had a wife and four children."

Elisabeth stood on tiptoe to kiss Jonathan's cheek, which was rough with a new beard. "I'm so sorry," she said gently. She'd set the oblong tin bathtub in the center of the kitchen floor earlier, and scouted out soap and a couple of thin, coarse towels. While Jonathan watched her bleakly, she began filling the tub with water from the reservoir and from various kettles on the stove. "Take off your clothes, Jon," she urged quietly when he didn't seem to make the connection. "I'll get you a drink while you're settling in."

He was unbuttoning his shirt with the slow, distracted motions of a sleepwalker when Elisabeth went into the dining room. Earlier, she'd found virtually untouched bottles of whiskey and brandy behind one of the doors in the china cabinet, and she took her time deciding which would be most soothing.

When she returned to the kitchen with the brandy, Jonathan was in the bathtub, his head back, his eyes closed. His bloody shirt and trousers were draped neatly over the back of a chair.

"You were telling the truth," he said when she knelt beside the tub and handed him a glass, "when you claimed to be a guardian angel."

Elisabeth wasn't feeling or thinking much like an angel. She was painfully, poignantly conscious of Jonathan's powerful body, naked beneath the clear surface of the water. "We all need someone to take care of us once in a while—no matter how strong we are.''

"I half expected you to be gone when I got back,'' Jonathan confessed, lifting the glass to his lips. He took a healthy swallow and then set the liquor aside on the floor. "I figured you might not want to be here, without Trista to act as an unofficial chaperone.''

Elisabeth couldn't quite meet his eyes. "I don't think I want to be chaperoned," she said.

Jonathan's chuckle was a raw sound, conveying despair and weariness, as well as amusement. "Ladies must be very forward where you come from," he teased. Elisabeth could feel him watching her, caressing her with his gaze.

She made herself look at him. "I guess compared to Victorian women, they are." She reached for soap and a wash cloth and made a lather. Jonathan looked pleasantly bewildered when she began washing his back. "The term 'Victorian,''' she offered, before he could ask, "refers to the time of Queen Victoria's reign.''

"I deduced that," Jonathan said with a sigh, relaxing slightly under Elisabeth's hand.

Bathing him was so sensual an experience that Elisabeth's head was spinning, and the warm ache between her legs had already reached such a pitch that it was nearly painful.

"You know, of course," Jonathan told her, leaning back as she began to wash his chest, "that I mean to take you directly from here to my bed and make love to you until you've given me everything?''

Elisabeth swallowed. Her heart was beating so hard, she could hear it. "Yes, Jon," she replied. "I know.''

He took the soap and cloth from her hand and, after watching her face for a long moment, set about finishing his bath. Elisabeth left the kitchen, climbing the stairs to his bedroom.

As soon as the door closed behind her, she began undressing. She had barely managed to wash and put on a thin white eyelet chemise she'd found when Jonathan entered the room.

His dark hair was rumpled, and he was naked except for the inadequate towel wrapped around his waist. Thunder rat-

tled the windows suddenly, like some kind of celestial warning, and Jonathan went to the fireplace and struck a match to
the shavings that waited in the grate. On top of them, he laid
several sticks of dry wood.

Elisabeth trembled, shy as a virgin, when he turned down
the kerosene lamps on the mantelpiece, leaving the room dark
except for the primitive crimson glow of the fire. He came to
her, resting his strong, skilled hands on the sides of her waist.

"Thank you," he said.

Heat was surging through Elisabeth's system, and she could
barely keep from swaying on her feet. "For what?" she managed to choke out as Jonathan began to caress her breasts
through the fabric of the chemise.

He bent, nibbling at her neck even as his thumbs chafed
her covered nipples into hard readiness for his mouth. "For
being here, now, tonight, when I need you so much."

Elisabeth gave a little moan and ran her hands up and down
his muscled, still-damp back. He smelled of soap and brandy
and manhood. "I need you, too, Jonathan," she admitted in
a whisper.

Jonathan drew back far enough to raise the chemise over
her head and toss it aside. His charcoal eyes seemed to smol-
der as he took in the curves and valleys of her body, bare
except for the rhythmic flicker of the firelight. He let the towel
fall away.

She hadn't meant to be bold, but he was so magnificent
that she couldn't resist touching him. When her fingers closed
around his heated shaft, he tilted his head back and gave a
low growl of fierce surrender. With one hand, she pressed
him gently backward into a chair, while still caressing him
with the other.

"Dear God, *Elisabeth*..." he moaned as she knelt between
his knees and began kissing the bare skin of his upper thighs.
"Stop..."

"I'm not going to stop," she told him stubbornly between
flicks of her tongue that made his flesh quiver. "I haven't
even begun to pleasure you."

He uttered a raspy shout of shock and delight when she

took him, his fingers entangling themselves in her hair. "Lizzie," he gasped. "Oh...Lizzie...my God..."

Elisabeth lightly stroked the insides of his thighs as she enjoyed him.

Finally, with a ragged cry, he clasped her head in his hands and forced her to release him. In a matter of seconds, he'd lifted her from the floor so that she was standing in the chair itself, her feet on either side of his hips. He parted her with the fingers of one hand and then brought her down onto his mouth.

There was no need to be quiet, since they were alone in the house, and that was a good thing, because such pleasure knifed through Elisabeth that she burst out with a throaty yell. Her hands gripped the back of the chair in a desperate bid for balance as Jonathan continued to have her.

She began to pant as her hips moved back and forth of their own accord, and a thin film of perspiration broke out over every inch of her. She could feel tendrils of her hair clinging to her cheeks as she blindly moved against Jonathan's mouth.

When she felt release approaching, she tried to pull away, wanting her full surrender to happen when Jonathan was inside her, but he wouldn't let her go. Gripping her hips in his work-roughened hands, he held her to him even as the violent shudders began, making her fling her head back and moan without restraint.

He was greedy, granting her absolutely no quarter, and Elisabeth's captured body began to convulse with pleasure. The firelight and the darkness blurred as she gave up her essence and then collapsed against the back of the chair, exhausted.

But Jonathan wasn't about to let her rest. Within five minutes her cries of delighted fury again rang through the empty house.

"Now you're ready for me," he informed her in a husky voice as he lowered her to his lap and then stood, carrying her to the bed.

Elisabeth's two releases had been so violent, so all-consuming, that she was left with no breath in her lungs. She lay gasping, gazing up at Jonathan as he arranged her in the center of the bed and put two fluffy pillows under her bottom.

He lay down beside her on the mattress, slightly lower so that he could take her nipple into his mouth while his hand stroked her tender mound.

"Jonathan," she managed to whisper. "Please—*oh*— please..."

Jonathan spread her legs and knelt between them, parting her to give her one more teasing stroke. Then he poised himself over her. He had played her body so skillfully that in the instant his shaft glided inside her, she came apart.

While she buckled under the slow, deliberate strokes of his manhood, her head tossed back and forth on the mattress and she sobbed his name over and over again.

Her vindication came when the last little whimper of satisfied surrender had been wrung from her, because that was when Jonathan's release began. She toyed with his nipples and talked breathlessly of all the ways she meant to pleasure him in the future. With a fevered groan and a curse, he quickened his pace.

"I'll put you back in that chair again," she told him as he moved more and more rapidly upon her, his head thrust back. "Only next time, I won't let you stop me...."

Jonathan gave a strangled shout and stiffened, his eyes glazed, his teeth bared as he filled Elisabeth with his warmth. She stroked his back and buttocks until he'd given up everything. He sank to the bed beside her, resting his head on her breasts.

A blissful hour passed and the fire was burning low before Jonathan rose on one elbow to look into her face. "Stay with me, Elisabeth," he whispered. "Be my wife, so that I can bring you to this room, this bed, in good conscience."

She plunged her fingers into his dark, freshly washed hair. "Jon," she sighed, "I'm a stranger. You have no idea what marrying me would mean."

He parted her thighs and touched her brazenly in that moist, silken place where small tremors of passion were already starting to stir again. "It would mean," he drawled, his eyes twinkling, "that I would either have to put a gag over your mouth or move Trista to a room downstairs."

Elisabeth blushed hotly, glad of the darkness. It wasn't like her to carry on the way she had; with Ian, she'd hardly made a sound. But then, there had been no reason to cry out. "You're a very vain man, Jon Fortner."

He laughed and kissed her. "Maybe so," he answered, "but you make me feel like something more than a man."

She blinked and tried to turn her head, but Jonathan clasped her chin in his hand and prevented that.

"Don't you think I'm—I'm cheap?" she whispered, only too aware of Victorian attitudes toward sex.

Jonathan got up and fed the fire, and then Elisabeth heard the chink of china. Only when he brought a basin of tepid water back to the bed and began gently washing her did he reply. "Because you enjoy having a man make love to you?" He continued to cleanse her, using a soft cloth. "Lizzie, it was refreshing to see you respond like that." He set the cloth and basin aside on the floor, but would not let her close her legs. "Did you mean what you said about the next time I sit in that chair?"

Elisabeth's face pulsed with heat, but she nodded, unable to break the link between his eyes and hers. "I meant it," she said hoarsely.

At that, he kissed her, his tongue teasing her lips until they parted to take him in. "I meant what I said, too," he told her presently, moving his lips downward, toward her waiting breasts. "I want you to be my wife. And I won't let you put me off forever."

God help us, Elisabeth thought, just before she succumbed to the sweet demands of her body, *we don't have forever.*

Elisabeth felt like a fraud, sitting there in church beside Jonathan the next morning, pretending to be his sister-in-law. Maybe these good people didn't know she'd spent most of the night tossing in his bed, but God did, and He was bound to demand an accounting.

All she could do was hope it made a difference, her loving Jonathan the way she did.

After the service, she and Jonathan and Trista went home, the three of them crowded into Jonathan's buggy. He saw to the horses while Elisabeth and Trista went inside to put a fresh ham in the oven.

When Jonathan appeared, just as the women finished peeling potatoes to go with the pork, he was carrying two simple bamboo fishing poles. Trista's eyes lit up at the prospect of a Sunday afternoon beside the creek, and Elisabeth's heart was touched. Jonathan led a busy, demanding life, and he and Trista probably didn't have a lot of time together.

"You'll come with us, won't you?" the little girl cried, whirling to look up into Elisabeth's face with an imploring expression.

Elisabeth glanced at Jonathan, who winked almost imperceptibly, then nodded. "If you don't think I'll be interrupting," she agreed.

The creek bank was theirs again, now that yesterday's picnickers had all gone home, taking their blankets and scraps with them. Elisabeth sat contentedly on her favorite rock while Jonathan and Trista dug worms from the loamy ground and then threw their lines into the water.

Trista's laughter was liquid crystal, like the creek sparkling in the sunshine, and Elisabeth's heart climbed into her throat. It wasn't fair that this beautiful child was destined to die in just a few short weeks—she'd never had a chance to live!

Neither Jon nor Trista noticed when Elisabeth got down from the boulder and walked away, trying to distract herself by gathering the wild daisies and tiger lilies that hadn't been crushed by the picnickers the day before. She was under the bridge, watching the water flow by, when Jonathan suddenly materialized at her side.

"Where's Trista?" she asked, looking away quickly in hopes that he wouldn't read too much from her eyes.

"She went back to the house to make a pitcher of lemonade," Jonathan answered sleepily, taking one of the tiger lilies from Elisabeth's bouquet and brushing its fragrant orange petals against the underside of her chin. When she turned her head, he kissed her and the tangle of flowers tumbled to the smooth pebbles at her feet. "I want to bring you here," he told her when he'd finally released her mouth, "and make love to you in the moonlight."

Elisabeth trembled as his fingers found the pins in her hair and removed them, letting the soft blond tresses fall around her face. His name was all the protest she managed before he kissed her again.

By the time Trista returned with the lemonade, Elisabeth was badly in need of something that would cool her off. She sat in the grass with the man and the child, sipping the tart drink and hoping she wasn't flushed. Trista chattered the whole time about how they'd have the trout they'd caught for breakfast, firmly maintaining that Vera and *her* father had certainly never caught so many fine fish in one single day.

They returned to the house in midafternoon to eat the lovely ham dinner, and Jonathan was called away before he could have dessert. He seemed to be contemplating whether to leave or stay with them as he kissed Trista on top of the head and gave Elisabeth's shoulder a subtle squeeze.

Just that innocent contact sent heated shards through her, and she couldn't help recalling what Jonathan had said about making love to her in the moonlight under the covered bridge.

She and Trista cleared the table when they were finished eating, then they went out to the orchard and sat on the same thick, low branch of a gnarled old tree. Elisabeth listened and occasionally prompted while Trista practiced her spelling.

They were back in the house, seated together on the piano bench and playing a duet that wouldn't be composed for another seventy years or so, when Jonathan returned. He was in much better spirits than he had been the night before.

"Susan Crenshaw had a baby girl," he said, his eyes clear.

Elisabeth wanted to kiss him for the happiness she saw in his face, but she didn't dare because Trista was there and because she wasn't entirely sure the air wouldn't crackle. "I guess delivering a healthy baby makes up for a lot of bad things, doesn't it?"

"That it does," he agreed, and his fingers touched her shoulder again, making her breasts ache. Elisabeth watched Jonathan as he walked away, disappearing into his study, and she dared to consider what it would be like to be his wife and share his bed every night.

"Your face is red," Trista commented, jolting her back to matters at hand. "Are you getting a fever?"

Elisabeth smiled. "Maybe," she replied, "but it isn't the kind you have to worry about. Now, let's trade places, and you can play harmony while I do the melody."

Trista nodded eagerly and moved to the spot Elisabeth had occupied.

Because Trista had had an exciting weekend—the picnic, spending the night with Vera and going fishing with her father and Elisabeth—she went to bed early. Jonathan read to his daughter, then came downstairs to join Elisabeth in the parlor.

Standing behind her chair in front of the fireplace, he bent and kissed the crown of her head. "Play something for me," he urged, and Elisabeth went immediately to the piano. Strange as it seemed, making music for his ears was a part of their lovemaking; it warmed Elisabeth's blood and made her heart beat faster and her breathing quicken.

She played soft, soothing Mozart, and she was almost able to believe that she belonged there in that untamed century, where life was so much more difficult and intense. When she'd finished, she turned on the piano bench to gaze at Jonathan, who was standing at the window.

"Have you decided?" he asked after a long interval of comfortable silence had passed.

Elisabeth didn't need to ask what he meant; she knew. Although Jonathan had never once said he loved her, he wanted her to marry him. She smoothed her skirts. "I've decided," she said.

He arched one eyebrow, waiting.

"I'll marry you," Elisabeth said, meeting his eyes. "But only on one condition—you have to promise that we'll go away on a wedding trip. We'll be gone a full month, and Trista will be with us."

Jonathan's expression was grim. "Elisabeth, I'm the only doctor between here and Seattle—I can't leave these people without medical care for a month."

"Then I have to refuse," Elisabeth said, although it nearly killed her.

Dr. Fortner held out a hand to her. "It seems you need a little convincing," he told her in a low voice that set her senses to jumping.

Elisabeth couldn't help herself; she went to him, let him enfold her fingers in his. "May I remind you," she said in a last-ditch effort at behaving herself, "that there's a child only a few rooms away?"

"That's why I'm taking you to the bridge." Jonathan led her through the dining room and the kitchen and out into the cool spring night. There was a bright silver wash of moonlight glimmering in the grass.

She had to hurry to keep up with his long, determined strides. She thought fast. "Jonathan, what if someone needs you...?"

"You need me," he answered without missing a beat, pulling her through the orchard, where leaves rustled overhead and crushed petals made a soft carpet under her feet. "I'm about to remind you how much."

In the shadow of the covered bridge, Jonathan dragged Elisabeth against his chest and kissed her soundly, and the mastery of his lips and tongue made her knees go weak beneath her. He pressed her gently into the fragrant grass, his fingers opening the tiny buttons of her high-collared blouse. He groaned when he found her breasts bare underneath, waiting for him, their sweet tips reaching.

Elisabeth surrendered as he closed his mouth around one nipple, sucking eagerly, and she flung her arms back over her head to make herself even more vulnerable. While he made free with her breasts, Jonathan raised Elisabeth's skirts and, once again, found no barrier between him and what he wanted so much to touch.

"Little witch," he moaned, clasping her in his hand so that

the heel of his palm ground against her. "Show me your magic."

He'd long since aroused Elisabeth with words and looks and touches, and she tugged feverishly at his clothes until he helped her and she could feel bare flesh under her palms. Finally, he lay between her legs, and she guided him into her, soothing Jonathan even as she became his conqueror.

"Prove it," Jonathan challenged in a whisper when he and Elisabeth had finally returned to the house. They were standing in the upstairs hallway, their clothes rumpled from making love on the ground beside the creek. Jonathan had lit the lamp on the narrow table against the wall. A light spring rain was just beginning to fall. "If you can leave this century at will, then show me."

Elisabeth paused, her hand resting on the knob of the door to the spare bedroom. "It's not a parlor trick, Jon," she told him with sad annoyance. "I don't have the first idea how or why it works, and there's always the chance that I won't be able to get back."

His eyes seemed to darken, just for a moment, but his gaze was level and steady. "If you want me to believe what you've been saying, Lizzie, then you'll have to give me some evidence."

"All right," she agreed with a forlorn shrug. She didn't like the idea of leaving Jonathan, even if it was only a matter of stepping over a threshold and back. "But first I want a promise from you. If I don't return, you have to take Trista away from this house and not set foot in it again until after the first of July."

Jonathan watched her for a moment, his arms folded, and then nodded. "You have my word," he said with wry skepticism in his eyes.

Elisabeth went silently into her room to collect the necklace from its hiding place. Then she went into Trista's room. After casting one anxious look at the sleeping, unsuspecting child,

Elisabeth put the chain around her neck. She could see Jonathan clearly, standing in the hallway.

She took a deep breath, closed her eyes, and stepped over the threshold.

In one instant, Elisabeth had been there, closing her eyes and wishing on that damned necklace as though it were some sort of talisman. In the next, she was gone.

Shock consumed Jonathan like a brushfire, and he sank against the wall, squinting at the darkened doorway, hardly daring to trust his own vision.

"Lizzie," he whispered, running one hand down his face. Then reason overcame him. It had to be a trick.

He thrust himself away from the wall and plunged through Trista's quiet room. The inner door was fastened tightly. Jonathan wrenched it open and bounded down the steep steps to the kitchen.

"Elisabeth!" he rasped, his patience wearing thin, his heart thrumming a kind of crazy dread.

Jonathan searched every inch of the downstairs, then carrying a lantern, he went out into the drizzling rain to look in all the sheds and check the barn. Finding nothing, he strode through the orchard and even went as far as the bank of the creek.

There was no sign of her, and fear pressed down on him as he made his way slowly back to the house, his hair dripping, his shirt clinging wetly to his skin. "Elisabeth," he said. Despair echoed in the sound.

Elisabeth stood smugly on the back porch of Jonathan's house, watching him cross the rainy yard with the lantern and waiting for him to look up and see her standing there on the step.

When he raised his eyes, he stopped and stared at her through the downpour.

"Get in here," she said, scurrying out to take Jonathan's free hand and drag him toward the door. "You'll catch something!"

"How did you do that?" he demanded, setting the lantern on the kitchen table and gaping at Elisabeth while she fed wood into the stove and urged him closer to the heat.

She tapped the side of the blue enamel coffeepot with her fingertips to see if it was still hot and gave an exasperated sigh. "Your guess is as good as mine," she said, fetching a mug from the cabinets and filling it with the stout coffee. "You must have seen *something,* Jonathan. Did I fade out, or was I gone in a blink?"

Jonathan sank into a chair at the table and she set the mug before him. He didn't even seem to be aware of his sodden shirt and hair. "You simply—disappeared."

This was no time for triumph; Jonathan's teeth were already chattering. Elisabeth got a dry shirt from his room and a towel from the linen chest upstairs and returned to the kitchen.

He was standing close to the stove, bare chested, sipping his coffee. "I've had enough nonsense from you, Lizzie," he said, shaking a finger at her. "You fooled me, and I want to know how."

Elisabeth laughed and shook her head. "I always thought my father was stubborn," she replied, "but when it comes to bullheaded, you beat him all to hell." Her eyes danced as she approached Jonathan, laying her hands on his shoulders. "Face it, Jon. I vanished into thin air, and you saw it happen with your own eyes."

His color drained away and he rubbed his temples with a thumb and forefinger. "Yes. Good God, Lizzie, am I losing my mind?"

She slipped her arms around his waist. "No. It's just that there's a lot more going on in this universe than we poor mortals know."

Jonathan pressed her head against his bare shoulders, and she felt a shudder go through him. "I want to try it," he said. "I want to see the other side."

It was as though Elisabeth had stepped under a pounding, icy waterfall. "No," she whispered, stepping away from him.

He allowed her to go no farther than arm's length. "Yes,"

he replied, his gaze locked with hers. "If this world you've been telling me about is really there, I want a glimpse of it."

Elisabeth began to shake her head slowly from side to side. "Jonathan, no—you'd be taking a terrible chance...."

His deft, doctor's fingers reached beneath her tousled hair to unclasp the necklace. Then, holding it in one hand, he rounded Elisabeth and started up the short stairway that led to Trista's room.

"Jonathan!" Elisabeth cried, scrambling after him. "Jonathan, *wait* there are things I need to tell you...."

She reached the first door just as he got to the one leading out into the main hallway. Her eyes widened when he stepped across the threshold. Like a rippling reflection on the surface of a pond, he diffused into nothingness. Elisabeth clasped one hand over her mouth and went to stand in the empty doorway.

She sagged against the jamb, half-sick with the fear that she might never see him again. Heaven knew how she would explain his absence to Trista or to Marshal Haynes and the rest of the townspeople. And then there was the prospect of living without him.

It was the damnedest thing Jonathan had ever seen.

A second ago, he'd been standing in Trista's bedroom, on a rainy night. Now, a fierce spring sun was shining and the familiar hallway had changed drastically.

There were light fixtures on the walls, and beneath his feet was a thick rug the color of ripe wheat. For a few moments, he just stood there, gripping the necklace, trying to understand what was happening to him. He was scared, but not badly enough to turn around and go back without seeing what kind of world Elisabeth lived in.

Once he'd regained his equilibrium, he crossed the hall and opened the door to the master bedroom.

Like the hallway, it was structurally the same, but there the similarities ended. Jonathan's scientific heart began to beat faster with excitement.

When the shrill sound of a bell filled the air, he jumped

and almost bolted. Then he realized the jangle was coming from a telephone.

He looked around, but there was no instrument affixed to the wall. Finally, he tracked the noise to a fussy-looking gadget resting on the vanity table and he lifted the earpiece.

"Hello!" he snapped, frowning. There were telephones in Seattle, of course, but the lines hadn't reached Pine River yet, and Jonathan hadn't had much practice talking into a wire.

"Who is this?" a woman's voice demanded.

"This is Jonathan Fortner," he answered, fascinated. "Who are you, and why are you telephoning?"

There was a pause. "I'm Janet Finch, Elisabeth's friend. Is she there?"

A slow grin spread across Jonathan's mouth. "I'm afraid not," he replied. And then he laid the receiver in its cradle and walked away.

Almost immediately, the jarring noise began again, but Jonathan ignored it. There were things he wanted to investigate.

Just as he was descending the front stairway, an old woman with fussy white hair and enormous blue eyes peered through one of the long windows that stood on either side of the door. At the sight of Jonathan, she gave a little shriek, dropped something to the porch floor with a clatter and turned to run away.

Jonathan went to the window, grinning, and watched her trot across the road, her legs showing beneath her short dress. If this was truly the future, the elderly lady probably thought he was a ghost.

He just hoped he hadn't scared her too badly.

With a sigh of resignation, Jonathan proceeded to the kitchen, where he made an amazed inspection. He figured out the icebox right away, and he identified the thing with metal coils on top as a stove by process of elimination. He turned one of the knobs and then moved on to the sink, frowning at the gleaming spigots. When he gave one a twist, water shot out of a small pipe, startling him.

One of the spirals on the stove was red hot when he looked

back, and Jonathan held his palm over it, feeling the heat and marveling.

By far the most interesting thing in the room, however, was the box that sat on the counter. It had little dials, like the stove, and a window made out of the same stuff as Elisabeth's medicine bottle, only clear.

Jonathan tampered with the knobs and suddenly the window flashed with light and the face of an attractive African woman with stiff hair loomed before him.

"Are you tired of catering to your boss's every whim?" she demanded, and Jonathan took a step backward, speechless. The woman was staring at him, as if waiting for an answer, and he wondered if he should speak to her. "Today's guests will tell you how to stand up for yourself and still keep your job!" she finished.

"What guests?" Jonathan asked, looking around the kitchen. Music poured out of the box, and then a woman with hair the same color as Elisabeth's appeared, holding up a glass of orange juice.

"No, thank you," Jonathan said, touching the knob again. The window went dark.

He ambled outside to look at the barn—it had fallen into a shameful state of disrepair—and stood by the fence watching automobiles speed by. They were all colors now, instead of just the plain black he'd seen on the streets of Boston and New York.

When half an hour passed and he still hadn't seen a single horse, Jonathan shook his head and turned toward the house. He walked around it, noting the changes.

The section that contained Trista's room and the second rear stairway was gone, leaving no trace except for a door in the second-story wall. Remembering what Elisabeth had said about a fire, he shoved splayed fingers through his hair and strode inside.

He could hear her calling to him the moment he entered, and he smiled as he started up the rear stairs.

"Damn you, Jonathan Fortner, you get back here! Now!"

Jonathan took the necklace from his pocket and held it in

one hand. Then he opened the door and stepped over the
threshold.

Elisabeth was wearing different clothes—a black sateen
skirt and a blue shirtwaist—and there were shadows under her
eyes. "Oh, Jonathan," she cried, thrusting herself, shuddering, into his arms.

He kissed her temple, feeling pretty shaken himself. "It's
all right, Lizzie," he said. "I'm here." He held her tightly.

She raised her eyes to his face. "People were starting to
ask questions," she fretted. "And I had to lie to Trista and
tell her you'd gone to Seattle on business."

Jonathan was stunned. "But I was only gone for an hour
or so...."

Elisabeth shook her head. "Eight days, Jonathan," she said
somberly. She pressed her cheek to his chest. "I was sure I'd
never see you again."

He was distracted by the way she felt in his arms, all soft
and warm. With a fingertip, he traced the outline of her trembling lips. "Eight days?" he echoed.

She nodded.

The mystery was more than he could assimilate all at once,
so he put it to the back of his mind. "You must have missed
me something fierce in that case," he teased.

A spark of the old fire flickered in her eyes, and a corner
of her mouth quivered, as though she might forgive him for
frightening her and favor him with a smile. "I didn't miss
you at all," she said, raising her chin.

He spread his hands over her rib cage, letting the thumbs
caress her full breasts, feeling the nipples just against the fabric in response. "You're lying, Lizzie," he scolded. His
arousal struck like a physical blow; suddenly he was hard and
heavy with the need of her. He bent and kissed the pulse point
he saw throbbing under her right ear. "Are we alone?"

Her breath caught, and her satiny flesh seemed to tremble
under his lips. "For the moment," she said, her voice breathless and muffled. "Trista isn't home from school yet, and
Ellen is out in the vegetable garden, weeding."

"Good," Jonathan said, thinking what an extraordinarily

long time an hour could be. And then he lost himself in Elisabeth's kiss.

Elisabeth knew her cheeks were glowing and, despite her best efforts, her hair didn't look quite the same as it had before Jonathan had taken it down from its pins.

"Imagine that," Ellen said, breaking open a pod and expertly scraping out the peas with her thumbnail. "The doctor came back from wherever he's been, but I didn't hear no wagon nor see a sign of a horse. Come to that, he never took his rig with him in the first place." She paused to cluck and shake her head. "Strange doin's."

Elisabeth was sitting on the front step, while Ellen occupied the rocking chair. Watching the road for Trista, Elisabeth brushed a tendril of pale hair back from her cheek. "There are some things in this life that just can't be explained," she informed the housekeeper in a moderate tone. She was tired of the woman's suspicious glances and obvious disapproval.

Ellen sniffed. "If you ask me—"

"I *didn't* ask you," Elisabeth interrupted, turning on the step to fix the housekeeper with a look.

Color seeped into Ellen's sallow cheeks, but she didn't say anything more. She just went on shelling peas.

When Elisabeth saw Trista coming slowly down the road from the schoolhouse, her head lowered, she smoothed her sateen skirts and stood. She met the child at the gate with a smile.

"Your papa is back from his travels," she said.

The transformation in Trista stirred Elisabeth's heart. The little girl fairly glowed, and a renewed energy seemed to make her taller and stronger in an instant. With a little cry of joy, Trista flung herself into Elisabeth's arms.

Elisabeth held the child, near tears. Over the past eight trying days, she'd seen the depths of the bond this child had with her father. To separate them permanently by sending Trista to Barbara, so far in the future, was no longer an option.

"I thought maybe he'd stay away forever, like Mama,"

Trista confided as the two of them went through the gate together.

Elisabeth had known what Trista was thinking, of course,
but there hadn't been much she could do to reassure the uneasy child. She squeezed Trista's shoulders. "He'll be home
for supper—if there isn't a baby ready to be born somewhere."

Ellen, in the meantime, had finished shelling the peas and
returned to the kitchen, where she was just putting a chicken
into the oven to roast. She sniffed again when she saw Elisabeth.

"I don't imagine I'll be needed around here much longer,"
she said to no one in particular.

So that was it, Elisabeth reflected. Ellen's tendency to be
unkind probably stemmed from her fear of losing her job, now
that the doctor's sister-in-law seemed to be a permanent fix-
ture in the house. The problem was really so obvious, but
Elisabeth had been too worried about Jonathan's disappearance into the twentieth century to notice.

Even now, Elisabeth couldn't reassure the woman because
she didn't know what Jonathan thought about the whole matter. He had talked about marriage, and he could well expect
Elisabeth to take on all the duties Ellen was handling then.
He might have been more progressive than most men of his
era, but he wouldn't be taking up the suffrage cause anytime
soon.

"I'll let Jon—the doctor know you're concerned," Elisabeth finally said, and Ellen paused and looked back at her in
mild surprise. "And for what it's worth, I think you do a very
good job."

Ellen blinked at that. Clearly, she'd had Elisabeth tagged
as an enemy and didn't know how to relate to her as a friend.
"I'd be obliged," Ellen allowed at last. "The family depends
on me, and if there ain't going to be a place for me here, I
need to be finding another position."

Elisabeth nodded and went back into the house to look
about. Lord knew, there weren't any labor-saving devices, and
she'd never been all that crazy about housework, but the idea

of being a wife to Jonathan filled her with a strange, sweet vigor. Maybe she *was* crazy, she thought with a crooked little smile, because she really wanted to live out this life fate had handed to her.

Twilight had already fallen when Jonathan returned, and the kitchen was filled with the succulent aroma of roasting chicken and the cheery glow of lantern light. Trista was working out her fractions while Elisabeth mashed the potatoes.

The moment she heard her father's buggy in the yard, Trista tossed down her schoolwork and bolted for the back door, her face flushed and wreathed in smiles.

Elisabeth watched with her heart in her throat as the child launched herself from the back step into Jonathan's arms, shrieking, "Papa!"

He laughed and caught her easily, planting a noisy kiss on her forehead. "Hello, sweetheart," he said. There was a suspicious glimmer in his eyes, and his voice was a little hoarse.

Trista's small arms tightened around his neck. "I missed you so much!" she cried, hugging him tightly.

Jonathan returned the child's embrace, told her he loved her and set her back on the steps. Only then did Elisabeth notice how tired he looked.

"I imagine your patients missed you, too," she said as he followed Trista into the house and set his bag in the customary place. One of the greatest sources of Elisabeth's anxiety, during Jonathan's absence, was the fact that people had constantly come by looking for him. It hadn't been easy, knowing patients who needed his professional attention were being left to their own devices.

He sighed, and Elisabeth could see the strain in his face and in the set of his shoulders. "There are times," he said, "when I think being a coal miner would be easier."

Although she wanted to touch him, to take him into her arms and offer comfort, Elisabeth was painfully aware that she didn't have that option—not with Trista in the room.

It was bad enough that they'd lied to the child, telling her Elisabeth was Barbara's sister. For the past week, Trista had been begging for stories of the childhood Elisabeth had supposedly shared with her mother.

"Sit down, Jon," Elisabeth said quietly, letting her hands rest on his tense shoulders for a moment after he sank into a chair at the kitchen table.

Trista, delighted that her father was home, rushed to get his coffee mug, but it was Elisabeth who filled it from the heavy enamel pot on the stove.

The evening passed pleasantly—by some miracle, no one came to call Jonathan away—and after Trista had been settled in bed, he came into the kitchen and began drying dishes as Elisabeth washed them.

That reminded her of Ellen's concerns. "You need to have a talk with your housekeeper," she said. "She wants to look for another job if you're planning to let her go."

Jonathan frowned. "Isn't her work satisfactory?"

Elisabeth couldn't help smiling, seeing this rugged doctor standing there with an embroidered dishtowel in his hands. "Her work is fine. But you have given the community—and me, I might add—the impression that I might be staying around here permanently." She paused, blushing because the topic was a sensitive one. "I mean, if I'm to be your wife...."

He put down the towel and the cup he'd been drying and turned Elisabeth to face him. Her hands were dripping suds and water, and she dried them absently on her apron.

His expression was wry. "I'm not as destitute as you seem to think," he said. "I had an inheritance from my father and I invested it wisely, so I can afford to keep a housekeeper *and* a wife."

Elisabeth flushed anew; she hadn't meant to imply that he was a pauper.

Her reaction made Jonathan laugh, but she saw love in his eyes. "My sweet Lizzie—first and foremost, I want you to be a wife and partner to me. And I hope you'll be a mother to Trista. But running a house is a lot of work, and you're going to need Ellen to help you." He tilted his head to one side, studying her more soberly now. "Does this mean you're going to agree to marry me?"

Elisabeth sighed. The motion left her partially deflated, like a balloon the day after a party. There was still the specter of the fire looming over them, and the question had to be resolved. "That depends, Jonathan," she said, grieving when he took his hands away from her shoulders. "You've been over the threshold now, you've experienced what I have. I guess it all distills down to one question—do you believe me now?"

She saw his guard go up, and her disappointment was so keen and so sudden that it made her knees go weak.

Jonathan shoved one hand through his dark, rumpled hair. "Lizzie…"

"You *saw* it, Jonathan!" she cried in a ragged whisper as panic pooled around her like tidewater, threatening to suck her under. "Damn it, *you were there!*"

"I imagined it," he said, and his face was suddenly hard, his eyes cold and distant.

Elisabeth strode over to the sidetable where his medical bag awaited and snapped it open, taking out the prescription bottle and holding it up. "What about this, Jonathan? Did you imagine this?"

He approached her, took the vial from her hands and dropped it back into the bag. "I experienced *something,*" he said, "but that's all I'm prepared to admit. The human mind is capable of incredible things—it could all have been some sort of elaborate illusion."

Elisabeth was shaking. Jonathan was the most important person in her topsy-turvy universe, and he didn't believe her. She felt she would go mad if she couldn't make him understand. "Are you saying we both had the same hallucination, Jon? Isn't that a little farfetched?"

Again, Jonathan raked the fingers of one hand through his hair. "No more than believing that people can actually travel back and forth between centuries," he argued, making an effort to keep his voice down for Trista's sake. "Lizzie, the past is gone, and the future doesn't exist yet. All we have is *this moment.*"

Elisabeth was in no mood for an esoteric discussion. For

eight days she'd been mourning Jonathan, worrying about him, trying to reassure his daughter and his patients. She was emotionally exhausted and she wanted a hot bath and some sleep.

"I'd like the kitchen to myself now, if you don't mind," she said wearily, lifting the lid on the hot-water reservoir to check the supply inside. "I need a bath."

Jonathan's eyes lighted with humor and love. "I'd be happy to help you."

Elisabeth glared at him. "Yes, I imagine you would," she said, "but I don't happen to want your company just now, Dr. Fortner. As far as I'm concerned, you're an imbecile and I'd just as soon you kept your distance."

He smiled and lingered even after Elisabeth had dragged the big tin bathtub in from the combination pantry and storage room. His arms were folded across his chest. It was obvious that he was stifling a laugh.

Elisabeth brought out the biggest kettle in the kitchen, slammed it down in the sink and began pumping icy well water into it. It was amazing, she thought furiously, that she wanted to stay in this backward time with this backward man, when she could have hot and cold running water and probably a Democrat with an M.B.A. if she just returned to the 1990s. She lugged the heavy kettle to the stove and set it on the surface with a ringing thump.

When she turned to face Jonathan, her hands were on her hips and her jaw was jutting out obstinately. "I wouldn't give a flying *damn* whether you believed me or not," she breathed, "if it weren't for the fact that your life is hanging in the balance—and so is Trista's! Half of this house is going to burn in the third week in June, and they're not going to find a trace of you or your daughter. What they are going to do is try *me* for your murders!"

It hurt that the concern she saw in his face was so obviously for her sanity and not for his safety and Trista's. "Lizzie, there are doctors back in Boston and New York—men who know more than I do. They might be able to—"

"Just get out of here," Elisabeth spat out, tensing up like a cat doused in ice water, "and let me take my bath in peace."

Instead, Jonathan brought out more kettles and filled them at the pump, then set them on the stove. "You took care of me when I needed you," he said finally, his voice low, his expression brooking no opposition, "and I'm going to do what I have to do to take care of you, Lizzie. I love you."

Elisabeth had never been so confused. He'd said the words she most wanted to hear, but it also sounded as though he was planning to pack her off to the nearest loony bin the first chance he got. "If you love me," she said evenly, "then trust me, Jon. You didn't believe your own eyes and ears and... well...I'm all out of ways to convince you."

He sat her down in a chair, then fed more wood to the fire so her bathwater would heat faster. He didn't look at her when he spoke. "There isn't going to be a fire, Lizzie—you'll see. The third week of June will come and go, just like it always does."

She stared at his back. "You're going to pretend it didn't happen, aren't you?" she said in a thick whisper. "Jonathan, you were gone for *eight days*. How do you explain that—as a memory lapse?"

Heat began to surge audibly through the pots of water simmering on the stove. "Frankly," he answered, "I'm beginning to question *my* sanity."

CHAPTER 11

Frantic pounding at the front door roused Elisabeth from a sound, dreamless sleep. She reached for the robe she'd left lying across the foot of the bed and hurried into the hallway, where she saw Jonathan leaving his room. He was buttoning his shirt as he descended the stairs.

She remembered the proprieties of the century and held back, sitting on one of the high steps and gripping a banister post with one hand.

"It's my little Alice," a man's voice burst out after Jonathan opened the door. "She can't breathe right, Doc!"

"Just let me get my bag," Jonathan answered with grim resignation. A few moments later, he was gone, rattling away into the night in the visitor's wagon.

Elisabeth remained on the stairway, even though it was chilly and her exhausted body yearned for sleep. She was still sitting there, huddled in her nightgown and robe when Jonathan returned several hours later.

He lit a lamp in the entryway and started upstairs, halting when he saw Elisabeth.

"What happened?" she asked, wondering if she was going to be in this kind of suspense every time Jonathan was summoned out on a night call. "Is the little girl..."

Jonathan sighed raggedly and shook his head. "Diphtheria," he said.

Elisabeth's knowledge of old-fashioned diseases was limited, but she'd heard and read enough about this one to know it was deadly. And very contagious. "Is there anything I can do to help?" she asked lamely, knowing there wasn't.

He advanced toward her, and his smile was rueful and sad. ''Just be Lizzie,'' he said hoarsely.

They went back to their separate beds then, but it wasn't long before someone else came to fetch the doctor for *their* sick child. When Elisabeth finally gave up on sleeping somewhere around dawn and got up, Jonathan had still not returned.

She built up the kitchen fire and put coffee on to brew. And then she waited. This, she supposed, would be an integral part of being the wife of a nineteenth-century country doctor—if, indeed, destiny allowed her to marry Jonathan at all.

Sipping coffee, her feet resting on the warm, chrome footrail on the front of the stove, Elisabeth thought of her old life with Ian. It was like a half-remembered dream now, but once, that relationship had been the focal point of her existence.

Tilting her head back and closing her eyes, Elisabeth sighed and contemplated the hole her leaving would rend in that other world. Her disappearence would make one or two local newscasts, but after a while, she'd just be another nameless statistic, a person the police couldn't find.

Ian would cock an eyebrow, say it was all a pity and call his lawyer to see if he and the new wife had any claim on Elisabeth's belongings.

Her father would suffer, but he had his career and Traci and the new baby. In the long run, he'd be fine.

Janet and Elisabeth's other friends in Seattle would probably be up in arms for a time, bugging the police and speculating among themselves, but they all had their own lives. Eventually, they'd go back to living them, and it would be as though Elisabeth had died.

Rue, of course, was an entirely different matter. She would come home from her travels, read the letter Elisabeth had written about her first experience with the threshold and be on the next plane for Seattle. Within an hour of landing, she'd be right here in this house, looking for any trace of her cousin, following up every lead, making the police wish they'd never heard of Elisabeth McCartney.

So close, Elisabeth thought, imagining Rue in these very rooms, her throat thickening with emotion, *and yet so far.*

The sound of Trista coming down the steps roused Elisabeth from her thoughts.

"What are you doing up so early?" Elisabeth asked, taking the child onto her lap.

Trista snuggled close. Although she was wearing a pinafore, black ribbed stockings and plain shoes with pointy toes, her dark hair hadn't been brushed or braided, and she was still warm and flushed from sleep. She yawned. "I kept hearing people knock on the door. Is Papa out?"

Elisabeth nodded, noting with a start that Trista's forehead felt hot against her cheek. *God, no,* she thought, pressing her palms to either side of the child's face. *No!* She made herself speak in an even tone of voice. "He's been gone for several hours," she said. "Trista—do you feel well?"

"My throat's sore," she said, "and my chest hurts."

Tears of alarm sprang to Elisabeth's eyes, but she forced them back. This was no time to lose her head. "Were you sick during the night?" She tightened her arms around the child, as if preparing to resist some giant, unseen hand that might wrench her away.

Trista looked up at Elisabeth. "I wanted to get into bed with you," she said shyly.

Elisabeth bit her lip and made herself speak calmly. "Well, I think we'd better forget about school and make you a nice, comfortable bed right here by the stove. We'll read stories and I'll play the piano for you. How would that be?"

A tremor ran through the small body in Elisabeth's arms. "I have to go to school," Trista protested. "There's a spelling bee today, and you know how hard I've been practicing."

There was an element of the frantic in the quick kiss Elisabeth planted on Trista's temple. "It would be my guess that there won't be any school today, sweetheart. And it's possible, you know, to practice too hard. Sometimes, you have to just do your best and then stand back and let things happen."

Trista sighed. "I *would* like to have a bed in the kitchen and hear stories," she confessed.

"Then let's get started," Elisabeth said with false cheer as she set Trista in a chair and automatically felt the child's face for fever again. "You stay right there," she ordered, waggling a finger. "And don't you dare think of even *one* spelling word!"

Trista laughed, but the sound was dispirited.

Elisabeth dragged a leather-upholstered Roman couch from Jonathan's study to the kitchen and set it as close to the stove as she dared. Then she hurried upstairs and collected Trista's nightgown and the linens from her bed.

By the time Jonathan came through the back door, looking hollow eyed and weary to the very center of his soul, his daughter was reclining on the couch, listening to Elisabeth read from *Gulliver's Travels.* The expression on his face as he made the obvious deduction was terrible to see.

Immediately, he came to his daughter's bedside, touched her warm face, examined her ears and throat. Then his eyes linked with Elisabeth's, over Trista's head, and she knew it might not matter that there was going to be a fire the third week in June. Not to this little girl, anyway.

They went into Jonathan's study to talk.

"Diphtheria?" Elisabeth whispered, praying he'd say Trista just had the flu or common cold. But then, those maladies weren't so harmless in the nineteenth century, either. There were so many medical perils at this time that a child would never encounter in Elisabeth's.

Jonathan was standing at one of the windows, gazing past the lace curtain at the new, bright, blue-and-gold day. He shook his head. "It's a virus I've never seen before—and there seems to be an epidemic."

Elisabeth's fingers were entwined in the fabric of her skirts. "Isn't there anything we can do?"

He shrugged miserably. "Give them quinine, force liquids...."

She went and stood behind him, drawn by his pain and the need to ease it. She rested her hands on his tense shoulders. "And then?"

"And then they'll probably die," he said, walking away from her so swiftly that her hands fell to her sides.

"Jon, the penicillin—there wouldn't be enough for all the children, but Trista..." Her sentence fell away, unfinished, when Jonathan walked out of the study and let the door close crisply behind him. Without uttering a word, he'd told Elisabeth he had neither the time nor the patience for what he considered delusions.

He'd left his bag on his cluttered desk in the corner. Elisabeth opened it and rummaged through until she'd found the bottle of penicillin tablets. Removing the lid, she carefully tipped the pills into her palm and counted them.

Ten.

She scooped the medicine back into its bottle and dropped it into her pocket.

Jonathan was stoking the fire in the kitchen stove when Elisabeth joined him, while Trista watched listlessly from the improvised bed. Elisabeth could see the child's chest rise and fall unevenly as breathing became more difficult for her.

Elisabeth began pumping water into pots and kettles and carrying them to the stove, and soon the windows were frosted with steam and the air was dense and hot.

"Let me take her over the threshold, Jon," Elisabeth pleaded in a whisper when Trista had slipped into a fitful sleep an hour later. "There are hospitals and modern drugs..."

He glowered at her. "For God's sake, don't start that nonsense now!"

"You must have seen the cars going by on the road. It's a much more advanced society! Jonathan, I can help Trista—I know I can!"

"Not another word," he warned, and his gray eyes looked as cold as the creek in January.

"The medicine, then—"

The back door opened and Ellen came in, looking flushed and worried. When her gaze fell on Trista, however, the high color seeped from her face. "I'm sorry I couldn't come sooner, but it's the grippe—we've got it at our place, and Seenie's so hot, you can hardly stand to touch her!"

Jonathan's eyes strayed to Trista for a moment, but skirted Elisabeth completely. "I'll be there in few minutes," he said.

Ellen hovered near the door, looking as though she might faint with relief, but Elisabeth felt nothing but frustration and despair.

"I'll get your bag," she said to Jonathan, and disappeared into the study.

When she returned, the doctor had already gone outside to hitch up his horse and buggy. Elisabeth gave the bag to Ellen, but there seemed to be no reassuring words to offer. A look passed between the two women, and then Ellen hurried outside to ride back to her family's farm with Jonathan.

Throughout the afternoon, Elisabeth kept the stove going at full tilt, refilling the kettles and pots as their contents evaporated. The curtains, the tablecloth, Trista's bedclothes—everything in the room was moist.

Elisabeth found fresh sheets and blankets and a clean nightgown for Trista. The child hardly stirred as the changes were made. Her breathing was a labored rattle, and her flesh was hot as a stove lid.

Elisabeth knelt beside the couch, her head resting lightly on Trista's little chest, her eyes squeezed shut against tears of grief and helplessness. This, too, was part of being a Victorian woman—watching a beloved child slip toward death because there were no medicines, no real hospitals. Now, she realized that she'd taken the vaccinations and medical advances of her own time for granted, never guessing how deadly a simple virus could be.

Presently, Elisabeth felt the pharmacy bottle pressing against her hip and reached into her pocket for it, turning it in her fingers. She was no doctor—in fact, she had virtually no medical knowledge at all, except for the sketchy first-aid training she'd been required to take to get her teaching certificate. But she knew that penicillin was a two-edged sword.

For most people, it was perfectly safe and downright magical in its curative powers. For others, however, it was a deadly poison, and if Trista had an adverse reaction, there would be nothing Elisabeth could do to help. On the other hand, an infection was raging inside the child's body. She probably wouldn't live another forty-eight hours if someone didn't intercede.

Resolutely, Elisabeth got to her feet and went to the sink. A bucket of cold water sat beside it, pumped earlier, and Elisabeth filled a glass and carried it back to Trista's bedside.

"Trista," she said firmly.

The child's eyes rolled open, but Trista didn't seem to recognize Elisabeth. She made a strangled, moaning sound.

The prescription bottle recommended two tablets every four hours, but that was an adult dose. Frowning, Elisabeth took one pill and set it on Trista's tongue. Then, holding her own breath, she gave the little girl water.

For a few moments, while Trista sputtered and coughed, it seemed she wouldn't be able to hold the pill down, but finally she settled back against the curved end of the couch and closed her eyes. Elisabeth sensed that the child's sleep was deeper and more comfortable this time, but she was so frightened and tense, she didn't dare leave the kitchen.

She was sitting beside Trista's bed, holding the little girl's hand, when the back door opened and Jonathan dragged in. "Light cases," he said, referring, Elisabeth hoped, to the children in Ellen's sizable family. "They'll probably be all right." He was at his daughter's side by then, setting his bag on the table, taking out his stethoscope and putting the earpiece in place. He frowned as he listened to Trista's lungs and heart.

Elisabeth wanted to tell him about the penicillin, but she was afraid. Jonathan was not exactly in a philosophical state of mind, and he wouldn't be receptive to updates on twentieth-century medicine. "You need some rest and something to eat," she said.

He smiled grimly as he straightened, pulling off the stethoscope and tossing it back into his bag. "This is a novelty, having somebody worry about me," he said. "I think I like it."

"Sit," Elisabeth ordered wearily, rising and pressing him into the chair where she'd been keeping her vigil over Trista.

She poured stout coffee for him, adding sugar and cream because he liked it that way, and then went to the icebox for eggs she'd gathered herself the day before and the leftovers from a baked ham.

Jonathan's gaze rested on his daughter's flushed face. "She hasn't been out of my thoughts for five minutes all day," he said with a sigh. "I didn't want to leave her, but you were here, and the others—"

Elisabeth stopped to lay a hand on his shoulder. "I know, Jon," she said softly. She found an onion and spices in the pantry and, minutes later, an omelette was bubbling in a pan on the stove.

"Her breathing seems a little easier," Jonathan commented when Elisabeth dished up the egg concoction and brought it to the table for him.

She didn't say anything, but her fingers closed around the little bottle of penicillin in the pocket of her skirt. Soon, when Jonathan wasn't looking, she would give Trista another pill.

He seemed almost too tired to lift his fork, and Elisabeth's heart ached as she watched him eat. When he finished his meal, she knew he wouldn't collapse into bed and sleep, as he needed to do. No, Jonathan would head for the barn, where he would feed and water animals for an hour. Then, provided another frantic father didn't come to fetch him, he'd sit up the rest of the night, watching over Trista.

Elisabeth woke the child while he was in the barn and made her swallow another penicillin tablet. By that time, her own body was aching with fatigue and she wanted to sink into a chair and sob.

She didn't have time for such luxuries, though, for the fire was waning and the water in the kettles was boiling away. Elisabeth found the wood box empty and, after checking Trista, she wrapped herself in a woolen shawl and went outside to the shed. There, she picked up the ax and awkwardly began splitting chunks of dry apple wood.

Jonathan was crossing the yard when she came out, her arms loaded, and he took the wood from her without a word.

Inside, he fed the fire while she pumped more water to

make more steam. Suddenly, she ran out of fortitude and sank against Jonathan, weeping for all the children who could not be saved, both in this century and in her own.

Jonathan embraced her tightly for a moment, kissed her forehead and then lifted her into his arms and started toward the stairs. "You're going to lie down," he announced in a stern undertone. "I'll bring you something to eat."

"I want to stay with Trista."

"You're no good to her in this condition," Jonathan reasoned, opening the door to her room and carrying her inside. He laid her gently on the bed and pulled off her sneakers, so incongruous with her long skirt and big-sleeved blouse. "I'll bring you a tray."

Elisabeth opened her mouth to protest, but it was too late. Jonathan had already closed the door, and she could hear his footsteps in the hallway.

She had to admit it felt gloriously, decadently good to lie down. She would rest for a few minutes, to shut Jonathan up, and then go back to Trista.

The doctor returned, as promised, bringing a ham sandwich and a glass of milk. Elisabeth ate, even though she had virtually no appetite, knowing she needed the food for strength.

Filling her stomach had a peculiar tranquilizing effect, and she sagged against her pillows and yawned even as she battled her weariness. She would just close her eyes long enough to make them stop burning, Elisabeth decided, then go back downstairs to sit with Trista.

There were shadows in the room and the bedside lamp was burning low when Elisabeth awakened with a start. Her throat was sore when she swallowed, but she didn't take time to think about that because she was too anxious to see Trista.

She was holding her breath as she made her way down the back stairway.

The kitchen lamps were lit, and Jonathan sat at the table, his head resting on his folded arms, sound asleep. Trista was awake, though, and she smiled shakily as Elisabeth approached the bed and bent to kiss her forehead.

"Feeling better?"

Trista nodded, though she was still too weak to talk.

"I'll bet you'd like some nice broth, wouldn't you?" Elisabeth asked, remembering the chicken Ellen had killed and plucked yesterday. And even though Trista shook her head and wrinkled her nose, Elisabeth took the poultry from the icebox and put it on the stove to boil.

Although she tried to be quiet, the inevitable clatter awakened Jonathan and he lifted his head to stare at Elisabeth for a few seconds, seeming not to recognize her. Then his gaze darted to his daughter.

Trista smiled wanly at the startled expression on his face.

A study in disbelief, Jonathan grabbed his bag and hastily donned his stethoscope. His eyes were wide with surprise when he looked at Elisabeth, who was grinning at him and holding up the little medicine bottle.

Jonathan snatched it out of her hands. "You gave her this?"

Elisabeth's delight faded. "Yes," she answered with quiet defiance. "And it saved her life."

He looked from the pills to his daughter's placid, if pale, face. "My God."

"It's safe to say He's involved here somewhere," Elisabeth ventured a little smugly. "You should give her one every four hours, though, until she's out of danger."

Jonathan groped for a chair and sank into it. He opened the bottle, this time with no assistance from Elisabeth, and dumped the remaining tablets out onto the table to stare at them as though he expected a magic beanstalk to sprout before his eyes. "Peni— What did you call them?"

"Penicillin," Elisabeth said gently.

"I didn't dream it," he whispered.

She shook her head and spread her hands over his shoulders. A glance at Trista showed her that the child was sleeping again, this time peacefully. "No, Jon—you were really there." She began to work the rigid muscles with her fingers. "You never told me what you saw, you know."

A tremor went through him. "There was a box with women inside," he said woodenly. "They spoke to me."

At the same time she was stifling a laugh, tears of affection burned in Elisabeth's eyes. "The television set," she said. "They weren't talking to you Jon—they were only pictures, being transmitted through the air."

"What else do they have in your world," Jonathan inquired wearily, "besides automobiles that travel too fast?"

Elisabeth smiled. So he *had* seen something of the real twentieth century. "We're exploring outer space," she said, continuing with the massage and knowing an ancient kind of pleasure as Jonathan's muscles began to relax. "And there have been so many inventions that I couldn't list them all— the most significant being a machine called a computer."

Jonathan listened, rapt, while Elisabeth told him what she knew about computers, which was limited. She went on to explain modern society as best she could. "There are still social problems, I'm afraid," she told him. "For instance, we have a serious shortage of housing for the poor, and there's a lot of drug and alcohol abuse."

He arched an eyebrow. "Which must be why you were so angry when I sedated you," he ventured.

Elisabeth's achy throat was tight as she nodded. He finally believed her, and if she'd had the energy, she would have jumped up and clicked her heels together to celebrate.

Jonathan sighed. "There are people now who use opium, but thank heaven it's not prevalent."

Elisabeth sat down beside him and cupped her chin in her hands. "Don't be too cocky, Dr. Fortner. You've got a lot of laudanum addicts out there, taking a tipple when nobody's looking. And the saloons are brimming with alcoholics. In approximately 1935, two men will start an organization to help drunks get and stay sober."

He rubbed his beard-stubbled chin, studying Elisabeth as though she were of some unfamiliar species. "Let's talk about that fire you've been harping on ever since you first showed up," he said. Then, remembering Trista, he caught Elisabeth's elbow in one hand and ushered her out of the kitchen and into the parlor, where he proceeded to build a fire against the evening chill. "You said Trista and I died in it."

"I said the authorities—Marshal Farley Haynes, to be specific—believed I killed you by setting the blaze. If—" she swallowed as bile rushed into her throat "—if bodies were found, the fact was hushed up. And the newspaper didn't give a specific date."

Jonathan rubbed the back of his neck and shook his head, watching as the fire caught on the hearth, sending orange and yellow flames licking around the apple-wood logs. "You'll understand," he said, still crouching before the grate, "if I find this whole thing a little hard to accept."

"I think I would in your place," Elisabeth conceded, taking a seat in a leather wing chair and folding her hands in her lap. "Jonathan, we can leave now, can't we? We can move to the hotel in town, at least during that week?"

To her surprise, he shook his head again as he rose to stand facing her, one shoulder braced against the mantelpiece. "We'll be especially careful," he said. "Surely being warned ahead of time will make a difference."

Elisabeth wasn't convinced; she had a sick feeling in the pit of her stomach, a sense of dire urgency. "Jonathan, please—you must have seen that the house was different in my time. If that isn't evidence that there really was a fire..."

Jonathan came to stand before her chair, bending to rest one hand on each of its arms and effectively trapping her. "There won't be a fire," he said, "because you and I are going to prevent it."

She closed her eyes tightly, defeated for the moment.

Jonathan's breath was warm on her face as he changed the subject. "I'm tired of lying in my bed at night, Elisabeth, aching for you. I want to get married."

She felt her cheeks heat as she glared up at him. "Now, that's *romantic!*" she murmured, moving to push him away and rise, but he stood fast, grinning at her. Raw pain burned her throat as she spoke, and the amusement faded from Jonathan's eyes.

He touched her forehead with his hand. "If you come from a time where some of our diseases no longer exist," he breathed, "you haven't built up any kind of immunity." Jonathan stepped back and drew Elisabeth to her feet, and she was instantly dizzy, collapsing against him. Her first thought was that the rigors of the past twenty-four hours had finally caught up with her.

As easily as before, Jonathan lifted her into his arms. The next thing she knew, she was upstairs and he was stripping her, tucking her into bed. He brought water and two of the precious pills, which Elisabeth wanted to save for Trista.

She shook her head.

But Jonathan forced her to swallow the medicine. She watched, her awareness already wavering, as he constructed a sort of tent around the bed, out of blankets. Presently, the air grew close and moist, and Elisabeth dreamed she was lost in a jungle full of exotic birds and flowers.

In the dream, she knew Jonathan was looking for her—she could hear him calling—but he was always just out of sight, just out of reach.

CHAPTER 12

Jonathan's fear grew moment by moment as he watched Elisabeth lapse further and further into the depths of the illness. As strong and healthy as she was, her body had no apparent defenses against the virus, and within a matter of hours, she was near death. Even the wonder pills she'd brought with her from the future didn't seem to be helping.

He was searching her dresser before he consciously acknowledged the desperate decision he'd made. Finding the necklace in a top drawer, under a stack of carefully laundered and folded pantaloons, he went back to Elisabeth's bedside and fastened the tarnished chain around her neck.

For a long time, he just stood there, staring down at her, marveling at how deeply he'd come to cherish her in the short time they'd had together. Even when he'd thought she was demented, he'd loved her.

The daylight was fading at the windows when he finally looked up. He turned and went rapidly down the rear stairway to check on Trista.

Earlier, he'd given her a bowl of Elisabeth's chicken broth. He found her sleeping now, and her fever had finally broken.

Jonathan bent and, smoothing back his daughter's dark hair with a gentle hand, kissed her forehead. ''I'll be back as soon as I can,'' he promised in a husky whisper.

Upstairs again, he lifted Elisabeth from the bed and carried her down the back stairs into the kitchen and then up the other set of steps leading to Trista's room. Within moments, they were standing at the threshold.

Although he'd never been a religious man, Jonathan prayed

devoutly in those moments. Then he closed his eyes and stepped across.

The immediate lightness in his arms swung a hoarse cry of despair from his throat. He was still in his time—the same pictures hung from the walls and the familiar runner was under his feet.

But Elisabeth was gone.

Miss Cecily Buzbee hovered and fretted while the young men from the county hospital lifted Elisabeth's inert form onto a gurney and started an IV flowing into a vein in her left hand.

"It's a lucky thing I came by to check on her, that's all I can say," Miss Cecily said, following as Elisabeth was carried down the stairs and out through the front door. "There's something strange going on in this house, you mark my words, and Sister and I have a good mind to telephone the sheriff...."

The paramedics lifted the stretcher into the back of the ambulance, and one of them climbed in with it.

"Heaven only knows how long she's been lying there in that hallway," Cecily babbled on, trailing after the second man as he walked around to get behind the wheel.

"Does Ms. McCartney have any allergies that you know about?" he asked, speaking to her through the open window on the driver's side of the ominous-looking vehicle.

Cecily had no idea and it was agony that she couldn't help.

The young man shifted the ambulance into gear. "Well, if she's got any family, you'd better get in touch with them right away."

The words struck Cecily like a blow. She didn't know Elisabeth well, but she cared what happened to her. Merciful heavens, the poor thing was too young and beautiful to die—she hadn't had a proper chance to live.

Cecily watched until the ambulance had turned onto the main road, lights slicing the twilight, siren blaring. Then she hurried back into the house and began searching for Elisabeth's address book.

* * *

"Jonathan?" The name hurt Elisabeth's throat as she said it, and she wasn't sure whether she was whispering or shouting. She tried to sit up, but she was too weak. And she was immediately pressed back to her pillows by a nurse anyway.

A nurse.

Every muscle in Elisabeth's limp and aching body tensed as a rush of alarm swept through her. Her eyes darted about the room wildly, looking for the one face that would make everything all right.

But there was no sign of Jonathan, and the reason was painfully obvious. Somehow, she'd found her way back into the twentieth century, though she had no conscious memory of making the transition. And that meant she was separated from the man she loved.

The nurse was a young woman, tall, with short, curly, brown hair and friendly eyes. "Just relax," she said. "You're safe and sound in the county hospital."

Elisabeth could barely control the panic that seized her. "How long have I been here?" she rasped, as the nurse—the tag on her uniform said her name was Vicki Webster—held a glass of cool water up so that Elisabeth could drink through a straw.

"Just a couple of days," Vicki replied. "One of your friends has been here practically the whole time. Would you like to see her?"

For a moment, Elisabeth soared with the hope that Rue had come back from her assignment, but in the next instant, she knew better. Rue was family and she would never have introduced herself to the staff as a friend.

Minutes later, Janet appeared, looking haggard. Her hair was a mess, her raincoat was crumpled and there were dark smudges under her eyes. "Do you know how worried I've been?" she demanded, coming to stand beside the bed. "First I talked to that strange man on the telephone, and then I couldn't get anyone to answer at all...."

Elisabeth gripped Janet's hand. "Janet, what day is this?"

Janet's brow furrowed with concern and she bit her lips. "It's the tenth of June," she said.

"The tenth..." Elisabeth closed her eyes, too drained to go on. Time was racing by, not only here, but in the nineteenth century, as well. Perhaps Jonathan and Trista were trapped in a burning house at that very moment—perhaps they were already dead!

Janet snatched a tissue from the box on the bedside stand and gently wiped away tears Elisabeth hadn't even realized she was shedding. "Beth, I know you're sick, and it's obvious you're depressed, but you can't give up. You've got to keep putting one foot in front of the other until you get past whatever it is that's troubling you so much."

Elisabeth was too tired to say any more, and Janet stayed a while longer, then left again. The next morning, a big bouquet of flowers arrived from Elisabeth's father, along with a note saying that he and Traci hoped she was feeling better.

As it happened, Elisabeth was feeling stronger, if not better, and she was growing more and more desperate to return to Jonathan and Trista. But here she was, too frail even to walk to the bathroom by herself. She fought off rising panic only because she knew it would drain her and delay the time when she'd be able to leave the hospital.

"I'm taking you home with me," Janet announced three evenings later. A true friend, she'd been making the drive to Pine River every day after she finished teaching her classes. "The term is almost over, so I'll have lots of time to play nurse."

Elisabeth smiled wanly and shook her head. "I want to go home," she said in a quiet voice. *To Jonathan, and Trista— please, God.*

Janet cleared her throat and averted her eyes for just a moment. When she looked back at Elisabeth, her gaze was steady. "Who was that man, Bethie—the one who answered the telephone when I called that day?"

Elisabeth imagined Jonathan glaring at the instrument as it rang, and she smiled again. "That was Jonathan," she said. "The man I love."

"So where is he?" Janet demanded, somewhat impatiently. "If you two are so wild about each other, why haven't I had so much as a glimpse of the guy?" She waved one hand to take in the flowers that banked the room—even Ian and his new bride had sent carnations. "Where's the bouquet with his name on the card?"

Elisabeth sighed. She was too tired to explain about Jonathan, and even if she attempted it, Janet would never believe her. In fact, she would probably go straight to the nearest doctor and the next thing Elisabeth knew, she'd be in the psychiatric ward, weaving potholders. "He's out of the...country," she lied, staring up at the ceiling so she wouldn't have to meet Janet's eyes. "And he's called every day."

When Elisabeth dared look at Janet again, she saw patent disbelief in her friend's face. "There's something very weird here," Janet said.

You don't know the half of it, Elisabeth thought. She was relieved when Janet left a few minutes later.

Almost immediately, however, the Buzbee sisters appeared with colorful zinnias from their garden and a stack of books that probably came from their personal library.

"I saw the ghost through the front window one day," Cecily confided to Elisabeth in a whisper, when her sister had gone down the hall to say hello to a friend who was recovering from gall-bladder surgery.

Elisabeth felt herself go pale. "The ghost?"

Cecily nodded. "Dr. Fortner it was—I'd know him anywhere." She took one of the books from the pile she'd brought, thumbed through it and held it out to Elisabeth. "See? He's standing second from the left, beside the little girl."

Elisabeth's throat tightened as she stared at the old picture, taken by the Pine River Bridge on Founder's Day 1892. Jonathan gazed back at her, and so did Trista, but that wasn't really what shook her, since this was a copy of the same book she'd checked out from the library and she'd seen the picture before. No, it was the fact that her own image had been added, standing just to Jonathan's right. Cecily probably hadn't noticed because Elisabeth looked very different in period clothes and an old-fashioned hairstyle, and because she'd been looking at the picture with the careless eyes of familiarity.

"You've seen this man, haven't you?" Cecily challenged, though not unkindly. She poured water for Elisabeth and held the straw to her lips, as though alarmed by Elisabeth's sudden pallor.

Tears squeezed past Elisabeth's closed eyelids and tickled in her lashes. "Yes," she said. "I've seen him."

Cecily patted Elisabeth's forehead. "There, there, dear. I'm sorry if I upset you. You've probably been frightened half out of your mind these past few weeks, and then you let yourself get run-down and you caught—what is it you caught?"

Elisabeth's disease had been diagnosed simply as a "virus," and she knew the medical community was puzzled by it. "I—I guess it's pneumonia," she said. She put her hand to her throat and turned pleading eyes on Cecily. "They took my necklace."

"I'll just get it right back for you," Cecily replied briskly. And she went out into the hallway, calling for a nurse.

Half an hour later, Elisabeth had her necklace back. Just wearing it made her feel closer to Jonathan and Trista.

That evening when the doctor came by on his evening rounds, he took the IV needle from Elisabeth's hand and pronounced her on the mend. His kindly eyes were full of questions as to where she could have contracted a virus modern medicine couldn't identify, but he didn't press her for answers.

"I want to go home," she announced when he'd finished a fairly routine examination. Weak as she was, she was conscious of every tick of the celestial clock, and it was hell not knowing what was happening to Jonathan and Trista.

The physician smiled and shook his head. "Not for a few more days, I'm afraid. You're in a very weakened state, Ms. McCartney."

"But I can recover just as well there as here...."

"Let's see how you feel on Friday," he said, overruling her. And then he moved on to the next room.

Elisabeth waited until it was dark before getting out of bed, staggering over to the door and peering down the lighted hallway to the nurses' station. One woman was there, her head bent over some notes she was making, but other than that, the coast was clear.

With enormous effort, Elisabeth put on the jeans and sweatshirt Janet had brought her from the house, brushed her tangled hair and crept out into the hallway. A city hospital would have been more difficult to escape, but this one was small and understaffed, and Elisabeth made it into the elevator without being challenged.

She leaned back, clutching the metal railing in both hands and summoning up all her strength. She still had to get to her house, which was several miles away. And Pine River wasn't exactly bustling with available taxi cabs.

Elisabeth didn't have her purse—that was locked away for safekeeping in the hospital and, of course, she didn't dare ask for it—but there was a spare house key hidden in the woodshed.

She started walking, and it soon became apparent that she was simply too weak to walk all the way home. Praying she wouldn't find herself hooked up with a serial killer, like women she'd read about, she stuck out her thumb.

Presently a rattly old pickup truck with one missing fender came to a stop beside her and a young man leaned across the seat to push open the door. His smile was downright ingenuous.

"Your car break down?" he asked.

Elisabeth eyed him wearily, waiting for negative vibes to strike her, but there weren't any. The kid kind of reminded her of Wally Cleaver. She nodded, not wanting to explain that she'd just sprung herself from the hospital, and climbed into the truck.

Just that effort exhausted her and she collapsed against the back of the lumpy old seat, terrified that she would pass out.

"Hey," the teenage boy began, shifting the vehicle into

gear and stepping on the gas with enthusiasm. "You sick or something? There's a hospital right back there...." He cocked his thumb over one shoulder.

Elisabeth shook her head. "I'm fine," she managed, rallying enough to smile. "I live out on Schoolhouse Road."

The young man looked at her with amused interest. "You don't mean that haunted place across from the Buzbees, do you?"

Elisabeth debated between laughing and crying, and settled on the former, mostly to keep from alarming her rescuer. "Sure do," she said.

He uttered an exclamation, and Elisabeth could see that he was truly impressed. "Ever see any spooks or anything like that?"

They were passing through the main part of town, and Elisabeth felt a bittersweet pang as she looked at the lighted windows and signs. She hoped to be back with Jonathan soon, and when that happened, the modern world would be a memory. If something that didn't exist yet could be called a memory.

"No," she said, pushing back her hair with one hand. "To tell you the truth, I don't believe in ghosts. I think there's a scientific explanation for everything—it's just that there are so many natural laws we don't understand."

"So you've never seen nothing suspicious, huh?"

As a teacher, Elisabeth winced at his grammar. "I've seen things I can't explain," she admitted. She figured she owed him that much, since he was giving her a ride home.

"Like what?"

Elisabeth sighed, unsure how much to say. After all, if he went home and told his parents she'd talked about traveling between one century and the next, the authorities would probably come and cart her off to a padded room. "Just—things. Shadows. The kind of stuff you catch a glimpse of out of the corner of an eye and wonder what you really saw."

Her companion shuddered as he turned into Elisabeth's driveway. She could tell the sight of the dark house looming in the night didn't thrill him.

"Thanks," she said, opening the door and getting out of the truck. Her knees seemed to have all the substance of whipped egg whites, and she clung to the door for a moment to steady herself.

The boy swallowed. "No problem," he answered. He gunned the engine, though it was probably an unconscious motion. "Want me to stick around until you're inside?"

Elisabeth looked back over her shoulder at the beloved house that had always been her refuge. "I'll be perfectly all right," she said. And then she turned and walked away.

Her young knight in shining armor wasted no time in backing out of the driveway and speeding away down the highway. Elisabeth smiled as she made her way around the house to the woodshed to extract the back door key from its hiding place.

The lights in the kitchen glowed brightly when she flipped the switch, and Elisabeth felt the need of a cup of tea to brace herself, but she didn't want to take the time. Her strength was about to give out, and she yearned to be with Jonathan.

Upstairs, however, she found the door to the past sealed against her, even though she was wearing the necklace. After a half hour of trying, she went into the master bedroom and collapsed on the bed, too weary even to cry out her desolate frustration.

In the morning, she tried once again to cross the threshold, and once again, the effort was fruitless. She didn't let herself consider the possibility that the window in time had closed forever, because the prospect was beyond bearing.

She listened listlessly to the messages on her answering machine—the last one was from her doctor, urging her to return to the hospital—then shut off the machine without returning any of the calls. She thumbed through her mail and, finding nothing from Rue, tossed the lot of it into the trash, unopened.

In the kitchen, she brewed hot tea and made toast with a couple slices of bread from a bag in the freezer. She was feeling a little better this morning, but she knew she hadn't recovered a tenth of her normal strength.

After finishing her toast, she wrote another long letter to Rue, stamped it and carried it out to the mailbox. By the time she returned, carrying a batch of fourth-class mail with her, she was on the verge of collapse.

Numbly, Elisabeth climbed the stairs again, found herself a fresh set of clothes and ran a deep, hot bath. After shampooing her hair, she settled in to soak. The heat revived her, and she had some of her zip back when she got out and dressed in black jeans and a T-shirt with a picture of planet Earth on the front.

Pausing in the hallway, she leaned against the door, both palms resting against the wood, and called, "Jonathan?"

There was no answer, and Elisabeth couldn't help wondering if that was because there was no longer a Jonathan. There were tears brimming in her eyes when she went back downstairs and stretched out on the sofa.

The jangle of the hallway telephone awakened her and, for a moment, Elisabeth considered not answering. Then she decided she'd caused people enough worry as it was, without ignoring their attempts to reach her.

She was shaky and breathless when she picked up the receiver in the hallway and blurted, "Hello?"

"What are you doing home?" Janet demanded. "Your doctor expressly told me you were supposed to stay until Friday, at least."

Elisabeth wound her finger in the cord, smiling sadly. She was going to miss Janet, and she hoped her friend wouldn't suffer too much over her disappearance. "I was resting until you called," she said, making an effort to sound like her old self.

"I'm wasting my time trying to get you to come to Seattle, aren't I?"

"Yes," Elisabeth answered gently. "But don't think your kindness doesn't mean a lot to me, Janet, because it does. It's just that, well, I'm up against something I have to work out for myself."

"I understand," Janet said uncertainly. "You'll call if you change your mind?"

Elisabeth promised she would, hung up and immediately dialed her father's number at Lake Tahoe. These conversations would be remembered as goodbyes, she supposed, if she managed to make it back to 1892.

The call was picked up by an answering machine, though, and Elisabeth was almost relieved. She identified herself, said she was out of the hospital and feeling fine, and hung up.

Early that afternoon, while Elisabeth was heating a can of soup at the stove, a light rain began to fall and the electricity flickered. She glanced uneasily at the darkening sky and wondered if it was about to storm where Jonathan and Trista were.

Just the thought of them brought a tightness to her throat and the sting of tears to her eyes. She was eating her soup and watching a soap opera on TV when a messenger from the hospital brought her purse. Later, if she felt better and she still couldn't get across the threshold, she would get into her car and drive to town for groceries. Because she'd been away so much, she had practically nothing in the cupboards except for canned goods.

Thunder shook the walls, lightning flashed and the TV went dead. Not caring, Elisabeth went upstairs. Once again, longingly, she paused in front of the door.

There was nothing beyond it, she told herself sternly, besides a long fall to the roof of the sun porch. She was having a nervous breakdown or something, that was all, and Jonathan and Trista were mere figments of her imagination. They were the family she'd longed for but never really had.

She leaned against the door, her shoulders shaking with silent sobs. The hope of returning was all she had to cling to, and even that was fading fast.

Presently, Elisabeth grew weary of crying and straightened. She knotted one fist and pounded. "Jonathan!" she yelled.

Nothing.

She splashed her face with cold water at the bathroom sink, then went resolutely downstairs. Amazed at how simple exertions could exhaust her, she got her purse and forced herself out to her car.

Shopping was an ordeal, and Elisabeth felt so shaky, she

feared she'd fall over in a dead faint right there in the super-market. Hastily, she bought fruit and a stack of frozen entrés and left the store.

At home, she found the electricity had been restored, and she put one of the packaged dinners into the microwave. She hardly tasted the food.

Following her solitary meal, Elisabeth spent a few discon-solate minutes at the piano, running her fingers over the keys. The songs she played reminded her too much of Trista, though, and of Jonathan, and she finally had to stop. And she had to admit she'd been hoping to hear the sound of Trista's piano echoing back across the century that separated them.

Figuring she might as well give up on getting back to 1892—for that day at least—Elisabeth gathered an armload of Aunt Verity's journals from one of the bookshelves in the parlor and took herself upstairs. After building a fire with the last of the wood, she curled up in the middle of the bed and began to read.

At first, the entries were ordinary enough. Verity talked about her marriage, how much she loved her husband, how she longed for children. After her mate's untimely death in a hunting accident, she wrote about sadness and grief. And then came the account of Barbara Fortner's appearance in the up-stairs hallway.

Elisabeth sat bolt upright as she read about the woman's baffled disbelief and Verity's efforts to make her feel at home. The words Elisabeth's aunt had written shed new light on the stories Verity had told her teenage nieces during their summer visits, and Elisabeth felt the pang of grief.

By midnight, Elisabeth's eyes were drooping. She closed the journals and stacked them neatly on the bedside table, then changed into a nightshirt, brushed her teeth and crawled into bed. "Jonathan," she whispered. His name reverberated through her heart.

She was never sure whether minutes had passed or hours when the sound of a child's sobs prodded her awake. *Trista.*

Elisabeth sat up and flung the covers back, her fingers grip-ping the necklace as she hurried into the hallway. Her hand trembled violently as she reached for the knob on the sealed door, praying with all her heart that it would open.

The child's name left her throat in a rush, like a sigh of relief, when the knob turned under her hand and the hinges creaked.

There was a lamp burning on Trista's bedside table, and she stared at Elisabeth as though she couldn't believe she was really seeing her. Then her small face contorted with childish fury. "Where were you? Why did you leave me like that?"

Elisabeth sat down on the edge of the bed and gathered the little girl into her arms, holding her very close. "I was sick, sweetheart," she said as joyous tears pooled in her eyes. "Believe me, the last thing I wanted to do was leave you."

"You'll stay here now?" Trista sniffled, pulling back in Elisabeth's embrace to look up into her face. "You won't leave us again?"

Elisabeth thought of Rue, her father, Janet. She would miss them all, but she knew she belonged here in this time, with these people. She kissed Trista's forehead. "I won't leave you again," she promised. "Were you all alone? Is that why you were crying?"

Trista nodded. "I was scared."

"Where's your papa?"

Jonathan's daughter allowed herself to be settled back on the pillows and tucked in. "He's just out in the barn, but I heard noises and I imagined Mr. Marley was coming down the hall, rattling his chains and moaning."

Elisabeth smiled at the reference to the Dickens ghost. "I'm the only apparition in this house tonight," she said. Then she kissed Trista again, turned down the wick in the lamp and went downstairs.

Before she went to Jonathan and told him she'd marry him if he still wanted her, before she threw herself into his arms, there was something she had to find out.

Elizabeth stood in the kitchen, staring helplessly at Jonathan's calendar. Never before had it been so crucial to know the exact date, but the small numbered squares told her nothing except that it was still June.

The sudden opening of the back door and a rush of cool, night air made her turn. Pure joy caused her spirit to pirouette within her. Jonathan was standing there, looking at her as though he didn't quite dare to trust his eyes.

With a strangled cry, she launched herself across the room and into his embrace, her arms tight around his neck.

"Lizzie," he rasped, holding her. "Thank God you're all right."

She tilted her head back and kissed him soundly before replying, "It was hell not knowing what was happening here. I was terrified I wouldn't be able to get back, and I was even more frightened by what I might find if I did."

Jonathan laughed and gave her a squeeze before setting her on her feet. His hand smoothed her hair with infinite gentleness, and his gaze seemed to caress her. "Are you well again?"

She shrugged, then slipped her arms around his lean waist. "I'm a little shaky, but I'm going to make it."

A haunted expression crossed his face. "I wanted to go with you, to make sure you got help, but when I stepped over the threshold, you vanished from my arms."

Elisabeth glanced back at the calendar. "Jonathan..."

He smiled and crooked a finger under her chin. "That's one thing you were wrong about," he said. "It's the twenty-third of June—Thursday, to be exact—and there's been no fire.''

His words lessened Elisabeth's dread a little. After all, she knew next to nothing about this phenomenon, and it was possible that she or Jonathan had inadvertently changed fate somehow.

In the next instant, however, another matter involving dates and cycles leapt into her mind, and the shock made her sway in Jonathan's arms.

He eased her into a chair. ''Elisabeth, what is it?''

''I...'' Her throat felt dry and she had to stop and swallow. ''My...Jonathan, I haven't had my...I could be pregnant.''

His eyes glowed bright as the kerosene lantern in the middle of the table. ''You not only came back to me,'' he smiled. ''You brought someone with you.''

Tears of happiness gathered on Elisabeth's lashes. Once, during her marriage, she'd gotten pregnant and then miscarried, and Ian had been pleased. He'd said it was for the best and that he hoped Elisabeth wouldn't take too long getting her figure back.

''Y-you're glad?''

Jonathan crouched in front of her chair and took her hands in his. A sheen of moisture glimmered in his eyes. ''What do you think? I love you, Lizzie. And a child is the best gift you could give me.'' He frowned. ''You won't leave again, will you?''

Elisabeth reached back to unclasp the necklace and place it in his palm. ''For all I care, you can drop this down the well. I'm here to stay.''

He put the pendant into his shirt pocket and stood, drawing Elisabeth with him. ''I'd like to take you straight to bed,'' he said, ''but you're still looking a little peaky, and we have to think about Trista.'' Jonathan paused and kissed her. ''Will you marry me in the morning, Lizzie?''

She nodded. ''I know it wouldn't be right for us to make love,'' she said shyly, ''but I need for you to hold me. Being apart from you was awful.''

He put an arm around her waist and ushered her toward the

rear stairs. "I'm not going to let you out of my sight," he answered gruffly.

In the spare room, he settled Elisabeth under the covers and then began stripping off his own clothes. She was grateful it was dark so she couldn't see what she was missing and *he* couldn't see her blushing like a virgin bride.

A few moments later, Jonathan climbed into the bed and enfolded Elisabeth in his arms, fitting her close against the hard warmth of his body. Despite the lingering effects of her illness and their decision not to make love again until they were man and wife, desire stirred deep within Elisabeth.

When his hand curved lightly over her breast, she gave an involuntary moan and arched her back. She felt Jon come to a promising hardness against her thigh and heard the quickening of his breath.

"I suppose we could be quiet," she whispered as he lifted her nightshirt and spread one hand over her quivering belly as though to claim and shelter the child within.

Jonathan chuckled, his mouth warm and moist against the pulsepoint at the base of Elisabeth's throat. "You?" he teased. "The last time I had you, Lizzie, you carried on something scandalous."

She reached back over her head to grasp the rails in the headboard as he began kissing her breasts. "I g-guess I'll just have to trust you to be a...to be a gentleman."

"You're a damn fool if you do," he said, just before he took a nipple into his mouth and scraped it lightly with his teeth.

Elisabeth flung her head from one side to the other, struggling with all her might to keep back the cries of surrender that were already crowding her throat. Rain pelted the window, and a flash of lightning lit the room with an eerie explosion of white. "Jonathan..." she cried.

He brought his mouth down onto hers at the same moment that he parted her legs and entered her. While their tongues sparred, her moans of impending release filled his throat.

Their bodies arched high off the mattress in violent fusion, twisting together like ribbons in the wind. Then, after long, exquisite moments of fiery union, they sank as one to the bed, both gasping for breath.

"We agreed not to do that," Elisabeth said an eternity later, when she was able to speak again.

Jonathan smoothed damp tendrils of hair back from her forehead, sighed and kissed her lightly. "It's a little late for recriminations, Lizzie. And if you're looking for an apology, you're wasting your time."

She blushed and settled close against his chest, which was still heaving slightly from earlier exertions. Thunder rattled the roof above their heads, immediately followed by pounding and shouting at the front door and a shriek from Trista's room.

"I'll see to her," Elisabeth said, reaching for her nightshirt while Jon scrambled into his clothes. "You get the door."

Trista was sobbing when Elisabeth stumbled into her room, lit the lamp on her bedside stand and drew the child into her arms. "It's all right, baby," she whispered. "You were just having a bad dream, that's all."

"I saw Marley's ghost," Trista wailed, shuddering against Elisabeth as she scrambled toward reality. "He was standing at the foot of my bed, calling me!"

Elisabeth kissed the little girl's forehead. "Darling, you're awake now and I'm here. And Marley's ghost isn't real—he's only a story character. You don't need to be afraid."

Trista clung to Elisabeth's shoulders, but she wasn't trembling so hard now, and her sobs had slowed to irregular hiccups. "I don't want to leave you and Papa," she said. "I don't want to die."

The words were like the stab of a knife, reminding Elisabeth of the fire. "You aren't going to die, sweetheart," she vowed fiercely, stretching out on top of Trista's covers, still holding the child. "Not for many, many years. Someday, you'll marry and have children of your own." Tears of determination scalded Elisabeth's eyes, and she reached to turn down the wick in the lamp, letting the safe darkness enfold them.

Trista sniffled, clutching Elisabeth as though she feared she would float unanchored through the universe if she let go.

"Will you promise to stay here with us?" she asked in a small voice. "Are you going to marry Papa?"

Elisabeth kissed her cheek. "Yes and yes. Nothing could make me leave you again, and your father and I are getting married tomorrow."

"Then you'll be my mother."

"I'll be your stepmother," Elisabeth clarified gently. "But I swear I love you as much as I would if you'd been born to me."

Trista yawned. It was a reassuring, ordinary sound that relieved a lot of Elisabeth's anxieties. "Will there be babies? I'm very good with them, you know."

Elisabeth chuckled and smoothed the child's hair. "Yes, Trista, I think you'll have a little brother or sister before you know it. And I'll be depending on your help."

She yawned again. "Did Papa go out?"

Elisabeth nodded. "I think so. We'll just go to sleep, you and I, and when we wake up, he'll be home again."

"All right," Trista sighed. And then she slipped easily into a quiet, natural sleep.

Jonathan had still not returned when Elisabeth and Trista rose the next morning, but Elisabeth didn't allow the fact to trouble her. He was a doctor, and he would inevitably be away from home a great deal.

While Ellen prepared oatmeal downstairs in the kitchen, Elisabeth brushed and braided Trista's thick, dark hair. After eating breakfast, the two of them went up to the attic to go through the trunks again. The school term was over, and Trista, who was still a little wan and thin from her illness, had a wealth of time on her hands.

Elisabeth found a beautiful midnight blue gown in the depths of one of the trunks and decided that would be her wedding dress.

Trista's brow crumpled. "Don't brides usually wear white?"

Draping the delicate garment carefully over her arm, Elisabeth went to sit beside Trista on the arched lid of one of the trunks. "Yes, sweetheart," she replied after taking a breath and searching her mind for the best words. "But I was married once before, and even though I wasn't very happy then, I don't want to deny that part of my life by pretending it didn't happen. Do you understand?"

"No," Trista said with a blunt honesty that reminded Elisabeth of Jonathan. The child's smile was sudden and blindingly bright. "But I guess I don't need to. You're going to stay and we'll be a family. That's what matters to me."

Elisabeth smiled and kissed Trista's forehead. It was odd to think that this child was her elder in the truest sense of the word. The dress in her arms and the dusty attic and the little girl had become her reality, however, and it was that other world that seemed like an illusion. "We are definitely going to be a family," she agreed. "Now, let's take my wedding gown outside and let it air on the clothesline, so I won't smell like mothballs during the ceremony."

Trista wrinkled her nose and giggled, but when her gaze traveled to the grimy window, she frowned. "It looks like it's about to rain."

There had been so much sunshine in Elisabeth's heart since she'd awakened to the realization that this was her wedding day, she hadn't noticed the weather at all. Now, with a little catch in her throat, she went over and peered out through the dirty panes of glass.

Sure enough, the sky was dark with churning clouds, and now that she thought of it, there was a hot, heavy, brooding feeling to the air. From where she stood, Elisabeth could see the weathered, unevenly shaped shingles on the roof of the front porch. They looked dry as tinder.

She tried to shake off a feeling of foreboding. Jonathan was right, she insisted to herself—if there was truly going to be a fire, it would have happened before this. Still, she was troubled, and she wished she and Jonathan and Trista were faraway from that place.

They took the dress down to Elisabeth's room and hung it near a window she'd opened slightly, then descended to the kitchen. Since Ellen was busy with the ironing, Elisabeth and Trista decided to gather the eggs.

Fetching a basket, she hurried off toward the hen house, expecting to be drenched by rain at any moment. But the sullen sky retained its burden, and the air fairly crackled with the promise of violence. *Jonathan,* Elisabeth thought nervously, *come home. Now.*

But she laughed with Trista as they filled the basket with brown eggs. Surprisingly, considering the threat of a storm, Vera appeared, riding her pony and carrying a virtually hairless doll. After settling the horse in the barn, the two children retreated to Trista's room to play.

Elisabeth joined Ellen in the kitchen and volunteered to take a turn at pressing Jonathan's shirts. The cumbersome flatirons were heated on the stove, and it looked like an exhausting task.

"You just sit down and have a nice cup of tea," Ellen ordered with a shake of her head. "It wasn't that long ago that you were sick and dying, you know."

There was a kind of grudging affection in Ellen's words, and Elisabeth was pleased. She was also enlightened; obviously, her disappearance had been easily explained. Jonathan had probably said she was lying in bed and mustn't be disturbed for any reason. "I'm better now," she allowed.

Ellen stopped ironing the crisp white shirts long enough to get the china teapot down from a shelf and spoon loose tea leaves into it. She added hot water from the kettle and brought the teapot and a cup and saucer to the table. "I guess you and the doctor will be getting married straight away."

Elisabeth nodded. "Yes."

The housekeeper frowned, but her expression showed curiosity rather than antagonism. "I can't quite work out what it is, but there's something different about you," she mused, touching the tip of her index finger to her tongue and then to the iron.

The resultant sizzle made Elisabeth wince. "I'm—from another place," she said, making an effort at cordiality.

Ellen ironed with a vehemence. "I know. Boston. But you don't talk much like she did."

By "she," Elisabeth knew Ellen meant Barbara Fortner, who was supposed to be Elisabeth's sister. Unfortunately, the situation left Elisabeth with no real choice but to lie. Sort of. "Well, I've lived in Seattle most of my adult life."

The housekeeper rearranged a shirt on the wooden ironing board and began pressing the yoke, and a pleasant, mingled scent of steam and starch rose in the air. "She never talked about you," the woman reflected. "Didn't keep your photograph around, neither."

Elisabeth swallowed, contemplating the tangled web that stretched before her. "We weren't close," she answered, and that was true, though not for the reasons Ellen would probably invent on her own. Elisabeth took a sip of tea and then boldly inquired, "Did you like her?"

"No," Ellen answered with a surprising lack of hesitation. "The first Mrs. Fortner was always full of herself. What kind of a woman would go away for months and leave her own child behind?"

Elisabeth wasn't about to touch that one. After all, she'd made a few unscheduled departures herself, and it hadn't been because she didn't care about Trista. "Maybe she was homesick, being so far from her family."

The housekeeper didn't look up from her work, but her reply was vibrant, like a dart quivering in a bull's eye. "She had you, right close in Seattle. Seems like that should have helped."

There was nothing Elisabeth could say to that. She carried her cup and saucer to the sink and set them carefully inside. Beyond the window, with its pristine, white lace curtains, the gloomy sky waited to remind her that there were forces in the universe that operated by laws she didn't begin to understand. Far off on the horizon, she saw lightning plunge from the clouds in jagged spikes.

If only the rain would start, she fretted silently. Perhaps that would alleviate the dreadful tension that pervaded her every thought and move.

"I'd like to leave early today, if it's all the same to you," Ellen said, startling Elisabeth a little. "Don't want to get caught in the rain."

Elisabeth caught herself before she would have offered to drive Ellen home in her car. If she hadn't felt so anxious, she would have smiled at the near lapse. "Maybe you'd better leave now," she said, hoping Ellen didn't have far to go.

Agreeing quickly, the housekeeper put away the ironing board and the flatirons and took Jonathan's clean shirts upstairs. Soon she was gone, but there was still no rain and no sign of Jonathan.

Elisabeth was more uneasy than ever.

She climbed the small stairway that led up to Trista's room and knocked lightly.

"Come in," a youthful voice chimed.

Smiling, Elisabeth opened the door and stepped inside. Her expression was instantly serious, however, when her gaze went straight to the pendant Vera was wearing around her neck. It took all her personal control not to lunge at the child in horror and snatch away the necklace before it could work its treacherous magic.

Vera preened and smiled broadly, showing a giant vacant space where her front teeth should have been. "Don't you think I look pretty?" she asked, obviously expecting an affirmative answer. It was certainly no mystery that her children had grown up to be adventurous; they would inherit Vera's innate self-confidence.

"I think you look very pretty," Elisabeth said shakily, easing toward the middle of the room, where the two little girls sat playing dolls on the hooked rug. She sank to her knees beside them, her movements awkward because of her long skirts.

Vera beamed into Elisabeth's stricken face. "I guess I shouldn't have tried it on without asking you," she said, reaching back to work the clasp. Clearly, she was giving no real weight to the idea that Elisabeth might have objections to sharing personal belongings. "Here."

Elisabeth's hand trembled slightly as she reached out to let

Vera drop the chain and pendant into her palm. Rather than make a major case out of the incident, she decided she would simply put the necklace away somewhere, out of harm's way. "Where did you find this?" she asked moderately, her attention on Trista.

Her future stepdaughter looked distinctly uncomfortable. "It was on top of Papa's dresser," she said.

Elisabeth simply arched an eyebrow, as if inviting Trista to explain what she'd been doing going through someone else's things, and the child averted her eyes.

Dropping the necklace into the pocket of her skirt, Elisabeth announced, "It's about to rain. Vera, I think you'd better hurry on home."

Trista looked disappointed, but she didn't offer a protest. She simply put away her doll and followed Vera out of the room and down the stairs.

Afraid to cross the threshold leading into the main hallway with the necklace anywhere on her person, Elisabeth tossed it over. Only as she was bending to pick the piece of jewelry up off the floor did it occur to her that she might have consigned it to a permanent limbo, never to be seen again.

She carried the necklace back to the spare room and dropped it onto her bureau, then went downstairs and out onto the porch to scan the road for Jonathan's horse and buggy. Instead, she saw the intrepid Vera galloping off toward home, while Trista swung forlornly on the gate.

"There was *supposed* to be a wedding today," she said, her lower lip jutting out just slightly.

Elisabeth smiled and laid a hand on a small seersucker-clad shoulder. "I'm sorry you're disappointed, honey. If it helps any, so am I."

"I wish Papa would come home," Trista said. She was gazing toward town, and the warm wind made tendrils of dark hair float around her face. "I think there's going to be a hurricane or something."

Despite her own uneasiness and her yearning to see Jonathan, Elisabeth laughed. "There won't be a hurricane, Trista. The mountains make a natural barrier."

As if to mock her statement, lightning struck behind the house in that instant, and both Trista and Elisabeth cried out in shock and dashed around to make sure the chicken house or the woodshed hadn't been struck.

Elisabeth's heart hammered painfully against her breastbone when she saw the wounded tree at the edge of the orchard. Its trunk had been split from top to bottom, and its naked core was blackened and still smoldering. In the barn, Jonathan's horses neighed, sensing something, perhaps smelling the damaged wood.

And for all of it, the air was still bone-dry and charged with some invisible force that seemed to buzz ominously beneath the other sounds.

"We'd better get inside," Elisabeth said.

Trista turned worried eyes to her face. "What about Vera? What if she doesn't get home safely?"

It was on the tip of Elisabeth's tongue to say they'd phone to make sure, but she averted the slip in time. She wished she knew how to hitch up a wagon and drive a team, but she didn't, and she doubted that Trista did, either.

She could ride, though not well. "Let's get out the tamest horse you own," she said. "I'll ride over to Vera's place and make sure she got home okay."

"Okay?" Trista echoed, crinkling her nose at the unfamiliar word.

"It means 'all right,'" Elisabeth told her, picking up her skirts and heading toward the barn. Between the two of them, she and Trista managed to put a bridle on the recalcitrant Estella, Trista's aging, swaybacked mare. Elisabeth asked for brief directions and set off down the road, toward the schoolhouse.

Overhead, black clouds roiled and rolled in on each other, and thunder reverberated off the sides of distant hills. Elisabeth thought of the splintered apple tree and shivered.

As she reached the road, she waved at the man who lived in an earlier incarnation of the house the Buzbee sisters shared. Heedless of the threatened storm, he was busy hammering a new rail onto his fence.

Just around the bend from the schoolhouse, Elisabeth found Vera sitting beside the road, her face streaked with dust, sobbing. The pony was galloping off toward a barn on a grassy knoll nearby.

"Are you hurt?" Elisabeth asked. She didn't want to get down from the horse if she could help it, because getting back on would be almost impossible, dressed as she was. It was bad enough riding with her skirts hiked up to show her bare legs.

Vera gulped and got to her feet, dragging one suntanned arm across her dirty face. Evidently, the sight of Elisabeth riding astride in a dress had been enough of a shock to distract her a little from the pain and indignity of being thrown. "I scraped my elbow," she said with a voluble sniffle.

Elisabeth rode closer and squinted at the wound. "That looks pretty sore, all right. Would you like a ride home?"

Vera gestured toward the sturdy-looking, weathered farmhouse five hundred yards from the barn. "I live close," she said. It appeared she'd had enough of horses for one day, and Elisabeth didn't blame her.

"I'll just ride alongside you then," she said gently as lightning ripped the fabric of the sky again and made her skittish mount toss its head and whinny.

Vera nodded and dried her face again, this time with the skirt of her calico pinafore. "I don't usually cry like this," she said as she walked along the grassy roadside, Elisabeth and the horse keeping pace with her. "I'm as tough as my brother."

"I'm sure you are," Elisabeth agreed, hiding a smile.

Vera's mother came out of the house and waved, smiling, apparently unruffled to see her daughter approaching on foot instead of on the back of her fat little pony. "It's good to see you're feeling better, Elisabeth," she called over the roar of distant thunder. "You're welcome to come in for pie and coffee if you have the time."

"I'd better get back to Trista," Elisabeth answered, truly sorry that she couldn't stay and get to know this woman better. "And I suppose the storm is going to break any minute now."

The neighbor nodded her head pleasantly, shepherding Vera into the house, and Elisabeth reined the mare toward home and rode at the fastest pace she dared, given her inexperience. As it was, she needn't have hurried, for even after she'd put Trista's horse back in the barn and inspected the unfortunate tree that had been struck by lightning earlier, there was no rain.

She muttered as she climbed the back steps and opened the kitchen door. The forlorn notes of Trista's piano plunked and plodded through the heavy air.

The rest of the afternoon passed, and then the evening, and there was still no word from Jonathan. The sky remained as black and irritable as ever, but not so much as a drop of rain touched the thirsty ground.

After a light supper of leftover chicken, Elisabeth and Trista took turns reading aloud from *Gulliver's Travels,* the book they'd begun when Trista had fallen ill. When they tired of that, they played four games of checkers, all of which Trista won with smug ease.

And Jonathan did not come through the door, tired and hungry, longing for the love and light of his home.

Elisabeth was beginning to fear that something had happened to him. Perhaps there had been an accident, or he'd had a heart attack from overwork, or some drunken cowboy had shot him....

Trista, who had already put on her nightgown, scrubbed her face and washed her teeth, was surprisingly philosophical— and perceptive—for an eight-year-old. "You keep going to the window and looking for Papa," she said. "Sometimes he's gone a long time when there's a baby on its way or somebody's real sick."

Self-consciously, Elisabeth let the curtain above the sink fall back into place. "What if you'd been here alone?" she asked, frowning.

Trista shrugged. "Ellen would probably have taken me

home with her.'' She beamed. ''I like going to her house because there's so much noise.''

The old clock on the shelf ticked ponderously, emphasizing the quiet. And it occurred to Elisabeth that Trista had been very lonely, with no brothers and sisters and no mother. ''You like noise, do you?'' Elisabeth teased. And then she bolted toward Trista, her hands raised, fingers curled, like a bear's claws.

Trista squealed with delight and ran through the dining room to the parlor and up the front stairway, probably because that was the long way and the pursuit could be drawn out until the last possible moment.

In her room, Trista collapsed giggling on the bed, and Elisabeth tickled her for a few moments, then kissed her soundly on the cheek, listened to her prayers and tucked her into bed.

Later, in the parlor, she sat down at the piano and began to play soft and soothing songs, tunes Rue would have described as cocktail-party music. All the while, Elisabeth listened with one ear for the sound of Jonathan's footsteps.

The touch of Jonathan's lips on her forehead brought Elisabeth flailing up from the depths of an uneasy sleep. The muscles in her arms and legs ached from her attempt to curl around Trista in a protective crescent.

For a moment, wild fear seized her, closing off her throat, stealing her breath. Then she realized that except for the rumble of distant thunder, the world was quiet. She and Trista were safe, and Jonathan was back from his wanderings.

She started to rise, but he pressed her gently back to the mattress and, in the thin light of the hallway lamp, she saw him touch his lips with an index finger.

"We'll talk in the morning," he promised, his low voice hoarse with weariness. "I trust you're still inclined to become my wife?"

Elisabeth stretched, smiled and nodded.

"Good." He bent and kissed her forehead again. "Tomorrow night you'll sleep where you belong—in my bed."

A pleasant shiver went through Elisabeth at the thought of the pleasures Jonathan had taught her to enjoy. She nodded again and then snuggled in and went contentedly back to sleep, this time without tension, without fear.

Jonathan couldn't remember being more tired than he was at that moment—not even in medical school, when he'd worked and studied until he was almost blind with fatigue. He'd spent most of the past twenty-four hours struggling to save the lives of a mother and her twins, losing the woman and one of the infants. The remaining child was hanging on to life by the thinnest of threads, and there was simply nothing more Jonathan could do at this point.

In his room, he poured tepid water from the pitcher into the basin, removed his shirt and washed, trying to scrub away the smell of sickness and despair. When he could at least stand the scent of himself, he turned toward the bed.

God knew, he was so exhausted, he couldn't have made love to Elisabeth even if the act somehow averted war or plague, but just having her lie beside him would have been the sweetest imaginable comfort. He ached to extend a hand and touch her, to breathe deeply and fill his lungs with her fragrance.

Wearily, Jonathan made his way toward his bed and then stopped, knowing he would lapse into virtual unconsciousness once he stretched out. Before he did that, he had to know Elisabeth wouldn't get it into her head to vanish again.

Picking up a small kerosene lamp, he forced himself out into the hallway and along the runner to the door of the spare room, where she normally slept. The necklace, left carelessly on top of the bureau, seemed to sparkle in the night, drawing Jonathan to it by some inexplicable magic.

Although he knew he would be ashamed of the action in the morning, he scooped the pendant into his hand and went back to his own room, where he blew out the lamp and sank into bed.

Even in sleep, his fingers were locked around the necklace, and the hot, thunderous hours laid upon him like a weight.

Somewhere in the blackest folds of that starless night, Elisabeth awakened with a wrench. She had to go to the bathroom, and that meant a trip to the outhouse if she didn't want to use a chamber pot—which she most assuredly didn't.

Yawning, she rose and pulled on a robe—Ellen and Trista always spoke of the garment as a wrapper—and, after her eyes had adjusted, made her way toward the inner door and down the back steps to the kitchen.

There was no wind, she noticed when she stepped out onto the back step, and certainly no rain. The air was ominously heavy, and it seemed to reverberate with unspoken threats.

With a little shiver, Elisabeth forced herself down the darkened path and around behind the woodshed to the privy.

She was returning when the unthinkable happened, paralyzing her in the middle of the path. As she watched, her eyes wide with amazement and horror, a bolt of lightning zigzagged out of the dark sky, like a laser beam from an unseen spacecraft, and literally splintered the roof of the house. For one terrible moment, the entire landscape was aglow, the trees and mountains like dazed sleepers under the glare of a flashlight.

Immediately, flames shot up from the roof, and Elisabeth screamed. The animals in the barn had heard the crash and had probably caught the scent of fire. They were going wild with fear. Elisabeth dared not take the time to calm them. She had to reach Jonathan and Trista.

She hurled herself through the barrier of terrified inertia that had blocked her way and ran into the house, coughing and shrieking Jonathan's and Trista's names.

The short stairway leading to Trista's room was filled with black, roiling smoke. The stuff was so noxious that it felt greasy against Elisabeth's skin. Breathing was impossible.

Beyond the wall of smoke, she could hear Trista screaming, "Papa! Papa!"

Elisabeth dragged herself a few more steps upward, but then she couldn't go farther. Her lungs were empty, and she was becoming disoriented, unsure of which way was up and which way was down. She began to sob, and felt herself slipping, the stairs bruising her as she lost her grip.

The next thing she knew, someone was grasping her by her flannel nightgown. Strong hands hoisted her into steely arms, and for a moment she thought Jonathan had found her and Trista, and that the three of them were safe.

But then Elisabeth heard a voice. She didn't recognize it. She felt a huge drop of rain strike her face, warm as bathwater, and opened her eyes to look into the haunted features of Farley Haynes.

Looking around her, she saw the man from across the road, along with his five sons. The shapes of other men moved through the hellish, flickering light of the flames, and Elisabeth saw that they'd formed a bucket brigade between the well and the house. Frantic horses had been released from the endangered barn into the pasture.

The barn won't burn, Elisabeth thought with despondent certainty, remembering the newspaper accounts she'd read in that other world, so faraway. *Only the house.*

Marshal Haynes set her down, and she stood trembling in the silky grass, her nightgown streaked with soot.

"Jonathan—Trista—" she gasped hoarsely, starting back toward the house.

But the marshal encircled her waist with one arm and hauled her back. "It's too late," he said, his voice a miserable rasp. "All three stairways are blocked."

At that moment, part of the roof fell in with a fierce crash, and Elisabeth screamed, struggled wildly in the marshal's grasp and then lost consciousness.

When she awakened, gasping, sobbing before she even became fully aware of her surroundings, Elisabeth found herself in a wagon, bumping and jostling along the dark road that led to town. She sat up, twisting to look at the man who sat in the box, driving the team.

She raised herself to her knees, hair flying wildly around her face, filthy nightgown covered with bit of hay and straw, and clasped the low back of the wagon seat. "Jonathan and Trista," she managed to choke out. "Did you get them out? Did anyone get them out?"

Marshal Haynes turned slightly to look back at her, but the night was moonless and she could see only the outline of his tall, brawny figure and Western hat. The rain that had begun to fall after she'd been pulled from the house started to come down in earnest in that moment, so that he had to raise his voice to be heard.

"That's somethin' you and I are going to have to talk about, little lady," he said.

Elisabeth remembered the sight of the roof of Jonathan's house caving in, and she closed her eyes tightly, heedless of the drops that were wetting her hair and her dirty nightgown. Nothing mattered, nothing in the universe, except Jonathan and Trista's safety. She knelt there, unable to speak, holding tightly to the back of the wagon seat, letting the temperate summer rain drench her.

Only when Farley brought the wagon to a stop in front of the jailhouse did Elisabeth's state of shock begin to abate. Bile rushed into her throat as she recalled the events she'd read about—the fire, no bodies found in the ruins, her own arrest and trial for murder.

And despite the horror of what she faced, Elisabeth felt the first stirring of hope. *No bodies.* Perhaps, just perhaps, Jonathan had found the necklace and he and Trista had managed to get over the threshold into the safety of the next century.

The marshal hoisted her down from the wagon and hustled her into his office. While Elisabeth stood shivering and looking around—the place was like something out of a museum—Marshal Haynes hung his sodden hat on a peg beside the door and crouched in front of the wood stove to get a fire going.

"Now, I suppose you're going to arrest me for murder," Elisabeth said, her teeth chattering.

Farley looked back at her over one shoulder, his expression sober. "Actually, ma'am, I just brought you here to wait for the church ladies. They'll be along to collect you any minute now, I reckon."

The guy was like something out of the late show. "You'll try me for murder," Elisabeth said with dismal conviction, stepping a little closer to the stove as the blaze caught and Farley closed the metal door with a clank. "I read it in the newspaper."

"I heard you were a little crazy," the marshal said thoughtfully. His eyes slid over Elisabeth's nightgown, which was probably transparent, and he brought her a long canvas coat that had been draped over his desk chair. "Here, put this on and go sit there next to the fire. All I need is for the Presbyterians to decide I've been mistreating you."

Elisabeth's knees were weak, and she couldn't keep her thoughts straight. She sank into the rocking chair he indicated, closing the coat demurely around her legs. "I didn't kill anybody," she said.

"Nobody is claiming you did," Farley answered, pouring syrupy black coffee into a metal mug and handing it to her. But he was staring at Elisabeth as though she were a puzzle he couldn't quite solve, and she wondered hysterically if she'd already said too much.

The chair creaked as Elisabeth rocked, and the heat from the stove and the terrible coffee began to thaw out her frozen senses. "Jonathan and Trista are not dead," she insisted, speaking over the rim of the cup. She had to cling to that, to believe it, or she would go mad, right then and there.

Farley looked pained as he finally shrugged out of his own coat and came to stand near the stove, giving Elisabeth a sidelong glance and pouring himself a cup of coffee. His beard-stubbled face was gray with grief, and his brown hair was rumpled from repeated rakings of his fingers and wet with the rain. His green-blue eyes reflected weariness and misery. "There's no way anybody could have survived a blaze like that, Miss Lizzie," he said with gruff gentleness. "They're dead, all right." He paused and sighed sadly. "We'll get their bodies out tomorrow and bury them proper."

Elisabeth felt the coffee back up into her throat in an acid rush, and it was only by monumental effort that she kept herself from throwing up on the marshal's dirty, plankboard floor. "No, you won't," she said when she could manage it. "You won't find their bodies because they're not there."

Farley sidled over and touched Elisabeth's forehead with the back of one big hand, frowning. Then he went back to his place by the stove. "What do you mean they're not there? Me and four other men tried to get in, and all the staircases were blocked. We couldn't get to Jonathan and the little girl, and we damn near didn't get to you."

A headache throbbed under Elisabeth's temples, and she could feel her sinus passages closing up. "Don't think I'm not grateful, Marshal," she said. "As for what I meant—well, I—" What could she say? That Jonathan and Trista might have disappeared into another time, another dimension? "I believe they got out and that they're wandering somewhere, perhaps not recalling who they are.''

"I've known Jonathan Fortner for ten years," Farley answered, staring off at some vision Elisabeth couldn't see. "He wouldn't have left that house unless he was taking everybody inside with him. He wasn't that kind of man.''

Elisabeth felt tears burn her eyes. No one was ever going to believe her theory that Jonathan and Trista had taken the only escape open to them, and she would have to accept the fact. Furthermore, even though the man she loved, the father of the baby growing inside her at that very moment, had not died, he might well be permanently lost to her. Perhaps he wouldn't be able to find his way back, or perhaps the mysterious passageway, whatever it was, had been sealed forever....

Farley fetched a bottle from his desk drawer and poured a dollop of potent-smelling whiskey into Elisabeth's coffee. "You mentioned murder a few minutes ago," he said, "and you talked of reading about what happened in the papers. What did you mean by that?''

Elisabeth normally didn't drink anything stronger than white wine, but she lifted the whiskey-laced coffee gratefully to her mouth, her hands shaking. "There hasn't been a murder. It's just that you're going to *think...''* Her voice failed as she realized how crazy any explanation she could make would sound. She squirmed in the chair. "You won't find any bodies in that house, Marshal, because no one is dead.''

A metallic ring echoed through the small, cluttered office when Farley set his cup on the stove top and disappeared into the single cell to drag a blanket off the cot. "Put this around you," he ordered, returning to shove the cover at Elisabeth. "You're out of your head with the shock of what you've been through.''

Elisabeth wrapped herself in the blanket. By that time, her mixed-up emotions had undergone another radical shift and she was convinced that Jonathan would come walking through the door at any moment, his clothes blackened and torn, to collect her and prove to the marshal that he was alive. Trista, she decided, was safe at Vera's house.

Farley stooped to peer into her face. "You didn't set that fire, did you?"

She jerked her head back, as though the words had been a physical blow. "Set it? Marshal, the roof was struck by lightning—I saw it happen!"

"Seems to me something like that would be pretty unlikely," he mused, rubbing his chin with a thumb and two fingers as he considered the possibilities.

"Oh, really?" Elisabeth demanded, frightened now because the scenario was beginning to go the way she'd feared it would. "Well, it split one of the apple trees in the orchard right down the middle. Maybe you'd like to go and see for yourself."

"Who are you?" Farley inquired, and Elisabeth was sure he hadn't heard a word she said. "Where did you come from?"

She swallowed. Jonathan had told various people in the community that she was his late wife's sister, and now Elisabeth had no choice but to maintain the lie. If—*when*—she saw him again, she was going to give him hell for getting her into this mess. "My name is Lizzie McCartney, and I was born in Boston," she said, her chin quivering.

"Yes, I remember that Barbara's family lived in Boston," the marshal answered calmly. "If you'll just give me your father's name and street address, I'll get in touch with your family and tell them you're going to need some help."

Elisabeth felt the color drain from her face. She couldn't relay the information the marshal wanted because she didn't know the answers to his questions. "I'd rather handle this on my own," she said after a hesitation that was a fraction too long.

The marshal took a watch from the pocket of his trousers, flipped the case open with his thumb and frowned at the time. "Now where do you suppose those Presbyterians are?" he muttered.

"I don't imagine they'll be coming by for me at all," Elisabeth ventured to say, and her throat felt thick because Jonathan and Trista were gone and she might have to live out what was left of her life alone in a strange place. "My guess would be the ladies of Pine River don't entirely approve of the fact that I've been staying in Jonathan's house."

"Well, you'd better get some sleep. You can bunk in there, on the cot." He pointed toward the cell and Elisabeth shuddered to think of some of the types who might have used it before her. "In the morning, we'll contact your people."

Elisabeth was shaking, and not in her wildest imaginings would she have expected to sleep, but she went obediently into the cell all the same. When the marshal had blown out all the lamps and disappeared into his own undoubtedly humble quarters out back, she stripped off the wet nightgown, wrapped herself tightly in the blanket and laid down on the rickety bed.

Two sleepless hours passed, during which Elisabeth alternately listened for Jonathan to storm the citadel and cried because she knew the twentieth century would never surrender him. She was tortured by worries about how he was faring and whether he and Trista had been hurt or not. Jonathan was a doctor and an extremely intelligent man, but Elisabeth wasn't sure he'd know how to get help in her world.

What if Jonathan and Trista were in pain? What if they weren't in the twentieth century at all, but some weird place in between? Worst of all, what if they *had* died in the fire and their remains simply hadn't been found yet?

The cell was brimming with sunshine when the marshal appeared, bearing an ugly brown calico dress in one hand. "You can put this on," he said, shoving it through the bars. Actually, he looked rather handsome in an Old West sort of way, with his brown hair brushed shiny, his jaw shaved and his substantial mustache trimmed.

"At least have the courtesy to turn your back," Elisabeth said, rising awkwardly in her scratchy blanket to reach for the garment.

Farley obliged, folding his beefy arms in front of his chest.

"Looks like you'll be staying with us for a while," he said with a sort of grim heartiness. "I had a talk with Jon's housekeeper, and she managed to find some family papers in the part of the house that didn't burn. Then I sent a telegram to Barbara's family, back there in Massachusetts. They wired me that they never had a daughter named Lizzie."

Elisabeth felt panic sweeping her toward the edge like a giant broom, but somehow she contrived to keep her voice even. "I guess I'm just lucky I didn't end up in the 1600s," she said, pulling on the charity dress and fastening the buttons. The thing was a good three sizes too big. "They probably would have burned me at the stake as a witch."

"I'd be careful about how I talked," Farley advised, turning around to face her. "The people around here don't hold much with witches and the like."

"I don't imagine they do," Elisabeth remarked sweetly, wondering how the heck she was going to get out of this one. "Tell me, whose dress is this?"

"Belongs to Big Lil over at the Phifer Hotel. She's the cook."

"And she's in the habit of lending her clothes to prisoners?"

Farley's powerful shoulders moved in an offhanded shrug. "Not really. I believe she left that here the last time I had to run her in for disturbing the peace."

Elisabeth gripped the bars in both hands and peered through with guileless eyes. "I hardly dare ask what Big Lil was wearing when she left."

To her satisfaction, the marshal's neck went a dull red, and he averted his eyes for a moment. "She had her daughter bring her some things," he mumbled.

If it hadn't been for the gravity of her situation and all the dreadful possibilities she was holding at bay, Elisabeth might have smiled. As it was, her sense of humor was strained to the breaking point.

"Exactly what am I charged with?" she asked as Farley went to the stove and touched the big enamel coffeepot with an inquiring finger. "You can't pin a murder on somebody if there aren't any bodies."

Farley stared at her, looking bewildered and just a touch sick. "What makes you so sure we didn't find...remains?"

He'd never buy the truth, of course. "I just know," Elisabeth said with a little shrug. She wriggled her eyebrows. "Maybe I am a witch."

The marshal hooked his thumbs under his suspenders and regarded Elisabeth somberly. "What did you do with them? Drop 'em down the well? Dump 'em into the river?"

Elisabeth spread her hands wide of her body and the horrendous brown dress that was practically swallowing her. "Do I look big enough to overcome a man Jonathan's size?"

Farley arched an eyebrow. "You could have poisoned him or hit him over the head. As for disposing of the bodies, you might even have had an accomplice."

Knowing the townspeople were going to believe some version of that story, Elisabeth cringed inwardly. Still, she had to at least try to save her skin. "What motive would I have for doing that?"

"What motive did you have for lying about who you are?" Farley countered, rapid-fire. "I'll bet you lied to Jonathan, too—told him you were family, so to speak. He took you in, and you repaid him by—"

"Before you whip out a violin," Elisabeth interrupted, "let me say that Jonathan *does* know who I am. And telling people I was Barbara's sister was his idea, not mine."

"Unfortunately, we don't have anybody's word for that but yours. And it wouldn't make a damn bit of difference if we did." He came to the cell door and glared at her through the bars, his hands gripping the black iron so hard that his knuckles went white. "What did you do to Dr. Fortner and his little girl?"

Elisabeth backed away from the bars because, suddenly, Farley looked fierce. "Damn it, I didn't do *anything* to them," she whispered. "To me, Jonathan and Trista are the most important people in the world!"

Glowering, Farley turned away. "Big Lil will be by with

your breakfast pretty soon,'' he said, taking a gun belt down from a hook on the wall and strapping it on with disturbing deftness. "See you don't try to escape or anything. Lil is mean as a wet badger and tall enough to waltz with a bear."

Again, Elisabeth had the feeling that she would have been amused, if her circumstances hadn't been so dire. "I'll be sure I don't try to dance with her,'' she replied, slumping forlornly on the edge of the cot.

Farley gave her a look over one broad shoulder and walked out, calmly closing the door behind him.

Elisabeth cupped her chin in her hands and tried to remember if the *Pine River Bugle* had said anything about a lynch mob. "Jonathan,'' she whispered, "where are you?"

When the door slammed open a few minutes later, however, it wasn't Jonathan filling the chasm. In fact, it could only have been Big Lil, so tall and broadly built was this woman who strode in, carrying a basket covered with a checked table napkin. She wore trousers, boots, suspenders and a rough-spun shirt. Her gray hair was tied back into a severe knot at the nape of her neck.

It occurred to Elisabeth that Big Lil might begrudge her the calico dress, and she reached back to pull the garment tight with one hand, hoping that effort would disguise it.

Big Lil fetched a ring of keys from the desk, unlocked the door and brought the basket into the cell. Her regard was neither friendly nor condemning, but merely steady. "So, you're the little lady what roasted the doctor like a trussed turkey," she said.

Elisabeth's appetite fled, and she swallowed vile-tasting liquid as she stared at the covered food. She jutted out her chin and glared defiantly at Big Lil, refusing to dignify the remark with an answer.

Big Lil gave a raucous, crowing laugh, then went out of the cell and locked the door again. "Folks around here liked the doc,'' she said. "I don't reckon they'll take kindly to what you did."

Still, Elisabeth was silent, keeping her eyes fixed on the

wall opposite her cot until she heard the door close behind the obnoxious woman.

Elisabeth was in the worst fix of her life, but in the next few moments, her appetite returned, wooed back by the luscious smells coming from inside the basket. She pushed aside the napkin to find hot buttered biscuits inside, along with two pieces of fried chicken and a wedge of goopy cherry pie.

She consumed the biscuits, then the chicken and half the piece of pie before Farley returned, followed by a hard-looking woman with dark hair, small, mean eyes and a pock-marked complexion.

"This is Mrs. Bernard," Farley said, cocking his thumb toward the lady. "She's a Presbyterian."

At last, Elisabeth thought, *the lynch mob.*

Mrs. Bernard stood at a judicious distance from the bars and told Elisabeth in on uncertain terms how God dealt harshly with harlots and liars and had no mercy at all for murderers.

Elisabeth's rage drew her up off the cot and made her stand tall, like a puppet with its strings pulled too tight. "There will certainly be no need to bring in a judge and try me fairly," she said. "This good woman apparently feels competent to pronounce sentence herself."

Mrs. Bernard's face turned an ugly, mottled red. "Jonathan Fortner was a fine man," she said after a long, bitter silence. She pulled a handkerchief from under her sleeve and dabbed at her beady eyes with it.

"I know that, Mrs. Bernard," Elisabeth replied evenly. The marshal made something of a clatter as he went about his business at the desk, opening drawers and shuffling papers and books.

"Which is not to say he didn't make his share of errors in judgment," the woman went on, as if Elisabeth hadn't spoken. She snuffled loudly. "In any case, the Ladies' Aid Society wishes to extend Christian benevolence. For that reason, I'll be bringing by some decent clothes for you to wear, and some of my companions will drop in to explain the wages of sin."

Elisabeth let her forehead rest against the cold bars. "And

I thought I didn't have anything but a hanging to look forward to,'' she sighed.

If Mrs. Bernard heard, she gave no response. She merely said a stiff goodbye to the marshal and went out.

"If you'll just bring a doctor in from Seattle," Elisabeth said, "he'll testify that human bones can't be destroyed in an ordinary house fire and you'll have to let me go."

"I'm not letting you go until you tell me what you did with the doc and that poor little girl of his," Farley replied, and although he didn't look up from his paperwork, Elisabeth saw his fist tighten around his nibbed pen.

"Well, at least send someone out to look for my necklace," Elisabeth persisted, but the situation was hopeless and she knew it. Farley simply wasn't listening.

It was the second week in July before the circuit judge showed up to conduct Elisabeth's trial, and by that time, she'd lost all hope that Jonathan and Trista would ever return. The townspeople were spoiling for a hanging, and even Elisabeth's defense attorney, a smarmy little man in an ill-fitting suit, made it clear that he would have preferred working for the prosecution.

If it hadn't been for the child nature was knitting together beneath her heart, Elisabeth wouldn't have minded dying so much. After all, she was in a harsh and unfamiliar century, separated from practically everyone who mattered to her, and even if she managed to be acquitted of killing Jonathan and Trista, she would always be an outcast.

And she would probably be convicted.

The thought of the innocent baby dying with her tightened her throat and made her stomach twist as she sat beside her lawyer in the stuffy courtroom—which was really the school-house with the desks all pushed against the walls.

The judge occupied the teacher's place, and there was nothing about his appearance or manner to reassure Elisabeth. In fact, his eyes were red rimmed, and the skin of his face settled awkwardly over his bones, like a garment that was too large. The thousands of tiny purple-and-red veins in his nose said even more about the state of his character.

"This court will now come to order," he said in a booming voice, after clearing his throat.

Elisabeth shifted uncomfortably in her chair beside Mr. Rodcliff, her attorney, recalling her reflection in the jailhouse mirror that morning. Her blond hair had fallen loose around her shoulders, her face looked pallid and gaunt, and there were purple smudges under her eyes.

She was the very picture of guilt.

Farley stood over by the wainscotted wall, slicked up for the big day, his hat in his hands. He caught Elisabeth's eye and gave a slight nod, as if to offer encouragement.

She looked away, knowing Farley's real feelings. He wanted to see her dangle, because he believed she'd willfully murdered his friend.

The first witness called to the stand was Ellen, Jonathan's erstwhile housekeeper. Tearfully, the plain woman told how Elisabeth had just appeared one day, seemingly out of nowhere, and somehow managed to bewitch the poor doctor.

Mr. Rodcliff asked a few cursory questions when his turn came, then sat down again.

Elisabeth folded her arms and sat back in her chair, biting down hard on her lower lip. Vera was the next to testify, saying Trista had told her some very strange things about Elisabeth—that she was really an angel come from heaven, and that she had a magic necklace and played queer music on the piano and claimed to know exactly what the world would be like in a hundred years.

Mr. Rodcliff gave Elisabeth an accusing sidelong glance, as if to ask how she expected him to defend her against such charges. When the prosecuting attorney sat down behind his table, Elisabeth's lawyer rose with a defeated sigh and told the judge he had nothing to say.

Elisabeth watched a fly buzzing doggedly against one of the heavy windows and empathized. She felt hot and ugly in her brown dress, and even though she'd borrowed a needle and thread from Farley and taken tucks in it, it still fit badly.

Hearing Farley's name called, Elisabeth jerked her attention back to the front of the room. He wouldn't meet her eyes, though his gaze swept over the jury of six men lined up under the world map. He cleared his throat before repeating the oath, then testified that he'd been summoned to the Fortner farm, along with the volunteer fire department, by one of Efriam

Lute's sons, who'd awakened because the livestock was fretful and seen the flames.

When he'd arrived, Farley said, he immediately tried to get up the main staircase, knowing the members of the household would be sleeping, it being the middle of the night and all. He allowed as how his way had been blocked by flames and smoke, so he'd tried both the other sets of stairs and met with the same frustration. He had, however, found Miss Lizzie half-conscious in the kitchen and had carried her out.

It was only later, he related, when she began saying odd things, that he started to suspect that something was wrong. When he'd learned she was lying about her identity, he'd filed charges.

While Farley talked, Elisabeth stared at him, and he began to squirm in his chair.

Mr. Rodcliff didn't even bother to offer a question when he was given the opportunity and, at last, Elisabeth was called to the stand. She was terrified, but she stood and walked with regal grace to the front of the crowded schoolroom and laid her left hand on the offered Bible, raising her right.

Benches had been brought in for the spectators, and the place was packed with them. The smell of sweat made Elisabeth want to gag.

"Do you solemnly swear to tell the truth, the whole truth and nothing but the truth?" asked the bailiff, who was really Marvin Hites, the man who ran the general store.

"I do," Elisabeth said clearly, even though she knew she couldn't tell the "whole truth" because these relatively primitive minds would never be able to absorb it. She would be committed, and Elisabeth's limited knowledge of nineteenth-century mental hospitals told her it would be better to hang.

There followed a long inquisition, during which Elisabeth was asked who she was. "Lizzie" was the only answer she would give to that. She was asked where she came from, and she said Seattle, which caused murmurs of skepticism among the lookers-on.

Finally, the prosecutor inquired as to whether Elisabeth had in fact "ignited the blazes that consumed one Dr. Jonathan Fortner and his small daughter, Trista."

The question, even though Elisabeth had expected it, outraged her. "No," she said reasonably, but inside she was screaming her anger and her innocence. "I loved Dr. Fortner. He and I were planning to be married."

The townswomen buzzed behind their fans at this statement, and it occurred to Elisabeth that many of them had probably either hoped to marry Jonathan themselves or had wanted to land him for a son-in-law or a nephew by marriage.

"You *loved* him," the prosecutor said in a voice that made Elisabeth want to slap his smug face. "And yet you did murder, Miss—Lizzie. You killed the man and his child *as they slept,* unwitting, in their beds!"

A shape moved in the open doorway, then a familiar voice rolled over the murmurs of the crowd like a low roll of thunder. "If I'm dead, Walter," Jonathan said, "I think it's going to come as a big shock to both of us."

He stood in the center aisle, his clothes ripped and covered in soot, one arm in a makeshift sling made from one of the silk scarves Elisabeth had collected in her other incarnation. His gray eyes linking with hers, he continued, "I'm alive, obviously, and so is Trista."

Women were fainting all over the room, and some of the men didn't look too chipper, either. But Elisabeth's shock was pure, undiluted joy. She flung herself at Jonathan and embraced him, being careful not to press against his injured arm.

He kissed her, holding her unashamedly close, his good hand pressed to the small of her back. And even after he lifted his mouth from hers, he seemed impervious to the crowd stuffing the schoolhouse.

It was Farley who shouldered his way to Jonathan and demanded, "Damn it, Jon, *where the hell have you been?*"

Jonathan's teeth were startlingly white against his soot-smudged face. He slapped the marshal's shoulder affectionately. "Someday, Farley, when we're both so old it can't make a difference, I may just tell you."

"Order, order!" the judge was yelling, hammering at the desk with his trusty gavel.

The mob paid no attention. They were shouting questions at Jonathan, but he ignored them, ushering a stunned Elisabeth down the aisle and out into the bright July sunshine.

"It seems time has played another of its nasty tricks on us," he said when he and Elisabeth stood beneath the sheltering leaves of a maple tree. He traced her jawline with the tip of one index finger. "Let's make a vow, Lizzie, never to be apart again."

Tears were trickling down Elisabeth's cheeks, tears of joy and relief. "Jonathan, what happened?"

He held her close, and she rested her head against his shoulder, not minding the acrid, smoky smell of him in the least. "I'm not really sure," he replied, his breath moving in her hair. "I woke up, Trista was screaming and there was no sign of you. I had the necklace in my hand. All three stairways were closed off, and the roof was burning, too. I grabbed up my daughter, offered a prayer and went over the threshold."

Elisabeth clung to him, hardly able even then to believe that he'd really come back to her. "How long were you there?" she asked.

He propped his chin on top of her head, and the townspeople kept their distance, though they were streaming out of the schoolhouse, chattering and speculating. "That's the crazy part, Elisabeth," he said. "A few hours passed at the most— I waited until I could be fairly sure the fire would be out, then I came over again, this time carrying Trista on my back. Climbing down through the charred ruins took some time."

"How did you know where to look for me?"

His powerful shoulders moved in a shrug. "There were a lot of horses and wagons going past. I stopped old Cully Reed, and he about spit out his teeth when he saw me. Then he told me what was going on and brought me here in his hay wagon."

Elisabeth stiffened, looking up into Jonathan's face, searching for any sign of a secret. "And Trista wasn't hurt?"

He shook his head. "She's already convinced the whole

thing was a nightmare, brought on by swallowing so much smoke. Maybe when she's older, we can tell her what really happened, but I think it would only confuse her now. God knows, it confuses me.''

The judge, who had been ready to send Elisabeth to the gallows only minutes before, dared to impinge upon the invisible circle that had kept the townspeople back. He laid a hand to Jonathan's shoulder and smiled. ''Looks like you need some medical attention for that arm, son.''

''The first thing I need,'' Jonathan answered quietly, his eyes never leaving Elisabeth's face, ''is a wife. Think you could perform the ceremony, Judge? Say in an hour, out by the covered bridge?''

The judge agreed with a nod, and Elisabeth thought how full of small ironies life is, not to mention mysteries.

''Will you marry me, Lizzie?'' Jonathan asked, a little belatedly. ''Will you throw away the necklace and live with me forever?''

Elisabeth thought only briefly of that other life, in that other, faraway place. She might have dreamed it, for all the reality it had, though she knew she would miss Rue and her friends. ''Yes, Jon.''

He kissed her again, lifting her onto her toes to do it, and the spectators cheered. Elisabeth forgave them for their fickleness because a lifetime of love and happiness lay before her, because Jonathan was back and she was carrying his baby, and because Trista would grow up to raise a family of her own.

As Elisabeth caught a glimpse of the half-burned house, what in her mind had been the very symbol of shattered hopes now, miraculously, became a place where children would laugh and run and work, a place where music would play.

''Oh, Jonathan, I love you,'' Elisabeth said, her arm linked with his as Cully Reed's hay wagon came to a stop in the side yard. They'd been sitting in the back, their feet dangling.

Jonathan kissed her smartly, jumped to the ground and lifted her after him with one arm. ''I love you, too,'' he answered huskily, and his eyes brushed over her, making her flesh tingle with the anticipation of his lovemaking. He waved at the driver. "Thanks, Cully. See you at the wedding."

Practical concerns closed around Elisabeth like barking dogs as she and Jonathan went up the front steps and into the house. "What am I going to wear?" she fretted, holding wide the skirts of Big Lil's brown calico dress. "I can't be married in this!"

Jonathan assessed the outfit and laughed. "Why not, Lizzie? This certainly isn't going to be a conventional wedding day anyhow."

Elisabeth sighed. There was no denying that. Nonetheless, she diligently searched the upstairs and was heartbroken to find nothing that wasn't in even worse condition than what she was wearing.

In his bedroom, Jonathan sank into a chair and unwrapped his wounded arm. Elisabeth winced when she saw the angry burn.

"Oh, Jon," she whispered, chagrined. She fell to her knees beside his chair. "Here I am, worrying about a stupid dress, when you're hurt...."

He bent to kiss her forehead. "I'll be all right," he assured her gruffly. "But after the wedding, I'd like to go first to Seattle and then San Francisco. There's a doctor in Seattle who might be able to help me keep full use of the muscles in my hand and wrist."

Elisabeth's eyes filled with tears. "I'll go anywhere, as long as I can be with you. You know that. But who will look after your patients here?" Even as she voiced the question, she thought of the young, red-haired physician who had been summoned from Seattle after Jonathan's disappearance.

"Whoever's been doing it in my absence," Jonathan replied, and there was pain in his eyes, and distance. "I won't be of use to anybody if I can't use my right hand, Lizzie."

Elisabeth watched unflinchingly as he began treating the burns with a smelly ointment. "That's not true. You're so important to me that I can't even imagine what I'd have done without you."

Before Jonathan could respond to that, Trista bolted into the room and hurled herself into Elisabeth's waiting arms.

"Vera said there was a trial and that she testified," the child chattered. Her brow was crimped into a frown when she drew back to search Elisabeth's face. "How could so much have happened while I was sleeping?"

Elisabeth kissed her cheek. "I don't think I can explain, sweetheart," she said truthfully enough, "because I don't understand, either. I'm just glad we're all together again."

"Vera's mother says there's going to be a wedding, and she's bringing over her own dress for you to wear. She says the least Pine River can do for you is see that things are done properly."

Soon Vera's mother did, indeed, arrive with a dress, and Elisabeth was so grateful that she forgot how the woman's child had practically called her a witch that very morning. She bathed in the privacy of the spare room, and brushed her hair until it shone, pinned it into a modified Gibson-girl and put on the lace-trimmed ivory silk dress her neighbor had so generously offered. The fabric made a rustling sound as Elisabeth moved, and smelled pleasantly of lavender. Trista gathered wildflowers and made a garland for Elisabeth's hair, and when the two of them reached the site Jonathan had chosen, next to the covered bridge, the doctor was waiting there with a handful of daisies and tiger lilies.

The townsfolk crowded the hillside and creek bank, and several schoolboys even sat on the roof of the bridge. Elisabeth marveled that she'd come so close to losing her life and then had gained everything she'd ever wanted, all in the space of a single day.

To be married by the very judge who would probably have handed down her death sentence was a supreme irony.

The ceremony passed in a sort of sparkling daze for Elisabeth; it seemed as though she and Jonathan were surrounded by an impenetrable white light, and the ordinary sounds of a summer afternoon blended into a low-key whir.

Only when Jonathan kissed her did Elisabeth realize she was married. When the kiss ended, she was flushed with the poignant richness of life. Instead of tossing her bouquet, she handed it to Trista and hugged the child.

"Now we're a family," Trista said, her gray eyes glowing as she looked up at her stepmother.

"We are, indeed," Elisabeth agreed, her throat choked with happy tears.

After the ceremony, there was corn bread and coffee at the hotel. There hadn't been enough advance warning for a cake, but Elisabeth didn't care. What stories she'd be able to tell her and Jonathan's grandchildren!

Trista would spend the night with Vera, it was agreed, and the Fortner family would leave on their trip the following morning. Once all the corn bread had been consumed and Jonathan and Elisabeth had been wished the best by everyone, from the judge who had married them to the man who swept out the saloon, the newlyweds retired to the room Jonathan had rented.

Beyond the window and the door, ordinary life went on. Buggies and wagons rattled by, and the piano player hammered out bawdy tunes in the saloon across the road. But Jonathan and Elisabeth were alone in a world no one else could enter.

She trembled with love and wanting as he slowly, gently undressed her, and it was an awkward process, since his right arm was still in a sling. "I'm going to have your baby, Jon," she said in a breathless whisper as he unbuttoned her muslin camisole and pushed it back off her shoulders, baring her breasts. "I'm sure of that now."

He bent his head, almost reverently, to kiss each of her firm, opulent breasts. "The first of many, I hope," he relied.

Elisabeth drew in a quick breath as she felt his mouth close over her nipple. "I missed you so much, Jon," she managed after a moment, tilting her head back and closing her eyes in blissful surrender as he enjoyed her. "I was terrified I would never see you again."

He suckled for a long, leisurely time before drawing back long enough to answer, "I was scared, too, wondering if you escaped the fire." He turned to her other breast, and Elisabeth moaned and entwined her fingers in his rich, dark hair, holding him close as he drank from her. If she never had another day to laugh and breathe and love, she thought, this one would be sweet enough to cherish through the rest of eternity.

Presently, he laid her down on the edge of the bed, running his hands along her inner thighs, easing her quivering legs apart for an intimate plundering. She felt her hair come undone from its pins and spread it over the covers with her fingers in a gesture of relinquishment.

Her soul was open to Jonathan now; there was no part of it he was not free to explore.

He knelt, his hands gripping the tender undersides of her knees, and nuzzled the moist delta where her womanhood nestled. "I love pleasing you, Elisabeth," he said. "I love making you give yourself up to me, totally, without reservation of any kind."

Elisabeth's breath was quick and shallow, and she could barely speak. "I need you," she whimpered.

Jonathan burrowed through and took her fiercely, and Elisabeth cried out, her body making a graceful arch on the mattress, her hands clutching and pounding at the blankets.

He consumed her until she was writhing wildly on the bed, until she was uttering low cries, until her skin was wet with perspiration and her muscles were aching with the effort of thrusting her toward him. He drove her straight out of herself and made her soar, and brought her back to earth with patient caresses and muttered reassurances.

She found him beside her on the lumpy hotel bed, after she'd returned to herself and could think and see clearly. Very gently, she touched his bandaged arm.

"Does it hurt much?"

He bent to scatter light kisses over her collarbone. "It hurts like hell, Mrs. Fortner. Just exactly how do you propose to comfort your husband in his time of need?"

She stretched like some contented cat, and he poised himself over her, one of his legs parting hers. "I intend to love him so thoroughly that he won't remember his name," she responded saucily, spreading her fingers in the coarse hair that covered his chest.

Jonathan groaned, touching his hardness to her softness, receiving warmth. Elisabeth guided him gently inside her, arching her back to take him deep within, and his magnificent gray eyes glazed with pleasure.

Slowly, slowly, she moved beneath him, tempting, teasing, taking and giving. With one hand thrust far into the mattress, the other resting against his middle in its sling and bandage, he met her thrusts, retreated, parried.

The release was sudden and ferocious, and it took Elisabeth completely by surprise because she'd thought she was finished, that all the responses from then on would be Jonathan's. But her body buckled in a seizure of satisfaction, and he lowered his mouth to hers, as much to muffle her cries as to kiss her.

When the last whimper of delight had been wrung from her, and only then, Jonathan gave up his formidable control and surrendered. He was like a magnificent savage as he lunged into her, drew back, and lunged again.

Finally, with a loud groan, he spilled himself inside her and then collapsed to lie trembling beside her on the mattress, his chest rising and falling with the effort to breathe. Elisabeth draped one leg across both of his and let her cheek rest against his chest.

For a long time, they were silent, and Elisabeth even slept for a while.

When she awakened, there were long shadows in the room and Jonathan's hand was running lightly up and down her back.

"I think you'll miss your world," he said sadly as she stirred against him and yawned. "Maybe you shouldn't stay, Elisabeth. Maybe you should take the necklace and go back and pretend that none of this ever happened."

She scrambled into a sitting position and stared down at him. "I'm not going anywhere, Jonathan Fortner. You're stuck with me and with our baby."

"But the medicine—the magic box..."

Elisabeth smiled and smoothed his hair, less anxious now. "In some ways the twentieth century is better," she conceded. "They've wiped out a lot of the diseases that are killing people now. And life is much easier, in terms of ordinary work, because there are so many labor-saving devices. But there are bad things, too, Jon—things I won't miss at all."

His forehead wrinkled as he frowned. "Like what?"

Elisabeth sighed. "Like nuclear bombs. Jonathan, my generation is capable of wiping out this *entire planet* with the push of a single button."

His frown deepened. "Would they actually be stupid enough to do that?"

"I don't know."

He sighed and settled deeper into the pillows. "Do you suppose all the rest of us would die, too, if they did? I mean, the past and the present are obviously connected in ways we don't understand."

Elisabeth was saddened. "Let's hope and pray that never happens."

Jonathan stroked her hair and held her close against his chest. "What else can you tell me about the twentieth century?"

"You're bound to experience some of it yourself, since it's only about eight years away," she answered, entwining an index finger in a curl of hair on his chest. She bit her lip, remembering history that hadn't happened yet. "But I'll see if I can't give you some previews of coming attractions. Around the turn of the century, America will declare war on Spain. And then, about 1914 or so, the Germans will decide to take over the world. France, England, Russia and eventually the United States will take them on and beat them."

Jonathan stared pensively into her face, waiting for more.

"Then, around 1929, the stock market will crash. If we're still around then, we'll have to make sure we invest the egg money carefully. After that—"

He laughed and held her close. "My little Gypsy fortune teller. After that, what?"

"Another war, unfortunately," Elisabeth confessed with a

sigh. "Germany again, and Japan. As awful as it was for everybody, I think most of the scientific and medical advances made in the twentieth century happened because—well, necessity is the mother of invention, and nothing creates necessity like war."

Jonathan shuddered. "Tell me the good things."

Elisabeth talked about airplanes and microwave ovens and Disneyland. She described movies, electric Christmas-tree lights, corn dogs and Major League Baseball games. Jonathan laughed when she swore that a former actor had served two terms as President of the United States, and he absolutely refused to believe that men were having themselves changed into women and vice versa.

When Elisabeth was finished with her tales of the future, she and Jonathan made slow, sweet love.

Later, they ate a wedding supper brought to them by Big Lil's daughter. They consumed the food hungrily, greedily, never remembering after that exactly what they'd been served. Then they made love again.

Early the next morning they rose, and Elisabeth put on the dress she'd been married in, since she had nothing else to wear. Jonathan kissed her, said she was beautiful and promised to buy her as many gowns as she wanted once they reached Seattle.

Elisabeth was nervous and distracted. Finally she brought up the subject they'd both been avoiding. "Jon, the necklace—where is it?"

He paused in the act of rebandaging his arm and studied her for a long moment. "I left it at the house," he said. "Why?"

"There's something I have to do," she replied, her gaze skirting his, her hand already on the doorknob. "Please—tell me where to find the necklace."

The expression in his eyes was a bleak one, but he didn't ask the obvious question. "All right, Elisabeth," he said. "All right."

They drove out to Jonathan's house—their house—in his

buggy. "The necklace is in my study," he said. "Under the ledger in the middle desk drawer."

As she hopped down from the rig, Elisabeth surveyed the ladder propped against the partially burned house. Apparently, the repair work had already begun.

She hummed as she went inside, found the necklace exactly where Jonathan had said it would be, and brought it out into the sunshine with her. Her husband stood beside the buggy, watching her pensively.

"I'm about to show you how much I love you, Jonathan Fortner," she said, and then she began climbing up the ladder.

"Lizzie!" Jonathan protested, bolting away from the buggy.

Elisabeth climbed until she reached the doorway that had once led from Trista's room into the main hallway. Holding her breath, she shut her eyes tightly, closed her fingers around the necklace and flung it over the threshold.

She was pleased when she opened her eyes and saw that the pendant had vanished. Holding her skirts aside with one hand, made her way quickly down the ladder.

Elisabeth Fortner had found the century where she belonged, and she meant to stay there.

HERE AND THEN

For Jane and Dick Edwards,
the kind of friends I always hoped I'd have

CHAPTER 1

Aunt Verity's antique necklace lay in an innocent, glimmering coil of gold on the floor of the upstairs hallway. An hour before, when Rue Claridge had been carrying her suitcases upstairs, it had not been there.

Frowning, Rue got down on one knee and reached for the necklace, her troubled gaze rising to the mysterious, sealed door in the outside wall. Beyond it was nothing but empty space. The part of the house it had once led to had been burned away a century before and never rebuilt.

Aunt Verity had hinted at spooky doings in the house over the years, tales concerning both the door and the necklace. Rue had enjoyed the yarns, but being practical in nature, she had promptly put them out of her mind.

Rue's missing cousin, Elisabeth, had mentioned the necklace and the doorway in those strange letters she'd written in an effort to outline what was happening to her. She'd said a person wearing the necklace could travel through time.

In fact, Elisabeth—gentle, sensible Elisabeth—had claimed she'd clasped the chain around her neck and soon found herself in the 1890s, surrounded by living, breathing people who should have been dead a hundred years.

A chill wove a gossamer casing around Rue's spine as she recalled snatches of Elisabeth's desperate letters.

You're the one person in the world who might, just might, believe me. Those wonderful, spooky stories Aunt Verity told us on rainy nights were true. There *is* another world on the other side of that door in the upstairs hall-

way, one every bit as solid and real as the one you and
I know, and I've reached it. I've been there, Rue, and
I've met the man meant to share my life. His name is
Jonathan Fortner, and I love him more than my next
heartbeat, my next breath.

A pounding headache thumped behind Rue's right temple,
and she let out a long sigh as she rose to her feet, her fingers
pressing the necklace deep into her palm. With her other hand,
she pushed a lock of sandy, shoulder-length hair back from
her face and stared at the sealed door.

Years ago there had been rooms on the other side, but then,
late in the last century, there had been a tragic fire. The dam-
age had been repaired, but the original structure was changed
forever. The door had been sealed, and now the doorknob was
as old and stiff as a rusted padlock.

"Bethie," Rue whispered, touching her forehead against
the cool, wooden panel of the door, "where are you?"

There was no answer. The old country house yawned
around her, empty except for the ponderous nineteenth-
century furniture Aunt Verity had left as a part of her estate
and a miniature universe of dust particles that seemed to per-
vade every room, every corner and crevice.

At thirty, Rue was an accomplished photojournalist. She'd
dodged bullets and bombs in Belfast, photographed and later
written about the massacre in Tiananmen Square, covered the
invasion of Panama, nearly been taken captive in Baghdad.
And while all of those experiences had shaken her and some
had left her physically ill for days afterward, none had frightened her so profoundly as Elisabeth's disappearance.

The police and Elisabeth's father believed Elisabeth had
simply fled the area after her divorce, that she was lying on
a beach somewhere, sipping exotic tropical drinks and letting
the sun bake away her grief. But because she knew her cousin,
because of the letters and phone messages that had been waiting when she returned from an assignment in Moscow, Rue
took a much darker view of the situation.

Elisabeth was wandering somewhere, if she was alive at

all, perhaps not even remembering who she was. Rue wouldn't allow herself to dwell on all the *other* possibilities, because they didn't bear thinking about.

Downstairs in the big kitchen, she brewed a cup of instant coffee in Elisabeth's microwave and sat down at the big, oak table in the breakfast nook to go over the tattered collection of facts one more time. Before her were her cousin's letters, thoughtfully written, with no indications of undue stress in the familiar, flowing hand.

With a sigh, Rue pushed away her coffee and rested her chin in one palm. Elisabeth had come to the house the two cousins had inherited to get a new perspective on her life. She'd planned to make her home outside the little Washington town of Pine River and teach at the local elementary school in the fall. The two old ladies across the road, Cecily and Roberta Buzbee, had seen Elisabeth on several occasions. It had been Miss Cecily who had called an ambulance after finding Elisabeth unconscious in the upstairs hallway. Rue's cousin had been rushed to the hospital, where she'd stayed a relatively short time, and soon after that, she'd vanished.

Twilight was falling over the orchard behind the house, the leaves thinning on the gray-brown branches because it was late October. Rue watched as a single star winked into view in the purple sky. *Oh, Bethie,* she thought, as a collage of pictures formed in her mind...an image of a fourteen-year-old Elisabeth predominated—Bethie, looking down at Rue from the door of the hayloft in the rickety old barn. "Don't worry," the woman-child had called cheerfully on that long-ago day when Rue had first arrived, bewildered and angry, to take sanctuary under Aunt Verity's wing. "This is a good place and you'll be happy here." Rue saw herself and Bethie fishing and wading in the creek near the old covered bridge and reading dog-eared library books in the highest branches of the maple tree that shaded the back door. And listening to Verity's wonderful stories in front of the parlor fire, chins resting on their updrawn knees, arms wrapped around agile young legs clad in blue jeans.

The jangle of the telephone brought Rue out of her reflections, and she muttered to herself as she made her way across the room to pick up the extension on the wall next to the sink. "Hello," she snapped, resentful because she'd felt closer to Elisabeth for those few moments and the caller had scattered her memories like a flock of colorful birds.

"Hello, Claridge," a wry male voice replied. "Didn't they cover telephone technique where you went to school?"

Rue ignored the question and shoved the splayed fingers of one hand through her hair, pulling her scalp tight over her forehead.

"Hi, Wilson," she said, Jeff's boyish face forming on the screen of her mind. She'd been dating the guy for three years, on and off, but her heart never gave that funny little thump she'd read about when she saw his face or heard his voice. She wondered if that meant anything significant.

"Find out anything about your cousin yet?"

Rue leaned against the counter, feeling unaccountably weary. "No," she said. "I talked to the police first thing, and they agree with Uncle Marcus that she's probably hiding out somewhere, licking her wounds."

"You don't think so?"

Unconsciously, Rue shook her head. "No way. Bethie would never just vanish without telling anyone where she was going...she's the most considerate person I know." Her gaze strayed to the letters spread out on the kitchen table, unnervingly calm accounts of journeys to another point in time. Rue shook her head again, denying that such a thing could be possible.

"I could fly out and help you," Jeff offered, and Rue's practical heart softened a little.

"That won't be necessary," she said, twisting one finger in the phone cord and frowning. Finding Elisabeth was going to take all her concentration and strength of will, she told herself. The truth was, she didn't want Jeff getting in the way.

Her friend sighed, somewhat dramatically. "So be it, Claridge. If you decide I have any earthly use, give me a call, will you?"

Rue laughed. "What?" she countered. "No violin music?"

In the next instant, she remembered that Elisabeth was missing, and the smile faded from her face. "Thanks for offering, Jeff," she said seriously. "I'll call if there's anything you can do to help."

After that, there didn't seem to be much to say, and that was another element of the relationship Rue found troubling. It would have been a tremendous relief to tell someone she was worried and scared, to say Elisabeth was more like a sister to her than a cousin, maybe even to cry on a sympathetic shoulder. But Rue couldn't let down her guard that far, not with Jeff. She often got the feeling that he was just waiting for her to show weakness or to fall on her face.

The call ended, and Rue, wearing jeans and a sweatshirt, put on a jacket and went out to the shed for an armload of the aged applewood that had been cut and stacked several years before. Because Rue and Elisabeth had so rarely visited the house they'd inherited, the supply had hardly been diminished.

As she came through the back door, the necklace caught her eye, seeming to twinkle and wink from its place on the kitchen table. Rue's brow crimped thoughtfully as she made her way into the parlor and set the fragrant wood down on the hearth.

After moving aside the screen, she laid twigs in the grate over a small log of compressed sawdust and wax. When the blaze had kindled properly, she added pieces of seasoned wood. Soon, a lovely, cheerful fire was crackling away behind the screen.

Rue adjusted the damper and rose, dusting her hands off on the legs of her jeans. She was tired and distraught, and suddenly she couldn't keep her fears at bay any longer. She'd been a reporter for nine eventful years, and she knew only too well the terrible things that could have happened to Elisabeth.

She went back to the kitchen and, without knowing exactly why, reached for the necklace and put it on, even before taking off her jacket. Then, feeling chilled, she returned to the parlor to stand close to the fire.

Rue was fighting back tears of frustration and fear, her forehead touching the mantelpiece, when she heard the distant tinkling of piano keys. She was alone in the house, and she was certain no radio or TV was playing....

Her green eyes widened when she looked into the ornately framed mirror above the fireplace, and her throat tightened: The room reflected there was furnished differently, and was lit with the soft glow of lantern light. Rue caught a glimpse of a plain woman in long skirts running a cloth over the keys of a piano before the vision faded and the room was ordinary again.

Turning slowly, Rue rubbed her eyes with a thumb and forefinger. She couldn't help thinking of Elisabeth's letters describing a world like the one she'd just seen, for a fraction of a second, in the parlor mirror.

"You need a vacation," Rue said, glancing back over her shoulder at her image in the glass. "You're hallucinating."

Nonetheless, she made herself another cup of instant coffee, gathered up the letters and went to sit cross-legged on the hooked rug in front of the fireplace. Once again, she read and analyzed every word, looking for some clue, anything that would tell her where to begin the search for her cousin.

Thing was, Rue thought, Bethie sounded eminently sane in those letters, despite the fact that she talked about stepping over a threshold into another time in history. Her descriptions of the era were remarkably authentic; she probably would have had to have done days or weeks of research to know the things she did. But the words seemed fluent and easy, as though they'd flowed from her pen.

Finally, no closer to finding Elisabeth than she had been before, Rue set the sheets of writing paper aside, banked the fire and climbed the front stairway to the second floor. She would sleep in the main bedroom—many of Elisabeth's things were still there—and maybe by some subconscious, instinctive process, she would get a glimmer of guidance concerning her cousin's whereabouts.

As it was, she didn't have the first idea where to start.

She showered, brushed her teeth, put on a nightshirt and

went to bed. Although she had taken the necklace off when she undressed, she put it back on again before climbing beneath the covers.

The sheets were cold, and Rue burrowed down deep, shivering. If it hadn't been for the circumstances, she would have been glad to be back in this old house, where all the memories were good ones. Like Ribbon Creek, the Montana ranch she'd inherited from her mother's parents, Aunt Verity's house was a place to hole up when there was an important story to write or a decision to work out. She'd always loved the sweet, shivery sensation that the old Victorian monstrosity was haunted by amicable ghosts.

As her body began to warm the crisp, icy sheets, Rue hoped those benevolent apparitions were hanging around now, willing to lend a hand. "Please," she whispered, "show me how to find Elisabeth. She's my cousin and the closest thing I ever had to a sister and my very best friend, all rolled into one— and I think she's in terrible trouble."

After that, Rue tossed and turned for a while, then fell into a restless sleep marred by frightening dreams. One of them was so horrible that it sent her hurtling toward the surface of consciousness, and when she broke through into the morning light, she was breathing in gasping sobs and there were tears on her face.

And she could clearly hear a woman's voice singing, "Shall We Gather at the River?"

Her heart thundering against her chest, Rue flung back the covers and bounded out of bed, following the sound into the hallway, where she looked wildly in one direction, then the other. The voice seemed to be rising through the floorboards and yet, at the same time, it came from beyond the sealed door of the outside wall.

Rue put her hands against the wooden panel, remembering Elisabeth's letters. There was a room on the other side, Bethie had written, a solid place with floors and walls and a private stairway leading into the kitchen.

"Who's there?" Rue called, and the singing immediately stopped, replaced by a sort of stunned stillness. She ran along the hallway, peering into each of the three bedrooms, then hurried down the back stairs and searched the kitchen, the utility room, the dining room, the bathroom and both parlors. There was no one else in the house, and none of the locks on the windows or doors had been disturbed.

Frustrated, Rue stormed over to the piano on which she and Elisabeth had played endless renditions of "Heart and Soul," threw up the cover and hammered out the first few bars of "Shall We Gather at the River?" in challenge.

"Come on!" she shouted over the thundering chords. "Show yourself, damn it! Who are you? *What* are you?"

The answer was the slamming of a door far in the distance.

Rue left the piano and bounded back up the stairs, because the sound had come from that direction. Reaching the sealed door, she grabbed the knob and rattled the panel hard on its hinges, and surprise rushed through her like an electrical shock when it gave way.

Muttering an exclamation, Rue peered through the opening at the charred ruins of a fire. A trembling began in the cores of her knees as she looked at blackened timbers that shouldn't have been there.

It was a moment before she could gather her wits enough to step back from the door, leaving it agape, and dash wildly down the front stairs. She went hurtling out through the front door and plunged around to the side, only to see the screened sun porch just where it had always been, with no sign of the burned section.

Barely able to breathe, Rue circled the house once, then raced back inside and up the stairs. The door was still open, and beyond it lay another time or another dimension.

"Elisabeth!" Rue shouted, gripping the sooty doorjamb and staring down through the ruins.

A little girl in a pinafore and old-fashioned, pinchy black shoes appeared in the overgrown grass, shading her eyes with a small, grubby hand as she looked up at Rue. "You a witch like her?" the child called, her tone cordial and unruffled.

Rue's heartbeat was so loud that it was thrumming in her ears. She stepped back, then forward, then back again. She stumbled blindly into her room and pulled on jeans, a T-shirt, socks and sneakers, not taking the time to brush her sleep-tangled hair, and she was climbing deftly down through the ruins before she had a moment to consider the consequences.

The child, who had been so brave at a distance, was now backing away, stumbling in her effort to escape, her freckles standing out on her pale face, her eyes enormous.

Great, Rue thought, half-hysterically, *now I'm scaring small children.*

"Please don't run away," she managed to choke out. "I'm not going to hurt you."

The girl appeared to be weighing Rue's words, and it seemed that some of the fear had left her face. In the next instant, however, a woman came running around the corner of the house, shrieking and flapping her apron at Rue as though to shoo her away like a chicken.

"Don't you dare touch that child!" she screeched, and Rue recognized her as the drab soul she'd glimpsed in the parlor mirror the night before, wiping the piano keys.

Rue had withstood much more daunting efforts at intimidation during her travels as a reporter. She held her ground, her hands resting on her hips, her mind cataloging material so rapidly that she was barely aware of the process. The realization that Elisabeth had been *right* about the necklace and the door in the upstairs hallway and that she was near to finding her, was as exhilarating as a skydive.

"Where did you come from?" the plain woman demanded, thrusting the child slightly behind her.

Rue didn't even consider trying to explain. In the first place, no one would believe her, and in the second, she didn't understand what was going on herself. "Back there," she said, cocking a thumb toward the open doorway above. That was when she noticed that her hands and the knees of her jeans were covered with soot from the climb down through the timbers. "I'm looking for my Cousin Elisabeth."

"She ain't around," was the grudging, somewhat huffy reply. The woman glanced down at the little girl and gave her a tentative shove toward the road. "You run along now, Vera.

I saw Farley riding toward your place just a little while ago. If you meet up with him, tell him he ought to come on over here and have a talk with this lady.''

Vera assessed Rue with uncommonly shrewd eyes—she couldn't have been older than eight or nine—then scampered away through the deep grass.

Rue took a step closer to the woman, even though she was beginning to feel like running back to her own safe world, the one she understood. ''Do you know Elisabeth McCartney?'' she pressed.

The drudge twisted her calico apron between strong, work-reddened fingers, and her eyes strayed over Rue's clothes and wildly tousled hair with unconcealed and fearful disapproval. ''I never heard of nobody by that name,'' she said.

Rue didn't believe that for a moment, but she was conscious of a strange and sudden urgency, an instinct that warned her to tread lightly, at least for the time being. ''You haven't seen the last of me,'' she said, and then she climbed back up through the charred beams to the doorway, hoping her own world would be waiting for her on the other side. ''I'll be back.''

Her exit was drained of all drama when she wriggled over the threshold and found herself on a hard wooden floor decorated with a hideous Persian runner. The hallway in the modern-day house was carpeted.

''Oh, no,'' she groaned, just lying there for a moment, trying to think what to do. The curtain in time that had permitted her to pass between one century and the other had closed, and she had no way of knowing when—or if—it would ever open again.

It was just possible that she was trapped in this rerun of *Gunsmoke*—permanently.

''Damn,'' she groaned, getting to her feet and running her hands down the sooty denim of her jeans. When she'd managed to stop shaking, Rue approached one of the series of photographs lining the wall and looked up into the dour face of an old man with a bushy white beard and a look of fanatical righteousness about him. "I sure hope *you're* not hanging around here somewhere," she muttered.

Next, she cautiously opened the door of the room she'd slept in the night before—only it wasn't the same. All the furniture was obviously antique, yet it looked new. Rue backed out and proceeded along the hallway, her sense of fascinated uneasiness growing with every passing moment.

"Through the looking glass," she murmured to herself. "Any minute now, I should meet a talking rabbit with a pocket watch and a waistcoat."

"Or a United States marshal," said a deep male voice.

Rue whirled, light-headed with surprise, and watched in disbelief as a tall, broad-shouldered cowboy with a badge pinned to his vest mounted the last of the front stairs to stand in the hall. His rumpled brown hair was a touch too long, his turquoise eyes were narrowed with suspicion, and he was badly in need of a shave.

This guy was straight out of the late movie, but his personal magnetism was strictly high-tech.

"What's your name?" he asked in that gravelly voice of his.

Rue couldn't help thinking what a hit this guy would be in the average singles' bar. Not only was he good-looking, in a rough, tough sort of way, he had macho down to an art form. "Rue Claridge," she said, just a little too heartily, extending one hand in friendly greeting.

The marshal glanced at her hand, but failed to offer his own. "You make a habit of prowling around in other people's houses?" he asked. His marvelous eyes widened as he took in her jeans, T-shirt and sneakers.

"I'm looking for my cousin Elisabeth." Rue's smile was a rigid curve, and she clung to it like someone dangling over the edge of a steep cliff. "I have reason to believe she might be in...these here parts."

The lawman set his rifle carefully against the wall, and Rue gulped. His expression was dubious. "Who are you?" he demanded again, folding his powerful arms. Afternoon sunlight streamed in through the open door to nowhere, and Rue could smell charred wood.

"I told you, my name is Rue Claridge, and I'm looking for my cousin, Elisabeth McCartney." Rue held up one hand to indicate a height comparable to her own. "She's a very pretty blonde, with big, bluish green eyes and a gentle manner."

The marshal's eyebrows drew together. "Lizzie?"

Rue shrugged. She'd never known Elisabeth to call herself Lizzie, but then, she hadn't visited another century, either. "She wrote me that she was in love with a man named Jonathan Fortner."

At this, the peace officer smiled, and his craggy face was transformed. Rue felt a modicum of comfort for the first time since she'd stepped over the threshold. "They're gone to San Francisco, Jon and Lizzie are," he said. "Got married a few months back, right after her trial was over."

Rue took a step closer to the marshal, one eyebrow raised, the peculiarities and implications of her situation temporarily forgotten. "Trial?"

"It's a long story." The splendid eyes swept over her clothes again and narrowed once more. "Where the devil did you get those duds?"

Rue drew in a deep breath and expelled it, making tendrils of her hair float for a few moments. "I come from another— place. What's your name, anyhow?"

"Farley Haynes," the cowboy answered.

Privately, Rue thought it was the dumbest handle she'd ever heard, but she was in no position to rile the man. "Well, Mr. Haynes," she said brightly, "I am sorry that you had to come all the way out here for nothing. The thing is, I know Elisabeth—Lizzie—would want me to stay right here in this house."

Haynes plunked his battered old hat back onto his head and regarded Rue from under the brim. "She never mentioned a cousin," he said. "Maybe you'd better come to town with me and answer a few more questions."

Rue's first impulse was to dig in her heels, but she was an inveterate journalist, and despite the fact that her head was still spinning from the shock of sudden transport from one time to another, she was fiercely curious about this place.

"What year is this, anyway?" she asked, not realizing how odd the question sounded until it was already out of her mouth.

The lawman's right hand cupped her elbow lightly as he ushered Rue down the front stairs. In his left, he carried the rifle with unnerving expertise. "It's 1892," he answered, giving her a sidelong look, probably wondering if he should slap the cuffs on her wrists. "The month is October."

"I suppose you're wondering why I didn't know that." Rue chatted on as the marshal escorted her out through the front door. There was a big sorrel gelding waiting beyond the whitewashed gate. "The fact is, I've—I've had a fever."

"You look healthy enough to me," Haynes responded, and just the timbre of his voice set some chord to vibrating deep inside Rue. He opened the gate and nodded for her to go through it ahead of him.

She took comfort from the presence of the horse; she'd always loved the animals, and some of the happiest times of her life had been spent in the saddle at Ribbon Creek. "Hello, big fella," she said, patting the gelding's sweaty neck.

In the next instant, Rue was grabbed around the waist and hoisted up into the saddle. Before she could react in any way, Marshal Haynes had thrust his rifle into the leather scabbard, stuck one booted foot in the stirrup and swung up behind her.

Rue felt seismic repercussions move up her spine in response.

"Am I under arrest?" she asked. He reached around her to grasp the reins, and again Rue was disturbed by the powerful contraction within her. Cowboy fantasies were one thing, she reminded herself, but this was a trip into the Twilight Zone, and she had an awful feeling her ticket was stamped "one-way." She'd never been on an assignment where it was more important to keep her wits about her.

"That depends," the marshal said, the words rumbling against her nape, "on whether or not you can explain how you came to be wearing Mrs. Fortner's necklace."

Leather creaked as Rue turned to look up into that rugged face, her mind racing in search of an explanation. "My—our aunt gave us each a necklace like this," she lied, her fingers straying to the filigree pendant. The piece was definitely an original, with a history. "Elis—Lizzie's probably wearing hers."

Farley looked skeptical to say the least, but he let the topic drop for the moment. "I don't mind telling you," he said, "that the Presbyterians are going to be riled up some when they get a gander at those clothes of yours. It isn't proper for a lady to wear trousers."

Rue might have been amused by his remarks if it hadn't been for the panic that was rising inside her. Nothing in her fairly wide experience had prepared her for being thrust unceremoniously into 1892, after all. "I don't have anything else to wear," she said in an uncharacteristically small voice, and then she sank her teeth into her lower lip, gripped the pommel of Marshal Haynes's saddle in both hands and held on for dear life, even though she was an experienced rider.

After a bumpy, dusty trip over the unpaved country road that led to town—its counterpart in Rue's time was paved— they reached Pine River. The place had gone into rewind while she wasn't looking. There were saloons with swinging doors, and a big saw in the lumber mill beside the river screamed and flung sawdust into the air. People walked along board sidewalks and rode in buggies and wagons. Rue couldn't help gaping at them.

Marshal Haynes lifted her down from the horse before she had a chance to tell him she didn't need his help, and he gave her an almost imperceptible push toward the sidewalk. Bronze script on the window of the nearest building proclaimed, Pine River Jailhouse. Farley Haynes, Marshal.

Bravely, Rue resigned herself to the possibility of a stretch behind bars. Much as she wanted to see the twentieth century again, she'd changed her mind about leaving 1892 right away—she meant to stick around until Elisabeth came back. Despite those glowing letters, Rue wanted to know her cousin was all right before she put this parallel universe—or whatever it was—behind her.

"Do you believe in ghosts, Farley?" she asked companionably, once they were inside and the marshal had opened a little gate in the railing that separated his desk and cabinet and wood stove from the single jail cell.

"No, ma'am," he answered with a sigh, hanging his disreputable hat on a hook by the door and laying his rifle down on the cluttered surface of the desk. Once again, his gaze passed over her clothes, troubled and quick. "But I do believe there are some strange things going on in this world that wouldn't be too easy to explain."

Rue tucked her hands into the hip pockets of her jeans and looked at the wanted posters on the wall behind Farley's desk. They should have been yellow and cracked with age, but instead they were new and only slightly crumpled. A collection of archaic rifles filled a gun cabinet, their nickel barrels and wooden stocks gleaming with a high shine that belied their age.

"You won't get an argument from me," Rue finally replied.

CHAPTER 2

Rue took in the crude jail cell, the potbellied stove with a coffeepot and a kettle crowding the top, the black, iron key ring hanging on a peg behind the desk. Her gaze swung to the marshal's face, and she gestured toward the barred room at the back of the building.

"If I'm under arrest, Marshal," she said matter-of-factly, "I'd like to know exactly what I'm being charged with."

The peace officer sighed, hanging his ancient canvas coat from a tarnished brass rack. "Well, miss, we could start with trespassing." He gestured toward a chair pushed back against the short railing that surrounded the immediate office area. "Sit down and tell me who you are and what you were doing snooping around Dr. Fortner's house that way."

Rue was feeling a little weak, a rare occurrence for her. She pulled the chair closer to the desk and sat, pushing her tousled hair back from her face. "I told you. My name is Rue Claridge," she replied patiently. "Dr. Fortner's wife is my cousin, and I was looking for her. That's all."

The turquoise gaze, sharp with intelligence, rested on the gold pendant at the base of Rue's throat, causing the pulse beneath to make a strange, sudden leap. "I believe you said Mrs. Fortner has a necklace just like that one."

Rue swallowed. She was very good at sidestepping issues she didn't want to discuss, but when it came to telling an outright lie, she hadn't even attained amateur status. "Y-yes," she managed to say. Her earlier shock at finding herself in another century was thawing now, becoming low-grade panic.

Was it possible that she'd stumbled into Elisabeth's nervous breakdown, or was she having a separate one, all her own?

The marshal's jawline tightened under a shadow of beard. His strong, sun-browned fingers were interlaced over his middle as he leaned back in his creaky desk chair. "How do you account for those clothes you're wearing?"

She took a deep, quivering breath. "Where I come from, lots of women dress like this."

Marshal Haynes arched one eyebrow. "And where is that?" There was an indulgent tone in his voice that made Rue want to knuckle his head.

Rue thought fast. "Montana. I have a ranch over there."

Farley scratched the back of his neck with an idleness Rue perceived as entirely false. Although his lackadaisical manner belied the fact, she sensed a certain lethal energy about him, an immense physical and emotional power barely restrained. Before she could stop it, Rue's mind had made the jump to wondering what it would be like to be held and caressed by this man.

Just the idea gave her a feeling of horrified delight.

"Doesn't your husband mind having his wife go around dressed like a common cowhand?" he asked evenly.

Color flooded Rue's face, but she held her temper carefully in check. Marshal Haynes's attitude toward women was unacceptable, but he was a man of his time and all attempts to convert him to modern thinking would surely be wasted.

"I don't have a husband." She thought she saw a flicker of reaction in the incredible eyes.

"Your daddy, then?"

Rue drew a deep breath and let it out slowly. "I'm not close to my family," she said sweetly. For all practical intents and purposes, the statement was true. Rue's parents had been divorced years before, going their separate ways. Her mother was probably holed up in some fancy spa somewhere, getting ready for the ski season, and her father's last postcard had been sent from Monaco. "I'm on my own. Except for Elisabeth, of course."

The marshal studied her for a long moment, looking pensive now, and then leaned forward in his chair. "Yes. Elisabeth Fortner."

"Right," Rue agreed, her head spinning. Nothing in her eventful past had prepared her for this particular situation. Somehow, she'd missed Time Travel 101 in college, and the Nostalgia Channel mostly covered the 1940s.

She sighed to herself. If she'd been sent back to the big-band era, maybe she would have known how to act.

"I'm going to let you go for now," Haynes announced thoughtfully. "But if you get into any trouble, ma'am, you'll have me to contend with."

A number of wisecracks came to the forefront of Rue's mind, but she valiantly held them back. "I'll just...go now," she said awkwardly, before racing out of the jailhouse onto the street.

The screech of the mill saw hurt her ears, and she hurried in the opposite direction. It would take a good forty-five minutes to walk back to the house in the country, and by the looks of the sky, the sun would be setting soon.

As she was passing the Hang-Dog Saloon, a shrill cry from above made Rue stop and look up.

Two prostitutes were leaning up against a weathered railing, their seedy-looking satin dresses glowing in the late-afternoon sun. "Where'd you get them pants?" the one in blue inquired, just before spitting tobacco into the street.

The redhead beside her, who was wearing a truly ugly pea green gown, giggled as though her friend had said something incredibly clever.

"You know, Red," Rue replied, shading her eyes with one hand as she looked up, and choosing to ignore both the question and the tobacco juice, "you really ought to have your colors done. That shade of green is definitely unbecoming."

The prostitutes looked at each other, then turned and flounced away from the railing, disappearing into the noisy saloon.

The conversation had not been a total loss, Rue decided, looking down at her jeans, sneakers and T-shirt. There was no telling how long she'd have to stay in this backward century, and her modern clothes would be a real hindrance.

She turned and spotted a store across the street, displaying gingham dresses, bridles and wooden buckets behind its fly-speckled front window. "'And bring your Visa card,'" she muttered to herself, "'because they *don't* take American Express.'"

Rue carefully made her way over, avoiding road apples, mud puddles and two passing wagons.

On the wooden sidewalk in front of the mercantile, she stood squinting, trying to see through the dirty glass. The red-and-white gingham dress on display in the window looked more suited to Dorothy of *The Wizard of Oz* fame, with its silly collar and big, flouncy bow at the back. The garment's only saving grace was that it looked as though it would probably fit.

Talking to herself was a habit Rue had acquired because she'd spent so much time alone researching and polishing her stories. "Maybe I can get a pair of ruby slippers, too," she murmured, walking resolutely toward the store's entrance. "Then I could just click my heels together and voilà, Toto, we're back in Kansas."

A pleasant-looking woman with gray hair and soft blue eyes beamed at Rue as she entered. The smile faded to an expression of chagrined consternation, however, as the old lady took in Rue's jeans and T-shirt.

"May I help you?" the lady asked, sounding as though she doubted very much that anybody could.

Rue was dizzied by the sheer reality of the place, the woman, the circumstances in which she found herself. A fly bounced helplessly against a window, buzzing in bewilderment the whole time, and Rue felt empathy for it. "That checked dress in the window," she began, her voice coming out hoarse. "How much is it?"

The fragile blue gaze swept over Rue once again, worriedly. "Why, it's fifty cents, child."

For a moment, Rue was delighted. Fifty cents. No problem. Then she realized she hadn't brought any money with her.

Even if she had, all the bills and currency would have looked suspiciously different from what was being circulated in the 1890s, and she would undoubtedly have found herself back in Farley Haynes's custody, post haste.

Rue smiled her most winning smile, the one that had gotten her into so many press conferences and out of so many tight spots. "Just put it on my account, please," she said. Rue possessed considerable bravado, but the strain of the day was beginning to tell.

The store mistress raised delicate eyebrows and cleared her throat. "Do I know you?"

Another glance at the dress—it only added insult to injury that the thing was so relentlessly ugly—gave Rue the impetus to answer, "No. My name is Rue...*Miss* Rue Claridge, and I'm Elisabeth Fortner's cousin. Perhaps you could put the dress on her husband's account?"

The woman sniffed. Clearly, in mentioning the good doctor, Rue had touched a nerve. "Jonathan Fortner ought to have his head examined, marrying a strange woman the way he did. There were odd doings in that house!"

Normally Rue would have been defensive, since she tended to get touchy where Elisabeth was concerned, but she couldn't help thinking how peculiar her cousin must have seemed to these people. Bethie was a quiet sort, but her ideas and attitudes were strictly modern, and she must surely have rubbed more than one person the wrong way.

Rue focused on the block of cheese sitting on the counter, watching as two flies explored the hard, yellow rind. "What kind of odd doings?" she asked, too much the reporter to let such an opportunity pass.

The storekeeper seemed to forget that Rue was a suspicious type, new in town and wearing clothes more suited, as Farley had said, to a cowhand. Leaning forward, she whispered confidentially, "That woman would simply appear and disappear at will. Not a few of us think she's a witch and that justice would have been better served if she'd been hanged after that trial of hers!"

For a moment, the fundamentals of winning friends and

influencing people slipped Rue's mind. "Don't be silly—
there're no such things as witches." She lowered her voice
and, having dispatched with superstition, hurried on to her
main concern. "Elisabeth was put on trial and might have
been hanged? For what?"

The other woman was in a state of offense, probably because one of her pet theories had just been ridiculed. "For a
time, it looked as though she'd murdered not only Dr. Fortner,
but his young daughter, Trista, as well, by setting that blaze."
She paused, clearly befuddled. "Then they came back. Just
magically reappeared out of the ruins of that burned house."

Rue was nodding to herself. She didn't know the rules of
this time-travel game, but it didn't take a MENSA member-
ship to figure out how Bethie's husband and the little girl had
probably escaped the fire. No doubt they'd fled over the
threshold into the next century, then had trouble returning. Or
perhaps time didn't pass at the same rate here as it did there....

It seemed to Rue that Aunt Verity had claimed the necklace's magic was unpredictable, waning and waxing under
mysterious rules of its own. Elisabeth had mentioned nothing
like that in her letters, however.

Rue brought herself back to the matter at hand—buying the
dress. "Dr. Fortner must be a man of responsibility, coming
back from the great beyond like that. It would naturally follow
that his credit would be good."

The storekeeper went pale, then pursed her lips and sighed,
"I'm sorry. Dr. Fortner is, indeed, a trusted and valued cus-
tomer, but I cannot add merchandise to his account without
his permission. Besides, there's no telling when he and that
bride of his will return from California."

The woman was nondescript and diminutive, and yet Rue
knew she'd be wasting her time to argue. She'd met third-
world leaders with more flexible outlooks on life. "Okay,"
she said with a sigh. She'd just have to check the house and
see if Elisabeth had left any clothes or money behind. Provided she couldn't get back into her own time, that is.

Rue offered a polite goodbye, only too aware that she might
be stuck on this side of 1900 indefinitely.

Although she power walked most of the way home—this
drew stares from the drivers of passing buggies and wagons—
it was quite dark when Rue arrived. She let herself in through
the kitchen door, relieved to find that the housekeeper had left
for the day.

After stumbling around in the darkness for a while, Rue
found matches and lit the kerosene lamp in the middle of the
table.

The weak light flickered over a fire-damaged kitchen, made
livable by someone's hard work. There was an old-fashioned
icebox, a pump handle at the sink and a big cookstove with
shiny chrome trim.

Bethie actually wanted to stay in this place, Rue reflected,
marveling. Her cousin would develop biceps just getting
enough water to make the morning coffee, and she'd probably
have to chop and carry wood, too. Then there would be the
washing and the ironing and the cooking. And childbirth at
its most natural, with nothing for the pain except maybe a
bullet to bite on.

All this for the mysterious Dr. Jonathan Fortner.

"No man is worth it, Bethie," Rue protested to the empty
room, but Farley Haynes did swagger to mind, and his image
was so vivid, she could almost catch the scent of his skin and
hair.

Desperately hungry all of a sudden, she ransacked the icebox, helping herself to milk so creamy it had golden streaks
on top, and half a cold, boiled potato. When she'd eaten, she
took the lamp and headed upstairs, leaving the other rooms to
explore later.

She'd had quite enough adventure for one day.

In the second floor hallway, Rue looked at the blackened
door and knew without even touching the knob that she would
find nothing but more ruins on the other side. Maybe she'd
be able to get back to her own century, but it wasn't going
to happen that night.

Reaching the master bedroom, Rue approached the tall armoire first. It soon became apparent that Bethie hadn't left

much behind, certainly nothing Rue could wear, and if there was a cache of money, it wasn't hidden in that room.

Finally, exhausted, Rue washed as best she could, stripped off her clothes and crawled into the big bed.

Farley didn't make a habit of turning up in ladies' bedrooms of a morning, though he'd awakened in more than a few. There was just something about this particular woman that drew him with a force nearly as strong as his will, and it wasn't just that she wore trousers and claimed to be Lizzie Fortner's kin.

Her honey-colored hair, shorter than most women wore but still reaching to her shoulders, tumbled across the white pillow, catching the early sunlight, and her skin, visible to her armpits, where the sheet stopped, was a creamy golden peach. Her dark eyelashes lay on her cheeks like the wings of some small bird, and her breathing, even and untroubled, twisted Farley's senses up tight as the spring of a cheap watch.

He swallowed hard. Rue Claridge might be telling the truth, he thought, at least about being related to Mrs. Fortner. God knew, she was strange enough, with her trousers and her funny way of talking.

"Miss Claridge?" he said after clearing his throat. He wanted to wriggle her toe, but decided everything south of where the sheet stopped was out of his jurisdiction. "Rue!"

She sat bolt upright in bed and, to Farley's guarded relief and vast disappointment, held the top sheet firmly against her bosom.

Farley Haynes was standing at the foot of the bed, his hands resting on his hips, his handsome head cocked to one side.

Rue sat up hastily, insulted and alarmed and strangely aroused all at once, and wrenched the sheets from her collarbone to her chin.

"I sure hope you're making yourself at home and all," Farley said, and the expression in his eyes was wry in spite of his folksy drawl. He wasn't fooling Rue; this guy was about as slow moving and countrified as a New York politician.

Although the marshal hadn't touched her, Rue had the odd-
est sensation of impact, as though she'd been hauled against
his chest, with just the sheet between them. "What are you
doing here?" she demanded furiously when she found her
voice at last. She felt the ornate headboard press against her
bare back and bottom.

He arched one eyebrow and folded his arms. "I could ask
the same question of you, little lady."

Enough was enough. Nobody was going to call Rue Claridge "honey," "sweetie" or "little lady" and get away with
it, no matter *what* century they came from.

"Don't call me 'little' anything!" Rue snapped. "I'm a
grown woman and a self-supporting professional, and I won't
be patronized!"

This time, both the intruder's eyebrows rose, then knit together into a frown. "You sure are a temperamental filly,"
Farley allowed. "And mouthy as hell, too."

"Get out of here!" Rue shouted.

Idly, Farley drew up a rocking chair and sat. Then he
rubbed his stubbly chin, his eyes narrowed thoughtfully.
"You said you were a professional before. Question is, a professional what?"

Rue was still clutching the covers to her throat, and she
was breathing hard, as though she'd just finished a marathon.
If she hadn't been afraid to let go of the bedclothes with even
one hand, she would have snatched up the small crockery
pitcher on the nightstand and hurled it at his head.

"You would never understand," she answered haughtily.
"Now it's my turn to ask a question, Marshal. What the *hell*
are you doing in my bedroom?"

"This isn't your bedroom," the lawman pointed out quietly. "It's Jon Fortner's. And I'm here because Miss Ellen
came to town and reported a prowler on the premises."

Rue gave an outraged sigh. The housekeeper had apparently
entered the room, seen an unwelcome guest sleeping there and
marched herself into Pine River to demand legal action.
"Hellfire and spit," Rue snapped. "Why didn't she drag
Judge Wapner out here, too?"

Farley's frown deepened to bewilderment. "There's no judge by that name around these parts," he said. "And I wish you'd stop talking like that. If the Presbyterians hear you, they'll be right put out about it."

Catching herself just before she would have exploded into frustrated hysterics, Rue sucked in a deep breath and held it until a measure of calm came over her. "All right," she said finally, in a reasonable tone. "I will try not to stir up the Presbyterians. I promise. The point is, now you've investigated and you've seen that I'm not a trespasser, but a member of the family. I have a right to be here, Marshal, but, frankly, you don't. Now if you would please leave."

Farley sat forward in his chair, turning the brim of his battered, sweat-stained hat in nimble brown fingers. "Until I get word back from San Francisco that it's all right for you to stay here, ma'am, I'm afraid you'll have to put up at one of the boardinghouses in town."

Rue would have agreed to practically anything just to get him to leave the room. The painful truth was, Marshal Farley Haynes made places deep inside her thrum and pulse in response to some hidden dynamic of his personality. That was terrifying because she'd never felt anything like it before.

"Whatever you say," she replied with a lift of her chin. Innocuous as they were, the words came out sounding defiant. "Just leave this room, please. Immediately."

She thought she saw a twinkle in Farley's gem-bright eyes. He stood up with an exaggerated effort and, to Rue's horror, walked to the head of the bed and stood looking down at her.

"No husband and no daddy," he reflected sagely. "Little wonder your manners are so sorry." With that, he cupped one hand under her chin, then bent over and kissed her, just as straightforwardly as if he were shaking her hand.

To Rue's further mortification, instead of pushing him away, as her acutely trained left brain told her to do, she rose higher on her knees and thrust herself into the kiss. It was soft and warm at first, then Farley touched the seam of her mouth with his tongue and she opened to him, like a night orchid worshiping the moon. He took utter and complete command before suddenly stepping back.

"I expect you to be settled somewhere else by nightfall," he said gruffly. To his credit, he didn't avert his eyes, but he didn't look any happier about what he'd just done than Rue was.

"Get out," she breathed.

Farley settled his hat on his head, touched the brim in a mockingly cordial way and strolled from the room.

Rue sent her pillow flying after him, because he was so insufferable. Because he'd had the unmitigated gall not only to come into her bedroom, but to kiss her. Because her insides were still colliding like carnival rides gone berserk.

Later, ignoring Ellen, who was watchful and patently disapproving, Rue fetched a ladder from the barn and set it against the burned side of the house. At least, she thought, looking down at her jeans and T-shirt, she was dressed for climbing.

She still wanted to find Elisabeth and make sure her cousin was all right, but there were things she'd need to sustain herself in this primitive era. She intended to return to the late twentieth century, buy some suitable clothes from a costume place or a theater troupe, and pick up some old currency at a coin shop. Then she'd return, purchase a ticket on a train or boat headed south and see for herself that Bethie was happy and well.

It was an excellent plan, all in all, except that when Rue reached the top of the ladder and opened the charred door, nothing happened. She knew by the runner on the hallway floor and the pictures on the wall that she was still in 1892, even though she was wearing the necklace and wishing as hard as she could.

Obviously, one couldn't go back and forth between the two centuries on a whim.

Rue climbed down the ladder in disgust, finally, and stood in the deep grass, dusting her soot-blackened hands off on the legs of her jeans. "Damn it, Bethie," she muttered, "you'd better have a good reason for putting me through this!"

In the meantime, whether Elisabeth had a viable excuse for being in the wrong century or not, Rue had to make the best of her circumstances. She needed to find a way to fit in—and fast—before the locals decided *she* was a witch.

Ellen had draped a rug over the clothesline and was busily beating it with something that resembled a snowshoe. Occasionally she glanced warily in Rue's direction, as though expecting to be turned into a crow at any moment.

Rue wedged her hands into the hip pockets of her jeans and mentally ruled out all possibility of searching Elisabeth's house for money while the housekeeper was around. There was only one way to get the funds she needed, and if she didn't get busy, she might find herself spending the night in somebody's barn.

Or the Pine River jailhouse.

The idea of being behind bars went against her grain. Rue had once done a brief stint in a minimum-security women's prison for refusing to reveal a source to a grand jury, but this would obviously be different.

Rue headed for the road, walking backward so she could look at the house and "remember" how it *would* look in another hundred years. A part of her still expected to wake up on the couch in Aunt Verity's front parlor and discover this whole experience had been nothing more than a dream.

Reaching Pine River, Rue headed straight for the Hang-Dog Saloon, though she did have the discretion to make her way around to the alley and go in the back door.

In a smoky little room in the rear of the building, Rue found exactly what she'd hoped for, exactly what a thousand TV Westerns had conditioned her to expect. Four drunk men were seated around a rickety table, playing poker.

At the sight of a woman entering this inner sanctum, especially one wearing pants, the cardplayers stared. A man sporting a dusty stovepipe hat went so far as to let the unlit stogie fall from between his teeth, and the fat one with garters on his sleeves folded his cards and threw them in.

"What the hell...?"

After swallowing hard, Rue peeled off her digital watch and tossed it into the center of the table. "I'd like to play, if you fellas don't mind," she said, sounding much bolder than she felt.

The man in the stovepipe hat had apparently recovered from the shock of seeing the wrong woman in the wrong place; he picked up the wristwatch and studied it with a solemn frown. "Never seen nothin' like this here," he told his colleagues.

Being one of those people who believe that great forces come to the aid of the bold, Rue drew up a chair and sat down between a long-haired gunfighter type in a canvas duster and the hefty guy with the garters.

"Deal me in," she said brightly.

"Where'd you get this thing?" asked the one in the high hat.

"K mart," Rue answered, reaching for the battered deck lying in the middle of the table. She thought of bumper stickers she'd seen in her own time and couldn't help grinning. "My other watch is a Rolex," she added.

Stovepipe looked at her in consternation and opened his mouth to protest, but when Rue shuffled the cards deftly from one hand to the other without dropping a single one, he pressed his lips together.

The gunfighter whistled. "Son of a— Tarnation, ma'am. Where'd you learn to do that?"

Rue was warming to the game, as well as the conversation. "On board Air Force One, about three years ago. A Secret Serviceman taught me."

Stovepipe and Garters looked at each other in pure bewilderment.

"I say the lady plays," said the gunslinger.

Nobody argued, perhaps because Quickdraw was wearing a mean-looking forty-five low on his hip.

Rue dealt with a skill born of years of practice—her grandfather had taught her to play five-card draw back in Montana when she was six years old, and she'd been winning matchsticks, watches, ballpoint pens and pocket change ever since.

Rue had taken several pots, made up mostly of coins, though she had raked in a couple of oversize nineteenth-century dollar bills, in this game when the prostitute in the pea green dress came rustling in.

The woman's painted mouth fell open when she saw Rue sitting at the table, actually playing poker with the men, and her kohl-lined eyes widened. She set a fresh bottle of whiskey down on the table with an irate thump.

"Be quiet, Sissy," Quickdraw said, talking around the matchstick he was holding between his teeth. "This here is serious poker."

Sissy's eyes looked, as Aunt Verity would have said, like two burn holes in a blanket, and Rue felt a stab of pity for her. God knew, nineteenth-century life was hard enough for respectable women. It would be even rougher for ladies of the evening.

Quickdraw picked up Rue's watch, which was lying next to her stack of winnings, and held it up for Sissy's inspection. "You bring me good luck, little sugar girl, and I'll give you this for a trinket."

"I think I may throw up," Rue murmured under her breath.

"What'd you say?" Stovepipe demanded, sounding a little testy. Losing at poker clearly didn't sit well with him.

Rue offered the same smile she would have used to cajole the president of the United States into answering a tough question at a press conference, and replied, "I said I'm sure glad I showed up."

Sissy tossed the watch back to the table, glared at Rue for a moment, then turned and sashayed out of the room.

Rue was secretly relieved and turned all her concentration on the matter at hand. She had enough winnings to buy that horrible gingham dress and rent herself a room at the boardinghouse; now all she needed to do was ease out of the game without making her companions angry.

She yawned expansively.

Garters gave her a quelling look, clearly not ready to give up on the evening, and the game went on. And on.

It was starting to get embarrassing the way Rue kept winning, when all of a sudden the inner door to the saloon crashed open. There, filling the doorway like some fugitive from a Louis L'Amour novel, was Farley Haynes.

Finding Rue with five cards in her hand and a stack of coins in front of her, he swore. Sissy peered around his broad shoulder and smiled, just to let Rue know she'd been the one to bring about her impending downfall.

"Game's over," Farley said in that gruff voice, and none of the players took exception to the announcement. In fact, except for Rue, they all scattered, muttering various excuses and hasty pleasantries as they rushed out.

Rue stood and began stuffing her winnings into the pockets of her jeans. "Don't get your mustache in a wringer, Marshal," she said. "I've got what I came for and now I'm leaving."

Farley shook his head in quiet, angry wonderment and gestured toward the door with one hand. "Come along with me, Miss Claridge. You're under arrest."

Farley Haynes set his jaw, took Miss Rue Claridge by the elbow and hauled her toward the door. He prided himself on being a patient man, slow to wrath, as the Good Book said, but this woman tried his forbearance beyond all reasonable measure. Furthermore, he just flat didn't like the sick-calf feeling he got whenever he looked at her.

"Now, just a minute, Marshal," Miss Claridge snapped, trying to pull free of his grasp. "You haven't read me my rights!"

Farley tightened his grip, but he was careful not to bruise that soft flesh of hers. He didn't hold with manhandling a lady—not even one who barely measured up to the term when it came to comportment. To his way of thinking, Rue Claridge added up just fine as far as appearances went.

"What rights?" he demanded as they reached the shadowy alley behind the saloon. He had the damnedest, most unmarshal-like urge to drag Rue against his chest and kiss her, right then and there, and that scared the molasses out of him. The thought of kissing somebody in pants had never so much as crossed Farley's mind before, and he hoped to God it never would again.

"Forget it," she said, and her disdainful tone nettled Farley sorely. "It's pretty clear that around this town, I don't *have* any rights. I hope you're enjoying this, because it won't be long until you find yourself dealing with the likes of Susan B. Anthony!"

"Who?" Farley hadn't been this vexed since the year he was twelve, when Becky Hinehammer had called him a coward for refusing to walk the ridgepole on the schoolhouse roof. His pride had driven him to prove her wrong, and he'd gotten a broken collarbone for his trouble, along with a memorable blistering from his pa, once he'd healed up properly, for doing such a damn-fool thing in the first place.

He propelled Miss Claridge out of the alley and onto the main street of town. Pine River was relatively quiet that night.

They reached the jailhouse, and Farley pushed the front door open, then escorted his captive straight back to the jail's only cell.

Once his saucy prisoner was secured, Farley hung his hat on a peg next to the door and put away his rifle. It didn't occur to him to unstrap his gun belt; that was something he did only when it was time to stretch out for the night. Even then, he liked to have his .45 within easy reach.

He found a spare enamel mug, wiped it out with an old dish towel snatched from a nail behind the potbellied stove, and poured coffee. Then he carried the steaming brew to the cell and handed it through the bars to Miss Claridge. ''What kind of name is Rue?'' he asked, honestly puzzled.

This woman was full of mysteries, and he found himself wanting to solve them one by one.

His guest blew on the coffee, took a cautious sip and made a face. At least she was womanly enough to mind her manners. Farley had half expected her to slurp up the brew like an old mule skinner and maybe spit a mouthful into the corner. Instead, she came right back with, ''What kind of name is Farley?''

If she wasn't going to give a direct answer, neither was he. ''You're a snippy little piece, aren't you?''

Rue smiled, revealing a good, solid set of very white teeth. Folk wisdom said a woman lost a tooth for every child she bore, but Farley figured this gal would probably still have a mouthful even if she gave birth to a dozen babies.

''And *you're* lucky I know you're calling me 'a piece' in the old-fashioned sense of the word,'' she said pleasantly. ''Because if you meant it the way men mean it where—

when—I come from, I'd throw this wretched stuff you call coffee all over you.''

Farley didn't back away; he wouldn't let himself be intimidated by a smudged little spitfire in britches. "I reckon I've figured out why your folks gave you that silly name," he said. ''They knew someday some poor man would rue the day you were ever born.''

A flush climbed Rue's cheeks, and Farley reflected that her skin was as fine as her teeth. She was downright pretty, if a little less voluptuous than he'd have preferred—or would be, if anybody ever took the time to clean her up.

Considering that task made one side of Farley's mouth twitch in a fleeting grin.

He saw her blush again, then lift the mug to her mouth with both hands and take a healthy swig.

''God, I can't believe I'm actually drinking this sludge!'' she spat out just a moment later. "What did you do, boil down a vat of axle grease?''

Farley turned away to hide another grin, sighing as he pretended to straighten the papers on his desk. ''The Presbyterians are surely going to have their hands full getting *you* back on the straight and narrow,'' he allowed.

Rue stared at Farley's broad, muscular back and swallowed. She was exhausted and confused and, since she hadn't had anything to eat in almost a century, hungry. She kept expecting to wake up, even though she knew this situation was all too real.

She sat on the edge of the cell's one cot, which boasted a thin, bare mattress and a gray woolen blanket that looked as though it could have belonged to the poorest private in General Lee's rebel army.

''Did you ever get around to having your supper?'' Farley's voice was gruff, but there was something oddly comforting about the deep, resonating timbre of it.

Rue didn't look at him; there were tears in her eyes, and she was too proud to let them show. ''No,'' she answered.

Farley's tone remained gentle, and Rue knew he had moved

closer. "It's late, but I'll see if I can't raise Bessie over at the Hang-Dog and get her to fix you something."

Rue was still too stricken to speak; she just nodded.

Only when the marshal had left the jailhouse on his errand of mercy did Rue allow herself a loud sniffle. She stood and gripped the bars in both hands.

Maybe because she was tired, she actually hoped, for a few fleeting moments, that the key would be hanging from a peg within stretching distance on her cell, like in a TV Western.

In this case, fact was not stranger than fiction—there was no key in sight.

She began to pace, muttering to herself. If she ever got out of this, she'd write a book about it, tell the world. Appear on *Donahue* and *Oprah.*

Rue stopped, the nail of her index finger caught between her teeth. Who would ever believe her, besides Elisabeth?

She sat on the edge of the cot again and drew deep breaths until she felt a little less like screaming in frustration and panic.

Half an hour had passed, by the old clock facing Farley's messy desk, when the marshal returned carrying a basket covered with a blue-and-white checkered napkin.

Rue's stomach rumbled audibly and, to cover her embarrassment at that, she said defiantly, "You were foolish to leave me unattended, Marshal. I might very well have escaped."

He chuckled, extracted the coveted key from the pocket of his rough spun trousers and unlocked the cell door. "Is that so, Miss Spitfire? Then why didn't you?"

She narrowed her eyes. "Don't be so damn cocky," she warned. "For all you know, I might be part of a gang. Why, twenty or thirty outlaws might ride in here and dynamite this place."

Farley set the basket down and moseyed out of the cell, as unconcerned as if his prisoner were an addlepated old lady. Rue was vaguely insulted that the lawman didn't consider her more dangerous.

"Shut up and eat your supper," he said, not unkindly.

Rue plopped down on the edge of the cot again. Farley had set the basket on the only other piece of furniture in the cell, a rickety old stool, and she pulled that close.

There was cold roast venison in the basket, along with a couple of hard flour-and-water biscuits and an apple.

Rue ate greedily, but the whole time she watched Farley out of the corner of one eye. He was doing paperwork at the desk, by the light of a flickering kerosene lamp.

"Aren't you ever going home?" she inquired when she'd consumed every scrap of the food.

Farley didn't look up. "I've got a little place out back," he said. "You'd better get some sleep, Miss Claridge. Likely as not, you'll have the ladies of the town to deal with come morning. They'll want to take you on as a personal mission."

Rue let her forehead rest against an icy bar and sighed. "Great."

When Farley finally raised his eyes and saw that Rue was still standing there staring at him, he put down his pencil. "Am I keeping you awake?"

"It's just..." Rue paused, swallowed, started again. "Well, I'd like to wash up, that's all. And maybe brush my teeth." *In my own bathroom, thank you. In my own wonderful, crazy, modern world.*

Farley stretched, then brought a large kettle from a cabinet near the stove. "I guess you'll just have to rinse and spit, since the town of Pine River doesn't provide toothbrushes, but I can heat up some wash water for you."

He disappeared through a rear door, returning minutes later with the kettle, which he set on the stove top.

Rue bit her lower lip. It was bad enough that the marshal expected her to bathe in that oversize bird cage he called a cell. How clean could a girl get with two quarts of water?

"This is a clear violation of the Geneva Convention," she said.

Farley looked at her over one sturdy shoulder, shook his head in obvious consternation and went back to his desk. "If you hadn't told me you and Lizzie Fortner were kinfolk, I'd have guessed it anyway. Both of you talk like you're from somewhere a long ways from here."

Rue sagged against the cell door and closed her eyes for a moment. "So far away you couldn't begin to comprehend it, cowboy," she muttered.

Farley's deep voice contained a note of distracted humor. "Since I didn't quite make out what you just said, I'm going to assume it was something kindly," he told her without looking up from those fascinating papers of his.

"Don't you have something waiting for you at home—a dog or a goldfish or something?" Rue asked. She didn't know which she was more desperate for—a little privacy or the simple comfort of ordinary conversation.

The marshal sighed and laid down his nibbed pen. His wooden chair creaked under his weight as he leaned back. "I live alone," he said, sounding beleaguered and a little smug in the bargain.

"Oh." Rue felt a flash of bittersweet relief at this announcement, though she would have given up her trust fund rather than admit the fact. Earlier, she'd experienced a dizzying sense of impact, even though Farley wasn't touching her, and now she was painfully aware of the lean hardness of his frame and the easy masculine grace with which he moved.

It was damn ironic that being around Jeff Wilson had never had this effect on her. Maybe if it had, she would have a couple of kids and a real home by now, in addition to the career she loved.

"You must be pretty ambitious," she blurted out. The sound of heat surging through the water in the kettle filled the quiet room. "Do you often work late?"

Farley put down his pen again and scratched the nape of his neck before emitting an exasperated sigh. "I don't plan on spending my life as a lawman," he replied with a measured politeness that clearly told Rue he wished she'd shut up and let him get on with whatever he was doing. "I've been saving for a ranch ever since I got out of the army. I mean to raise cattle and horses."

At last, Rue thought. Common ground.

"I have a ranch," she announced. "Over in Montana."

"So you said," Farley replied. It was plain enough that, to him, Rue's claim was just another wild story. He got up and crossed the room to test the water he'd been heating. "Guess this is ready," he said.

Rue narrowed her eyes as he came toward the cell, carrying the kettle by its black iron handle, fingers protected from the steam by the same rumpled dish towel he'd used to wipe out the mug earlier.

"I'm not planning to strip down and lather up in front of you, Marshal," she warned, standing back as he unlocked the cell door and came in.

He laughed, and the sound was unexpectedly rich. "That would be quite a show," he said.

Rue wasn't sure she appreciated his amusement. She just glared at him.

Farley set the kettle down in the cell, then went out and locked the door again. He handed Rue a rough towel and a cloth through the bars, then ambled over to collect his hat and canvas duster.

"Good night, Miss Claridge." With that, he blew out the kerosene lantern on his desk, plunging the room into darkness except for the thin beams of moonlight coming in through the few windows.

It was remarkable how lonely and scared Rue felt once he'd closed and locked the front door of the jailhouse. Up until then, she'd have sworn she wanted him to go.

She waited until she was reasonably sure she wouldn't be interrupted before hastily stripping. Shivering there in that cramped little cell, Rue washed in the now-tepid water Farley had brought, then put her clothes back on. After wrapping herself in the Civil War blanket, she lay down on the cot and closed her eyes.

Although Rue fully expected the worst bout of insomnia ever, she fell asleep with all the hesitation of a rock dropping to the bottom of a deep pond. She awakened to a faceful of bright sunlight and the delicious smell and cheerful sizzle of bacon frying.

At first, Rue thought she was home at Ribbon Creek, with her granddaddy cooking breakfast in the ranch house kitchen. Then it all come back to her.

It was 1892 and she was in jail, and even if she managed to get back to her own time, no one was ever, *ever* going to believe her accounts of what had happened to her.

She would definitely write a novel. A movie would inevitably follow. Priscilla Presley could play Rue, and they could probably get Tom Selleck for Farley's role, or maybe Lee Horsely....

Rue rose from the bed and immediately shifted from one foot to the other and back again.

"'Morning," Farley said with a companionable smile. He was standing beside the stove, turning the thick strips of pork in a cast-iron skillet.

"I have to go to the bathroom," Rue told him impatiently. "And don't you dare offer me a chamber pot!"

The marshal's white teeth flashed beneath his manly mustache. Expertly, he took the skillet off the heat, setting it on a trivet atop a nearby bookshelf, then ambled over to face Rue through the bars.

"Don't try anything," he warned, gesturing for Rue to precede him into freedom.

She stepped over the grubby threshold, concentrating on appreciating the sweet luxury of liberty, however brief it might be.

The marshal ushered her outside and around the back of the small building. Behind it was a small, unpainted cabin, and beyond that was an outhouse.

Rue wrinkled her nose at the smell, but she was in no position to be discriminating.

She went inside and, peering through the little moon some facetious soul had carved in the door, saw Farley standing guard a few feet away, arms folded.

When they were back in the jailhouse, he gave her soap and a basin of water to wash in before setting the bacon on to finish cooking. Rue felt a little better after that, though she longed for a shower, a shampoo and clean clothes.

"I suppose you'll be releasing me this morning," she said after Farley had brought her a metal plate containing three perfectly fried slices of bacon, a dry biscuit and an egg so huge, it could have been laid by Big Bird's mother. "After all, if playing poker were a crime, you'd have to arrest Stovepipe and Garters and Quickdraw."

Farley, who was perched on the edge of his desk, consuming his breakfast, laughed. Then he chewed a bite of bacon with such thoroughness that Rue grew impatient.

Finally, he responded. "I reckon you're referring to Harry and Micah and Jim-Roy, and you're partly right. It isn't against the law for *them* to play poker, but Pine River has an ordinance about women entering into unseemly behavior." Farley paused, watching unperturbed as Rue's face turned neon pink with fury. "You not only entered in, Miss Claridge—you set up housekeeping and planted corn."

"That's the most ridiculous thing I've ever heard!" Rue thought about flinging her plate through the bars like a Frisbee and beaning Farley Haynes, but she hadn't finished her breakfast and she was wildly hungry. "It's downright discriminatory!"

Farley went to the stove and speared himself another slab of bacon from the skillet. "Nevertheless," he went on, "I can't ask the good citizens of this town to support you forever."

"If you'd just wire Elisabeth in San Francisco—"

"Nobody's heard from Jon and Lizzie," Farley interrupted. "They were in such a hurry to get started on their honeymoon, they didn't bother to tell anybody where they were going to stay once they got to California. They weren't planning to return until Jon's hand has healed and he's ready to start doctoring again."

Rue finished her breakfast with regret. Although loaded with fat and cholesterol, the food had tasted great. "People have mentioned a little girl. Did they take her with them?"

Farley nodded. "Yes, ma'am. Looks like we'll just have to wait until Jon decides to write a letter to somebody around here. When he left, he wasn't thinking of much of anything besides Lizzie.''

After handing her empty plate through the bars, Rue folded her arms and sighed. "They're really in love, huh?"

The marshal's blue eyes sparkled. "You might say that. Being within twelve feet of those two is like being locked up in a room full of lightning."

Rue took comfort in the idea that this whole nightmare might not have been for nothing. If Bethie was really happy and truly in love with the country doctor she'd married, well, that at least gave the situation some meaning.

"I understand there was a fire and that nobody really knows how Dr. Fortner and his little girl escaped."

Farley stacked his plate and Rue's neatly on the trivet and poured the bacon grease from the frying pan into a crockery jar. "That's right. Of course, what's important is, they're alive. There are a lot of goings-on in this world that don't lend themselves to reasoning out."

"Amen," agreed Rue, thinking of her own experiences.

After fetching a bucket of water from outside, Farley put another kettle on to heat.

"You are going to give back my poker winnings, aren't you?" Rue asked nervously. She needed that money to buy some acceptable clothes and pay for a room. Provided she could find someone willing to rent her one, that is.

Farley took a mean-looking razor from his desk drawer, along with a shaving mug and a brush. "It'd serve you right if I didn't," he said calmly, studying his reflection in a cracked mirror affixed to the wall near the stove. "But I'll turn the money over to you as soon as I decide to let you go."

Rue's temper simmered at his blithely officious attitude, but she held her tongue. It was a technique she usually remembered after a conflagration, not before.

She watched, oddly fascinated, when Farley poured water from the kettle into a basin and splashed his face. Then, after moistening his shaving brush, he turned the bristles in the mug and lathered his beard.

Presently, he began using the straight razor with what seemed to Rue to be extraordinary skill.

The whole process was decidedly masculine, and it had a very curious—and disturbing—effect on Rue. Every graceful motion of his hands, every turn of his head, was like a caress; it was as though Farley were removing her clothes and taking the time to explore each new part of her as he bared it. And that odd feeling that she'd just collided with a solid object was back, too; she gripped the bars tightly to hold herself up.

When Farley gave her a sidelong look and grinned, she felt as though the bones in her pelvis had turned to warm wax.

Rue had spent a lot of time on a ranch, and she'd traveled and met people, read hundreds of books, watched all sorts of movies, so she had a pretty fundamental understanding of what was happening in her body. What she *didn't* comprehend was exactly what it would be like to make love, because that was something she hadn't gotten around to doing quite yet. It wasn't that she was scared or even especially noble—she just hadn't found the right man.

Farley finished shaving, humming a little tune all the while, rinsed his face and dried it with the towel draped around his neck.

The jailhouse door opened, and Rue noticed that Farley's hand flashed with instinctive speed and grace to the handle of the six-gun riding low on his hip.

His fingers relaxed when a big woman dressed in black bombazine entered. Her eyes narrowed in her beefy face when she caught sight of the prisoner. Two other ladies in equally somber dress wedged themselves in behind her.

"Something tells me the Presbyterians have arrived," Rue murmured.

"Worse," Farley whispered. "These ladies head up the Pine River Society for the Protection of Widows and Orphans, and they're really mean."

The trio stared at Rue, their mouths dropping open as they took in her jeans, sneakers and T-shirt.

"Poor misguided soul," one visitor said, raising bent fingers to her mouth in consternation and pity.

"Trousers!" breathed another.

The heavy woman whirled on Farley, and Rue noticed that a muscle twitched under his right eye.

"This is an outrage!" the lady thundered, as though he were somehow to blame for Rue's existence. "Where on earth did she get those dreadful clothes?"

"I can speak for myself," Rue said firmly, and the other two women gasped, evidently at her audacity. "This is called a T-shirt," Rue went on, indicating the garment in question, "and these are jeans. I know none of you are used to seeing a woman dressed the way I am, but the fact is, these clothes are really quite practical, when you think about it."

"Well, I never!" avowed the leader of the pack.

Rue's mouth twitched. "Never what?" she inquired sweetly.

Farley rolled his eyes, but offered no comment. It was plain that, although he wasn't really intimidated by these women, he wasn't anxious to cross them, either.

"Are you a saloon woman?" demanded the leader of the moral invasion. The moment the words were out of her mouth, she drew her lips into a tight line and retreated a step, no doubt concerned that sin might prove contagious.

Rue smiled. "No, Miss— What was your name, please?"

"My name is *Mrs.* Gifford," that good lady snapped.

Holding one hand out through the bars, Rue smiled again, winningly. "I'm very glad to meet you, Mrs. Gifford. My name is Rue Claridge, and I'm definitely not a 'saloon woman.'" She dropped her voice to a confidential whisper. "Just between you and me, I think I'm probably overqualified for that kind of work."

Mrs. Gifford turned away and gathered her bombazine-clad troops into a huddle. While the conference went on, Rue stood biting her lower lip and wondering whether or not Farley would turn her over to these people. She thought she'd rather take her chances with a lynch mob, if given the choice.

Farley scratched the back of his neck and sighed. Judging from his body language, Rue was pretty sure he wanted to let her go and get on with the daily business of being a living, breathing antique.

Finally, Mrs. Gifford approached the cell again. "There will be no more prancing up and down the street in trousers and no more poker playing," she decreed firmly.

Under any other circumstances, Rue would have defended her right to dress and gamble as she liked, but she wasn't about to risk getting herself into still more trouble. For all she knew, *Mr.* Gifford was a judge with the power to lock her away in some grim prison.

"No more poker playing," Rue conceded in a purposely meek voice. "As for the—trousers, I promise I won't wear them any farther than the general store. I mean to go straight over there and buy a dress as soon as the marshal here lets me out of the pokey."

The delegation put their heads together for another consultation. After several minutes, Mrs. Gifford announced, "Rowena will walk down to the mercantile and purchase the dress," she said, indicating one of the other women.

"Great," Rue responded, shifting her gaze to the marshal. "Will you give Rowena fifty cents from my winnings so I can get out of here?" If the Society tried to make her go with them, she'd make a break for it.

Rowena, who was painfully thin, her mousy brown hair pulled back tightly enough to tilt her eyes, swallowed visibly and backed up when Farley held out the money.

"Poker winnings," she said in horror. "My hands will never touch filthy lucre!"

Now it was Rue who rolled her eyes.

"*I'll* get the dress," Farley bit out furiously, grabbing his hat from its peg and putting on his long canvas duster. A moment later, the door slammed behind him.

The church women stared at Rue, as though expecting her to turn into a raven and fly out through the barred window.

Thank God I didn't land in seventeenth-century Salem, Rue thought wryly. *I'd surely be in the stocks by now, or dangling at the end of a rope.*

Basically a gregarious type, Rue couldn't resist another attempt at conversation, even though she knew the effort was probably futile. "So," she said, smiling the way she did when she wanted to put an interviewee at ease, "what do you do with yourselves every day, besides cooking and cleaning and tracking down sinners?"

CHAPTER 4

When Farley returned from his mission to the general store, looking tight jawed and grim, he opened the cell door and handed a wrapped bundle to Rue.

Rue's fiery, defiant gaze swept over Mrs. Gifford and her cronies, as well as the marshal, as she accepted the package. "If you people think I'm going to change clothes with the four of you standing there gawking at me, you're mistaken," she said crisply.

Farley seemed only too happy to leave, although the Society hesitated a few moments before trooping out after him.

If she hadn't been so frazzled, Rue would have laughed out loud at the sheer ugliness of that red-and-white gingham dress. As it happened, she just buttoned herself into the thing, tied the sash at the back and tried with all her might to hold on to her sense of humor.

When the others returned, Farley slid his turquoise gaze over Rue in an assessing fashion, and she thought she saw the corner of his mouth twitch. The ladies, however, were plainly not amused.

"Just let me out of here before I go crazy!" Rue muttered.

Farley unlocked the cell again and stepped back, holding the door wide. In that moment, an odd thought struck Rue: she would miss being in close contact with the marshal.

Their hands brushed as he extended the rest of her poker winnings, and Rue felt as though she'd just thrust a hairpin into a light socket.

"I'll try to stay out of trouble," she said. All of a sudden, her throat felt tight, and she had to force the words past her vocal cords.

Farley grinned, showing those movie-cowboy teeth of his. "You do that," he replied.

Rue swallowed and went around him, shaken. She'd been in an earthquake once, in South America, and the inner sensation had been much like what she was feeling now. It was weird, but then, so was everything else that had happened to her after she crossed that threshold and left the familiar world on the other side.

The Society allowed her to leave the jailhouse without interference, but the looks the women gave her were as cool and disapproving as before. It was plain they expected Rue to go forth in sin.

Once she was outside, under a pastel blue sky laced with white clouds, Rue felt a little stronger and more confident. The air was fresh and bracing, though tinged with the scent of manure from the road. Rue's naturally buoyant spirits rose.

She set out for the house in the country, determined to take another crack at returning to her own time. Not by any stretch of the imagination had she given up on finding Elisabeth and hearing her cousin tell her face-to-face that she was truly happy, but Rue needed time to regroup.

She figured a couple of slices of pepperoni pizza with black olives and extra cheese, followed by a long, hot bath, wouldn't hurt her thinking processes, either.

Soon Rue had left the screeching of the mill saw and the tinny music and raucous laughter of the saloons behind. Every step made her more painfully conscious of the growing distance between her and Farley, and that puzzled her. The lawman definitely wasn't her type, and besides...talk about a generation gap!

When Rue finally reached Aunt Verity's house, she stood at the white picket fence for a few moments, gazing up at the structure.

Even with its fire-scarred side, the place looked innocent, just sitting there in the bright October sunshine. No one would have guessed, by casual observation, that this unassuming

Victorian house was enchanted or bewitched or whatever it was.

Rue drew a deep breath, let it out in a rush and opened the gate. With her other hand, she touched the necklace at her throat and fervently wished to be home.

The gate creaked as she closed it behind her. Rue proceeded boldly up the front walk and knocked at the door.

When the crabby housekeeper didn't answer, Rue simply turned the knob and stepped inside. *Remarkable,* she thought, shaking her head. Bethie and her new husband were off in California and the maid had probably left for the day, and yet the place was unlocked.

"Hello?" Rue inquired with a pleasantry that was at least partially feigned. She didn't like Ellen and would prefer not to encounter her.

There was no answer, no sound except for the loud ticking of a clock somewhere nearby.

Rue raised her voice a little. "Hello! Anybody here?"

Again, no answer.

Rue hoisted the skirts of her horrible gingham dress so she wouldn't break her neck and bounded up the front stairway. In the upper hall, she stood facing the burned door for a moment, then pushed it open and climbed awkwardly out onto a charred beam, praying it would hold her weight.

The antique necklace seemed to burn where it rested against her skin. Clutching the blackened doorjamb in both hands and closing her eyes, Rue whispered, "Let me go home. *Please,* let me go home."

A moment later, she summoned all her courage and thrust herself over the threshold and into the house.

When she felt modern carpeting beneath her fingers, jubilation rushed through Rue's spirit, though there was a thin brushstroke of sorrow, too. She might never see her cousin Elisabeth again.

Or Farley.

Rue scrambled to her feet and gave a shout of delight because she was back in the land of indoor plumbing, fast food and credit cards. Looking down at the red-and-white dress, with its long skirts and puffy sleeves, she realized the gown was tangible proof that she actually had been to 1892. No one else would be convinced, but Rue didn't care about that; it was enough that *she* knew she wasn't losing her mind.

After phoning the one restaurant in Pine River that not only sold but delivered pizza, Rue stripped off the dress, took a luxurious bath and put on khaki slacks and a white sweater. She was blow-drying her hair when the doorbell rang.

Snatching some money off the top of her bureau, Rue hurried downstairs to answer.

The pizza delivery person, a young man with an outstandingly good complexion, was standing on the porch, looking uneasy. Rue smiled, wondering what stories he'd heard about the house.

"Thanks," she said, holding out a bill.

The boy surrendered the pizza, but looked at the money in confusion. "What country is this from?" he asked.

Rue could smell the delicious aromas rising through the box, and she was impatient to be alone with her food. "This one," she replied a little abruptly.

Then Rue's eyes fell on the bill and she realized she'd tried to pay for the pizza with some of her 1892 poker winnings. The mistake had been a natural one; just the other day, she'd left some money on her dresser. Apparently, she'd automatically done the same with these bills.

"I'm a collector," she said, snatching back the bill. "Just a second and I'll get you something a little more...current."

With that, Rue reluctantly left the pizza on the hall table and hurried upstairs. When she returned, she paid the delivery boy with modern currency and a smile.

The young man thanked her and hurried back down the walk and through the front gate to his economy car. He kept glancing back over one shoulder, as though he expected to find that the house had moved a foot closer to the road while he wasn't looking.

Rue smiled and closed the door.

In the kitchen, she consumed two slices of pizza and put

the rest into the refrigerator for later—or earlier. In this house, time had a way of getting turned around.

On one level, Rue felt grindingly tired, as though she could crawl into bed and sleep for two weeks without so much as a quiver of her eyelids. On another, however, she was restless and frustrated.

As a newswoman, Rue especially hated not knowing the whole story. She wanted to find her cousin, and she wanted to uncover the secret of this house. If there was one thing Rue was sure of, it was that the human race lived in a cause-and-effect universe and there was some concrete, measurable reason for the phenomenon she and Elisabeth had experienced.

She found her purse and the keys to her Land Rover and smiled to herself as she carefully locked the front door. Maybe the dead bolt would keep out burglars and vandals, but here all the action tended to be on the *inside*.

Rue drove into town, past the library and the courthouse and the supermarket, marveling. It had only been that morning—and yet, it had *not* been—that the marshal's office and the general store and the Hang-Dog Saloon had stood in their places. The road, rutted and dusty and dappled with manure in Farley's time was now paved and relatively clean.

Only when she reached the churchyard did Rue realize she'd intended to come there all along. She parked by a neatly painted wooden fence and walked past the old-fashioned clapboard church to the cemetery beyond.

The place was a historical monument—there were people buried here who had been born back East in the late seventeen hundreds.

Rue paused briefly by Aunt Verity's headstone, crouching to pull a few weeds, then went on to the oldest section. Almost immediately, she found the Fortner plot, a collection of graves surrounded by a low, iron fence.

She opened the little gate, which creaked on rusty hinges, and stepped inside.

Jonathan Fortner's grave was in the center and beside his stone was another one, marked Elisabeth Fortner. Rue felt tears sting her eyes; maybe Bethie was still alive in that other dimension, but she was long dead in this one. So were her husband and all her children.

After she'd recovered from the shock of standing beside Bethie's grave, Rue studied the other stones. Sons, daughters, sons-in-law and daughters-in-law, even grandchildren, most of whom had lived to adulthood, were buried there. Obviously, Jonathan and Elisabeth's union had been a very fruitful one, and that consoled Rue a little. More than anything else, her cousin had wanted a lot of children.

When Rue turned, she was startled to see a handsome young man crouched by the metal gate, oiling the creaky hinges. He smiled, and something about the expression was jarringly familiar.

"Friend of the family?" he asked pleasantly. Rue had him pegged for the kind of kid who had played the lead in all the high school drama productions and taken the prettiest girl in his class to the prom.

Rue allowed herself a slight smile. "You might say that. And you?"

"Jonathan and Elisabeth Fortner were my great-great-grandparents," he said, rising to his feet. He looked nothing like Bethie, this tall young man with his dark hair and eyes, and yet his words struck a note of truth deep inside Rue.

For a moment, she was completely speechless. It seemed that every time she managed to come to terms with one element of this time-travel business, another aspect presented itself.

Rue summoned up a smile and offered her hand. "I guess you could say Bethie—Elisabeth—was my great-great-cousin. My name is Rue Claridge."

"Michael Blake," he replied, clasping her fingers firmly.

Rue searched her memory, but she couldn't recall Aunt Verity ever mentioning this branch of the family. "Do you live in Pine River, Michael?"

He shook his head and, once again, Rue felt a charge of recognition. "Seattle—I go to the university. I just like to come out here once in a while and—well—I don't know exactly how to explain it. It's like there's this unseen connection and I'm one of the links. I guess this is my way of telling them—and myself—that I haven't broken the chain.''

Rue only nodded; she was thinking of the overwhelming significance a simple decision or random happenstance could have. If Bethie hadn't stumbled into that other dimension or whatever it was, then Michael would probably never have existed. In fact, just a few months before, when Elisabeth had not yet stepped over the threshold to meet and fall in love with her country doctor, there had surely been no Michael Blake. That would explain why Aunt Verity had never talked about him or his family.

On the other hand, Michael had grown to youthful manhood; he had a life, a history. He was as solid and real as anyone she'd ever met.

Rue's head was spinning.

"Are you all right?" Michael asked, firmly taking her elbow and helping her to a nearby bench. "You look pale."

Rue sat down gratefully and rubbed her right temple with a shaking hand. "I'm fine," she said hastily. "Honestly."

"I could get you some water...."

"No," Rue protested. "I'm okay. Really."

Michael brought a small black notebook from his jacket pocket, along with a stub of a pencil. "My grandmother would really like to meet you, since you're a shirttail relation and everything. She lives with my mom and dad in Seattle. Why don't you give her a call sometime?"

Rue grinned at the ease with which he invited a total stranger into the inner circle of the family, but then that was the sort of thing kids did. "Thanks, Michael."

He wedged one hand into the pocket of his jacket, holding the can of spray lubricant in the other. "Well, I guess I'd better be getting back to the city. Nice meeting you."

"Nice meeting you," Rue said hoarsely, looking away. *Did you think about what it means to change history, Bethie?* she thought. *I know I never did.*

Michael had long-since driven away in a small blue sports car when Rue finally rose from the bench and went to stand beside her cousin's grave once again.

"Maybe I should just leave it all alone," she murmured as a shower of gold, crimson and chocolate-colored leaves floated down onto the little plot from the surrounding maple trees. "Maybe it would be better to walk away and pretend I believe the official explanation for your disappearance, Bethie. But I just can't do it. Even though I know I could stir up ripples that might be felt all the way into this century, I have to hear you say, in person, that you want to stay there. I have to look into your eyes and know that you understand your decision."

And I have to see Farley Haynes again.

The stray, ragtag thought trailed in after the others, and Rue immediately evicted it from her mind. For all practical intents and purposes, Farley was just a figment of her imagination, she reminded herself, little more than a character she'd seen in a movie or read about in a book.

The idea left a keen, biting sense of loneliness in its wake, but Rue was determined to accept the fact and get on with her life.

Of course, before she could do that, she had to see Bethie just once more.

Instead of going home, Rue drove into Seattle.

She visited a coin shop first, where she purchased an expensive selection of bills and coins issued between 1880 and 1892. After that, Rue visited a dusty little secondhand store tucked away in an alley behind a delicatessen, and bought herself a graceful ivory gown with tatting on the cuffs and collar, and a waist-length capelet to match. A little searching unearthed a pair of brown, high-button shoes and a parasol.

Rue coughed as the shop's proprietress shook out the ancient garment and prepared to wrap it. "Is this a theatrical costume, or was it a part of a real wardrobe?"

The other woman smiled wistfully. "I suspect this gown came from a camphor trunk in someone's attic, since it's in relatively good condition. If you'll look closely at the handwork, you'll see it's made to last."

"Is it washable?"

"I wouldn't try that. The fabric is terribly old; water or dry-cleaning solution might dissolve the fibers."

Rue nodded, feeling fond of that romantic old relic of a dress already, and hoping she could make it hold together long enough to get back to 1892, have a couple of practical calico dresses made and find Elisabeth. Between her poker winnings and the old currency she'd purchased at the coin shop, Rue figured she'd have enough money to catch a boat or a train to San Francisco, where Elisabeth and Jonathan were supposed to have gone.

As Rue was driving back to Pine River, a light rain began to fall. She found a classical station on the car radio—Rue's musical tastes covered the full range, but on that particular night, Mozart had the greatest appeal.

It truly startled her to realize, just as she reached the outskirts of Pine River, that there were tears on her face.

Rue rarely cried, not because she was in any way above it, but because she'd long ago learned that weeping solved nothing. In fact, it usually just complicated matters.

Nevertheless, her cheeks seemed as wet as the windshield, and her feelings were an odd, explosive tangle. Methodically, she began to separate them.

Meeting Michael Blake had given her a shattering sense of the gossamer threads that link the past with the present and the future. If for some reason Elisabeth changed her mind about staying in 1892 and following through with the new destiny she'd created for herself by making that choice, Michael and a lot of other people would simply be obliterated.

To make matters worse, the problem wouldn't stop with Michael's generation. Whole branches of the family tree that might have lived and loved, laughed and cried, would never come into being at all.

Rue's hands began to tremble so badly that she had to pull over to the side of the road and sit with her forehead resting against the steering wheel.

Finally, after several minutes, she was able to drive on, but she was still crying, and there were more feelings to be faced and dealt with.

Next came the most prickly fact of all, the one Rue could no longer deny: she was lonely. From an emotional standpoint, she sometimes felt as though everyone on the planet had stepped into a parallel dimension. She could see them and hear their voices, but they seemed somehow inaccessible, forever out of reach.

Only her grandfather, Aunt Verity and Elisabeth had been able to reach through the invisible barrier to touch her, and now they were all gone.

Rue sniffled. There was one positive aspect to this experience she and Elisabeth shared, however: it opened the door to all sorts of possibilities. Maybe the philosophers and poets were right and she *would* see her loved ones again someday. Maybe Aunt Verity and Gramps were carrying on happy lives in some other time and place, just as Elisabeth seemed to be.

It was all too mystical for a pragmatic mind like Rue's.

Darkness had fallen by the time she reached home but, as always, the atmosphere of the house was friendly.

After carefully hanging up the dress she'd purchased and setting the high-button shoes side by side on the floor of the armoire, Rue went downstairs and made supper: a grilled cheese sandwich and a cup of microwave soup.

She was too tired and overwrought to think clearly or make further plans. After a warm bath, Rue crawled into bed, read two chapters of a political biography and promptly drifted off to sleep.

In the early hours of the morning, Rue dreamed she was back in Baghdad, at the start of the Gulf War, hiding out in the basement of a hotel with several other news people and trying not to flinch every time a bomb exploded. She forcibly woke herself from the nightmare, but the loud noises continued.

Rue's fingers immediately rushed to the necklace at her throat. Once again, the pendant felt warm, almost hot, to the touch. And the predawn air reverberated with gunshots.

Muttering, Rue tossed back the covers and stumbled through the hallway to the sealed door. Sure enough, it opened when she turned the knob, and now she could hear drunken male laughter and the nervous whinnying of horses on the road, though the thick darkness prevented her from seeing anything.

There was more shooting, and Rue cringed. Obviously, a few of the boys where whooping it up, as they used to say on TV, and that made her furious. Someone could be shot!

She gripped the sooty sides of the doorframe and yelled, "Hey, you guys! Knock it off before you hurt somebody!"

Surprisingly, an immediate silence fell. Rue listened for a moment, smiled and closed the door. True, she had unfinished business in 1892, but she wasn't going to attend to it in her nightgown.

There was no point in trying to go back to sleep, thanks to the James Gang. Rue set up her portable computer at the kitchen table and brewed a cup of herbal tea in the microwave. Then she sat down, her toes hooked behind the rung of her chair, and began tapping out an account of the things that had happened to her. Like Bethie with her letters, Rue felt a fundamental need to record her experiences with an orderly succession of words.

Rue had been writing steadily for over half an hour, and the first thin light was flowing in through the window above the sink, when suddenly the keyboard vanished from beneath her fingertips.

Rue looked up, stunned to see that the room had changed completely. Dr. Fortner's cast-iron cookstove stood near the back door. There was no tile, only rough wood flooring, and the wooden icebox had returned, along with the bulky pump handle and the clunky metal sink.

Just as quickly, the modern kitchen appeared. The computer keyboard materialized in front of Rue, and the sleek appliances stood in their customary places.

Rue swallowed hard, remembering the time she'd been standing in the front parlor, looking into the mirror above the mantel. The room had altered that day, too, and she'd even caught a glimpse of a woman dusting a piano.

These experiences gave new credence to Aunt Verity's hazy theory that the necklace had a mind of its own.

She sat back in her chair, pressing her palms to her cheeks, half expecting to find she had a raging fever. Instead, her face felt cool.

After a few moments spent gathering her composure, Rue got out Elisabeth's letters and read them again, carefully, word by word. Not once did Bethie mention seeing a room change; she'd gone back and forth between the present and the past all right, but only by way of the threshold upstairs.

Clearly, the common denominator was the necklace.

Rue rubbed the antique pendant thoughtfully between her thumb and forefinger. She, unlike her cousin, had twice caught glimpses of that other world while just going about her business. Did that mean the invisible passageway between the two eras was changing, expanding? If that were the case, it might also shrink just as unpredictably, or disappear entirely.

Forever.

Rue sighed and shoved splayed fingers through her hair, then began pounding at the keys of her computer again, rushing to record everything. She had always believed that reality was a solid, measurable thing, but there was something going on in and around the house that superceded all the normal rules.

There were no more incidents that day, and Rue spent the time resting and making preparations to return to old-time Pine River. She carefully aired and pressed the fragile dress she'd bought, watched a few soap operas and made herself a tuna sandwich for lunch.

Then on a foray into the dusty attic, she found one of Aunt Verity's many caches of unique jewelry and helped herself to a brooch and set of tarnished, sterling combs.

Later, in her bedroom, she put on the dress and sat at the vanity table, putting her hair up and learning to use the combs strategically. When she'd mastered the technique, Rue sat looking at her reflection for a long time, liking the wistful, romantic image she made.

The faintly musty scent of the fabric was a subtle reminder, however, that she and the garment belonged to two distinctly different times.

Carefully, Rue unpinned her hair, took off the dress and got back into her jeans and sweatshirt. She felt a strong draw to 1892, but she wasn't quite ready to go back. She needed to gather all her internal forces and make this trip count.

Just to make certain there wouldn't be any unscheduled visits to the Outer Limits, Rue unclasped the necklace and carefully placed it inside an alabaster box on the vanity. She wondered briefly if the pendant was capable of slipping back and forth between then and now all on its own.

That concept caused Rue a case of keen, if momentary, panic. She reached for the necklace, drew back her hand, reached again. Finally, she turned purposefully and walked away, determined not to be held hostage by a chunk of antique gold on a chain.

The pull of the necklace was strong, though, and Rue had to leave the house to keep away from it.

She decided to call on the Buzbee sisters, the two spinsters who lived on the other side of the road, and find out if they could shed any light on the situation.

Roberta Buzbee, a plain and angular woman, greeted Rue at the door. She seemed pleased to have company and, after explaining that her sister was "indisposed," invited Rue in for tea.

They sat in the front parlor before a blazing applewood fire. It was a cozy room, except for the shrunken head prominently displayed on top of the piano. Rue didn't ask how the sisters had come to acquire the memento because she was pretty sure Miss Roberta would tell her. In detail.

"Have there been any developments in the search for your cousin Elisabeth?" Miss Roberta asked. The sisters had been among the first people Rue had spoken with when she'd arrived in Pine River and begun to look for Bethie, and she knew they'd never bought the official theories.

Rue shrugged and avoided the older woman's gaze for a moment, wishing she dared admit the truth. The situation was simply too delicate. "I'm going to find her," she said, and all the considerable certainty she possessed was contained in those words. "No matter what it takes, no matter what I have to do, I'm going to see Bethie and make sure she's okay."

Miss Roberta nodded primly and took a graceful sip of her tea.

Rue cleared her throat softly and began again. "Miss Roberta, have other people disappeared from that house? Temporarily or permanently?"

The other woman looked distinctly uncomfortable. "Not just that. People have *appeared,* too," she confided. "Folks in old-timey clothes, mostly."

This was new to Rue; she scooted to the edge of her chair. "Like who?" she asked, wide-eyed.

"Well, there was a woman—never liked her. Verity took her under her wing, though, and she finally left town. Once in a while, Sister and I catch sight of a buggy that comes along and turns in at your driveway. And there's another woman who can be seen hanging out clothes on a fine spring morning."

Ellen, Rue thought. Lizzie's housekeeper. "Ghosts?" Rue asked, to keep the spinster talking.

Miss Roberta clucked her tongue. "Oh, my, no. There aren't any such things—just places where the curtain between our time and theirs has worn a little thin, that's all. Time's all of a piece, Sister and I believe, like a big tapestry. Would you like some lemon cookies? I just baked them this morning."

Rue loved homemade sweets, no matter how agitated her state of mind might be, and she eagerly agreed.

While her hostess was in the kitchen, though, Rue was restless. She picked up a small book that was lying on the coffee table—the title, *My Life in Old Pine River,* suggested the subject was local history. She began thumbing through page after page of old pictures in the center of the book.

Rue's heart twisted when she came across a photograph of Elisabeth standing with the townsfolk in front of a new-looking covered bridge, a slight and mysterious smile curving her lips.

CHAPTER 5

Seeing an impossibly old photograph of Elisabeth left Rue shaken. Even though she knew from personal experience that time travel was possible, the mysteries of it all still boggled her mind.

"Is something wrong, dear?" Miss Roberta asked as she appeared in the doorway with the promised cookies. "You look as though you wouldn't trust your knees to hold you up."

Rue sighed and rubbed her temple. "This picture..."

Miss Roberta put the platter of cookies down on the coffee table and bent to look at the book in Rue's lap.

Even as she acted, Rue knew discretion would have been a better course than valor, but she was tired of being the only one who knew. She needed the understanding and support of another human being.

She tapped the page lightly with an index finger, and when she spoke, her voice was thready and hoarse. "This woman, standing here by the bridge...this is Elisabeth."

The spinster perched gracefully on the arm of the sofa, took the volume from Rue and raised it for a closer view. "My land, that does *look* like Elisabeth. I've been through this book a thousand times.... This little girl sitting on the big rock by the stream grew up to be our mother...but I swear I've never noticed this woman. Well, well, well. What do you make of that?"

"What, indeed?" Rue murmured, longing to take an aspirin.

Miss Roberta was pensive. "Maybe she was an ancestor of

yours. That would account for the resemblance. What I can't understand is how something so obvious could have escaped my attention.''

Rue accepted the book when it was offered and scrutinized the picture again. The woman standing in that crowd was definitely Elisabeth herself, not just someone who resembled her, and the handsome, dark-haired man at her side was probably Jonathan Fortner.

Rue smiled, though she could just as easily have cried, so fragile were her emotions. Elisabeth and Jonathan looked right together.

"Next thing you know," Miss Roberta said irritably, "we'll be appearing on *Unsolved Mysteries,* the whole lot of us. We'll have our pictures on the front of those dreadful newspapers they sell at the supermarket, and all because of that troublesome old house of Verity's."

Lowering her head for a moment to hide her smile, Rue nodded. She suspected the neighbor woman secretly hoped an explosion of notoriety would thrust the boundaries of Pine River outward, thus bringing some excitement to an otherwise humdrum town.

Rue ate a cookie and finished her tea, but only to be polite. Now that she'd seen the photograph of Elisabeth, she was more anxious than ever to make contact with her cousin. Bethie looked happy in that old picture, but that didn't mean she wasn't in over her head in some way. After all, during her marriage to Ian McCartney, Elisabeth had put a brave face on things, but she'd also been miserable for the duration.

Dr. Fortner looked like a hard-headed, autocratic type, though there was no denying he was a formidable hunk, and the male sex had virtually ruled the world in the nineteenth century. Maybe the good doctor was dominating Elisabeth in some way, forcing her to stay when she really wanted to come back to her own time.

Just the idea made Rue's blood simmer. Nobody, but *nobody* was allowed to mistreat Elisabeth.

When she could leave without seeming hasty, Rue thanked Miss Roberta for the cookies and tea, and set out for the other side of the road. By that time, it was already getting dark, and a crisp autumn wind was stirring the flame-colored trees.

Reaching the house, Rue built a fire and then carefully assembled all the items she'd purchased for her journey back to 1892—the dress, the brown high-button shoes, the musty, fragile old money, the silver combs.

Since she hadn't bought stockings, Rue made a concession and wore panty hose. She put on a bra, too, because there were certain comforts she just wasn't willing to sacrifice, even for the sake of authenticity. Besides, nobody in 1892 was going to get a look at her underwear, anyway.

Once she'd donned the dress—she had to suck in her stomach and fasten the buttons in front, then turn the gown around again and put her hands through the armholes—Rue did up her hair. Then, reluctantly, wishing she could wear her sneakers as she had before, she slipped her feet into the pinchy-toed shoes.

She folded the money she'd bought in the coin shop, along with the funds she'd won in the poker game, and tucked the bundle securely into her bodice. The hated red-and-white gingham dress was carefully folded into a neon pink designer sports bag, along with a toothbrush and toothpaste, a paperback book, a bottle of aspirin and some snack-size candy bars.

Once she was seated at the kitchen table, the bag perched on her lap, Rue put on the necklace and waited. A sense of urgent excitement buzzed in her stomach, and she was certain something was about to happen.

Rue sat waiting for so long that she finally unzipped the bag and brought out the novel. She was halfway through chapter two when suddenly the necklace started to vibrate subtly and the light changed, dimming until she could barely see.

The first thing Rue was aware of after that was an incredibly bad smell. The second was the moon shape cut out of the crude wooden door in front of her.

Realizing she'd landed in somebody's outhouse, Rue bolted to her feet, sending the book and the sports bag tumbling to the floor. "*Yuk,*" she grumbled, snatching up her belongings again and then turning the loosely nailed piece of wood that served as a primitive lock and bolting out into the sunlight.

An elderly cowboy touched his hat and smiled at her, and the gaps between his teeth made Rue think of a string of Christmas-tree lights with some of the bulbs burned out. "No hurry, ma'am," he said. "I can wait."

Rue's face throbbed with the heat of embarrassment. It was disconcerting enough to be flung back and forth between two different centuries. Landing helter-skelter in somebody's privy was adding insult to injury.

She hurried past a line of laundry flapping in the breeze, not recognizing the house in front of her or the ones on either side, possessed by an entirely new fear. Maybe she wasn't in 1892, or even in Pine River, for that matter.

Rue's hand tightened on the handle of her bag. Reaching a side gate in the white picket fence, she opened it and stepped out onto a wooden sidewalk. She glanced wildly up and down the street, looking for anything familiar.

She swayed slightly, so great was her relief when she saw Farley come out of a saloon and amble toward her, holding his rifle casually in one hand. With his free hand, he pushed his hat back a notch, and the sigh he gave was one of exasperation.

"You're back," he said.

Rue wrinkled her nose. "How long was I gone?"

Farley's marvelous turquoise eyes narrowed as he studied her. "How long were you...what the sam hill are you talking about?"

"An hour?" Rue shrugged and smiled charmingly, pleased that she was confusing Marshal Haynes. He deserved it for being so arrogant. "Two hours? A week?"

"I haven't seen you in about four days." He frowned, and his expression was pensive now. "I figured you'd gone back to your folks or something."

Rue wanted to ask if he'd missed her, but she couldn't quite bring herself to take the risk. "I've been...around," she said, holding out the skirts of the gown she'd bought especially for this trip. "Like my dress?"

Farley wasn't looking at her outfit, however. He was staring at the blindlingly pink bag she was carrying. "That's the damnedest colored satchel I've ever seen," he muttered, reaching out to touch the material. "Where did you get that?"

"Nordstrom," Rue answered with a slight grin. "It's a store in Seattle." Obviously, she couldn't go into much more detail. As it was, if Farley went looking for the place in the Seattle *he* knew, he'd never find it.

"Where are you staying?" he asked suspiciously.

Much as Rue enjoyed Farley's company, she had no desire to do another stretch in his jail. She looked around, biting her lip, and fortunately caught sight of a sign swinging from the lowest branch of an elm tree in a yard down the street. "There," she said. "At Mrs. Fielding's Rooming House."

Farley sighed again. "That's interesting," he commented at some length, "because Geneva Fielding only takes in gentleman boarders, as a rule."

Rue bit her lower lip. "Okay, so I lied," she blurted out in a furious whisper. "If I'd told you the truth, you wouldn't have believed me. I don't *have* a place to stay, since you won't let me set foot inside Elisabeth's house, but you don't need to worry. I'm not going to loiter or anything. I plan to buy a ticket on the next stagecoach out of town."

The marshal raised one eyebrow. "That so? There won't be one leaving for nearly a week."

"Damn!" Rue ground out. If it weren't for the inconvenience this news was bound to cause her, she would have laughed at the expression of shock on Farley's face. She set the bag on the sidewalk and placed her hands on her hips. "Now I suppose you're going to say it's illegal for a lady to swear and I'm under arrest!"

One corner of Farley's mouth twitched almost imperceptibly. "It's true enough that a lady can't cuss on the street and still be within the law. Thing is, I'm not sure whether that ordinance could cover *you* or not."

Rue opened her mouth, closed it again. As a child, she'd been a tomboy, and as an adult, she'd thought more in terms of being a woman than a lady. It hurt that Farley wasn't sure how to classify her.

He allowed her a smile so brief it might have been nothing more than a mirage, then took her elbow in his free hand. "Miss Ella Sinclair takes in roomers now and again. Do you still have that poker money you won the other night?"

It was a moment before Rue could speak, since a series of small shocks was still jolting through her system from the place where Farley was touching her. "Ah...er...yes, I have a little money." She swallowed hard, awed at the cataclysmic shifts taking place in the deepest, most private passages of her spirit. Farley began to walk purposefully onward, and Rue hurried to keep up. "I've got to be careful, though, because I don't know how much I'll need for train fare to San Francisco."

"It'll cost you about seventy-five cents to go from here to Seattle by stage. As for the train ticket, that'll be considerably more."

Mentally, Rue was counting the currency tucked into her bodice, but she kept having to start over because of the distracting sensations Farley's grip on her elbow was causing. She figured she probably had enough money for the trip, provided she skimped on meals and didn't run into any emergencies.

"Is there a place around here where a woman can get a job?" she asked. Farley stopped in front of a narrow blue house with a white weather vane on the roof.

His look was one of wry annoyance as he cocked his thumb back toward the main part of town. "Sure. They're always looking for dancing girls at the Hang-Dog Saloon."

"Very funny," Rue whispered, stepping away from him. "I'll have you know that I'm a trained journalist, with a college education...."

Farley grinned. He plainly knew full well that what he was going to say would infuriate Rue, and so did she...long moments before he actually spoke. "I guess that's where your kinfolks went wrong. Sending you to college, I mean. That's probably how you got all those muddleheaded ideas you're always spouting.''

After telling herself silently that it would be immature to stomp on the man's instep, Rue managed to reply in a relatively moderate tone of voice. ''It would serve you right if I told you *exactly* where I got all my 'crazy ideas,' Mr. Haynes. However, since you'd almost certainly be too boneheaded to absorb the information, I won't bother.'' She opened the gate latch. ''Goodbye.''

Farley was right beside Rue as she strode up the flagstone walk. ''You'll need me to vouch for you,'' he said, his eyes laughing at her even though his sensual mouth was somber. ''Even that might not be enough, given the reputation you've made for yourself in this town by wearing pants, playing poker and getting yourself thrown into jail.''

Before Rue could answer, the front door of the house swung open and a woman appeared. She was tall, with blue eyes and thin, blond hair, and she wore a paisley shawl pulled tightly around her shoulders. Her smile was tremulous and hopeful—and it was entirely for Farley.

A laughable stab of jealousy knifed through Rue, but she didn't feel at all amused.

Farley touched his hat brim in a courtly way. ''Miss Ella, this is...er...a friend of mine. Miss Rue Claridge.'' Rue didn't miss the fact that he'd remembered her last name, though she had no idea what conclusions to draw from the discovery. ''She needs a place to stay, just until the stage pulls out on Tuesday.''

Miss Ella folded her arms and assessed Rue with disapproving eyes, and her nostrils flared slightly in rebellion. ''I'm sorry, Farley.'' Her voice was irritatingly shrill. ''I don't have a single room left.''

''Then I guess she'll just have to stay at my place,'' Farley said, resigned. With that, he took hold of Rue's elbow again and propelled her back toward the gate.

Miss Ella took only a few moments to weigh the implications of that. The hard leather heels of her shoes clicked purposefully against the floorboards of the porch as she hurried after Farley and Rue. "Wait!" she warbled. "There is Mama's old sewing room.... It's just a matter of moving out a few trunks and the like."

Rue smiled to herself, though in some ways she'd found the idea of being Farley's houseguest appealing.

Farley winked at her, causing Rue's heart to go into arrest for at least five beats, before turning to look back at Miss Ella. "That's very kind of you," he said cordially.

For the first time, it occurred to Rue that Farley Haynes was a well-spoken man, for a small-town, nineteenth-century marshal. Silly questions boiled up in her heart and rose into her mind like vapor, and Rue was grateful that he'd be going on about his business soon. Hopefully before she made a complete fool of herself.

Sure enough, he escorted the ladies only as far as the porch, then tugged at his hat brim, muttered a polite farewell and left.

Rue felt as though she'd been abandoned on a distant planet.

The look in Miss Ella's eyes was not a friendly one as the woman opened the front door and swept into the thin, blue house.

Rue followed, lugging her pink bag. By that time, sleeping in somebody's barn sounded a shade more inviting than rooming with Miss Ella Sinclair.

"That'll be one dollar in advance," the spinster said, holding out one hand, palm up.

Pulling her money from her bodice embarrassed Rue, but she did it defiantly all the same, to let the landlady know she wasn't intimidated. "Here," she said, peeling off a bill.

"Thank you," Miss Ella replied crisply. "I'll just go and ready up that room I mentioned." With that, she swept off, leaving Rue standing awkwardly in the front parlor, still holding her bag.

The landlady returned in a surprisingly short time for someone who'd allegedly had to move trunks out of a sewing room. Of course, Rue knew there had never been a shortage of beds in this house in the first place; Miss Sinclair was smitten with Farley, and she didn't want him taking in a female boarder.

Rue's quarters turned out to be a closet-size room wedged underneath the stairway. There was very little light and even less air. Someone had made a disastrous attempt at decoration, papering the place with hideous red cabbage roses against a pea green background. It looked as though a child had stood on the threshold and pitched overripe tomatoes at the walls.

"Dinner is at seven," Miss Ella announced. "Please be prompt, because Papa is always ravenous when he returns from a day at the bank."

Rue nodded and set her bag on the foot of the narrow cot she'd be sleeping on every night until the stagecoach came through and she could be off to Seattle. It hardly looked more comfortable than the bed in Pine River's solitary jail cell.

"Thank you." Rue rushed on without thinking, and the instant the question was out of her mouth, she regretted it. "Where's the bathroom?"

"There's a chamber pot underneath the bed," the landlady answered with a puzzled frown. "And as for bathing, well, each boarder is assigned one particular night when he can bathe in the kitchen. Yours will be..." She paused, tapping her mouth with one finger as she considered. "Thursday."

Rue sat down on the edge of the cot with a forlorn sigh. She didn't mind being in the wrong century, she didn't even mind boarding in a house where she wasn't wanted, but not being able to take a shower every day was practically unbearable.

Miss Ella waggled her fingers in farewell and went out, closing the squeaky door behind her.

Rue got out her paperback book, stretched out on the lumpy cot and sighed. She'd stayed in worse places, though most of them had been in third-world countries.

Somewhere between chapters four and five, Rue dozed off. When she awakened, she had a headache and cramps in all her muscles, and she was clutching her sports bag like some pitiful orphan abandoned at Ellis Island.

Since crying wasn't a workable method of operation, she

got up, poured tepid water from a chipped pitcher into a mismatched bowl and splashed her face. After that, she opened the window a crack and took a few deep breaths.

Soon Rue was feeling better. She ferreted out the supply of candy bars tucked away in her bag and ate a single piece, then decided to brave Miss Sinclair's parlor. She would borrow a cloak, if she could, and go out for a walk before dinner.

The landlady was nowhere to be found, as it happened, but a young woman who introduced herself as Miss Alice McCall volunteered a long woolen cape. Gratefully, Rue wrapped herself against the evening chill and went out.

There were no streetlights in this incarnation of Pine River, and certainly no neon signs. The blue-gray color of television screens didn't flicker beyond the windows, but oil lanterns sent out a wavering glow.

A crushing wave of loneliness washed over Rue, a bruising awareness that the lights behind those thick panes of glass didn't shine for her.

She was a stranger here.

In the center of town, the golden glimmer of lamps spiced with bawdy piano tunes spilled out of the saloon windows into the streets. Rue was drawn not by the drinking and the ugliness, but by the light and music.

The sudden flare of a match startled her, and she jumped. Farley was leaning against the outer wall of the feed and grain, his trusty rifle beside him, smoking a thin brown cigar.

"Looking for a poker game?" he inquired dryly.

Rue tossed her head to let him know just how much contempt she had for his question, then gestured toward the cigar. "Those things will kill you," she said. She didn't really expect to turn Farley from his wicked ways; she just wanted to make conversation for a few minutes.

He chuckled and shook his head. "You have an opinion on just about everything, it seems to me."

Rue sighed. It wasn't the first time someone had called her opinionated, and it probably wouldn't be the last. "There are worse things," she said, drawing her borrowed cloak more tightly around her. She hoped she would catch up with Elisabeth before too long, because she didn't have the clothes for cold weather.

"I can't deny that," Farley confessed good-naturedly. He started walking along the board sidewalk, and Rue just naturally strolled along beside him.

"Miss Sinclair is—what did you people call it?—oh, yes. She's sweet on you, Marshal. She's set her cap for you."

Now it was Farley who sighed. "Umm," he said.

"Typical male answer," Rue replied briskly. "Who are you, Farley? Where did you go to school?"

His boots made a rhythmic and somehow comforting sound on the wooden walk as he moved along, keeping a thoughtful silence. Finally, he countered, "Why do you want to know?"

"I'm just curious," Rue said. They'd reached the end of the main street, and Farley crossed the road and started back the other way, the ever-present rifle in his hand. "You're educated, and that isn't all that common in the old...in the West."

Farley laughed, and the sound was low and rich. The smell of his cigar was faint and somehow a comfort in the strangeness of that time and place. "My pa was a hard-scrabble farmer in Kansas," he said, "and my ma never got beyond the fourth grade in school, but she loved books, and she taught me to read from the Bible and the *Farmer's Almanac*. Once in Texas, I herded cattle for a man who must have had two hundred books in his house, and he let me borrow as many as I could carry." Farley paused, smiling as he remembered. "I stayed on with that outfit for three years, even though the money wasn't for spit, and I read every damn one of those books."

Rue felt a swell of admiration, along with the usual jangling this man always caused in her nervous system. And she wished she could take him by the hand and show him the library her grandfather had built up on the ranch in Montana. "Awesome," she said.

"Awesome," Farley echoed. They were passing one of the saloons, and he glanced in over the swinging doors, apparently just making sure all was well with the warm-beer set. "I've never heard that word used that way."

Rue smiled. "Kids say 'awesome' in...Seattle." It was true enough. They just weren't saying it *yet.* "I'm impressed, Farley. That you've read so many books, I mean."

"If you ever want to borrow any," he said with an endearing combination of modesty and shyness Rue had never dreamed he was capable of, "just let me know. I've got some good ones."

They had reached the residential part of town, and Rue knew seven o'clock must be getting close. "Thanks," she said, lightly touching Farley's arm. "I might do that."

The instant her fingers made contact with the hard muscles of his forearm, Rue knew she'd made a mistake. The ground seemed to tremble beneath her feet, and she felt more than slightly dizzy.

When Farley leaned his rifle against a building and gripped the sides of her waist to steady her, the whole situation immediately got worse. He gave a strangled groan and bent his head to kiss her.

His tongue touched either side of her mouth, then the seam between her lips. She opened to him as she had never done for another man, and he took full advantage of her surrender.

Much to Rue's chagrin, it was Farley who finally broke away. He gripped her shoulders and held her at a distance, breathing hard and muttering an occasional curse word.

"I'll see you back to the Sinclair place," he said after a long time.

Rue was shaken and achy, wanting the marshal of Pine River as she had never in her life wanted a man before. "Farley, what's wrong?" she asked miserably.

He took her elbow and started hustling her along the walk. "Nothing. You're leaving for Seattle on Tuesday and I'm staying here to start a ranch. Let's remember that."

For the first time, Rue fully understood how Elisabeth could care enough about a man to give up every comfort and convenience of the twentieth century. Her own attraction to Farley Haynes had just reached a frightening pitch.

She swallowed. "I guess you'll marry someone like Miss Sinclair, once you're ready to settle down. A man out here needs a wife."

Farley didn't look at her. "I guess so," he said, and his voice sounded gruff. They'd reached the Sinclair's front gate, and he reached down to unfasten the latch. "In the future, Miss Claridge," he said tightly, "it might be a good idea if you didn't go out walking after dark. It's not safe or proper, and the good people of the town don't set much store by it."

Rue was riding an internal roller coaster, had been ever since Farley had kissed her, and she'd exhausted her supply of sensible remarks. "Good night," she said, turning and rushing toward the house.

The Sinclairs and their boarders were just sitting down to supper, and Rue joined them only because she was famished. This was one night when she would definitely have preferred room service.

"What do you do, Miss Claridge?" the head of the household asked pleasantly. He was a tall, heavy man with slate gray hair and a rather bulbous red nose. "For a living, I mean?"

His daughter smiled slyly and lowered her eyes, obviously certain that the new boarder was about to make a fool of herself.

"I'm an heiress," Rue said. The statement was true; it was just that her money was in another dimension, stamped with dates that would be nothing but science fiction to these people. "My family has a ranch in Montana."

"What brings you to Pine River, Miss Claridge?" asked the young woman who had loaned Rue her cloak earlier.

"I came to see my cousin, Elisabeth Fortner."

Mr. Sinclair put down his fork, frowning, but his daughter did not look at all surprised. Of course, Rue would have been the subject of much female conjecture in the dull little town.

"Jonathan's wife?" Mr. Sinclair inquired, frowning heavily. "The woman we tried for murder?"

"Yes," Rue answered. "The woman you tried...and acquitted."

Pointing out Elisabeth's innocence of any crime didn't seem to lighten the mood at the table. It was as though being accused had been enough to taint not only Bethie, but all who came before and all who could come after.

Once again, Rue wondered how happy her cousin could expect to be in this town. Probably the memory of Elisabeth McCartney Fortner's murder trial would live on long after Bethie herself was gone, and time would undoubtedly alter the verdict.

"More chicken and dumplings, Miss Claridge?" cooed Miss Sinclair with particular malice.

Rue's stomach had suddenly closed itself off, refusing to accept so much as one more forkful of food. "No, thank you," she said. Then she excused herself from the table, carried her dishes into the kitchen and took refuge in her room under the stairway.

After making a reluctant trip to the privy behind the house—Rue refused to use the chamber pot under any circumstances—she washed and brushed her teeth, then climbed into bed. There was one lamp burning on the bedside stand, but the oil was so low that reading was out of the question.

Rue turned down the wick until the room was in darkness, then lay back on her pillow, thinking about Farley and the way she'd felt when he kissed her. She raised one hand to her chest, amazed at the way her heart was pounding against her breastbone, and that was when she made the frightful discovery.

The necklace was gone.

Rue bounded out of bed, lit the lamp and tore through her sheets and blankets in a panic. There was no sign of the necklace.

Only too aware that she would be trapped in this backward century if she didn't find the antique pendant, she sank to her knees and went over every inch of the floor.

Rue was rifling through her sports bag when the last of the lamp oil gave out and the tiny room went dark. For a long moment, she just knelt there on the splintery wood, breathing hard and fighting a compulsion to scream hysterically.

Finally, reason prevailed. She couldn't retrace her steps through town until morning. Flashlights hadn't been invented yet and, besides, if Farley caught her out prowling the sidewalks at that hour, he'd probably toss her back in jail just on general principle.

Lying very still, Rue forced herself to concentrate on her breathing until she was calmer. Soon her heartbeat had slowed to its regular rate and the urge to rush wildly around Pine River upending things in search of the missing necklace had abated slightly. For all her self-control, Rue didn't manage to sleep that night.

Finally the sun peeked over the blue-green, timber-carpeted hills, and Rue bolted out of her room like a rubber-tipped dart shot from a popgun. She'd long since washed, dressed and brushed her teeth.

She went over every step she'd taken the day before, hoping to find the necklace wedged between one of the boards in the sidewalk or lying beside the Sinclairs' gate or on the path to the privy. After a full morning of searching, however, Rue still had no necklace, and she was pretty forlorn.

In a last-ditch effort, she made her way to Farley's office. The front door was propped open with a rusty coffee can filled with ordinary speckled rocks.

"Hello?" Rue called, peering around the frame.

Farley was just hanging his hat on its customary peg, and a large, rumpled-looking man was snoring away on the cot in the cell.

When Farley smiled in recognition, Rue felt as if two of the floorboards had suddenly switched places beneath her feet. "Good day, Miss Claridge," the marshal said.

He acted as though he hadn't kissed her the night before, and Rue decided to go along with the pretense.

She stepped into the room reluctantly, torn between approaching the marshal and bolting down the sidewalk in utter terror. Rue hadn't felt this awkward around a guy since junior high. "I wonder if you would mind checking your lost-and-found department for my necklace," she said, sounding as prim as Miss Ella Sinclair or one of the Society.

Farley's dark eyebrows knit together for a moment, then he went to the stove and reached for the handle of the coffeepot. "We've never seen the need for a lost-and-found department here in Pine River," he said with a good-natured patience that nonetheless rankled. "Folks pretty much know what belongs to them and what doesn't."

Rue sagged a little. "Then no one has reported finding a gold necklace?"

Farley studied her sympathetically and shook his head. "Coffee?"

Rue had never been a frail woman, but these were stressful circumstances, and she knew a dose of Farley's high-octane brew would probably turn her stomach inside out. "No, thanks," she said distractedly. "Did you know it's been proven that caffeine aggravates P.M.S.?"

"What aggravates what?"

"Never mind." Rue turned to go, muttering. "I've got to find that necklace...."

There was nowhere else to look, however, so Rue returned to the Sinclair house. The place was empty and, since she'd probably missed lunch, Rue headed for her room. As she was opening the door, a distraught, feminine moan drifted down the stairway.

Holding the skirts of her secondhand dress, Rue swept around the newel post and up the stairs. The sound was coming from beneath the first door on the right. She knocked lightly. "Hello? Are you all right in there?"

"Yes." The answer was a fitful groan.

Rue opened the door a crack and saw Alice McCall lying on a narrow bed in her chemise. A crude hot-water bottle lay on the lower part of her stomach.

"Cramps?" Rue inquired.

"It's the curse," Alice replied, whispering the words as though confessing to some great sin.

Remembering the aspirin in her bag, Rue said, "I think I can help you. I'll be right back." She raced downstairs to her room to fetch the miracle drug she'd brought from her own century and then, after pausing in the kitchen to battle the pump for a glass of water, returned to Alice's room.

The poor girl was pale as death, and her wispy, reddish blond hair was limp with perspiration.

She looked at the pair of white tablets in Rue's palm and squinted. "Pills?"

"They're magic," Rue promised with a teasing lilt to her voice. Aspirin would probably work wonders for someone who had never taken it before. "Just swallow them and you'll see."

Alice hesitated only a moment. Then she took the tablets and washed them down, one by one, with delicate sips of water.

"Would you like me to fix you a cup of tea?" Rue asked.

"You're very kind, but, no," Alice responded, her face still pinched with pain. It would be a while before the aspirin worked.

Rue sat down at the foot of the bed, since there was no chair, and took in the small, tidy room at a glance. Although

Alice's bedroom had a window and the wallpaper was actually tasteful, the place was as sparsely furnished as a monk's cell. Two dresses hung on pegs on the wall, one for everyday and one for Sundays and special occasions. Over the bureau, with its four shallow drawers, was a mirror made of watery greenish glass. A rickety washstand held the requisite pitcher and bowl.

Above the bed was a calendar, clearly marked 1892, with a maudlin picture of two scantily clad children huddling close in a blizzard. The month of October was on display, and the twenty-third was circled in a wreath of pencil lines.

"Is your birthday coming up?" Rue asked, knowing Alice had seen her glance at the calendar.

Alice smiled wanly. "No. That's the day of the Fall Dance at the schoolhouse."

Rue wondered if Alice, like Miss Ella Sinclair, was sweet on Marshal Haynes. The idea took a little of the sparkle off her charitable mood. "Are you hoping to dance with anybody special?"

Color was beginning to return to Alice's cheeks, though Rue couldn't be sure whether that was due to the aspirin or the prospect of spending time with that special someone. "Jeffrey Hollis," she confided. "He works at the mill."

"Are the two of you dating?"

Alice looked puzzled. "Dating?"

"Courting," Rue corrected herself.

Alice laughed softly. "*I* am definitely courting Jeffrey," she replied, "but I think somebody will have to tell him that he's supposed to be courting me in return." She lay back on the pillow, her lashes fluttering against her cheeks, and then, without further adieu, she floated off to sleep.

Rue covered her newfound friend with a plaid woolen blanket and sneaked out of the room. Back in her own quarters, she ate another candy bar, read two more chapters of her book, and closed her eyes to meditate on the problem of the lost necklace.

Mentally, she retraced every step she'd taken the day before, from the moment she'd found herself in a stranger's privy until she lay down in bed and realized the pendant was gone. And again the chilling thought came to her that that weird, spooky piece of jewelry might have taken to traveling through time all on its own.

Rue squeezed her eyes shut and dragged in a series of slow, deep breaths in an effort to keep her cool, all the while feeling like a one-woman riot.

If she got stuck in this place, she vowed silently, she would pay Elisabeth back by moving into her house like a poor relation. She would stay for fifty years and consciously work at getting more eccentric with every passing day.

Rue brought herself up short. She refused to worry about the future or about the missing necklace. It was time to stop thinking about problems and start looking for solutions.

The first order of business was to find Elisabeth. Once she'd done that, once she knew for a fact that her cousin really wanted to stay in the Victorian era, she could worry about getting home. Or about making a life for herself right there in old Pine River.

With Farley.

She imagined cooking for him, pressing his shirts, washing his back.

The images stirred hormones Rue hadn't even known she had, and a schoolgirl flush rolled from her toes to the roots of her hair in a single crimson wave.

Good grief! she thought, bolting upright on the cot. *Cooking? Ironing?* Washing his back? *What's happening to me? I'm regressing at warp speed!*

Rue sighed and rose from the bed. Lying around in her room in the middle of the day was a waste of daylight. She would check on Alice, then go out and retrace her steps again. Maybe she would find the necklace, or maybe some earth-shaking idea would come to her.

Miss McCall was still sleeping, and some of the color had returned to her cheeks, so Rue knew the aspirin was doing its work. She closed the door of Alice's room carefully and turned toward the front stairway.

Mr. Sinclair was standing there, barring her way, a worrisome smile on his face. He was a portly man, with gray hair, shrewd brown eyes, florid cheeks and a somewhat bulbous nose.

"Miss Claridge," he said, as though Rue might have forgotten her name and he was generous enough to enlighten her.

Rue retreated a step, feeling uneasy. She'd seen that look in a man's eyes many times during her travels, and she knew the banker had decided to make a pass. "Good afternoon," she said warily, with a little nod.

"Exploring the house?" He crooned the words, and somehow that was more unnerving than if he'd shouted them.

Rue raised her chin a notch, still keeping her distance. "Of course not," she said with cool politeness.

"Your room is on the first floor, I believe." Sinclair's eyes never linked with hers all the while he was speaking. Instead, his gaze drifted over her hair, her throat, her shoulders and then her breasts.

"I was looking in on Miss McCall," Rue said, folding her arms to hide at least one part of her anatomy from his perusal. "She's suffering from—feminine complaints."

In the next instant, the master of the house reached out with one beefy hand and took hold of Rue's jaw. While his grip was not painful, it was definitely an affront, and she immediately tried to twist free.

"Now, now," Sinclair murmured, as though soothing a fractious child, "don't run away. I wouldn't want to have to tell Farley I caught you going through my personal belongings and get you thrown back into jail."

Rue felt the blood drain from her face. This kind of bore was easy enough to deal with in her own time, but just then the year was 1892 and Sinclair was probably among the most influential men in town. "What do you want?" she asked, hoping she was wrong.

She wasn't.

He ran a sausage-size thumb over her mouth. "Just an hour of your time, Miss Claridge. That's all."

Rue thrust herself away from him. "I wouldn't give you a *moment*," she ground out, "let alone an hour!"

Smiling genially, Sinclair hooked his thumbs in his vest pockets. "That's a pity. More jail time will surely ruin what little is left of your reputation."

Rue inched backward toward the stairway leading down to the kitchen. "I'll deny everything. And Farley will believe me, too!" She wasn't too sure about that last part, but she wanted to keep Sinclair distracted until she was out of lunging distance.

His bushy eyebrows rose in mocking amusement. "Silly child. What the marshal believes doesn't amount to a hill of beans. Not against the say-so of a man who controls everybody's finances."

Knowing she had reached the stairs, Rue whirled and raced down them. She snatched her bag from the little room she had occupied so briefly and fled out the front door.

Now, for all practical intents and purposes, she was homeless. She couldn't go back to her own century because she'd lost the necklace, and since Farley would probably take Sinclair's word over hers, arrest was no doubt imminent.

Much as Rue enjoyed Farley's company, she wasn't about to be locked up again. One stretch in the hoosegow on trumped up charges was more than enough; she had no intention of serving another.

Even so, Rue was forced to admit to herself that she was drawn to Farley's quiet strength. She made her way through the deep grass behind the mercantile and the Hang-Dog Saloon, stopping now and then to crouch down when she heard voices. After nearly half an hour of evasion tactics, she reached the little barn behind the marshal's house and slipped inside.

Farley's horse, a big roan gelding, nickered companionably from its stall.

"At least somebody around here likes me," Rue said, looking around the small structure and deciding the loft would make the best hiding place.

After letting out a long sigh, she tossed her bag up and then climbed the rickety ladder—not an easy task in a long skirt.

The hay in the loft was sweet smelling, and afternoon sunlight flooded in through a gap in the roof. Rue sat cross-legged and automatically unzipped the side flap on her bag, since that was where she had hidden her money.

The currency, like Aunt Verity's necklace, had vanished.

Rue gave a little cry of frustration and fell backward into the hay. A few minutes later, she checked the main compartment of the bag, but nothing was missing. Evidently the thief—possibly even Sinclair himself—had stumbled upon the money first and been content with that.

Despite her fury, Rue had to smile, wondering what the robber would have made of her miniature candy bars and other modern inventions.

Following that, she took the advice her grandfather had given her long ago and quietly accepted the fact that she was in big trouble. As much as she would like things to be different, the reality was that her money was gone, one of Pine River's most prominent citizens planned to accuse her of stealing, and she'd lost the only means she'd had of returning to her own time. Only when she'd faced these problems squarely would solutions begin to present themselves.

At least, she *hoped* solutions would begin to present themselves. Nothing came to her right away.

The sun was setting and crickets were harmonizing in the quack grass outside the barn when she heard sounds below and rolled over to peer through a crack between the floorboards of the loft.

Farley was there. He filled a feedbag and slipped it over the gelding's head, then began currying the animal. The graceful play of the muscles in the marshal's back and shoulders did odd things to Rue's heartbeat, but she couldn't help watching him work.

The lawman caught her completely off guard when he suddenly whirled, drew his pistol and pointed it at the underside of the loft.

"All right, just come down from there," he ordered. "And keep your hands where I can see them."

Some days, Rue reflected dismally, it just didn't pay to get out of bed.

"Don't shoot, Marshal," she said. "It's only me, Rue Claridge, Pine River's Most Wanted."

When Rue peered over the top of the ladder, Farley was just sliding his pistol back into its holster. He'd hung his hat on a peg on the wall, and his attractively rumpled brown hair glimmered even in the fading light. "What the hell are you doing up there?" he demanded, setting his hands on his hips.

Rue sighed and swung her legs over the side of the loft, gripping the pink sports bag in one hand. "Holding, of course. When Mr. Sinclair put the moves on me, I told him to get lost, and he said he'd have you arrest me...."

Farley scratched his head, obviously impatient and puzzled.

Rue tossed her bag to the floor and then climbed resignedly down the ladder to face her fate. "Here." She held out her hands, wrists together. "Handcuff me."

The marshal looked sternly down his nose at Rue. "You've gone and gotten yourself thrown out of the only boarding-house that would have you?"

Sudden color pulsed in Rue's cheeks. "Didn't you hear a word I've said? Sinclair wanted me to—to be intimate with him. I refused, of course, and he said he'd have me arrested for robbing his house."

Farley's turquoise eyes narrowed. "Let's see that satchel," he said brusquely.

Rue resented the invasion of privacy, but she also knew she had no real choice, so she handed over the bag.

The marshal turned it end over end, trying to find the opening, and Rue finally reached out and pulled back the zipper herself.

Farley stared at the small mechanism as though it were a bug under a microscope. "What the—"

"It's called a zipper," Rue said with a sigh. "They won't be invented for another twenty-five or thirty years, so don't bother looking for them in your favorite store."

Now Farley studied Rue with the same thoroughness as he'd examined the zipper on her neon pink bag. "You don't talk like anybody I've ever known before, except for Mrs. Fortner, of course. Where did you come from?" he asked quietly.

Rue folded her arms. She might as well tell the truth, she decided, since nobody was going to believe her anyway. "The future. I came from the far end of the twentieth century." She snatched the bag from his hands, suddenly anxious to convince him, to have one person on the face of the earth know what was happening to her. "Here," she said, pulling the paperback spy novel out and thrusting it in Farley's face. "Look. Did you ever see a book like this before, with a soft cover? And read the copyright date."

Farley turned the book in his hands, clearly amazed by the bright red cover and the gold-foil lettering spelling out the title and the author's name.

"Nobody can come from the future," he insisted stubbornly, but Rue could see that the paperback puzzled him.

"I did," she said. After setting the bag down, she politely took the book, opened it to the copyright page and held it out again. "There. Read that."

Farley took in the printed words, then raised baffled eyes to Rue's face. "It's a trick," he said.

"How could it be?" Rue demanded, growing impatient even though she'd known she would never convince him. "Paperback books and zippers don't exist in 1892, Farley!"

"You could have gotten those things at some fancy science exhibition in St. Louis or Chicago or somewhere." Clearly, Farley meant to stand his intellectual ground, even though it was eroding under his feet. "All I know is, it's got to be some kind of hoax."

Rue rolled her eyes. Then she bent and pulled out one of her precious snack-size candy bars. "How about this?" she challenged, holding out the morsel. "Did I get this at an exhibition, too?"

Farley frowned, examining the wrapper.

"You have to tear off the paper," Rue prompted. "Then you eat what's inside."

Farley looked suspicious, but intrigued, also. He tore away the paper, letting it drift to the floor.

Rue picked the litter up and crumpled it on one hand, while Farley carried the candy bar over to the doorway and studied it in the last light. The look of consternation on his face was amusing, even under the circumstances.

"Go ahead, Farley," she urged. "Take a bite."

The marshal glanced at her again, then nibbled cautiously at one end of the chocolate bar. After a moment, he smiled. "I'll be damned," he muttered, then consumed the rest of the candy. "Got any more of those?"

"Yes," Rue answered, thrusting out her chin, "but I'm not going to let you wolf them down. Especially not when you're about to arrest me for something I didn't do."

"I'm not going to arrest you," Farley replied reasonably, looking at Rue with curious amusement. "We've only got one jail cell here in Pine River, as you know, and it's already occupied. I'll just have to give you my bed and bunk out here in the barn until you get on that stage next Tuesday."

Rue didn't protest, nor did she turn the conversation back to the reality of time travel. Farley was still telling himself he was the victim of some elaborate prank, no doubt, but at least she had the satisfaction of knowing she'd planted the seed of possibility in his mind. Maybe after some rumination, he'd begin to take the idea seriously.

It the meantime, they were clearly going to pretend nothing out of the ordinary was going on.

If someone had to sleep in the barn, Rue reasoned, better Farley than she. She lowered her eyes. "There's a problem with my leaving on the stage," she confessed. "Somebody snitched all my money."

Farley sighed. "With luck like yours, it's purely a wonder you ever managed to win at poker the other night," he said, gesturing toward the door. "Come on, Miss Rue. Let's go in and rustle up some supper. We'll figure out what to do with you later."

Rue picked up her bag, straightened her shoulders and preceded him through the doorway of the barn. An inky twilight was working its way down the timbered hills toward them, and there was a bite in the air.

The inside of Farley's log cabin was cozy and surprisingly neat. Books lined one whole wall, from roof to floor, and a stone fireplace faced the door. An attached lean-to housed a small kitchen area, and Rue suspected the tattered Indian blanket hanging from the ceiling hid Farley's bed.

She went to stand beside the fireplace, hoping the warmth would dispel the sweet shivers that suddenly overtook her. She had a peculiar sense, all of a sudden, of being a piece on some great celestial board game, and she'd just been moved within easy reach of both victory and defeat.

"Hungry?" Farley asked, clattering metal against metal in the lean-to kitchen.

"Starved," Rue said, too tired, confused and frustrated for any more deep thought. She'd missed both breakfast and lunch, and the candy bars weren't taking up the slack.

Farley came out of the lean-to. "The stew'll be warmed up in a few minutes," he said. As he went around the cabin lighting kerosene lamps, he seemed uncharacteristically nervous.

Rue, on the other hand, felt totally safe. "So you're a cook as well as a reader," she said, wanting to hear him talk because she liked the sound of his voice, liked knowing he was there.

He grinned and shook his head. "No, ma'am," he replied. "My food is provided as a part of my wages, like this cabin. The ladies of the town take turns cooking for me."

The thought made Rue violently jealous, and that was when she realized the horrible truth. Somehow, she'd fallen in love with Farley Haynes.

Talk about Mr. Wrong.

"Oh," she said finally.

Farley shook his head and crouched to add wood to the fire. "Maybe you shouldn't stand so close," he said, and his voice was suddenly hoarse. ''Ladies have been known to catch their skirts afire doing that.''

Rue moved away to look at Farley's collection of books, and her voice shook when she spoke. ''Have you really read all these?''

''Most of them more than once,'' Farley replied. She heard him retreat into the lean-to, then he called to her to join him. ''Stew's warm,'' he said.

After drawing a deep breath, raising her chin and pushing back her shoulders, Rue marched into the tiny kitchen.

Farley had set a place for her at the small, round table, and there was a lantern flickering on a shelf nearby. The atmosphere was cozy.

He ladled stew into two bowls, set a loaf of hard bread on a platter and sat down across from her.

Once she'd taken several bites of the stew, which was delicious, Rue was a little less shaky, both inwardly and outwardly. She smiled at Farley. ''This is quite a place you've got here.''

''Thank you,'' Farley replied, ''but I'll be glad when I can take up ranching and let somebody else wear my badge.''

A bittersweet sadness touched Rue's heart. ''Have you got a place picked out?'' she asked, breaking off a piece of bread.

Farley nodded. ''There's a half section for sale north of town. I've almost got enough for the down payment, and the First Federal Bank is going to give me a mortgage.''

''Mr. Sinclair's bank,'' Rue murmured, feeling less festive.

Farley was chewing, and he waited until he'd swallowed to answer. ''That's right.''

An autumn wind tested the glass in the windows, and Rue was doubly glad Farley had taken her in. ''If there was any justice in this world, you'd go right over there and arrest that old lecher right this minute for sexual harassment.''

A modest flush tinted Farley's weathered cheekbones. ''He hasn't broken the law, Rue. And that means he can't be arrested.''

''Why?'' Rue demanded, only vaguely registering the fact that Farley had called her by her first name. ''Because he's a man? Because he's a banker? I was innocent of any crime, and that didn't keep you from slapping *me* behind bars."

"I've never slapped a woman in my life," Farley snapped, looking outraged.

Rue sat back in her chair, her eyes brimming with tears she was too proud to shed. "It's hopeless," she said. "Absolutely hopeless. You and I speak different languages, Farley Haynes."

"I would have sworn we were both talking English," he responded, reaching calmly for his glass of water.

"I give up!" Rue cried, flinging out her hands.

Farley reached for her bowl and carried it to the stove. "What you need," he said, "is some more stew."

Rue watched him with a hunger she would have been too embarrassed even to write about in the privacy of her journal, and she swallowed hard. "Stew," she said. "Right."

The stew was remarkably good, hot and savory and fresh, and Rue consumed the second helping without quibbling. She was fiercely hungry, and the food eased her low-grade headache and the shaky feeling that invariably overtook her when she failed to eat regular meals.

After supper, Farley heated water on the stove, and Rue insisted on washing the dishes. It was fun, sort of like playing house in an antique store.

The lean-to was a small place, though, and when Farley poured himself a cup of coffee and then lingered at the table, flipping thoughtfully through a stack of papers, Rue was more painfully conscious of his presence than ever. She tried not to think about him, but it was an impossibility. He seemed to fill the little room to its corners with his size, his uncompromising masculinity and the sheer strength of his personality.

In Rue's opinion, the effect on her nerves, her muscles and her most-secret parts was all out of proportion to the circumstances, strange as they were. She felt like a human volcano; lava was burning and bubbling in the farthest reaches of her body and her spirit. Simple things like drying the chipped crockery bowls they'd eaten from and setting them on the shelves took on the significance of epic poetry.

She was wrestling with the enormous enamel coffeepot, trying to pour herself a cupful, when she felt Farley looming behind her. He displaced her grip on the pot's handle and filled her cup.

He was only standing at her back, it was nothing more dramatic than that, yet Rue felt a devastating charge radiate from his body to hers. In the next moment, the invisible field, woven of lantern light, cosmic mystery, half-forgotten dreams and stardust enfolded her, and she sagged backward against Farley's steely stomach and chest.

Farley made no sound. He simply took the cup from Rue's hand, set it on the stove and closed his strong arms lightly around her waist. For all that she had never been in such trouble, even on her most memorable assignments as a journalist, Rue felt as though she'd stumbled upon some magical sanctuary where nothing and no one could ever hurt her.

In the meantime, the seismic tumult was building inside Rue, gaining force moment by moment. She knew the inevitable eruption would be more than physical; it would be an upheaval of the soul, as well. And she wanted it despite the danger.

Presently—whether a minute or an hour passed, Rue could not have said—Farley raised his hands slowly, gently, to weigh her breasts. When his thumbs moved over her nipples, making them harden and strain against the fabric of her dress, Rue groaned and tilted her head back against his shoulder.

He touched his lips to her temple, warming the delicate flesh there, and then he bent his head slightly to nibble the side of her neck. Rue would have throttled any other man for taking such liberties, but her need for Farley had sneaked up on her, and it was already so pervasive that she couldn't tell where the craving stopped and her own being began.

When he lifted her into his arms, Rue's logical left brain finally struggled to the surface and gurgled out a protest, but it was too late. The fanciful right side of her brain was hearing rapturous symphonies, and the notes drowned out all other sounds.

Farley carried her out of the kitchen—Rue was vaguely aware of the fire as they passed the hearth—then he took her behind the Indian blanket that served as a curtain. There was a look of grim resignation on his face as he laid her on the neatly made bed and stood gazing down at her for a long moment. It was as if he thought she'd cast a spell over him and he was trying to work out some way to break it.

She couldn't tell him that she was under an enchantment, too, that she had never done anything like this before. All she could do was lie there, all but the most primitive essence of her identity seared away by the heat of her desire, needing him. Waiting.

He took off her funny, old-fashioned shoes and tossed them aside, then began unbuttoning her dress. Only when she lay completely naked on his bed, totally vulnerable, did he speak.

"God help me," he said in a raw whisper, "I've wanted to see you like this since that day I found you wandering in Doc Fortner's house. I've wanted to touch you...."

Rue took his hand in hers, emboldened by the turquoise fire in his eyes and the frantic fever in her own spirit, and pressed his palm and fingers to her breast. "Touch me," she said softly, and the words were both a plea and an affirmation.

Farley complied for a long, torturously delicious interval, then while Rue waited in sweet agony, he withdrew. She watched, dazed, as he removed his clothes.

His body had the stealth and prowess of a stalking panther as he stretched out beside her on the rough, woolen blanket that served as a bedspread. Then he kissed her, first caressing her lips with his, then commanding her mouth to open for the entrance of his tongue.

The conquest was a triumphant one, far more potent than any ordinary kiss. Rue's body arched beside Farley on the bed, and he reached beneath her to cup her bottom in one hand and press her close against his thighs and the solid demand of his manhood.

She was afraid when she felt him, terrified of his size and power, and yet this knowledge did nothing to stem the furious tide of her passion.

Farley kissed Rue, again and again, all the while caressing and shaping her with his hands, until she was in a virtual delirium of need. Perspiration shimmered on every inch of her flesh, and tendrils of her hair clung wetly to her neck and temples.

At last, Farley positioned himself between her legs, then put his hands under her shoulder blades and raised her breasts for conquering. When he captured one eager nipple with his mouth, Rue cried out in despairing surrender, begging him to take her.

For all her travels, for all her reading and her sophistication, when Farley entered her, Rue was startled. There was pain, and it lingered, but it was also promptly overshadowed by a consuming, joyous rage made up of heavenly light and dragon's fire.

Rue pressed her hands to Farley's back, and the play of his muscles under her palms was as much a part of their love-making as the ferocious rhythm of joining and parting that was even then transforming them both.

For all the breathless promise of the past half hour or so, when Rue finally achieved satisfaction, she was all but swept away by the force of it. She strained beneath Farley in wild, glorious and totally involuntary spasms, her teeth clenched against the shouts of triumph rattling in the back of her throat. She was just settling back to the bed, breathless and disoriented, when Farley clasped her bottom hard in his hands, pressed her tightly against him and made a series of deep, abrupt thrusts. To Rue's surprise, she reached another climax when Farley had his; her release was a soft, languid implosion, like a blessing on the tempest that had preceded it.

When he'd finally spent the last of his energy, Farley collapsed beside Rue, his breathing hard and raspy. She pressed her face into the taut, moist flesh on his shoulder, at once hiding from her lover and seeking him out.

"I knew it would be like that," Farley muttered after they'd lain entwined for a long time, listening to the beating of each other's hearts, the crackle of the fire and the night sounds of the lively timber town beyond the cabin walls.

Rue's eyes filled with tears, but she wasn't mourning the time before, when she and Farley had been innocent of each other. No matter what happened, whether she lived the rest of her life with this man or without him, in this century or another, she'd given herself truly and totally to Farley Haynes, and she would never forget the splendor of it.

"I thought it was a lie," she finally confessed. "What people said about making love, I mean. I never knew—until now.''

Farley sighed and raised his head to look through her eyes, as though they were clear as windowpanes, and straight into her soul. He kissed her forehead and then rested his scratchy chin where his lips had just touched. ''I'm sorry,'' he said, his voice low and hoarse. ''I offered you safe haven here, and then I took advantage.''

Rue had just been transported to a whole other plane of womanhood, and the journey had had just as great an impact on her senses and emotions as being tossed from one time period to another. She was incapable, for the moment, of working out whether Farley's apology was appropriate or not. ''It's not as though you threw me down on the bed and forced me,'' she pointed out, loving the feel of his back, supple skin over firm muscles. ''I wanted you.''

Farley drew back to search her eyes again, and the gesture made her feel more naked than she had earlier when he'd methodically relieved her of her clothes. ''You are the most forward-thinking female I have ever encountered,'' he said somberly, but then a grin broke over his face. ''I think I like that about you.''

Rue swallowed, and her ability to think in rational terms was beginning to dissipate like fog in bright sunshine. Farley was joined to her, and he was getting hard again, and she didn't want him to leave her. ''Stay inside me, Farley. Please.''

Bracing himself by pressing his hands on the mattress on either side of her, Farley began to move slowly. ''I'll find out the truth about you,'' he said, his words growing short and breathy as he increased his pace, ''if it's the last thing I ever do.''

Pressing her shoulders deep into the feather pillows and tilting her head back in magnificent surrender, Rue gasped out, ''I'd love to tell you—I'd love to show you the place I came from....'' And from that moment on, Rue was beyond speaking.

Farley dipped his head to lave one of her distended nipples

with his tongue. His attentions were merciless and thorough, and soon Rue was pitching under him like a wild mare trying to shake off a rider.

Once that session had ended, Rue cuddled against Farley's side—his rib cage had about as much flexibility as the staves of a wooden barrel—and promptly drifted off to sleep. When she awakened, the Indian blanket that separated the bed from the rest of the cabin was framed in silvery moonlight and Farley's side of the mattress was empty.

Rue scrambled off the bed, found one of Farley's shirts hanging from a peg in the wall and shoved her arms through the sleeves. The clock on the plain, board mantel over the fireplace read 3:17 and despite the fact that she had no claim on the marshal's time, a sense of alarm crowded her throat.

Obviously, Farley had gone out for some reason—maybe there had been shouts or a frantic knock at the door or even shots fired, and she'd been too drunk on lovemaking to hear. In fact, she hadn't even noticed when Farley left.

Rue's imagination tripped into overdrive. She'd seen enough Clint Eastwood movies to know what awful things could happen to a lone lawman. The difference was that now she wouldn't be able to toss away her popcorn box, fish her car keys out of her purse and go home to an apartment filled with modern conveniences. This was the real thing, and she just happened to be hopelessly in love with the peace officer in question.

On some level, Rue had known from the moment she met Farley that something significant was going to happen between them. But she hadn't expected the event to be on a par with the destruction of the dinosaurs or the formation of the Grand Canyon.

Rue groped her way into the lean-to kitchen, blinded by her emotions rather than a lack of light, and looked at herself in Farley's shaving mirror. Except that her hair was tangled and she was wearing a man's shirt, she seemed unchanged. Inside, however, Rue was wholly different; she'd been converted, not into someone else, but into a better, richer and more genuine version of herself.

Trembling, Rue poured a cup of coffee from the pot on the stove and sank into one of the two chairs at the table. Since it had been sitting on the heat for hours, the brew was black as coal oil and only slightly more palatable. Rue figured there was probably enough caffeine in the stuff to keep her awake well into the next century—be it the twentieth or the twenty-first—but she took a second sip anyway.

Through the closed windows and thin walls of Farley's house, Rue could hear the sounds of laughter and bad piano music and an ongoing argument between a man and a woman. She was overwhelmingly relieved when the door opened and the marshal himself walked in.

He set his rifle in the corner, hung his hat and long canvas duster on their pegs and then began unfastening his gun belt. All the time, he watched Rue in the dim, icy glow of the moonlight.

Rue didn't want to express her relief at seeing him; she didn't have the right. "I hope I didn't keep you from your work," she said with as much dignity as a person wearing only a man's shirt and a glow of satisfaction can be expected to summon up.

Farley didn't answer. He simply came to the table, took Rue's hand and brought her to her feet. He took her back to the bedside, and she crawled under the covers, her heart turning to vapor and then gathering in her throat like a summer storm taking shape on the horizon.

She watched as Farley took off his clothes for the second time that night, more shaken than before by his magnificence and quiet grace.

He stretched out beside her under the blankets and with a few deft motions of one hand, relieved her of the long shirt she wore. Having done that, Farley curved one arm around Rue and arranged her close against his side, her head resting on his shoulder.

Farley did not make love to Rue; instead, he simply held her, sheltering her in his solidity and strength. For Rue, the experience was, in its own way, just as momentous as full surrender had been earlier. The simple intimacy met fundamental needs that had not only been unsatisfied before, but unrecognized.

Rue slept soundly that night and awakened with the first light of dawn, when Farley gently displaced her to get out of bed.

"What do I do now?" Rue asked softly. Sadly. "I can't stay here. The whole town will know if I do."

"The whole town already knows," Farley answered, pulling on a pair of dark trousers and disappearing around the edge of the blanket curtain. "There aren't many secrets in a place like Pine River."

Rue slipped under the covers with a groan of mortification, but she could still hear the clatter and clink of stove lids, the working of a pump handle, the opening and closing of a door.

Presently, the smell and sounds of sizzling bacon filled the air, along with the aroma of fresh coffee. Rue got up, struggled back into her clothes and peered around the blanket.

She could see Farley in the lean-to, standing at the stove. The sight of him, with his hair wetted down and combed, a meat fork in one hand, filled her with a tenderness so keen that it was painful.

Rue approached hesitantly. For the first time in her life, she didn't know what to say.

Farley turned a strip of bacon in the black skillet and ran his turquoise eyes companionably over her length. For an instant, Rue was beneath him again, in the throes of complete physical and spiritual communion, and the sensation left her disconcerted.

The marshal made short work of her poetic mood. "If you're sore," he said, "I've got some balm out in the barn."

Rue sighed. This was the same man who had evoked such violently beautiful responses from her the night before and had later held her snugly against his side, making no demands. Now he was offering her the same medicine he would use on a cow or a horse.

"Thanks," she answered belatedly, "but I'll be fine."

Farley shrugged, took two plates down from a shelf and began dishing up breakfast.

"Interesting," she murmured thoughtfully, pulling back a chair.

He set a plate filled with fried food in front her. "What's interesting?"

"You," Rue reflected. "You're a nineteenth-century male, and here you are cooking for a woman. Even waiting table."

Farley arched an eyebrow. "It's that or risk letting you do the cooking," he replied.

Rue laughed, but her amusement faded as daylight strengthened the thin glow of the lanterns and reality settled in around her. It was morning now; the enchanted night was over and she was stranded in the wrong century, with the wrong man.

"Farley, what am I going to do?" she asked again. "My money is gone, I don't have anywhere to stay and it's beginning to look like my cousin and her husband are going to make their home in San Francisco and never contact anybody in Pine River again."

"Jon and Lizzie will come back when they're ready," Farley said with certainty. "And you can stay here with me."

"Oh, right," Rue snapped, irritated not with Farley for making the suggestion, but with herself for wanting to go on sharing his life and his bed for as long as possible. "The good women of Pine River will love that."

Farley grinned. "No, they won't."

"You're being pretty cocky right now," Rue pointed out, annoyed, "but the truth is, you're afraid of those women, Farley Haynes. They have the power to make both our lives miserable, and you know it."

Farley's smile tightened to a look of grim obstinance, and Rue wondered hopefully if the night before had worked some ancient, fundamental magic in the deepest parts of his being, the way it had in hers.

"Those old hens will just have to do their scratching and pecking in somebody else's dooryard," he said.

"What the devil is that supposed to mean?" Rue countered, reaching for another slice of crispy bacon. The man made love with the expertise of a bard taking up the pen, and he had some pretty modern attitudes, but sometimes he talked in cowboy riddles.

Farley got up to refill his coffee mug and Rue's. "Hell," he grumbled, "even the prissy Eastern lieutenants and captains I knew in the army didn't boss a man around the way those old biddies do."

Rue stifled a giggle, but said nothing.

Farley came back to the table, set their mugs down and shook an index finger at her. "Mind you don't take to carrying on the way they do, because I won't put up with it."

Rue swallowed, unsure how to react. On the one hand, it was an affront, Farley's presuming to issue orders that way. On the other, though she would have chewed one of Aunt Verity's antique crystal doorknobs before admitting as much to him, she liked the gentle forcefulness of his manner. Here, at last, was a person as strong as she was.

"I don't see where my actions are any concern of yours," she finally managed to say.

He sighed and shook his head, as though marveling that someone so simpleminded could have reached adulthood without being seriously injured in the process. "After last night," Farley told her, making an insulting effort at clarity as he spoke, "there's nothing we can do but get married."

Rue wouldn't have been more stunned if he'd thrown his food all over her. *"Married?"* she squeaked. In that instant, she realized that it was the dearest, most secret wish of her heart to marry Farley Haynes. At the same time, she knew she'd have to be demented even to entertain the idea.

Okay, so she loved Farley, she thought. He didn't feel the same way toward her; in mentioning marriage, he was probably just following the code of the West, or something like that. And there was still the matter of their coming from two different centuries, two different *worlds*. To love Farley, to stay in this time with him, would be to give up everything she knew and much of what she was.

Rue was a strong woman, and that was both her blessing and her curse. Not even for Farley and a lifetime of the tempestuous dances he'd taught her in the night just past could she give up her own identity. She was of another time; she was a journalist, a person with many more bridges to cross, both professionally and personally.

Of course, if she did marry the marshal, she would have a place to stay until she made contact with her cousin, found the necklace and returned to her own century. Farley would undoubtedly make thorough love to her practically every night, and the mere prospect of that brought all Rue's feminine forces to a state of hypersensitivity.

"I'll send somebody over to the next town for the justice of the peace," Farley said, as if the matter had been settled.

"Now just a minute," Rue protested, thumping the tabletop lightly with one fist. "I haven't said yes to your proposal, if you can call it that. It just so happens that I don't want to get married—I don't even plan to stay around here, once I've seen my cousin."

Farley looked untroubled by this announcement. "What if we made a baby last night?" he asked, figuratively pulling the rug out from under Rue's feet. "I don't think things are any different in Seattle or Boston or wherever it is you really come from. Life is damn near impossible for an unmarried woman with a child."

Rue laid both her hands to her stomach. Nature might very well be knitting a tiny being in the warm safety of her womb. She was filled with wanting and fear. "Oh, my God," she whispered.

Farley stood and carried his plate to the sink. Then he came back to the table, stood beside Rue's chair and bent to simultaneously taste her lips and rub her lower abdomen with one hand. "If there's no baby inside you now," he said huskily, "I'll put one there when I get back."

A hot shiver shook Rue; she was amazed anew at the depths of the passion this man could rouse in her with a few words and caresses. "When will that be?"

He nibbled at her lower lip before answering. "About noon, if nothing goes wrong," he said. Then he walked away to strap on his gun belt, reload his pistol and shrug into his duster. Farley put on his battered hat and reached for his rifle in a smooth, practiced motion. "Try to stay out of trouble until I can get you married," he urged, grinning slightly. Then he opened the door and left.

Rue was restless, and the choices confronting her seemed overwhelming. Go or stay. Love or pretend to be indifferent. Follow her heart or her head. Laugh or cry.

More to keep herself busy than because she was a devotee of neatness, Rue heated water on the cookstove, washed the dishes, wiped off the table and swept the floor. Following that, she made the bed. It was while she was doing that that she found the stash.

Her foot caught on a loose floorboard as she was plumping the pillows, and she crouched to press the plank back into place. The same curiosity that had made her such a good journalist made her a very bad houseguest; Rue couldn't resist peeking underneath.

A cigar box was tucked away in the small, dark place, and Rue lifted the lid to find a respectable collection of five-dollar gold pieces. This money, surely, was meant to be the down payment on Farley's ranch.

Kneeling now, Rue set the box on the side of the bed and studied one of the coins. Where she came from, the small, ornate bit of gold would be worth far more than five dollars, but here it was ordinary money.

Carefully, Rue closed the lid and set the box back in its place. If Farley had been anyone but who he was, she might have taken that money, used it to get to San Francisco, but she couldn't steal his dreams.

The best thing to do was look for the necklace.

The day was chilly, and Rue wished for a shawl as she walked along the sidewalks of Pine River, searching for the lost piece of jewelry that was her only link with the world she knew.

She searched all morning without any luck, and her shoulders were sagging with discouragement when she started toward Farley's office. Hopefully, since he was willing to give her a baby, he might also offer lunch.

As she was passing Ella Sinclair's boarding house, Rue

realized there was one place she hadn't looked—the outhouse she'd materialized in. Her heart started to pound. She wasn't sure which one it was, but she knew it was in this neighborhood.

Lifting her skirts, Rue dashed around the house she'd been passing, avoiding manure and mud in the yard as best she could, and hurtled herself into the outhouse she found there, but to no avail—the necklace wasn't there. She began to run through backyards, entering and searching each outhouse she came to. So intent was she on finding the lost necklace that she was barely aware of the rumbles of consternation, shock and amusement around her.

When she spotted her pendant caught between two boards—thank the Lord—she let out a shriek of delighted triumph and snatched it up.

In practically the same instant, a strong arm curved around her from behind, and Rue was yanked backward against an impervious chest. She knew by the quivering in her spirit and the straightforward method of operation that she'd been apprehended by Farley Haynes. Again.

"I was only getting my necklace," she told him, wriggling to get free. "I lost it in the back of this wagon the other day, when I hitched a ride into town."

With his free arm, Farley swept off his hat and wiped his forehead with his sleeve. "That's just fine," he drawled, obviously furious. "Now I suggest you start apologizing to these people you've been disturbing."

Rue wanted to laugh and to cry, she was so relieved at finding the necklace. She dropped it into her skirt pocket. "Anything you say, Marshal," she responded sweetly. "Are we still getting married?"

The question stirred a buzz in the crowd that had gathered, and Rue was amused. Farley had just assumed she was up to no good, plundering the good citizens' outhouses for heaven only knew what scurrilous purpose, and she wouldn't have put it past him to arrest her. Therefore, in her opinion, a little embarrassment served him right, because after the previous night's activities, he should have trusted her more.

''Yes,'' he said as grimly as a judge pronouncing a death sentence.

Rue smiled all the while as she offered her apology to the crowd, every once in a while reaching into her pocket to make sure the necklace was there. She could not yet return to her own time because she hadn't found Elisabeth, but the door was no longer closed to her, and that was the important thing.

Some thoughtful citizen had brought fried chicken, biscuits and gravy for Farley's lunch, and he shared the feast with the solitary prisoner and Rue. The marshal's eyes were narrowed, however, as he regarded her across the surface of his messy desk.

"I thought I told you to stay out of trouble," he said.

Rue's cheeks pulsed a little as she thought of the episode. "I was only looking for my necklace, Farley," she answered reasonably. She took a bite from a crispy fried chicken leg and chewed thoroughly before going on. "If you had any idea how important that pendant really is, you wouldn't make such a big deal about a little disturbance."

Farley's frown deepened. He took another piece of chicken from the lunch basket, which was lined with a blue-and-white cotton napkin. "I know ladies like their trinkets," he allowed. "My mother had a brooch made of marcasite and jet that she wouldn't have parted with to save her own scalp. But I have a feeling this necklace of yours is important for some other reason."

He was remarkably astute, Rue thought, but she wasn't about to explain the necklace's peculiar power—mainly because she didn't begin to understand it herself.

She reached into her pocket and touched the twisted chain, and that was when she felt the strange warning vibration. By instinct, she realized that the pendant was up to its old tricks again; she was about to be sent helter-skelter into some other part of history, and not necessarily the one she belonged in, either.

No, she thought desperately, *not now. Not without saying goodbye....*

The room seemed to waver and shift, like a reflection in old bottle glass. Glimpses of the orchard behind Aunt Verity's house were superimposed over the stove, the bars in the cell door, Farley himself. Rue wrenched her hand from her pocket and the visions faded instantly, along with the sense of an impending spiritual earthquake.

She gripped the edge of Farley's desk with both hands, swaying slightly with mingled sickness and relief.

Farley immediately jumped up to bring her a dipperful of cold well water from the bucket near the stove.

"Are you sick?" he demanded. "Do you want me to go and get the doc?"

Rue smiled thinly and squeezed her eyes shut for a moment, still trying to regain her equilibrium. "Yes. Find Dr. Jonathan Fortner, please," she joked. "And his wife Elisabeth, while you're at it."

Farley crouched beside her chair, looking up into her face with troubled eyes, eyes of such a beautiful Arizona turquoise that it hurt Rue's heart to return their gaze. "What just happened here?" he demanded quietly.

I almost left you, Rue answered in stricken silence.

"Rue," Farley insisted, setting the empty dipper on the desk and holding both her hands in his. "Are you suffering from some sickness of the head? Is that your big secret? Did you run away from one of those mental hospitals?"

Rue laughed, a little hysterically, but with genuine amusement. She could answer only one of his questions with an unequivocal no. The other two he would have to take on trust. She shook her head. "I didn't escape from an asylum, Farley," she said softly.

She could see by his face that he believed her, maybe only because he wanted to, and that was the biggest relief she'd had since finding the necklace in the outhouse.

"I sent for the justice of the peace," he said. "He'll be here in a few hours."

Rue had never, in all her life, had to deal with such a degree of temptation. She wanted so much to marry Farley, to have the right to share his joys and sorrows, his table and his bed, but to vow eternal fidelity when she fully intended to return to her own time as soon as possible would be unthinkable. She would simply disappear, and Farley would be left to wonder, to the end of his days, what had become of her.

"We can't," she said.

"We will," he replied, rising and walking away to hang the dipper on its nail near the bucket.

Nothing was resolved when, fifteen minutes later, Rue left the jailhouse. Since she had nowhere in particular to go, she set out for the house in the country where all this had begun. She meant to find a tree in the orchard, climb up as high as she could and sit there and think, her back to the rough trunk, the way she'd done as a child, in a time far in the future.

She was surprised to find a fancy carriage in the yard next to the farmhouse. There was lots of bustle and activity; a little girl ran full tilt, first in one direction, then another, her small arms outspread in a child's joy at simply existing. A handsome, dark-haired man was taking bags and satchels from the vehicle's boot....

It was only then that the belated realization struck Rue.

Elisabeth was back from San Francisco.

A tearful joy filled her. She struggled with the latch on the front gate, grew impatient and vaulted over the low fence, catching her skirts on the pickets. "Bethie!" she cried in breathless, exultant frustration; even though she had not yet caught sight of her cousin, she knew she was there somewhere.

Sure enough, Elisabeth came bursting through the doorway of one of the outbuildings at the sound of Rue's voice. She heedlessly dropped the crock she was carrying to the ground, and her blond hair tumbled around her shoulders as she ran.

"Rue!" she shrieked, laughing and sobbing the name. "Rue!"

Rue was dimly aware of the man and the little girl looking on in confusion, but she could only think of Elisabeth in those moments. Elisabeth, her best friend, her only real family.

"Bethie," Rue said, and then the two women were embracing and weeping, as women have always done, and probably will do, when meaningful separations end.

Finally, Bethie gripped Rue's upper arms in hands that had been strengthened by life in simpler but more physically demanding times, her blue-green eyes shimmering with tears, her face bright with joy.

"What are you doing here?" she wanted to know.

Rue laughed even as she wiped her cheek with one palm. "I sort of stumbled onto the place, the way I suspect you did," she confessed. "Once I got here, I was determined to find you, to make sure you were all right."

"I'm more than all right," Elisabeth answered, touching her stomach. "I never thought it was possible to be so happy, Rue. I'm going to have a baby."

The man and the child gravitated toward the two cousins while Rue was absorbing this news. She felt a pang of jealousy, which surprised her, and she even went so far as to hope she was pregnant herself—which was ridiculous, because that could only complicate matters.

"This is my husband Jonathan," Elisabeth said, and her skin took on the lustrous glow of a fine pearl as she introduced him. The child, who was as lovely as her father was handsome, huddled against Bethie's side and smiled shyly up at Rue. "And this is Miss Trista Fortner," Elisabeth added, as proudly as if she'd somehow produced the little girl herself, just that very moment. "Jonathan, Trista, I'd like you to meet my cousin Rue."

Elisabeth's husband was movie-star gorgeous, in a smooth, urbane way. Farley was just as good-looking, but he was the rugged type, exactly the kind of man Rue had always avoided.

"Hello," Jonathan said. He started to offer his right hand, which was scarred, then shrugged, grinned sheepishly and eased his arm back to his side. Rue recalled Farley saying the doctor had been injured.

Bethie smiled and linked elbows with Rue, marching her double-time toward the house. "I want to hear everything," she told her cousin. *"Everything."*

They sat at the kitchen table, and Rue, hardly knowing where to begin, told the story. She explained that the search had begun after she'd read Elisabeth's amazing letters about traveling through time, and admitted she'd first thought her cousin needed professional help. Then she'd found the necklace on the floor of the upstairs hallway, she went on, and made the trip herself.

For some reason she didn't fully understand—under normal circumstances Rue would have told Bethie *anything*—she didn't mention the passion she'd developed for Farley Haynes.

Elisabeth told Rue about her honeymoon, blushing intermittently and looking impossibly happy, and explained how Jonathan had hurt his hand. A fire had broken out and, while Farley had dragged Elisabeth out, Jon and Trista had been trapped upstairs. Jon had had the necklace in his possession and he'd escaped with the little girl over the threshold into 1992. The flow of time did not run parallel on both sides of the threshold, as Rue had already discovered, and when Dr. Fortner and his child finally managed to return, they'd found Elisabeth on trial for their murder.

Jon had made a dramatic entrance, Elisabeth said, eyes glowing with the memory, thus exonerating her of all charges, and they'd been married that day.

With help from Rue and Trista, Elisabeth began preparing dinner. She did it as naturally as if she'd been born in the nineteenth century instead of the twentieth. By then, the cousins had begun to speculate about the necklace. Although she couldn't explain why, Elisabeth believed the pendant's magic was different, depending on whose hands it fell into. She cautioned Rue to be careful about her choices.

Lanterns were lit as twilight tumbled silently down around the house and rose past the windows, and Jonathan moved, whistling, between the house and the barn.

"You truly do belong here," Rue marveled to her cousin later that night, when Jonathan had gone out to check on his regular patients and Trista was tucked away in one of the upstairs bedrooms.

Elisabeth nodded, lifting a kerosene lamp from the center of the table and leading the way into the parlor. A cozy fire crackled on the hearth and one other light burned on the mantelpiece. "I never knew it was possible for a woman to love a man the way I love Jonathan," she said softly, and there was a dreamy, faraway expression in her eyes as she gazed out the window toward the barn and the orchard and the covered bridge beyond. "It's like I was never whole before I came here. I felt like the odd woman out in some game of musical chairs—there was never a place for me to sit in that other world. The place is like a dream to me now, and I might even have convinced myself I'd imagined it all if it hadn't been for your appearance."

Rue thought of Farley and wondered if he was worried about her or if he'd even noticed she wasn't around. She sighed. "Don't you ever get scared? I mean, if a thing like this can happen, it changes everything. We're like players in some game, and none of us knows the rules."

Elisabeth turned to meet Rue's eyes. "They say that realizing how little we truly understand is the beginning of wisdom. But I've got a handle on this much—when you love with everything that's inside you, you take a terrible risk. I'm vulnerable in a way I never was before I knew Jonathan and Trista, and, yes, that scares me."

Reaching into her pocket, Rue found the necklace and brought it out, dangling it from her fingers. "Here's your ticket out," she said. "If you don't want to be vulnerable, all you have to do is go back home."

Elisabeth actually recoiled, her blue-green eyes round. "*This* is home," she said. "For heaven's sake, put that thing away before something awful happens."

Rue smiled and hurriedly dropped the pendant back into her pocket. After her experience in the jailhouse at lunchtime, when she'd seen one world taking shape on top of another, she was still a little shy about holding it for too long.

"Then I guess you've decided the risk is worth taking," she said, taking a place on a settee, resting one elbow on the arm and propping her chin in her hand. "Don't you miss it,

Bethie? Don't you ever wish you could see a movie or eat frozen yogurt in a mall?''

Elisabeth moved to the fireplace and stood looking down at the fire on the hearth. ''I miss hot baths,'' she said, ''and supermarkets and books on tape. I *don't* miss traffic jams, jangling telephones and the probability of one marriage out of two biting the proverbial dust.''

''Would you want to go back if it weren't for Jonathan and Trista?''

Bethie thought for a long time before answering, ''I'm not sure. Things are difficult here—the old saying about a woman's work never being done certainly holds true—but there's an intensity to life, a *texture,* that I never found in the twentieth century. I feel as though I've come home from some long journey of the soul.''

Rue sighed. ''Well, I guess this completes my mission,'' she said. ''I can go home now.''

Elisabeth looked alarmed. ''Oh, please say you'll stay for a few days, at least. After all, once you leave...'' She paused, lowered her head for a moment, then finished bravely, ''Once you leave, we may never see each other again.''

''I can't stay,'' Rue said miserably. She reminded Elisabeth how the power of the necklace seemed to be changing, how she no longer needed to step over the threshold to return to her own century, how she'd seen images of the orchard in the middle of Farley's office that day.

In typical Victorian fashion, Elisabeth laid spread fingers to her bosom. ''You're right,'' she said. ''You mustn't take the risk. Do you suppose it's possible for a person to end up in another time period entirely, or another place? Say, medieval England, or Boston during Revolutionary days?''

''I'm the wrong person to ask, Bethie,'' Rue answered. Her heart was aching at the prospect of leaving her cousin and, she could almost admit it to herself, of leaving Farley. ''I don't have any idea what laws govern this crazy situation, or even if there are any. Maybe it's covered by Einstein's Theory of Relativity or something.''

Elisabeth's beautiful eyes were glazed with tears. ''A day

won't go by that I don't think of you," she said. "Oh, Rue, I want you to be as happy as I am. Will you try to go back tonight?"

Rue thought of Farley. "Yes, but there's something I have to do first," she said. She glanced at the clock on the mantel, then at the darkened windows. "Oh, my gosh! I forgot I was supposed to get married!"

"What?"

Rue was hurrying toward the front door. "I wasn't really going to marry Marshal Haynes," she babbled. "He just thought we should because we've slept together and everything." She pulled open the door and would have bolted out into the starry night if Elisabeth hadn't caught her firmly by the arm.

"Now just a minute!" Rue's cousin protested. "You can't just go traipsing off to town through the dark of night! And what's this about your sleeping with Farley?"

Rue sagged against the doorjamb, heedless of the biting chill of the November night, and she began to cry. "I'm in love with him," she whispered brokenly, then sniffled. Her eyes found Elisabeth's worried face in the dim light of the moon and the glow of lanterns from the parlor. "I'm not like you, Elisabeth. I can't stay here—I can't be happy in a place where there's no UPS, no PBS, no CNN!"

Elisabeth laughed and put an arm around Rue's shoulders. "Come in and sit by the fire. I'll brew us a pot of tea and we'll work out this whole problem."

When Jonathan returned an hour later, Elisabeth and Rue were no closer to a solution. However, the doctor had brought a surprise along with him, a coldly angry Farley Haynes.

"The justice of the peace came and went," Farley said when Jonathan had taken Elisabeth's hand and led her out of the room so that Rue and the marshal were alone. He rested his hands on the sides of her chair, effectively pinning her between his arms.

Rue studied Farley's craggy, handsome face fondly, trying to make a memory that would last for all time. "I'm sorry, Farley," she said, touching his beard-stubbled cheek with one hand. ''But I'm not the girl for you, and you wouldn't be happy with me.''

Farley set his hands on either side of her waist, stepped back and hauled Rue unceremoniously to her feet. The necklace slipped to the floor, with a *chink* that seemed to echo throughout eternity, and she bent to grab for it. The marshal's hand tightened around her upper arm, as though he thought she might try to escape his hold, and then it happened.

There was a wild spinning effect, as if the parlor were a merry-go-round gone berserk. Colors and shapes collided and meshed. Rue, hurled to the floor, wrapped both arms around Farley's right leg and held on with all her strength to keep from being flung into the void.

''Jumpin' Juniper,'' Farley said when the wild ride subsided.

Rue couldn't let go of his leg, but she did look around, seeing that while they were still in that same parlor, the furniture was different. There was a TV in the corner with a VCR on top.

''What the hell just happened here?'' Farley whispered. Rue had to admire his cool. She was trembling as she shinnied up his thigh and finally stood on her own two feet.

She wanted to laugh, hysterically, joyously. She was home, and Farley was with her. On the other hand, she would probably never see Elisabeth again, and that made her want to weep.

''You've just aged almost a hundred years,'' Rue said, resting her forehead against Farley's shoulder and almost automatically slipping her hands around his waist. ''I've got a lot to show you, Marshal Haynes, but first I'd better give you a little time to absorb the shock.''

Farley went to the television set and touched one of the buttons. The head and shoulders of a late-night talk-show host appeared on the screen in an instantaneous flash of light and color.

The marshal recoiled, though only slightly, his wonderful, weathered face crumpled into a frown. ''Where's the rest of that fellow?'' he demanded. Before Rue could reply, he tapped the screen with his knuckles. "I'll be damned. It's a picture."

Rue set the necklace on the mantelpiece. Suddenly, she was filled with pizza lust and the yearning for a long, hot shower. She went to the telephone and punched out a number.

"One large pepperoni with extra cheese, sausage, green peppers and mushrooms," she said. Then she gave the address and hung up.

Farley had left the television to examine the phone. He picked up the receiver and put it to his ear, as Rue had done, then handed it back. "It's a telephone," she said. "A later version of those big wooden boxes with hand cranks and chrome bells." At his look of puzzlement, Rue added, "I'll explain later. Right now, I'm perishing for pizza." She looked down at her Victorian clothes. "I'd better change or the delivery person will spread a vicious rumor that we're having a costume party."

The marshal, who would certainly have carried off the prize for the most authentic getup at such a gathering, went over to one of the chairs and sank into it. He looked pale beneath his deep tan, and understandably bewildered.

"Where are Mrs. Fortner and the doctor?" he asked. "What happened here?"

"Listen, Farley," Rue said, sitting on the arm of his chair and slipping one arm reassuringly around his shoulders, "it's all pretty complicated, though if you'll remember, I tried to tell you about it before. Anyway, it's going to take a while for you to absorb the fact that this is really happening, let alone process a whole new universe. We just jumped a hundred years, you and I. Technically, Bethie and Jonathan are long dead. On the other hand, they're alive and well on the other side of some kind of cosmic chasm we don't understand."

"Thanks, Rue. That made everything clear as creek water," Farley said wryly. He was clearly still unnerved, as anyone would have been, but that lethal intelligence of his was stirring, too. Rue could see it in his eyes, hungry, wanting to comprehend everything. "Am I losing my mind?"

"No more so than I am, or Elisabeth. You just crossed from one dimension to another, somehow. All I know is that it has to do with my necklace."

"Good God," Farley sighed, rubbing his chin.

"Now you know how I felt," Rue said, polishing his badge with the sleeve of her dress. After that, she stood again. "Since you're company," she teased, "you can have the first shower."

"The first what?"

Rue laughed and took his hand. "Come on. I'll show you." She led the befuddled lawman up the stairs, along the hallway and into the main bathroom, reserving the one off the master bedroom for herself. There, she gave Farley soap and shampoo and showed him where to find the towels, then adjusted the shower spigots.

Farley's eyes went wide with puzzled amazement, but he was already starting to strip off his clothes when Rue slipped out of the room. She'd gotten only partway down the hall when a shout of stunned annoyance echoed from behind the door.

Thinking she should have explained that one spigot brought forth hot water and one cold, Rue smiled. She hoped it was ice Farley had just doused himself with, and not fire.

In the master bedroom, where all her things were still in the drawers and the closet, Rue had an urge to kneel and kiss the floor. She didn't, however. She just laid out jeans, underwear, socks and a bulky, white sweater, then took a shower.

The doorbell was ringing when she reached the upper hallway, and she heard voices roll up the front stairs.

"Here's the pizza, sir," said a voice, teenage and masculine. "That'll be fifteen dollars and seventy-five cents."

"For one flat box?" Farley boomed. "You'd better take your wares someplace else, boy."

Grinning, Rue hurried down the stairs. Farley was wrapped in a pink chenille bedspread taken from one of the guest bedrooms, and his freshly washed hair was standing up on top of his head.

"It's okay," Rue said quickly. She paid the young man,

took the pizza and closed the door. Then looking up at Farley, she started to laugh. With the bedspread draped around him, toga-style, all he needed was a wreath of laurel leaves on his head to make him a very convincing Roman. "Don't tell me, I know. A funny thing happened to you on the way to the forum."

Farley was clearly not amused. "I'm in no mood for any of your fancy double-talk, woman," he said, glowering.

Rue opened the lid on the pizza box. "Mellow out, Marshal. This will fix you up—prepare to experience one of the best things about modern life." She pried a gooey slice loose and handed it to him. "Go ahead," she urged. "Eat it."

He took a cautious bite, tightened his bedspread toga with a nervous gesture of one hand and took another.

"Good, isn't it?" Rue said, talking with her mouth full.

Farley answered by taking another piece.

Rue had waited too long for this pizza to stand on ceremony. They went into the parlor and sat cross-legged on the floor in front of the empty hearth.

"Bet none of the Pine River ladies ever brought you anything like this for dinner," Rue said smugly.

He lifted a slice to look under it. "Damnedest pancake I've ever seen," he said in all seriousness.

Rue's attention had shifted to the bedspread. "We're going to have to get you some clothes, big fella. I think you're the button-fly-jeans type."

"I've got clothes," Farley protested. Rue hoped he wasn't going to pick now, of all times, to get stubborn.

"Chenille bedspreads have been out of style for a long time," she said. For Farley, the situation was gravely confusing, Rue knew that, but she couldn't help being happy that the two of them hadn't been separated. She would face the lingering pain of saying goodbye to Elisabeth later, and begin learning to live with it. She sighed. "Life is very complicated, Farley."

He glared at her, probably thinking she was a witch or a creature from another planet, that she'd deliberately uprooted him from the world he knew.

"Okay, so maybe that was kind of an obvious statement," Rue conceded. "I can't explain what happened to you, for the simple reason that I don't have the first idea myself. The fact is, you're in the 1990s instead of the 1890s, and you can probably go back if you want to just by holding the necklace in one hand." She started to rise to get the pendant from the mantel, but Farley stopped her by grasping her arm.

"Will you go with me?" he asked hoarsely.

Rue hesitated, then shook her head. "I belong here," she said. If she hadn't realized that before, she reflected, traveling back to 1892 had certainly cleared the matter up for her. She had a suspicion Farley belonged, too, because of his insatiable mind and progressive attitudes, but he would have to discover that for himself. It was not something she could decide for him.

Farley swallowed hard, the last slice of pizza forgotten in his hand, and Rue knew he was making a costly decision.

"I ought to go back where I came from," he finally said. "There are things I left undone and people I need to say goodbye to. But, damn it, scared as I am, I want to see this place." Farley gestured toward the TV set. "I want to see what other machines there are and how they work." He reached out from where he sat and touched the dangling cord of a lamp. "And these lanterns. Does the kerosene come in through this wire?"

Rue kissed his forehead. "You've got quite an adventure ahead of you, cowboy."

Farley finished the pizza, thoughtfully examining Rue's jeans and sweater. "I guess women must dress like that here, then?" he inquired, and it was obvious that he didn't wholly approve of the look.

She nodded. "Chinese women have worn pants for centuries," she said. "Here in the United States, the style didn't really catch on until the Second World War."

"There was a war involving the whole world?" Farley's eyes were wide and haunted with the horrible images of such an event.

"There were two," Rue said. "And all of us are praying like crazy that there'll never be a third."

Awkwardly, Farley got to his feet, still carefully clutching the bedspread that preserved his modesty, and started toward the back of the house. "The privy still in the same place?"

Again, Rue laughed. "The outhouse was filled in sometime in the thirties, Farley." She wriggled her fingers to summon him to the downstairs bathroom, showed him how to flush. "There's another one upstairs. I guess you missed it when you took your shower."

He whistled. "That's one fine invention."

"Wait until you see what we can do with computers," she countered, leaving the room and closing the door. She hung up Farley's sheepskin coat, his badge still gleaming on the lapel, and gingerly set his gun belt on top of the highboy in the smaller parlor. Then she dropped his socks, trousers and shirt into the washer. He'd need something to wear while they shopped for contemporary clothes the next day.

By this time, Farley was standing behind her, wearing just a bath towel around his middle now. Obviously, he was feeling a little more comfortable in the circumstances.

"What is that thing doing?" he asked, frowning at the washer.

Rue explained, and Farley grinned at the wonderment of such a thing, flashing his white teeth. He lifted the washer's lid to look inside. The agitator promptly stopped.

Rue closed the lid again and patted the top of the washer's companion appliance. "This is the drier. I'll put your shirt and pants in here after the washer stops, and they'll be ready to wear in less than half an hour."

Farley looked mesmerized. "Will you teach me how to work these things?" he asked.

"Count on it," Rue agreed. She was a firm believer in training a man right in the first place. That way, maybe he wouldn't be dropping socks and wet towels on the bathroom floor and leaving dirty dishes in the kitchen sink.

Upstairs, she gave him a new toothbrush from the supply in the linen closet, along with a tube of paste. He was standing at the sink in the main bathroom, happily foaming at the mouth when Rue retired to the master bath.

When she came out, Farley was sitting on the edge of the bed, still clad in the towel. Which was almost worse than nothing, because it sent Rue's fertile imagination spinning.

He discovered the switch on the bedside lamp and flipped it on and off three or four times before he was apparently satisfied that the same thing would happen ad infinitum, until either the mechanism wore out or he did.

When Farley turned his eyes to Rue and ran them over her short, cotton nightgown, she knew he'd gone a long way toward adjusting to his situation. He smiled broadly and said, "Hope you don't mind sharing your bed. I'm scared of the dark, and, besides, this was supposed to be our wedding night."

Rue hesitated in the doorway, fighting a disconcerting urge to fling herself at Farley in unqualified surrender. She'd always found other men highly resistible, no matter how famous or accomplished they might be, but this self-educated nineteenth-century marshal could send her pulse careening out of control with a look, a simple touch or a few audacious words.

"Are you sure it would be wise for us to sleep together?" she finally managed in a thin voice. "After all, we don't exactly know where our relationship is headed."

"Relationship," Farley repeated with a thoughtful frown, stretching out on the bed. At least *he* was comfortable. Rue was a mass of warm aches and quivering contradictions. "That's a peculiar-sounding word. If it means what I think it does, well, I don't believe all of that has to be worked out tonight. Do you?"

Rue ran the tip of her tongue nervously over dry lips. "No, but—"

Farley arched one eyebrow. "But...?" he prompted, not unkindly.

Rue hugged herself and unconsciously took a step closer. "I'm not sure you're going to understand this, being a man, but when we made love, I opened myself up to you in a way that I never had before. There was no place for me to hide, if you know what I mean, and intimacy of that kind—"

He rose, graceful in his bath towel, and came to stand directly in front of her. "Did I hurt you?" he asked.

Rue shook her head. "No," she croaked after a long moment of silence. "It's just that I felt so vulnerable."

Gently, Farley took Rue's hand, raised it to his mouth, brushed the knuckles with his lips. "I'll make you a bargain," he said. "If I'm loving you and you get scared, all you have to do is say stop, and I will. No questions, no arguments."

Gazing into Farley's eyes, Rue knew he was telling the truth. Color pooled in her cheeks. "You know as well as I do," she told him with a rickety smile, "that once you start kissing and touching me, stopping will be the last thing on my mind."

He eased her to the side of the bed, pulled the nightgown off over her head and tossed it aside. Then he feasted on her with his eyes, and that alone made Rue feel desirable and womanly.

Her breasts seemed to swell under Farley's admiring gaze, the nipples protruding, eager. Her thighs felt softer and warmer, as if preparing to cradle his hard weight, and the most secret reaches of her womanhood began a quiet, heated throbbing.

When Farley spread splayed fingers through her freshly combed hair and bent her head back for his kiss, Rue gave an involuntary whimper. She was terrified, and the sensation of his mouth against hers was something like hurtling down the face of Mount Rainier on a runaway toboggan.

Rue felt Farley's towel fall away as he gripped her bottom, raised her slightly and pressed her against him, never slackening the kiss. Most of her wits had already deserted her, but she knew somehow that Farley was afraid, too, as she had been when she'd suddenly found herself in an alien century. He needed her comfort as he might never need it again, and if Rue hadn't already been incredibly turned on, that knowledge alone would have done the trick.

Passion made her bold. Farley broke the kiss with a gasp of surprised pleasure when she closed her hand around his manhood and instinctively began a fiery massage. Finally, Rue knelt and took him into her mouth, and his fingers delved into her hair, frantic, worshiping. A low groan rolled beneath the washboard muscles of his stomach before escaping his throat.

Farley allowed Rue to attend him for a long time—it was

amazing, but somehow he was still in charge of their lovemaking, even while she was subjecting him to exquisite rap-
ture. Finally he stopped her, raised her to the bed and gently
laid her there.

He said something to her in a low, rumbling voice, and
then repaid her thoroughly for the sweet torment she'd given
him. He did not bring her to the brink again and again, as
Rue had done to him, however. Instead, Farley took her all
the way, pursuing her relentlessly, until her heels dug deep
into the mattress and her cries of satisfaction echoed off the
ceiling.

When at last he took her, Rue didn't expect to have anything left to give. Her own instant, fevered response came as
a shock to her, and so did the deep wells of sensation Farley
plumbed with every thrust. He was exposing parts of her emotional life, places in her very soul, that had never seen the
light.

Afterward, as before, he held Rue close, and her soaring
heart returned from the heavens and settled itself inside her
like a storm-ruffled bird that has finally found a roosting place.
A tear brimmed the lower lashes of Rue's right eye and then
zigzagged down her cheek, catching against the callused side
of Farley's thumb.

Maybe he knew she didn't need consoling, that she was
crying because life was life, because she was so grateful for
the steady beat of her heart and the breath in her lungs. In
any case, all Farley did was hold her a little tighter.

"It's strange," she said after a very long time, "to think
that Elisabeth and Jonathan and Trista are in this house, too,
even though we can't see or hear them."

Farley's hand moved idly against her hair, her temple, her
cheek. "I'm still trying to figure out that thing you've got
downstairs, the box with the pictures inside. There's no point
in vexing my poor brain with how many people are traipsing
around without us knowing about it."

Rue smiled, spreading her fingers over the coarse patch of
hair on Farley's chest. "It's nice, though, to think Bethie and

the others are so close by, that they're not actually dead but just in another dimension."

He reached over to cover her lips with an index finger. "I'm not even going to ask what you mean by 'another dimension,'" he said, "because I'm afraid you'll tell me."

She turned over, resting her leg on top of his and curling her foot partway around his ankle. Then she gave one of his nipples a mischievous lick before smiling into his eyes. "There is so much I want to show you, Farley. Like my ranch, for instance."

"Your what?"

"You remember. I told you I had a ranch in Montana."

He chuckled. "I thought you were just pulling my leg about that. How did you come to have your own land?"

"I inherited it from my grandfather. Let's go there, Farley—tomorrow. As soon as we've bought you some new clothes."

Farley stiffened, and his tone, though as quiet as before, had an edge to it. "The duds I've got will do just fine."

Rue sighed. "This is no time to have a fit of male pride, Marshal. Times have changed, and if you go around in those clothes, people will think you're a refugee from a Wild West show."

"I don't accept what I haven't earned," he replied. He'd clamped his jaw with the last word, and even in the thin moonlight Rue could see that his eyes had gone hard as marbles.

"Good," Rue said. "I need a foreman at Ribbon Creek anyway; my lawyers have been complaining about the one I've got ever since Gramps died."

In the next few seconds, it was as though Farley's masculine pride and desire for a ranch had taken on substance even though they remained invisible. Rue could feel them doing battle right there in the room.

"What are you going to do if you don't work for me, Farley?" she pressed quietly. "You're one of the most intelligent men I've ever known, but believe me, you don't have the kind of job skills you'd need to make a decent living in this day and age.''

He was quiet for such a long time that Rue feared he'd drifted off to sleep. Finally, however, Farley replied, ''Let's go and have a look at this ranch of yours, then.''

Rue laid her cheek against his chest, smiled and closed her eyes.

When she awakened in the morning, Farley was sitting in a chair next to the bed, wearing his regular clothes. Although there were pulled threads shriveling the fabric in places, and the pants looked an inch or two shorter, he was still handsome enough to make Rue's heart do a happy little spin.

''I was beginning to think you meant to lay there till the Resurrection,'' Farley grumbled, and Rue ascertained in that moment that, despite the fact that he'd gotten up comparatively early, the marshal was not a morning person.

''Low blood sugar,'' Rue diagnosed, tossing back the covers and sitting up. She'd put her nightgown back on during the night, so she didn't feel as self-conscious as she might have otherwise. ''Don't let it bother you. I have the exact same problem. If I don't eat regularly—and junk food is worse than nothing—I get crabby, too.''

Farley was already at the door. ''I don't know what the hell you're talking about, but if you're saying I'm hungry, you're right. I was planning to make breakfast, and I took some wood from the basket by the parlor fireplace, but I'll be damned if I could figure out where to kindle the fire in that kitchen stove of yours.''

Rue grinned and preceded him out of the bedroom and down the stairs. ''It's not the kind of stove you're used to, Marshal. Remember the cords on the lamp? Most everything in the kitchen works the same way, by electricity.'' She'd explained the mysteries of that science as best she could the night before, but in a way it was like trying to illustrate their trip through time. Rue couldn't very well clarify things she barely understood herself. ''Never fear,'' she finished. ''There's a set of books at the ranch that covers that type of thing—Gramps had a penchant for knowing how things worked.''

She crossed the kitchen and opened the refrigerator, knowing ahead of time what she'd find. Nothing edible, except for three green olives floating in a jar. The other stuff had been there when she arrived at the house days—weeks?—before.

Rue opened the freezer and took out a box of toaster waffles. ''I'm afraid this will have to hold us until we can get to Steak Heaven out on Highway 18.''

Farley watched in consternation as Rue opened the carton, pulled apart the inner wrapper and popped two waffles into the toaster. While they were warming, she scouted out syrup and put two cups of water into the microwave for instant coffee.

''How does this contraption work?'' Farley asked, turning to the stove that had so confounded him earlier.

Rue checked the oven on a hunch and found kindling sticks neatly stacked on the middle rack. She struggled not to laugh as she removed them, thanking heaven all the while that Farley had not gone so far as to light a blaze.

''These knobs on the top control everything,'' she said when she could trust herself to speak. With one arm, she held the applewood while pointing out the dials with her free hand.

Farley listened earnestly to her explanation, then nodded with a grin. It was plain that he was a quick study; no doubt he would take in information as fast as it could be presented.

They breakfasted on the waffles and coffee, and then Rue hurriedly showered and dressed. She wasn't afraid of her Aunt Verity's house, even after all that had happened to her and to Elisabeth here; she could never have feared that benevolent place. Still, Rue felt an urgency to be gone, a particular fear she didn't like facing.

Perhaps away from here, the necklace would have no power. If it did, however, Farley could disappear at any moment.

Getting the marshal to leave his gun belt behind required some of the fastest talking Rue had ever done, but in the end, she succeeded by promising him access to the big collection of firearms that had belonged to her grandfather.

It was almost noon when she and Farley locked the house and set out. Rue had brought her laptop computer, clothes and personal things, but she'd deliberately left the necklace behind; in its own way, the thing was as dangerous as the marshal's Colt .45.

Farley was fascinated by the Land Rover. He walked around it three or four times before getting in.

Thinking her guest might be interested in seeing how Pine River had developed over the decades since he'd been its marshal, Rue drove him down Main Street, showed him the movie house and the library and the local police station. She avoided the churchyard without looking too closely at her reasons.

Farley was, of course, amazed by the changes, and would have insisted on getting out and exploring, Rue was sure, if he hadn't been so fascinated by their mode of transportation.

He spent the entire ride to Steak Heaven opening and closing the glove compartment, turning the dials on the radio, switching on the heat, then the air-conditioning, then the heat again.

"Soon as we get to Ribbon Creek," Rue promised from her position behind the wheel, "I'll teach you to drive."

Farley beamed at the prospect.

When they reached the restaurant, Farley turned his attention from the dashboard and stared in amazement at the crowded parking lot. "Jumpin' Juniper," he said. "Does everybody in this place have one of these newfangled buggies?"

Rue smiled. "Almost," she answered, "but they come in all shapes, sizes and colors, as you can see."

Farley paused to inspect a pricey red sports car as they passed, giving a low whistle of appreciation. It only went to prove, Rue thought in amusement, that some things transcend time. Maybe men had always been fascinated by methods of transportation.

The noise and bustle of the inside of the restaurant made Farley visibly nervous. His face took on a grim expression, and Rue saw him touch his outer thigh once or twice while they waited to be seated. Probably he was unconsciously seeking reassurance that wasn't there—his gun.

"Smoking or nonsmoking?" a waitress asked pleasantly.

Farley's turquoise eyes widened as he took in the girl's short skirt, and Rue realized he'd never seen a female show so much leg in public.

"Non," Rue answered, linking her arm with Farley's and propelling him between the crowded tables as the girl led the way.

"Tarnation," Farley muttered, looking around and seeing that not only other waitresses but customers were dressed in the same way. "If the Presbyterians saw this, they'd be spitting railroad spikes."

Rue chuckled. "Some of these people probably *are* Presbyterians, Farley. This is an accepted way for women to dress."

They reached their booth, and Farley slid into the seat across from Rue, still looking overwhelmed. His eyes narrowed. "It's bad enough to see a woman in pants," he whispered pointedly. "I hope you don't plan on parading around in one of these getups you call a dress, with your knees sticking out. I'm the only one who should see you like that."

Rue rested her plastic-coated menu against her forehead for a moment, hiding her face while she battled amusement and her natural tendency to protest his arbitrary words. Finally, she met his gaze over the steaming cups of coffee between them, and said, "Even if we were married, which we're not, I wouldn't let you tell me what to wear, Farley. That would be like allowing you to tell me how to vote."

He stared at her. "You can vote?"

She sighed and rolled her eyes heavenward. "I can see this is going to be quite a project, acclimatizing you to the twentieth century."

The waitress returned, and Rue ordered a club sandwich and a diet cola, since it was lunchtime. Farley, having read his own menu, asked for sausage and eggs. Plainly, the toaster waffles hadn't seemed like breakfast to him.

When the food came, he loaded it down with pepper, except for the toast, and consumed every bite, leaving nothing on his plate but a few streaks of egg yoke.

Rue paid the check with a credit card, and when the cashier handed it back, Farley intercepted and studied the card intently.

"This is money?" he asked, handing the card to Rue as they crossed the parking lot a few minutes later.

"The plastic variety," Rue affirmed with a nod. She stopped and looked up into Farley's wonderful eyes, feeling so much love for him that it was painful. "I know everything seems pretty bewildering," she said gently, "but you're a very intelligent man and you'll figure things out."

He looked the Land Rover over speculatively as they approached. "I'd like to drive now," he announced.

"No way," Rue answered, pulling her keys from the pocket of her jeans. "Cars move a whole lot faster than horses, Farley, and when they collide, people get killed."

Although the marshal looked disappointed, he didn't argue.

Where before his attention had been taken up by the gizmos on the dashboard, now Farley was intent on the other cars, the buildings, the power lines alongside the highway. As they drove toward Seattle, he asked a million questions about the pavement, the road signs, the cars and trucks in the other lanes.

When Seattle itself came into view, with its busy harbor and the picturesque Space Needle, Farley was apparently struck dumb by the sight. He stared intently, as though his eyes couldn't take in enough to suit him, and he kept turning in different directions.

Rue drove through the city, knowing Farley couldn't have absorbed explanations just then, and kept going until they reached a large mall.

She parked and they entered the concourse. Rue still didn't speak because Farley was so busy absorbing the sights and sounds that he probably wouldn't have heard her anyway.

He studied a colorful display in front of a bookstore with an attitude that seemed like reverence to Rue. She was touched by the depth of his wonder, knowing it must be some-thing like what she felt when he made love to her.

Suddenly she wanted to give him the world, show him ev-erything there was to see.

"I remember that you like reading," she said, her voice a little shaky. She proceeded into the store, located the instruc-tional section and found a comprehensive volume on how things work. Then from another shelf, she took a novel set in the twenty-fifth century. It was the only way she could think of to prepare Farley for the fact that human beings could fly now, that a few brave souls had even visited the moon.

Farley watched as she paid. "You can buy books with plas-tic money?" he asked as they left.

"You can buy almost anything with plastic money," Rue replied, handing him the bag.

They went on to the men's department of one of the big chain stores, and Farley was soon outfitted with jeans, shirts, underwear and socks. He refused to part with his boots, and Rue didn't press the issue.

Soon they were on the freeway again, headed east. Farley alternated between staring out the window and thumbing through the books Rue had bought for him. When he opened one and started to read, she protested.

"You shouldn't read in a moving car, Farley," she said, amazed at how silly she sounded even as she was saying the words. "It'll make you sick."

Farley wet the tip of an index finger, turned a page and read on. "If you can go around with your knees showing in one of those short skirts," he said without even glancing in her direction, "I can read whenever I want to. And I want to."

"Fine," Rue replied, because there was nothing else she could say. She was glad, in a way, that Farley hadn't given in, because his stubborn strength was one of the qualities she loved most. Without looking away from the road, she took a cassette tape from the box between the seats and shoved it into the slot below the radio.

Farley jumped and then lowered the book when Carly Simon's voice filled the Land Rover.

"I think the closest thing you had to this in 1892 was the music box," Rue said without smugness. She knew Farley's curiosity had to be almost overwhelming. "Or maybe a hand organ."

"I'm getting a powerful headache," Farley confessed, rubbing his eyes. "How could so much have happened in a hundred years?"

She didn't tell him about automatic-teller machines and laser surgery, out of simple courtesy. "There were many factors involved," she said gently. "A lot of historians think the nation turned a corner during the Civil War. There were other conflicts later. As wretched and horrible as war is, it forced science to advance, in both good ways and bad, because of the awesome needs it creates."

Farley sat up rigidly straight—clearly some dire thought had just occurred to him—and rasped, "The Union—it still stands, doesn't it?"

Rue nodded and reached out to pat his arm reassuringly. "Oh, yes," she said. "There are fifty states now, you know."

"Canada is a state?"

She laughed. "Hardly. Canada is still a great nation in her own right. I was talking about Arizona, Utah, New Mexico, Oklahoma, Alaska and Hawaii."

Farley was quiet.

That evening, they pulled in at a truck stop to buy gas and have supper. Rue showed Farley how to work the gas pump, and his pride in the simple task was touching.

In the bright, busy restaurant adjoining the filling station, Farley consumed a cheeseburger deluxe, fries and a chocolate milk shake. "Anything that good has got to be kissing cousin to original sin," he commented cheerfully, after making short work of the food.

Rue shrugged and smiled slightly. "Only too true," she agreed with regret, deciding to save the nutritional lectures for later.

Farley cleared his throat. "I suppose these folks have filled in their outhouse, too," he said seriously.

Rue laughed, pushed away the last of her own chef's salad, and slid out of the booth. "This way, cowboy," she said. She pointed out the men's room, which was at the end of a long hallway, and paid the bill for their supper.

Farley reappeared shortly, his thick hair damp and finger-combed.

They were cruising along the freeway toward Spokane, a star-dappled sky shining above, before he spoke again.

"I keep thinking I must have gotten hold of some locoweed or something," he said in a low, hoarse voice. "How could this be happening to me?"

Rue understood his feelings well, having experienced the same time-travel process, and she was sympathetic. "You're not crazy, Farley," she said, reaching over to touch his arm briefly. "That much I can promise you. There's something really strange going on here, though, and I owe you an apology for dragging you into it the way I did. I'm sorry."

He turned to her in apparent surprise. "It wasn't your fault."

Rue sighed, keeping a close eye on the road. "If I hadn't attached myself to your leg the way I did when the necklace started acting up again and the room was spinning, you probably wouldn't be here now."

Farley chuckled and gave a rueful shake of his head. "I'd be back there wondering just how a lady could be standing in front of me one moment and gone without a trace the next."

"I think the thing that bothers me the most about this whole situation is not knowing, not being able to pick up a thread of reason and follow it back to its spool, so to speak. I don't like mysteries."

Farley was going through Rue's collection of cassettes. "Speaking of mysteries," he marveled, turning a tape over in his hand. "This is the damnedest thing, the way you people can put a voice and a whole bunch of piano players and fiddlers into a little box like this. Back there at that place where we ate, they were selling these things.''

"Tapes are available almost everywhere. They don't just have music on them, either—you can listen to books and to all sorts of instructional stuff.''

Farley grinned. ''I saw one back at the truck stop that interested me,'' he said. ''It was called, *Red-hot Mamas on Wheels.*''

Again, Rue laughed. ''I didn't say it was all literature, Farley.''

"What exactly is a red-hot mama?''

"I'll tell you when you're older.''

"I'm thirty-six!''

"And then some,'' Rue agreed, and this time it was Farley who laughed.

Several hours later, they reached Spokane, and Rue stopped at a large motel, knowing Farley would be uncomfortable with the formality of a city hotel. As it happened, he was pretty Victorian when it came to the subject of sharing rooms.

"It didn't bother you last night!'' Rue whispered impatiently. She'd asked for a double, and Farley had immediately objected, wanting two singles. The clerk waited in silence for a decision to be made, fingers poised over the keyboard of his computer, eyebrows raised.

Farley took Rue's hand and hauled her away from the desk. They were partially hidden behind a gigantic jade tree, which only made matters worse, as far as Rue was concerned.

"We're not married!'' he ground out.

"Now there's a flash,'' Rue said, her hands on her hips. "We weren't married *last* night, either!''

"That was different. This is a public place.''

Rue sighed. ''Like the beds are in the lobby or something.'' But then she conceded, ''Okay, you win. Explaining this is obviously going to be a monumental task, and I'm too tired to tackle the job. We'll compromise.'' She went back to the desk, credit card in hand, and asked for adjoining rooms.

Her quarters and Farley's were on the second floor, along an outside balcony.

"Good night," she said tightly, after showing Farley how to unlock his door with the plastic card that served as a key. There was an inner door connecting the two rooms, but Rue had promised herself she wouldn't use it. "Don't eat the peanuts or drink the whiskey in the little refrigerator," she warned. "Everything costs about four times what it would anywhere else."

Farley's tired blue eyes were twinkling with humor. "I'm only looking out for your reputation as a lady," he said, plainly referring to their earlier row over shared accommodation.

"I have a reputation as a reporter," Rue replied, folding her arms. "Nobody ever accused me of being a lady."

Farley put down her suitcase and curled his fingers under the waistband of her jeans, pulling her against him with an unceremonious jerk. "Somebody's accusing you of it right now," he argued throatily, and then he gave Rue a long, thorough, lingering kiss that left her trembling. "You're all woman, fiery as a red-hot branding iron, and the way you fuss when I have you, everybody in this place would know what was happening. I don't want that—those gasps and cries and whimpers you give belong to me and me alone."

Rue's face was crimson by that time. She'd heard much blunter statements—while traveling with other journalists and camera crews, for instance—but this was intimate; it was personal. "Good night," she said again, trying to wrench free of Farley's grasp.

He held on to her waistband, the backs of his fingers teasing the tender flesh of her abdomen, and he kissed her again. When he finally drew back, her knees were so weak, she feared she might have to *crawl* into her room.

"Good night," Farley said. Then he went into his room and closed the door.

That night, Farley experienced a kind of weariness he'd never had to endure before—not after forced marches in the army or herding cattle across three states or tracking outlaws through the worst kind of terrain. No, it wasn't his body that was worn out—he hadn't done a lick of honest work all day long—it was his mind. His spirit. There was so much to understand, to absorb, and he was bewildered by the onslaught of information that had been coming down on him in a continuous cascade ever since his abrupt arrival in the 1990s.

He moved to toss his hat onto the bed, with its brown striped spread, and stopped himself at the last second. Where he came from, to do that was to invite ill fortune. In this strange place where everything was bigger, brighter and more intense, he hated to think what plain, old, sorry luck might have developed into.

After a little thought, he went to the wardrobe, which was built into the wall, and put his hat on the shelf. The conveniences were right next to that, and he couldn't help marveling at the sleek and shiny bathtub, the sink and commode, the supply of thick, fluffy towels.

Except for Rue, who was just beyond a puny inside door, he was most attracted by the box on the bureau facing the bed. Rue had called the machine a TV, describing it as a shirttail relation to the camera, and Farley found the device wonderfully mystifying.

Facing it, he bent to squint at the buttons arrayed down one side, then touched the one that said Power.

Immediately, a black man with hair as flat as the top of a

windswept mesa appeared, smiling in a mighty friendly way. He said something Farley didn't quite catch, and a lot of unseen people laughed.

Farley punched another button and found an imposing-looking fellow standing behind the biggest pulpit he'd ever seen in his life. Beginning to catch on to the system, the marshal pressed still another button.

A lady wearing one of those skimpy dresses appeared, pushing something that might have been a carpet sweeper. There was a block in one side of the window, listing several different figures.

Farley proceeded to the next button, and this time he got a faceful of a bad-natured galoot with a long, red mustache and six-guns as big as he was. He was moving and talking, this noisy little desperado, and yet he wasn't real, like the other TV people had been. He was a *drawing*.

Farley sat down on the end of the mattress, enthralled. Next came a rabbit who walked upright, jabbered like an eager spinster and would do damn near anything for a carrot.

Finally, Farley turned off the machine, removed his boots and stretched out on the bed with a sigh. This century was enough to terrify a body, though he couldn't rightly admit that out loud, being a United States marshal and all.

On the other side of the wall, he heard a deep voice say, ''This is CNN,'' and smiled. A month ago, even a day ago, he'd have torn the place apart, hearing that. He'd have been convinced there was a man in Rue's room, bothering her. Now he knew she was only watching the TV machine.

He imagined her getting ready for bed, brushing her teeth, washing her face, maybe padding around in one of those thin excuses for a nightdress that made his whole body go hard all at once. He could have been in there with her—it was torture knowing that—but he didn't want anybody thinking less of her because she'd shared a room with a man who wasn't her husband. She was too fine for that, too special.

Farley got up after a time, stripped off his clothes and ran himself a bath in the fancy room with the tiles that not only covered the floor but climbed most of the way up the wall.

When the tub was full, he tested the steaming water with a toe, yelped in pain, and studied the spigots, belatedly recalling that *H* meant hot and *C* meant cold.

He had scrubbed himself from head to foot and settled into bed with one of the books Rue had bought for him when the ugly contraption on the bedside stand started to make a jangling noise. Farley frowned, staring as though to intimidate it into silence. Then, remembering the brief lecture Rue had given him at her house, he recognized it as a telephone.

He picked up the removable part and heard Rue's voice, tinny and small, saying, "Farley? Farley, are you there?"

He put the device to his ear, decided the cord wasn't supposed to dangle over his eye and cheek, and turned it around. "Rue?"

"Who else would it be?" she teased. "Did I wake you?"

He glowered at the contrivance, part of which still sat on the bedside table. If the TV machine was family to the camera, this thing must be kin to the telegraph. Now that he thought about it, the conclusion seemed obvious. "No," he said. "I wasn't sleeping." Farley liked talking to Rue this way, there was a strange intimacy to it, but he surely would have preferred to have her there in the bed with him. "I was watching that TV box a little while ago."

There was a smile in her voice, though not the kind meant to make a man feel smaller than he should be. "What did you see?"

Farley shook his head, still marveling. "Pictures—drawings—that moved and talked. One was supposed to be a person, but it wasn't."

Rue was quiet for a moment, then she said, again without a trace of condescension in her voice, "That was a cartoon. Artists draw and paint figures, and then they're brought to life by a process called animation. I'll tell you more about it tomorrow."

Farley wasn't sure he was really that interested, not when there were so many other things to puzzle through, but he didn't want to hurt Rue's feelings, so he would listen when the time came. They talked for a few minutes more, then said good-night, and Farley put the talking part of the telephone back where he'd found it.

He'd mastered light switches—to his way of thinking it was diabolical how the damn things were in a different place on every lamp—so he twisted a bit of brass between his fingers and the room became comparatively dark.

He was as exhausted as before, maybe more so, and he yearned, body and soul, for the comfort Rue could give him. He closed his eyes, thinking he surely wouldn't be able to sleep, and he promptly lost consciousness.

He must have rested undisturbed for a few hours, but then the dream was upon him, and it was so real that he felt the texture of the sheets change beneath him, the firmness of the mattress. Indeed, Farley felt the air itself alter, become thinner, harder to breathe.

The traffic sounds from the nearby highway turned to the twangy notes of saloon pianos, the nickering of horses, the squeaks and moans of wagon wheels.

Farley was back in his own lifetime.

Without Rue.

He let out a bellow, a primitive mixture of shock and protest, and sat bolt upright in bed. His skin was drenched with sweat, and he was gasping for breath, as though he'd been under water the length of the dream.

The dream. Farley wanted to weep with relief, but that, too, was something unbefitting a United States marshal. There was an anxious knock at the door separating his room from Rue's, and then, just as Farley switched on the lamp, Rue burst in.

"Good grief, Farley, are you all right? It sounded like you were being scalped!"

He was embarrassed at being caught in the aftermath of a nightmare, and that made him a little angry. "Do you always barge in on people like that?"

Rue was wearing a white cotton nightdress that barely reached the top of her thighs. Her eyes were narrowed, and her hands were resting on her hips. "I seem to recall asking you a similar question," she said, "when I woke up in the master bedroom at Pine River a hundred years ago and found you standing there staring at me." She paused, drew a deep breath and went on, a fetching pink color rising in her cheeks. "Your virtue is in no danger, Farley. I just wanted to make sure you were okay. I mean, you could have slipped in the bathtub or something."

He arched one eyebrow after casting an eye over her nightclothes—there were little bloomers underneath the skimpy gown, with ruffles around the legs—and then her long, slender legs. Lordy, she looked as sweet as a sun-warmed peach.

"Suppose I *had* fallen in the bathtub," he responded huskily, leaning back against the padded headboard and pulling the sheets up to his armpits. One of them had to be modest, and it sure as hell wasn't going to be Rue, not in the getup she had on. "How would you have known?"

She ran impudent eyes over the length of his frame. "The walls are thin here, Marshal. And you would have made quite a crash." She folded her arms, thus raising the nightdress higher. "Stop trying to evade the subject and tell me what made you let out a yell like that."

Farley sighed. Now that he'd stalled long enough to regain most of his composure, he figured he could talk about what happened without breaking into a cold sweat. "I dreamed I was back in 1892, that's all," he said.

Rue came and sat on the foot of the bed, cross-legged like an Indian. "Was I there?"

Farley hoped the tremendous vulnerability he was feeling wasn't audible in his voice. "No," he said. "Don't you have a dressing gown you can put on? I can't concentrate with you wearing that skimpy little nightgown."

She gave him a teasing grin. "You'll just have to suffer."

He fussed with his covers for a few moments. He was suffering, all right; it felt like he had a chunk of firewood between his legs. He changed the subject.

"Can one or the other of us be sent back even if that damn necklace is nowhere around?"

Rue's smile faded. She bit her lower lip for a moment. "I don't know, Farley," she said quietly. "When I first found the necklace, I had to be wearing or holding it to travel through time, and I had to pass through a certain doorway in the upstairs hall of my aunt's house. It was the same for Elisabeth. Later, it was as though the two time periods were meshing somehow, and I no longer had to go over the threshold to reach 1892.''

''But you always had the necklace?''

She nodded. ''Things are obviously changing, though. It seems to me that if people can step backward or forward in time, anything can happen.''

Farley had another chill, though this was only a shadow of the one that had gripped him during the nightmare. Maybe he wouldn't be allowed to stay in this crazy, mixed-up century, with this crazy, mixed-up woman. The idea was shattering.

Rue was as vital to him as the blood flowing through his veins, and there was so much he wanted to see, so much he wanted to know.

He moved over and tossed back the covers to make room for her. He hadn't changed his mind about the impropriety of sharing a bed in a public inn, but he needed to sleep with his arms around her.

She switched off the lamp and crawled in beside him, all warm and soft and fragrant. When she snuggled close, Farley let out an involuntary groan.

Rue smoothed the hair on his chest with a palm. ''Let's hope we don't do any time traveling while we're making love,'' she teased. ''We could make an embarrassing landing, like in the horse trough in front of the feed and grain, or on one of the pool tables at the Hang-Dog Saloon. I don't mind telling you, Marshal, the Society would be livid!''

Farley laughed, rolled onto his side and gathered her close with one arm. There was no use in trying to resist her; she was too delicious, too funny, too sweet.

''What am I going to do with you?'' he asked in mock despair.

Rue started nibbling at his neck, and murmured, ''I have a few suggestions.''

When Rue awoke the next morning, Farley was already up. He'd showered and dressed in some of his starchy new clothes, and he was sitting at the requisite round table by the windows, reading *USA Today*. "It seems to me that politicians haven't changed much," he commented without lowering the newspaper.

Rue smiled. She was hypersensitive, but in a pleasant way; the feel of Farley's hands and mouth still lingered on her lips, her throat, her breasts and stomach. "Some things stay the same no matter how much time passes," she replied, sitting up and wrapping her arms around her knees.

He peered at her over the colorful masthead. "I agree," he said solemnly, folding the paper and setting it aside. Having done that, Farley shoved one hand through his gleaming brown hair. "It's wrong for us to—to do what we did last night, Rue. That's something that should be confined to marriage."

Rue would have rolled her eyes if she hadn't known Farley was dead serious. She reached for the telephone and punched the button for room service. "Are you trying to tell me that you were married to every woman you ever slept with?" she inquired reasonably.

"No, ma'am," replied the youthful masculine voice at the other end of the line.

Hot color surged into Rue's face, and she would have hung up in mortification if she hadn't wanted coffee so much. "I wasn't talking to you," she told the room-service clerk with as much dignity as she could manage. Farley had clearly figured out what had happened, and he was chuckling.

Rue glared at him, then spoke into the receiver again, giving the room number and asking for a pot of coffee, fresh fruit and toast.

The moment she hung up, Farley gave a chortle of amusement.

"Well?" Rue demanded, not to be deterred. "*Were* you married to everyone you've ever made love with?"

Farley cleared his throat and reddened slightly. "Of course not. But this is different. A nice woman doesn't—"

Rue interrupted with an imperious upward thrust of one

finger and, "Don't you dare say it, Farley Haynes!" She stabbed her own chest with that same digit. "*I* slept with you, and I'm one of the 'nicest women' you'll ever hope to meet!"

"You only did it because I took advantage of you."

"What a crock," Rue muttered, flinging back the covers and standing. "Did I act like I was being taken advantage of?"

"You should have just stayed in your own room," Farley grumbled.

"So now it's my fault?"

The marshal sighed. "I think it would probably be easier to change General Custer's mind about strategy than win an argument with you. Damn it, Rue, what I'm trying to say is, I think we should be married."

Rue sat down on the edge of the bed again. She loved Farley, and she hadn't agreed to marry him in 1892 because she'd known she didn't want to stay in that dark and distant century. This proposal, however, was quite another matter.

"It might be difficult getting a marriage license," she said awkwardly after a long time. "Considering that you have no legal identity."

While Farley was still puzzling that one out, the food arrived. Rue wrapped herself in one of the big shirts they'd bought the day before to let the room-service waiter in and sign the check.

Once they were alone again, she sat at the round table, feet propped on the edge of the chair, and alternately sipped coffee and nibbled at a banana.

"What do you mean, I don't have a legal identity?" Farley wanted to know. He added two packets of sugar to his coffee and stirred it with a clatter of spoon and china. "Is there a gravestone with my name on it somewhere back there in the long ago?"

A chill made Rue shiver and reach to refill her coffee cup. "I can show you where Elisabeth and Jonathan are buried," she said, not looking at him. "But that's different, because they stayed in the past. You came here."

"So if we find my marker, say around Pine River some-place, that'll mean I'm going back. It would have to."

Rue's head was spinning, but she understood Farley's meaning only too well. Elisabeth had a grave in the present because she'd returned to the past and lived out her life. Coming across Farley's burial place would mean he wasn't going to stay with her, in the here and now, that he was destined to return.

"You're right," she blurted, "we should get married."

A slow smile spread across Farley's rugged face. "What are we going to do about my identity?"

Rue bit her lip, thinking. "We'll have to invent one for you. I know a guy who used to work with the Witness Protection Program—those people can come up with an entire history."

After giving the inevitable explanations, Rue finished her breakfast and took a shower. Farley brought her things from the room next door, so she was able to dress and apply light makeup right away.

They were checked out of the motel and on the road to Montana while the morning was still new.

As they passed out of eastern Washington into Idaho and then Montana, the scenery became steadily more majestic. There were snow-capped mountains, their slopes thick with pine and fir trees, and the sheer expanse of the sky was awe inspiring.

"They call Montana the 'Big Sky Country,'" Rue said, touched by Farley's obvious relief to be back in the kind of unspoiled territory he knew and understood. She'd have to tell him about pollution and the greenhouse effect sooner or later, but this wasn't the time for it.

"Are we almost there? At your ranch, I mean?"

Rue shook her head. "Ribbon Creek is still a few hours away."

They stopped for an early lunch at one of those mom-and-pop hamburger places, and Farley said very little during the meal. He was clearly preoccupied.

"We should have stopped at the cemetery in Pine River"

was the first thing he said, much later, when they were rolling down the highway again.

Just thinking of standing in some graveyard reading Farley's name on a tombstone made Rue's eyes burn. "I'll call the church office and ask if you're listed in the registry for the cemetery," she said. Even as Rue spoke the words, she knew—she who had never been a procrastinator—that this was a task she would put off as long as possible.

In the late afternoon, when the sun was about to plunge beneath the western horizon in a grand and glorious splash of crimson and gold, Rue's spirits began to lift.

Roughly forty-five minutes later, the Land Rover was speeding down the long, washboard driveway that led to the ranch house.

Farley had opened the door and gotten out almost before the vehicle came to a stop. Rue knew he was tired of being confined, and he was probably yearning for the sight of something familiar, too.

Soldier, a black-and-white sheepdog, met them in the dooryard, yipping delightedly at Rue's heels and giving Farley the occasional suspicious growl. There were lights gleaming in the kitchen of the big but unpretentious house, and Rue had a sweet, familiar sensation of being drawn into an embrace.

The screen door at the side of the house squeaked, and so did the old voice that called, "Who's that?"

"Wilbur, it's me," Rue answered happily, opening the gate and hurrying along the little flagstone walk that wound around to the big screen porch off the kitchen. "Rue."

Wilbur, who had worked for Rue's grandfather ever since both were young men, gave a cackle of delight. Now that he was elderly, he had the honorary title of caretaker, but he wasn't expected to do any real work. "I'll be ding danged," he said, limping Walter Brennan-style along the walk to stand facing Rue in the glow of the porch light. His rheumy blue eyes found Farley and climbed suspiciously to a face hidden by the shadow of the marshal's hat brim.

"Who might this be?" Wilbur wanted to know and, to his credit, he didn't sound in the least bit intimidated by Farley's size or the aura of strength that seemed to radiate from the core of his being.

"Farley Haynes," the marshal answered, taking off the hat respectfully and offering one hand.

Wilbur studied Farley's face for a long moment, then the still-extended hand. Finally, he put his own palm out for a shake. "Since it ain't none of my business," the old man said, "I won't ask who you are or what your errand is. If Miss Rue here says you're welcome at Ribbon Creek, then you are."

"Thank you," Farley said with that old-fashioned note of courtliness Rue found nearly irresistible. Then he turned and went back to the Land Rover for their things, having learned to open and close the tailgate when they left the motel that morning.

"He gonna be foreman now that Steenbock done quit?" Wilbur inquired in a confidential whisper that probably carried clear to the chicken coop.

Rue looked back at Farley, wishing they could have arrived before sunset. When he got a good look at the ranch, the marshal would think he'd been carried off by angels. "Mr. Haynes is going to be my husband," she said with quiet, incredulous joy. "That means he'll be part owner of the place."

The inside of the house smelled stale and musty, but it was still the same beautiful, homey place Rue remembered. On the ground floor were two parlors—they'd been her grandmother's pride—along with a study, a big, formal dining room, two bathrooms and an enormous kitchen boasting both a wood stove and the modern electric one. Upstairs, above the wide curving staircase, there were five bedrooms, one of which was huge, each with its own bath.

"This looks more like a palace than a ranch house," Farley said a little grimly when they'd made the tour and returned to the kitchen.

Rue took two steaks from the freezer in the big utility room and set them in the microwave to thaw. "This is a working ranch, complete with cattle and horses and the whole bit," she said. "Tomorrow, I'll show you what I mean."

Farley shoved a hand through already-rumpled hair. "What about you? What are you going to do way out here?"

"What I do best," Rue said, taking two big potatoes from a bin and carrying them to the sink. "Write for magazines and newspapers. Of course, I'll have to travel sometimes, but you'll be so busy straightening this place out that you won't even notice I'm gone."

When she looked back over one shoulder and saw Farley's face, Rue regretted speaking flippantly. It was plain that the idea of a traveling wife was not sitting well with the marshal.

She busied herself arranging the thick steaks under the broiler. After that, she stabbed the potatoes with a fork so they wouldn't explode and set them in the microwave.

"Farley, you must have already guessed that I have plenty of money," she said reasonably, bringing plates to the table. "I'm not going to be rushing out of here on assignment before the ink's dry on our marriage license. But I have a career, and eventually I'll want to return to it."

Farley pushed back his chair, found the silverware by a lucky guess and put a place setting by each of the plates. He was a Victorian male in the truest sense of the word, but he didn't seem to be above tasks usually regarded as women's work. Rue had high hopes for him.

"Farley?" She stood behind one of her grandmother's pressed-oak chairs, waiting for his response. Quietly demanding it.

His wonderful turquoise eyes linked with hers, looking weary and baffled. "What if we have a baby?" he asked hoarsely. "A little one needs a mother."

Rue smiled because he'd spoken gently and because the picture filled her with such joy. "I quite agree, Mr. Haynes," she said, yearning to throw her arms around Farley's neck and kiss him soundly. "When we have a child, we'll take care of him or her together," she assured him.

She turned the steaks and wrapped the microwaved potatoes in foil. Soon, Rue and Farley were sitting at the table, like any married couple at the end of a long day, sharing a late supper. Farley ate hungrily of the potatoes and steak, but he politely ignored the canned asparagus Rue had heated on the stove. To him, the vegetable probably looked as though it had been boiled to death.

When they'd finished, they cleaned up the kitchen together.

"Sleepy?" she asked.

Farley's wind-weathered cheeks blushed a dull red. He was going to get stubborn about the marriage thing again, she could tell.

"Look," Rue said with a sigh, "you can have your own room until after the wedding. After that, there will be no more of this Victorian-virgin stuff, understand?"

Farley stared at her for a moment, then smiled. "Absolutely," he agreed, his voice throaty and low.

Rue led the way upstairs. On the second floor, she paused in front of an electrical panel and switched off the downstairs lights. "This will be our room eventually," she said, opening the door to the large master suite with its fireplace and marble hot tub, "so you might as well get used to sleeping here. I'll be just down the hall."

Farley's throat worked visibly as he swallowed and nodded his agreement. Rue wanted him to sleep alone in the big bed, to imagine her sharing that wonderful room with him.

She stood on tiptoe to kiss the cleft in his stubbly chin. "Good night," she said.

"Good night," he replied. The words were rough, grating against each other like rusty hinges.

Rue went down the hall to her own room, whistling softly.

It was comforting to be back where she had sometimes slept as a child. When she was small, she'd spent a lot of time at the ranch, but later, her mother and grandfather had had some sort of falling out. That was why she'd ended up at Aunt Verity's when her parents had finally been divorced.

She unpacked, took a quick bath and climbed into bed. For a long time, Rue lay in the darkness, letting her eyes adjust, remembering. Once, a long time ago, she'd dreamed of living out her whole life on this ranch, marrying, raising her children here. Now it seemed that fantasy was about to come true.

Not that Farley wasn't going to have a hard time adjusting

to the idea of having a working wife. He was fiercely proud, and he might never regard the ranch as a true home.

"Stop borrowing trouble," Rue scolded herself in a sleepy whisper. "Farley's always wanted a ranch. You know that."

She tossed restlessly from one side to the other. Then she lay flat on her back and spread her hands over her stomach. *Let there be a baby,* she thought. *Oh, please, let there be a baby.*

Imagining a child with turquoise eyes and unruly brown hair like Farley's made her smile, but her pleasure faded as she remembered his terrible dream the night before. He'd been flung back to his own time without her.

Rue squeezed her eyes closed, trying to shut out the frightening possibilities that had stalked her into this quiet place. It was hopeless; she knew Farley could disappear at any time, maybe without any help from the necklace. And if that was going to happen, there was a grave somewhere, maybe unmarked, maybe lost, and he would have to lie there eventually, like a vampire hiding from the light.

A tear trickled over Rue's cheekbone to wet the linen pillowcase. Okay, she reasoned, love was a risk. *Life* was a risk, not just for her and Farley, but for everyone. The only thing to do was ante up her heart and play the hand she'd been dealt with as much panache as possible.

CHAPTER 11

Rue was out of bed with the first crow of Wilbur's pet rooster, but when she reached the kitchen, wearing boots, jeans and a chambray work shirt left behind on her last visit, Farley was already there. He'd built a fire in the wood cookstove and had used Gramps's old enamel pot to brew coffee. He was reading intently from his how-things-work book.

She decided to demonstrate the automatic coffeemaker another time; Farley would have enough to think about, between grasping the ways ranching had changed since the 1890s and dealing with the cowboys. He would not be given their respect and allegiance simply because he was the foreman; he would have to earn them.

Rue kissed the marshal's cleanly shaved cheek and glanced again at the book he was devouring with such serious concentration. He was studying the inner workings of the combustion engine, and she could almost hear his brain cataloging and sorting the new information.

"'Morning," he said without looking up from the diagram that spanned two pages.

Rue got a cup and went to the stove for coffee. The warmth of the wood fire seemed cozier, somehow, than the kind that flowed through the heat vents from the oil furnace. "Good morning, Mr. Ford."

"Mmm-hmm," Farley said.

Rue was gazing out the window over the sink, watching as big, wispy flakes of November snow began to drift down past the yard light from a gray-shrouded sky. Silently, she marveled that she'd stayed away from the land so long, loving it the way she did. She'd let things go where the ranch was concerned, having her accountants go over the books, but never examining them herself, hiring one foreman after another by long-distance telephone without meeting them, sizing them up.

Sorry, Gramps, she said silently.

Wilbur had bacon and eggs in the refrigerator—he had spent the night in the bunkhouse with the other men now that Rue was back—so she made a high-fat, high-cholesterol and totally delicious breakfast. "We'll have to go into town and stock up on groceries," she said, serving the food. "Then I'll introduce you to the men, and you can choose a horse."

By that time, Farley had finished reading about car engine motors, but he looked sort of absentminded, as if he was still digesting facts and sorting ideas. A light went on in his eyes, though. "A horse?" he echoed.

Rue grinned, a slice of crisp bacon in one hand. "Horses are still fundamental to ranching," she said.

"Is this a big spread?"

She told him the acreage, and he whistled in exclamation. "You raise mostly cattle?"

Rue nodded. "Some horses, too. I'd like to pursue that further, start breeding show stock." She got up and pulled a newspaper clipping she'd spotted earlier from the bulletin board. Wilbur had a habit of saving unusual accounts. "As you can see," she went on, placing the picture of a miniature pony and its trainer next to Farley's plate, "horses come in all shapes and sizes these days."

Farley frowned, studying the photograph. "Tarnation. That little cayoose doesn't even reach the man's belt buckle. Can't be more than two feet high at the withers."

"People breed miniature ponies to show and sell," Rue said, reaching for her coffee. She was prattling, but she didn't care. She enjoyed talking to Farley about anything. "Horses used to be about the size of house cats back in prehistoric times. Did you know that?"

"What good is a two foot horse?" Farley asked practically, letting the history lecture pass without comment. "I don't imagine you could housebreak them like an old lady's pet dog.''

Rue laughed. "True enough. And just imagine what it would be like if they jumped up in your lap, the way a cat or a puppy might do." Seeing Farley's consternation, she spoke seriously. "I know in your time every animal had to have a distinct function. Nowadays, people raise all kinds of creatures just because they enjoy it. I know of a woman who raises llamas, for instance, and a man who keeps a little pig as a pet. It even rides in his car."

"You know some strange people," Farley said, and he clearly wasn't kidding.

Rue smiled. "Yes," she agreed. "And the strangest one of all is a United States marshal from 1892."

Farley smiled back, but he was obviously a little tense. He probably felt nervous about meeting the ranch hands; after all, up until then, Rue had been the only twentieth-century person he'd had any real dealings with. Now he would have to integrate himself into a world he'd only begun to understand.

Rue touched his hand. "Everything will be fine," she promised. "Hurry up and finish your breakfast, please. I'll show you the horse barn, and then I want to get the grocery shopping out of the way."

After giving her a humorously ironic look, Farley carried his plate to the sink. "Don't nag me, woman," he teased.

Widening her eyes in feigned innocence, Rue chirped, "Me? Nag? Never!"

With a lift of one eyebrow, Farley put on his hat and the canvas coat he'd been wearing when he and Rue were suddenly hurled into the latter part of the twentieth century. Rue put on a heavy jacket, gloves and a stocking cap, knowing the wind would be ferocious.

The sun had yet to rise, the snow was still coming down, and the cold was keen enough to bite, but Rue's heart brimmed with happiness all the same. Although she hadn't consciously realized the fact before, this ranch was home, and Farley was the man she wanted to share it with.

When they reached the horse barn, the lights were on and

one of the hands was helping Wilbur feed and water the valuable geldings and mares. Soldier, the sheepdog, was overseeing the project, and he ran over to bark out a progress report when Rue and Farley appeared.

Farley grinned and affectionately ruffled the animal's ears, one of which was white, the other black. "Good boy," he said.

Rue proceeded along the center of the barn until she came to the stall that held her own mare, Buttermilk. It had been too long since she'd seen the small, yellow horse, and she longed to ride, but there were other things that had to be done first.

She went on to meet Wilbur, who was hobbling toward her.

"Where is that stallion you wrote me about? The one we bought six months ago?"

Wilbur ran his fingers through hair that existed only in his memory. "That would be Lobo. His stall is on the other side of the concrete wall. Had to keep him away from the mares, of course, or he'd tear the place apart."

"Lobo," Rue repeated, well aware of Farley towering behind her. "That's a silly name. You've been watching too many cowboy movies, Wilbur."

The old man winked, not at Rue, but past her right shoulder, at Farley. Obviously Wilbur had pegged the marshal as a kindred soul. "No such thing as too many cowboy movies," he decreed. "Ain't possible. Hell, when the Duke died, those Hollywood folks just stopped making good Westerns altogether."

Rue could feel Farley's questions and his effort to contain them until they were alone again.

"Movies," she said as they rounded the concrete wall Wilbur had mentioned, headed for Lobo's private suite, "are pictures, like on TV, put together to make a story."

"Who's this Duke Wilbur was talking about? I thought we didn't have royalty in America."

Rue grinned, working the heavy latch on the door to the inner stable. "There was a very popular actor called John Wayne. His nickname was the Duke."

Inside his fancy stall, the stallion kicked up a minor fuss. Rue supposed it was some kind of macho thing, a way of letting everybody know he was king of the stables.

"Easy, Lobo," she said automatically.

Farley let out a long, low whistle of admiration as he looked at the magnificent animal through the heavy metal slats of the stall door. "You broke to ride, fella?" he asked, stepping closer.

Rue had been around horses a lot, but she felt as nervous then as she would have if Farley had stood on the threshold of that mysterious doorway in Aunt Verity's house with the necklace in his hand. Either way, he'd have been tempting fate.

"Sure is," Wilbur replied from behind them, before Rue had a chance to answer.

She looked at the horse and then at Farley. "I don't think—"

"Where can I find a saddle?" Farley broke in. The line of his jaw and the expression in his eyes told Rue he would not be dissuaded from riding the stallion.

Wilbur produced the requested tack, along with a bridle and saddle blanket, and Farley opened the stall door and stepped inside, talking quietly to Lobo. Beyond the windows, the snow continued to tumble through the first gray light of morning.

Rue bit her lip and backed up, knowing Farley would never forgive her if she protested further. He was a grown man, he'd probably ridden horses most of his life, and he didn't need mothering.

Wilbur stood back, too, watching closely as Farley slipped the bridle over Lobo's gleaming, ebony head, then saddled the horse with an expertise that made a lump of pride gather in Rue's throat. Finally, he led the animal from the stall and through the outer doorway into the paddock.

Lobo was fitful, nickering and tossing his head and prancing to one side.

"You're sure that stallion is broken to ride?" Rue asked Wilbur, watching as Farley planted one booted foot in the stirrup and swung himself into the saddle.

"Pretty much," Wilbur answered laconically.

Lobo gave a shriek of outrage at the feel of a man's weight on his back. He set his hind legs, and his coal black flanks quivered as he prepared to rebel. Several of the ranch hands had gathered along the paddock fence to watch.

"Damn it," Rue ground out, "this isn't funny!" She was about to walk up to Lobo and grab hold of his bridle when Wilbur reached out and caught hold of her arm.

"Let the man show what he's made of," he said, and Rue could have sworn those words came not from the mischievous old man beside her, but from her grandfather.

"That's stupid," Rue protested in a furious whisper, even though she knew Wilbur was absolutely right.

Lobo had finished deliberating. He "came unwrapped," as Rue's grandfather used to say, bucking as if he had a twenty pound tomcat burying its claws in his hide.

Farley looked cool and calm. He even spurred the stallion once or twice, just to let Lobo know who was running the show.

Finally, with a disgruntled nicker, the stallion settled down, and permitted Farley to ride him around the paddock once at a trot. The watching ranch hands cheered and whistled, and Rue knew Farley had taken the first step toward making a place for himself at Ribbon Creek.

Farley rode over to the fence and spoke to the men who remained there, and soon he was bending from Lobo's back to shake hands.

Rue gave Wilbur a look fit to scorch steel, then crossed the paddock to speak to Farley. She smiled so that no one, least of all the marshal himself, would get the idea she was trying to boss him around.

"I guess we'd better be getting to town if we're going to get our business done," she said.

Farley nodded and rode toward the stables without protest, dismounting to lead Lobo through the doorway.

The cowboys at the fence greeted Rue pleasantly and then went on about their own tasks. When she stepped inside the stable, Farley had already unsaddled Lobo and was praising the horse in a low voice as he curried him.

"That was some fancy riding, Marshal," she said.

Farley didn't look away from the horse. "This is some pretty fancy stallion," he replied.

Rue nodded and wedged her hands into the pockets of her jacket. "The men seem to like you. I guess you know they'll play some pranks and bait you a little, to see if they can get a rise out of you."

"I know about ranch hands, Rue," he said with gentle amusement in his voice. "Don't worry yourself. The boys and I will get on just fine."

Rue sighed. "Maybe I'm like Wilbur," she said. "Maybe I've seen too many Westerns on TV."

He looked back at her over one shoulder, grinned and shook his head.

"In the movies, the new arrival on the ranch always has to prove himself by showing that he's got the hardest fists and the quickest draw," Rue said a little defensively.

Farley ran those saucy eyes of his over her in a searing sweep. "I haven't seen anybody around this place I couldn't handle," he said. He gave the horse a last wistful look before joining Rue to walk toward the house.

She put a hand on his arm. "Don't worry, Marshal. You'll be back here and in the saddle before you know it."

Since it was a two-mile stretch to the main highway, Rue let Farley drive on the first leg of the journey to town. He swerved right off the road once, and sent the Land Rover barrelling through the creek that had given the ranch its name, whooping like a Rebel soldier leading a raid.

Rue decided he was better at riding horses.

The drive into town took another half an hour. By the time they arrived, the community's one supermarket was open for business.

Even though he'd been to the mall outside Seattle and had driven across three states with Rue, Farley was still stricken mute with amazement when he walked into the market and saw the wide aisles and the colorful, complicated displays of boxes and cans and bottles. He jumped when the sprayers came on over the produce, and his eyes widened when he saw the pyramids of red apples and plump oranges. In the meat department, he stood watching a mechanized cardboard turkey until Rue finally grabbed his sleeve and pulled him away.

When they finally returned to the parking lot to load two bulging cartfuls of food into the back of the Land Rover, the marshal was looking a little dazed. All during the ride home, he kept turning around in the passenger seat and plundering products from the bags. He read the boxes and labels letter by letter, it seemed to Rue, frowning in consternation.

"No wonder you women are getting into so much trouble with your short dresses and all," he finally remarked when they were turning off the highway onto the ranch. "Everything can be cooked in five or ten minutes, and you've got all sorts of contraptions besides, like that washing machine. You've got too much free time."

Rue smiled. "I'm going to let you get by with that chauvinistic observation just this once, since for all practical intents and purposes, you're new in town."

"Chauvinistic?" Farley looked puzzled, but certainly not intimidated.

"It's another word for a hardheaded cowboy from 1892," Rue replied. Then she proceeded to explain the finer points of the definition.

Farley sighed when it was over. "I still think you've got too much free time," he said. He was gazing out at the snow-dusted plains of the ranch, and the longing to escape the confines of the Land Rover was clearly visible in his face.

"I guess you'll want to saddle one of the horses and look the place over on your own," Rue observed, pulling to a stop in front of the house.

He grinned with both relief and anticipation, and the moment they'd taken the grocery bags into the house, he headed for the barn.

Knowing Farley needed private time to acclimatize himself, Rue put away the food, then retired to the study to make some calls. Farley's old-fashioned insistence that they needed to be married had never been far from her mind and, due to her wide travels, she had contacts in virtually every walk of life.

It wasn't long before she'd arranged a legal identity for Farley, complete with a birth certificate, Social Security number, S.A.T. scores and even transcripts from a midwestern college. All the necessary paperwork was on its way by express courier.

Farley hadn't returned by noon, when a new snow began to powder the ground, so Rue made a single serving of vegetable-beef soup and sat by the big, stone fireplace in the parlor, her feet resting on a needlepoint hassock.

Once she was finished eating, Rue immediately became bored. She went to the woodshed and split a pile of pine and fir for the fireplace. She was carrying the first armload into the house when Farley appeared, striding toward her from the direction of the barn.

His smile was as dazzling as sunlight on ice-crusted snow as he wrested the wood from Rue's arms and carefully wiped his feet on the mat outside the back door. Obviously the ride had lifted his spirits and settled some things in his mind, and she found herself envying him the fresh air and freedom.

"At least you haven't come up with a machine to chop wood," he said good-naturedly, carrying his burden through the kitchen after seeing that the box by the cast-iron cookstove was full.

Rue followed, marveling at the intensity of her reactions to his impressive height, the broad strength of his shoulders, the muscular grace of his arms and legs. "We can get married in a few days," she said, feeling slightly foolish for her eagerness. "The system recognizes you as a real, flesh-and-blood person."

Farley laid the wood on the parlor hearth, pulled aside the screen and squatted to feed the fire. "That sounds like good news," he commented wryly, "though I've got to admit, I can't say I'm entirely sure."

Rue smiled. "Trust me," she said. "The news is good. Are you hungry?"

Farley closed the fireplace screen and stood. "Yes, but I

can see to my own stomach, thank you." He went into the kitchen, with Rue right behind him, and took a frozen entrée from the fridge.

Rue watched with amusement as Farley read the instructions, then set the dish inside the microwave and stood staring at the buttons. She showed him how to set the timer and turn on the oven.

He took bread from the old-fashioned metal box on the counter, and his expression was plainly disapproving as he opened the bag and pulled out two slices. "If a man tried to butter *air,* it would hold up better than this stuff," he remarked scornfully, evidently wanting to let Rue know that not everything about the twentieth century was an improvement over the nineteenth. He held up a slice and peered at Rue through a hole next to the crust. "It's amazing you people aren't downright puny, the way you eat."

Rue laughed and startled Farley by jumping up and flinging her arms around his neck. "I never get tired of listening to you talk, lawman," she said, and her voice came out sounding husky. "Tell me you won't ever change, that you're always going to be Farley Haynes, U.S. Marshal."

He set the bread aside and cupped her chin in one hand. "Everybody changes, Rue," he said quietly, but there was a light in his eyes. She knew he was going to kiss her, and the anticipation was so intense that she felt unsteady and interlocked her fingers at his nape to anchor herself.

The bell on the microwave chimed, and hunger prevailed over passion. Farley stepped gracefully out of Rue's embrace and took his food from the oven.

It was a curious thing, being moved emotionally and spiritually by the plain sight of a man eating spaghetti and meatballs from a cardboard plate, but that was exactly what happened to Rue. Every time she thought she'd explored the depths of her love for this man, she tumbled into some deeper chasm not yet charted, and she was amazed to find that the inner universe was just as vast as the outer one.

Shaken, she tossed her hair back over one shoulder and stood with her hands resting on her hips. "I'm really in trouble here, Farley," she said, only half in jest. "It seems I want to cook for you and wash your clothes and have your babies. We're talking rapid retrograde, as far as women's rights are concerned."

Farley smiled and stabbed a meatball with his fork. "I imagine you'll be able to hold your own just fine," he said, and Rue wondered if he knew how damnably appealing he was, if his charm was deliberate.

That afternoon, while Farley was out somewhere with Wilbur and the dog, Rue dusted off her grandmother's old cookbooks and hunted down a recipe for bread. When the marshal returned, the dough was rising in a big crockery bowl, and the air was still clouded with tiny, white particles.

Farley's turquoise eyes danced as he hung up his hat and gunslinger coat. "Somebody dynamite the flour bin?"

Rue was covered in white dust from head to foot, but, by heaven, those Presbyterians back in 1892 Pine River had nothing on her. As soon as the dough had puffed up for the second time, she would set it in the oven to bake, and Farley would have the kind of bread he was used to eating.

Sort of.

She thought of the vast differences between them, and the very real danger that they might be parted by forces they could neither understand nor control. All the rigors of past days caught up with her...all of a sudden, and Rue felt some barrier give way inside her.

She was stricken with what women of Farley's generation would have called "melancholia," she guessed, or maybe she was pregnant. The only thing she was certain of was that for the next little while, she wasn't going to be her usual, strong self.

Rue let out a wail of despair, covered her floury face with her floury hands and sobbed. Out on the utility porch, Soldier whined in unison.

Smelling of soap and clean, country snow, Farley came to her and gently pulled her hands down. His mouth quirked at one corner, and his eyes were still shining with humor.

"Stop that crying," he scolded huskily, wiping a tear from

her cheekbone with the side of one thumb. "You're going to paste your eyelids together."

"I don't...even know...why I'm...acting like this!" Rue babbled.

Farley kissed her forehead, no doubt leaving lip prints. "You've been through a whole lot lately, and you're all tired out," he said. Then he led her into one of the downstairs bathrooms, ran warm water into the sink and tenderly, carefully washed her face.

The experience in no way resembled lovemaking, and yet the effect was just as profound.

After that, Farley carried her into the parlor, laid her on the big leather sofa and covered her with the lovely plaid throw she'd brought home from a trip to Scotland. She lay sniffling while Farley went to build up the fire.

"This is really unlike me," she whimpered.

"I know," he answered, his voice low and laced with humor. "Just close your eyes and rest awhile, Rue. I'll look after you."

Rue was used to taking care of herself, for the most part. Aunt Verity and Elisabeth had coddled her when she came down with a head cold or the flu, but having a man's sympathy was an entirely new experience. The sensation was decadently delicious, but it was frightening, too. She was afraid that if she laid down her sword even for a little while, it would prove too heavy to lift when the time came to fight new battles.

Rue hadn't suffered through her bread-baking crisis for nothing. After she'd enjoyed the crackling parlor fire and Farley's pampering for half an hour, she returned to the kitchen and tackled the remainder of the job.

While the loaves were baking, filling the room with a very promising fragrance, Rue put game hens on the portable rotisserie, washed some russet potatoes for baking in the microwave and poured a can of cooked carrots into a saucepan to heat.

Farley had gone out to help with the evening chores, and when he returned, Rue had set the kitchen table with her grandmother's favorite china and silver. She'd exchanged her flour-covered clothes for a set of black lounging pajamas with metallic silver stripes, put on a little makeup and swept up her hair.

When the cold Montana wind blew Farley in, he stood staring at her, at the same time trying unsuccessfully to hang his hat on the peg next to the door. "How soon did you say we'd be getting married?" he asked.

Rue smiled, pleased, and lifted one shoulder. "Three or four days from now, if all goes well." She sighed. "Too bad you're such a prude. Montana nights can get very cold, and it would be nice to have somebody to snuggle with."

Farley was unbuttoning his coat. "Seems to me Montana nights can turn hot even in the middle of a snowstorm," he retorted hoarsely. He walked to the sink, rolling up the sleeves of his shirt as he went, and washed his hands as thoroughly as any surgeon would have done.

Proudly, Rue served the dinner she'd made, and Farley made it obvious that he enjoyed the fare, and even though the bread was a little on the heavy side, he didn't comment.

After eating, they washed and dried the dishes together—Rue never mentioned the shiny, perfectly efficient built-in dishwasher—and they went into the parlor. Rue had hoped for a romantic interlude in front of the fire, but Farley, having apparently absorbed everything in his how-things-work book, had gone to Gramps's bookshelf for another volume. This time, it seemed, he'd decided to investigate the secrets of indoor plumbing.

Resigned, Rue got out her laptop computer, and soon her fingers were flying over the keyboard. It seemed more important than ever to record what had happened to Elisabeth, and to her and Farley because of the strange antique necklace Aunt Verity had left as a legacy.

Rue had written several pages when she realized Farley was watching her. She glanced at him over her shoulder. He was next to her on the couch, holding his place in his book with a thumb. He'd already read nearly half the volume, which was incredible, given the technical nature of the material.

She smiled, reading the questions from his eyes and the furrows in his brow. "This is a computer, Farley. If I were you, I'd make that my next reading project. The modern world runs on these handy little gadgets."

Farley had seen the laptop before, of course, but never while it was running. "Light," he marveled. "You're writing words with *light* instead of ink."

As usual, his wonderment touched Rue deeply. He'd made such a profound difference in her life simply by being who he was, and even though she had been happy and fulfilled before she'd met him, Rue cherished the special texture and substance he gave to her world.

She showed him how to work the keyboard, and she watched with delight as he read from the screen.

All in all, it was a wonderful evening.

In the morning, Farley was up and gone before Rue even opened her eyes. She stumbled in and out of the shower, dressed warmly and went down to the kitchen for coffee. Since Soldier was whimpering on the back porch, she let him in to lie contentedly on the hooked rug in front of the old cookstove.

Farley had left a note on the table, and Rue read it while the water for her instant coffee was heating in the microwave.

Rue,
   It might be a long day. The snow is getting deeper, and Wilbur and the others think some of the cattle may be in trouble out on the range. Stay close to the house; folks have been lost in weather like this. Warm regards,
                                                      F.H.

"'Warm regards,'" Rue scoffed, turning to the dog, who lifted a single ear—the black one—in polite inquiry. "I give the man my body, and he signs notes 'warm regards.' And this command to stay in the house! What does he think I am? A child? A greenhorn? Next he'll be tying a rope between the back porch and the chicken coop so I don't get lost in the blizzard when I gather the eggs!"

Soldier whimpered and lowered his muzzle to his outstretched paws, eyeing Rue balefully.

"Oh, you're right," she conceded, though not in a generous way. "I'm being silly. Farley is a man of the 1890s, and it's perfectly natural that he sees things from a very different angle."

She went to the window and felt a vague sense of alarm at the depth of the snow. The drifts reached halfway up the fences and mounded on the sills, and shimmering, pristine flakes were still whirling down from a fitful sky.

Rue drank her coffee, poured herself a bowlful of cereal and began to pace. She was an active person, used to a hectic schedule, and the sense of being trapped in the house made her feel claustrophobic.

She went upstairs and made her bed, and even though she tried to resist, she couldn't. Rue opened the door to the master suite, intending to make Farley's bed, as well, and stopped cold on the threshold.

Farley had already taken care of the task, but that wasn't what troubled Rue so much. A golden chain lay on the bedside table, shimmering in the thin, winter light, and she knew without taking a single step closer it was *the* necklace, the magical, deadly, ticket-through-time necklace she'd purposely left on Aunt Verity's parlor mantel.

Rue sagged against the doorjamb for a moment, one hand cupped over her mouth. The discovery had been as startling as a sudden earthquake, and the implications crashed down on her head with all the weight of timbers shaken loose from their fittings.

Farley knew about the pendant, knew about its power. He could only have brought it along for one reason: he didn't intend to stay in the twentieth century with Rue, despite all his pretty talk about their getting married. This was only a cosmic field trip to him; he planned to return to 1892, to his jailhouse and his horse and women who never wore pants!

She started toward the necklace, possessed by a strange, tender spite, fully intending to carry the thing into the master bathroom and flush it. In the end, though, she retreated into the hallway, afraid to touch the pendant for fear that it might send her spiralling into some other period in time.

The distant toot of a horn distracted her, and she was grateful. She ran down the main staircase, one hand trailing along the banister, and bounded out onto the porch without bothering to put on her coat.

A white van had labored up the road from the highway. The logo of an express-courier company was painted brightly on its side, and the driver came cheerfully through the gate in the picket fence and up the unshoveled walk.

"Rue Claridge?" he inquired.

Rue nodded, hugging herself against the cold, her thoughts still on the necklace.

The courier handed her a package and pointed out a line for her signature. "Sure is a nasty day," he said.

Rue had long ago made a personal pledge to fight inanity

wherever she encountered it, but she was too distracted to do battle that day. "Yes," she muttered, scrawling her name. "Thank you."

She fled into the house a moment later and tore open the packet. Inside were the papers her somewhat shady acquaintance had assembled for Farley.

Tears filled her eyes, and her throat thickened. Maybe he didn't intend to marry her at all. Or perhaps he'd planned to go through with the ceremony and then blithely return to 1892, leaving his bride behind to cope as best she could....

Soldier was in the kitchen, and he suddenly started to bark. Grateful for the distraction, Rue headed in that direction, the express packet still in her hand.

Through the window in the back door, she saw Wilbur standing on the porch, smiling at her from beneath the brim of his hat. She was surprised, having gotten the impression from Farley's note that the old man had gone out to help with the cattle.

Rue opened the door. "Hi, Wilbur. Got time for a cup of coffee?"

Her grandfather's old friend looked a little wan. "It isn't often that I turn down the opportunity for a chat with a pretty lady," he said, "but the truth is that I'm under the weather today. I wondered if you could pick up my prescription for me, if you were going to town or anything."

Rue took a closer look at the old man. "You come in here and sit down this instant," she ordered in a firm but friendly tone. "Of course, I'll get your medicine, but why didn't you have the store deliver it?"

"Costs extry," said Wilbur, hanging up his hat and slowly working the buttons on his ancient coat. He took a chair at the kitchen table and accepted the coffee Rue brought to him with a philosophical sigh.

"For heaven's sake," she scolded good-naturedly, sitting down with her coffee, "you're not poor, Wilbur." She knew that was true; Gramps had provided well for the faithful employee in his will. "Besides, you can't take it with you."

Wilbur smiled, but his hand trembled as he lifted his cup

to his mouth. "You young people gotta spend a nickel or it burns a hole in your pocket."

Rue leaned forward, frowning. "What kind of medicine are you taking, anyway?"

"Just some stuff that jump starts the old ticker," he replied with a sort of blithe weariness.

In the next instant, as quickly and unexpectedly as Rue and Farley had been thrust from the nineteenth century into the twentieth, Wilbur's coffee clattered to the table. Brown liquid stained the cloth, and the old man clutched at his chest, a look of helpless bewilderment contorting his face.

"Oh, my God," Rue gasped, jumping up, rushing to him and grabbing his shoulders. "Wilbur, don't you do this to me! Don't you dare have a heart attack in my kitchen!" Even as she spoke the words, she knew how inane they were, but she couldn't help saying them.

He started to fall forward, making a choking sound in his throat. Soldier hovered nearby, whimpering in concern. Rue gently lowered her friend to the floor and loosened the collar of his shirt—a handmade one, Western cut with pearl snaps—that was probably older than she was.

"Hold on," she said urgently. "I'll have some help out here right away. Just hold on!"

She stumbled to the phone on the wall, punched out 911. Wilbur lay moaning on the floor, while Soldier helpfully licked his face.

"This is Rue Claridge out at Ribbon Creek," she told the young man who answered her call. "A man has collapsed, and I think he's having a heart attack."

"Is he conscious? Breathing?"

Rue glanced nervously toward her patient. "Yes. I think he's in extreme pain."

The operator was reassuringly calm. "We're on our way, Miss Claridge, but the roads are bad and the trip is bound to take some time. Are you trained to administer CPR?"

Rue nodded, then realized that was no help and blurted out, "Yes. Tell the paramedics to hurry, will you? We're in the kitchen of the main house."

"Would you like me to stay on the line with you?"

She looked at Wilbur, and her eyes filled with tears at his fragility. "I'd appreciate that—I think I'd better put some blankets over him, though."

"I'll be right here waiting," the dispatcher answered, and the unruffled normalcy of his tone gave Rue a badly needed dose of courage.

She quickly snatched thick woolen blankets from a chest in one of the downstairs bedrooms and rushed back to the kitchen to cover Wilbur, then rushed back to the phone.

"Should I give him water?"

"No" was the brisk and immediate response on the other end of the line. "Can the patient speak?"

Rue rushed back to the old man's side. He was looking up at her with glassy, frightened eyes, and she found herself smoothing his thin hair back from his forehead. "You'll be all right, Wilbur," she said. "Help is on the way. Can you talk?"

He grimaced with effort, but only an incoherent, helpless sound came from his lips. His hands were still pressed, fingers splayed and clutching, against his chest.

Rue spent the next half hour running back and forth between the telephone and the place where Wilbur lay, but it seemed like much longer to her. When she heard a siren in the distance, she felt like sobbing with relief.

"The cavalry's just about to come over the rise," she told Wilbur. "Hold on."

Farley and the others must have heard the siren, too, for the paramedics had just finished loading their charge into the ambulance when the whole yard seemed to be crowded with horses.

"What happened?" Farley asked, reaching Rue's side first. He was gazing speculatively at the vehicle with the spinning red light. "Is this what was making all that racket?"

Rue linked her arm through his and let her head rest against the outside of his shoulder. She hadn't forgotten that he'd brought the necklace to Ribbon Creek, knowing full well what could happen, but she was still in the throes of the current crisis and unable to pursue the point.

Yet.

"Wilbur came by to ask me to pick up his prescription if I went to town," she said. "After a few minutes, he grabbed his chest—" Emotion overcame her, and Farley held her close against his side.

Life was so uncertain, so damn dangerous, she thought. Here today, gone tomorrow. No guarantees. Catch as catch can.

One of the paramedics slammed the rear doors of the ambulance, then the vehicle was reeling away through the ever-worsening weather. The light flung splashes of crimson onto the snow, and the sound of the siren was like big needles being pushed through Rue's eardrums.

With Farley holding her close, Rue's heart was mended, if only briefly, and she could almost believe he hadn't planned to desert and betray her.

She forced herself to look up into his wonderful, rugged, unreadable face. "Are the cattle all right?"

He nodded, this man she loved, this man she'd hoped to spend her life with. "For the moment. Let's get you back in the house before you start sprouting icicles." With that, he ushered her away toward the warmth and light of the kitchen.

And the danger of the necklace.

Perhaps because she was used to crises, Rue quickly regained her composure. There was no point in worrying about Wilbur until she'd heard something from the hospital, and she wasn't sure how to broach the subject of the antique pendant.

"We can get married now," she said with only a slight tremor in her voice, after showing him the paperwork. They were in the parlor, by the fire, sitting on the raised hearth and drinking hot coffee laced with Irish cream. She watched him closely after making the announcement.

"Today? Tomorrow?"

Rue was heartened by his response, but only a little. "I think there's a three-day waiting period and, of course, it would be foolish to try to get into town today."

Farley grinned. "We could make it if we went on horse-back."

Rue's heartbeat quickened, but she sternly reminded herself how sneaky men could be. Words were cheap; it was what a person *did* that counted. "Okay, cowboy," she said testily, thrusting out her chin. "You're on."

Farley looked at his feet and the gleaming hardwood floor immediately surrounding them. "On what?"

"I'm accepting your challenge. We're going to put the Land Rover into four-wheel drive and head for town. Just don't blame me if we get stuck and freeze to death!"

The marshal narrowed his eyes, not in hostility, but in confusion. "Wilbur was just saying the other day that women are odd creatures, and he was right. What the devil's gotten into you, Rue?"

"You kept the necklace!" she cried, surprising herself as much as Farley. "How could you do that? How could you pretend that I meant something to you, that you were planning to stay here with me, when all the time you intended to go back!"

Farley gripped her shoulders and lifted her onto her toes. While the gesture was in no way painful, it was certainly intimidating. "I thought you'd forgotten the damn thing," he said, his eyes darkening from turquoise to an intense blue. "I was trying to help."

Rue longed to believe him, and she felt herself wavering. "Sure," she threw out. "That's why you didn't mention it."

He closed his eyes for a moment, jawline clamped down tight, and if he wasn't feeling pure frustration, he was doing a good job of projecting that emotion. "It's not every day a man jumps a hundred years like a square on a checkerboard, Rue. I've been thinking about electricity and gasoline engines and computers and supermarkets and shopping malls—and how much I want to sleep with you again. There just wasn't room in my head for that blasted necklace!"

Rue felt herself sagging, on the inside at least. She wondered, not for the first time, whether this man sapped her strength or nurtured it. She let her forehead rest against his shoulder, and he slipped his arms lightly around her waist and kissed the top of her head.

"Let's hitch up your Land Rover," he said with a smile in his voice. "I think I'd better hurry up and marry you before you decide Wilbur's the man for you."

Rue laughed and cried and finally dried her eyes.

Then she grabbed the false papers proving Farley was a real person, smiling at the irony of that, and the two of them headed for town. The conditions were bad, but the snowplows and gravel trucks were out, and the Land Rover moved easily over the slippery highways.

At the courthouse in Pigeon Ridge, Farley and Rue applied for a marriage license, then went to the town's only restaurant to celebrate. The establishment was called the Roost, to Rue's amusement.

She called the hospital in the next town, while Farley's cheeseburger and her nachos were being made, and asked about Wilbur. He had arrived, the nurse told her, but was still in the emergency room.

Farley was poking the buttons on the fifties-style jukebox at their table, frowning the way he always did when something puzzled him.

Rue smiled, fished a couple of coins out of her wallet and dropped them into the slot. "Push a button," she said.

Farley complied, and a scratchy sound followed, then music. A country-western ballad filled the diner, an old song that would, of course, be totally new to the marshal. He grinned. "Cassette tapes," he said triumphantly.

"Close," Rue replied, fearing the strength of the love she felt for this man, the depth and height and breadth of it. She explained about 45-r.p.m. records and jukeboxes while they ate. After the meal, she called the hospital again.

Farley was having a second cup of coffee when she returned. "How is Wilbur?" he asked.

Rue sighed and slid back into the booth. "He's going to make it, thank God. He definitely had a heart attack, but he could live a long time yet, if he takes care of himself. I mean to see that he does."

"If Wilbur were a younger man, I'd be jealous."

Rue smiled at Farley's teasing, knowing he was trying to help her over a slick place, so to speak. "You should be. A guy like Wilbur can drive a woman mad with passion."

"Can we see him?"

She shook her head. "Not today. He needs to rest."

The trip back to the ranch was even more treacherous than the journey into town. Even with four-wheel drive, the Land Rover fishtailed on the icy highway, and finally Farley braced both hands against the dashboard and let out an involuntary yelp of alarm.

"For heaven's sake, Farley," Rue snapped, managing the steering wheel with a skill her grandfather had taught her, "get a grip!"

He thrust himself backward in the seat and pushed his hat down over his eyes, and Rue knew for certain that it wasn't because he wanted to sleep.

She spared one hand from the wheel just long enough to thump Farley hard in the shoulder. "I suppose you think you could do better!"

He pushed the hat back and glared at her. "Lady, I *know* I could do better."

"This superior, know-it-all attitude is one of the many things I don't like about men!" Rue yelled. She wasn't sure *why* she was yelling; maybe it was the stress inherent in the day's events, the tension of driving on such dangerous roads or frustration because it would be three days before she and Farley could be married and he had suddenly decided he had to be a virgin groom. Then again, it could have been because she'd thought she'd escaped the power of Aunt Verity's necklace, only to find that it had followed her.

Very carefully, she pulled to the side of the road.

"All right, wise guy," she challenged, "you can drive the rest of the way home. But when we're both in the emergency room, shot full of painkillers and wrapped in surgical tape and looking like a couple of fugitives from the King Tut exhibit, don't say I didn't warn you!"

Farley had already unfastened his seat belt, and he was

opening the door before Rue even finished speaking. "I don't have the first idea what you're talking about," he said evenly, "but I know a dare when I hear one and, furthermore, I don't care for your tone of voice."

They traded places, Rue grimly certain they'd end up in the ditch before they'd traveled a mile, Farley quiet and determined. Much to Rue's relief and, though she wouldn't admit it, her disappointment, they reached the ranch without incident, and Soldier met them in the yard.

"There's a blizzard blowing in," Farley announced, looking up at the sky before he wrapped one arm around Rue and shuffled her toward the house. Even though the gesture was protective, there was something arrogant and proprietary about it, too.

Within an hour, the power had gone off. Farley built up the fire in the kitchen stove, and Rue lit a couple of kerosene lamps she'd found on the top shelf of the pantry. While she read the book she'd started earlier, Farley went over the account books for the ranch. He made notes, paused periodically to slip into deep thought, then went back to the study for more reports and files.

If Rue hadn't known better, she'd have sworn he was auditing her income tax return.

"I'm sorry," she said.

"About what?" Farley asked without looking up. He was making notes on a pad of paper, and every once in a while, he stopped to touch the tip of the pencil to his tongue.

"For yelling before. It's just that—well—it's the necklace. It's really bugging me."

That made him lay down the pencil and regard her somberly. "'Bugging' you?"

"Troubling. Irritating. Farley, this is no time for a lesson in twentieth-century vocabulary. I love you, and I'm afraid. That necklace has the power to separate us."

Farley reached across the table and took her hand in his. For a moment, she really thought he was going to say he loved her, too, she believed she saw the words forming in the motion of his vocal cords. In the end, though, he simply replied,

"We're going to be married. I don't know how to make my intentions any plainer, Rue."

She traced his large knuckles with the pad of her thumb. When Farley declared his love, it had to be by his own choice and not because she'd goaded him into it. She suspected, too, that men of his time had an even more difficult time talking about their feelings than the contemporary variety did.

"Okay," she finally responded, "but I'm still scared."

Farley gripped her hand and gently but firmly steered her out of her chair and around the table, then into his lap. "Don't be," he muttered, his lips almost touching hers. "Nothing and no one will hurt you as long as the blood in my veins is still warm."

Rue could certainly vouch for the warmth of the blood in *her* veins. She ached with the need to give pleasure to Farley, and to take it, and when he kissed her, tentatively at first and then with the audacity of a plundering pirate, her whole body caught fire.

"Just tell me," she pleaded breathlessly when Farley finally freed her mouth, "that you won't go back to 1892 without me."

The stillness descended on the room suddenly, with all the slicing, bitter impact of a mountain snowslide. Farley thrust Rue firmly off his lap and onto her feet. "I can't promise that," he said.

CHAPTER 13

Rue clenched her hands into fists and stood beside the table, staring down into Farley's stubborn, guileless face. "What do you mean, you can't promise you won't go back without me?" The question was a whispery hiss, like the sound of water spilling onto a red-hot griddle.

Farley reached out and pulled her back onto his lap. He splayed his fingers between her shoulder blades, offering slight and awkward comfort. "Rue, I was the marshal of Pine River, and I had responsibilities. People trusted me. One day, I just vanished without a fare-thee-well to anybody. Sooner or later, I have to find a way to let those folks know I'm not lying in some gully with a bullet through my head, that I didn't just ride out one day and desert them. I can't make a new life with you until I've made things right back there."

Rue looked away, but she didn't have the strength to escape his embrace again. The day had been long and stressful, and she was drained. "So I was right in the first place," she said miserably. It wasn't often that Rue wanted to be wrong, but this time she would have given her overdraft privileges at the bank for it. "You brought the necklace to Ribbon Creek because you knew you were going back, just like I said. When you claimed you thought I'd forgotten it, well, that was just a smoke screen."

Farley paused, obviously stuck on the term "smoke screen," then he met Rue's gaze squarely. "I'm not the kind of man the Presbyterians entirely approve of," he confessed in a grave tone of voice, "but there's one thing I'm definitely not, and that's a liar. And if you'll search your memory, you'll find that I never promised to stay here."

Rue was aghast. "We took out a marriage license today," she whispered. "Didn't that mean anything to you? Was it just something to do?"

He laid his strong hands to either side of her face, forcing her to look at him, making her listen. "There's nothing I want more than to be your husband," he said evenly. "Unless you change your mind and call off the wedding, we *will* be married. We'll fill this big house with children, and I think I can even set aside my pride long enough to accept the fact that my place at Ribbon Creek came to me by marriage instead of honest effort. But the longer I talk, the more certain I get that I can't leave that other life unfinished."

Rue was exasperated, even though she could see the merit in his theory only too well. "What are you going to do, Farley?" she demanded, and something in her tone made Soldier whimper fretfully from his place on the hooked rug by the stove. "Grab the necklace, click your heels together, make a dramatic landing in 1892 and tell everybody you're a time traveler now?"

He shook his head. "I wouldn't talk about what really happened with anybody but Jon Fortner or your cousin Elisabeth." He frowned, his brows knitting. "You don't suppose they're in any sort of trouble over our being gone all of a sudden like that, do you? After all, we were in their parlor when we disappeared."

Rue was ashamed to realize that the possibility had never crossed her mind. "I imagine the townspeople think I spirited you away to some den of never-ending iniquity. Besides, Jon and Bethie had no motive for foul play. Jon is—was—your friend, and everybody knew—knows."

Farley didn't look reassured, and Rue was almost sorry she'd ever confronted him about the necklace. It was plain that if he'd had any intention of using the pendant to escape her and an admittedly hectic modern world, he hadn't been consciously aware of the fact. No, the marshal had only begun to seriously consider returning to 1892 to tie up loose ends *after* Rue had reminded him that such a thing was possible.

She laid her head against his shoulder. "Don't try to send me off to bed alone tonight, Marshal, because I'm not stepping out of reaching distance. If I have to attach myself to you like one sticky spoon behind another, I'll do it. And I don't give a damn about your silly ideas about keeping up appearances, either. Everybody within a fifty-mile radius of this ranch thinks we're making mad, passionate love every chance we get."

Farley kissed her forehead. "We'll be married soon enough," he said.

The house was cooling off rapidly, since the furnace wasn't working, and the kitchen was the only logical place to sleep. Rue took one of the lamps and went in search of sleeping bags, making a point of going nowhere near the necklace. She returned sometime later to find Farley still absorbed in paperwork. He reminded her of Abraham Lincoln, sitting there in the light of a single lantern, reading with such solemn concentration.

She built up the fire in the wood stove and spread the sleeping bags within the warm aura surrounding it. "What are you doing?" she asked, sitting cross-legged on the floor to watch him.

He scribbled something onto a yellow legal pad and then glanced at her distractedly. "Doing? Oh, well, I'm just writing up some changes we could make—in the way the ranch is being run, I mean."

Rue was heartened that he was thinking of the ranch from a long-range perspective, but her fear of being abandoned hadn't abated. Afraid or not, though, she was tired, and after brushing her teeth and washing her face, she stripped to her T-shirt and stretched out on one of the sleeping bags.

The power outage wasn't bothering Farley a bit; lantern light and wood fires were normal to him. Rue wasn't above wishing he were a little spooked by the encroaching darkness and the incessant howl of the wind; she would have liked for him to join her in front of the stove. With his arms around her, she might have been able to pretend there was no danger, just for a little while.

She yawned and closed her eyes. Sleeping on the kitchen floor reminded her of other nights, long ago, when Aunt Verity had sometimes allowed Rue and Elisabeth to ''camp out'' on the rug in front of the parlor fire. They had turned out all the lights, munched popcorn and scared each other silly with made-up stories about ghosts and vampires and rampaging maniacs—never dreaming that something with equally mysterious powers, an old-fashioned pendant on a gold chain, lay hidden away among their aunt's belongings.

Waiting.

Farley continued to read and work on the rough outline of his plans for the ranch, but every once in a while, his gaze strayed to Rue, who lay sleeping in a bedroll in front of the cookstove. Looking at her tightened his loins and made barbs catch in the tenderest parts of his heart, but he wouldn't let himself approach her.

He sighed and took a cold, bitter sip from his mug, rather than pass Rue to get fresh coffee from the pot on the stove. If he got too close, he knew he'd end up pulling that peculiar-looking nightdress off over her head and making love to her until the sun came up.

The lights flared on just as dawn was about to break, and Farley switched them off so Rue wouldn't be disturbed, then he went upstairs to shower and change clothes. After last night's storm, there would be plenty to do.

As he entered the room he would soon be sharing with Rue, Farley looked at the big, welcoming bed and wondered if he was losing his mind. Rue was so beautiful, and he wanted her so much. Refusing to sleep with her now was like putting the lid back on the bin after the mice had gotten to the potatoes, and he knew she was right in believing that her reputation was long gone. Still, he wanted to offer her a tribute of some sort, and honor was all he had.

The necklace glittered on the nightstand, as if to attract his attention, and he reached for it, then drew back his hand. He'd be returning to 1892, all right, but only long enough to put his affairs in order. Then he would come straight back to Rue. He didn't intend to go before he'd married her, at any rate, nor would he leave without saying goodbye.

He made his way into the bathroom, kicked off his boots and peeled away his clothes. By then he'd figured out the plumbing system, thanks to one of the books he'd found in the study, and when there was no hot water, he knew it was going to take a while for the big heater downstairs to return to the proper temperature.

Resigned, Farley went back to the bed, crawled under the covers because he was naked and the room was still frigidly cold, and immediately felt the fool for being afraid of a little geegaw like that necklace. He reached out and closed his hand over it and, in the next instant, the room rocked from side to side. It was as though somebody had grabbed the earth and yanked it out from under the house like a rug.

Farley felt the firm mattress go feathery soft beneath him, and he bolted upright with a shout. "Rue!" He was sweating, and he could feel his heart thundering against his breastbone, as if seeking a way to escape.

He knew immediately that he was in a different room, in a different house. He could make out blue wallpaper, and the bed, an old four-poster with a tattered canopy, faced in another direction. And those things were the least of his problems.

Not only had Farley landed in a strange bed, there was someone sharing it. At his shout, a plump middle-aged woman in a nightcap let out a shriek loud enough to hasten the Resurrection, bounced off the mattress and snatched up a poker from the nearby hearth.

She continued to scream while Farley frantically clutched the necklace and willed himself back to the 1990s and Rue. The poker was coming toward his head when the mattress turned hard again and the wallpaper changed to paneling. He hadn't had more than two seconds to acclimatize himself when the bedroom door flew open and Rue burst in. She hurled herself over the foot of the bed and scrambled the rest of the way to Farley on her knees, throwing her arms around his neck when she reached him.

"I heard you yell. You saw something, didn't you? Something happened."

Farley tossed the necklace aside and embraced Rue. She was real and solid, thank God. "Yes," he finally rasped when his breathing had slowed to the point where speech was possible. "Yes."

"What?"

"I don't know. A woman with a poker in her hand—"

Rue drew back, her hands resting on the sides of his face, her eyes full of questions. "You're sure you weren't dreaming?"

Farley laughed, though amusement was about the last thing he felt. "I wasn't dreaming. That woman was as real as you are, and she wasn't pleased to find a naked cowboy in her bed, I can tell you that. Another second and she would have changed the shape of my skull."

Rue turned her head, looking at the necklace lying a few feet away on the carpet. "Farley, let's throw the pendant away before something terrible—and irrevocable—happens. Surely the good people of Pine River hired a new marshal, and Jonathan and Elisabeth *must* have found a way to explain your disappearance."

Farley gathered Rue close and held her, taking comfort from the soft, fragrant, womanly substance of her. "We can't do that, Rue," he reasoned after a long time. "There's no way of predicting what the consequences might be. Suppose somebody found it, a child maybe? No, we've got to hide that pendant and make damn sure it stays put."

She buried her face in his chest, that was all, but the surface of Farley's skin quivered in response, and he felt himself come to attention. "I'm scared," she said, her voice muffled by his flesh.

Farley wanted Rue more than ever, having been separated from her by a wall of time, but he was strong and stubborn, and so were his convictions. The next time he made love to

Rue, she would bear his name as well as the weight of his body.

Her hand trailed slowly down over his chest and belly, leaving a sparkling trail of stardust in its wake. Then she captured him boldly.

He groaned in glorious despair. "Damn it, Rue, let go."

She did not obey. "You're bigger and stronger," she teased in a whimpery voice. "But I declare, Marshal, I don't see you trying to wrest yourself free of my sinful attentions."

Farley fully intended to pull her fingers away, but his hands went instead to the sides of her head. With a strangled cry, he kissed her, his tongue invading her mouth, plundering. And still she worked him mercilessly with her hand.

He broke away from the kiss, gasping. "Oh, God, *Rue*—"

She teased his navel with the tip of her tongue. "You promised not to make love to me again until we were married," she said, and he trembled in anticipation, knowing what was going to happen. "I, on the other hand, never said anything of the kind."

Farley felt her moving downward and groaned, but he could not make himself stop her. When Rue took him, he gave a raspy cry of relief and surrendered to her.

Later, Farley left the bed, showered and went about the business of running a ranch. Rue took a pair of tweezers from her makeup case, picked up the necklace, which was still lying on the floor where Farley had thrown it after his unscheduled flight into history, and dropped it gingerly into a big envelope.

She held the envelope by a corner, carrying it downstairs and laying it on the desk in the study. She opened the safe hidden behind her grandmother's bad painting of a bowl of grapes, expecting to find it empty since she had long since gone through all her grandfather's papers. To her surprise, however, there was a thin envelope of white vellum inside, and when she pulled it out, a chill went through her.

The handwriting on the front was old and faded and very familiar, and it read, "Miss Rue Claridge, Ribbon Creek, Montana." There was even a zip code, a fact that might have made Rue smile if she hadn't been so shaken. The date on the postmark was 1892.

She let the other envelope, containing the necklace, drop forgotten to the floor and sank into a chair, her heart stuffed into her throat.

Apparently the letter had been delivered to Gramps, and he'd saved it for her, probably never noticing the postmark or the antiquated ink.

Rue drew in a deep breath and sat up very straight. If the letter had been delivered to the ranch, why hadn't she found it before, when she'd settled Gramps's affairs? Come to that, why was any of this happening at all?

The only explanation Rue could think of was that Farley was going back to 1892 in the near future, if he hadn't done so already. And this was the only way he could contact her, by writing a letter that would be misplaced and passed from person to person for a hundred years.

Fingers trembling, Rue opened the envelope and pulled out a single, thin page. Stinging tears came instantly to her eyes. These words had been written a century before by a man she'd brazenly made love to only that morning.

My Dearest Rue,
I'm writing this to say goodbye, even though I know my words will be confusing to you when and if you ever lay eyes on them. Maybe you'll not see this page at all, but I don't mind admitting I take some comfort from the writing of it.

I never meant to leave you forever, Rue, especially not on our wedding day; I want you to know that. My love for you is as constant as my breath and my heartbeat, and I will carry that adoration with me into the next world, where the angels will surely envy it.

I have every confidence that if a child is born of our union, you will raise our son or daughter to be strong and full of honor.

I'm staying here at the Pine River house, having been shot last week when there was a robbery at the bank.

Oftentimes, I wonder if you're in another room some-where, just beyond the reach of my eyes and ears.

When last I saw your cousin Lizzie, which was just a little while ago when she came to change my bandages, she was well. She saw that I was writing you and prom-ised to help me think of a way to get the letter to you, and she asked me to give you her deepest regards.

I offer mine as well.

With love forever,
Farley.

Rue folded the letter carefully and tucked it back into the envelope, even though there was a wild fury of panic storming within her. She wanted to scream, to sob, to refuse to accept this fate, but she knew it would be useless.

Farley was going back; the letter was tangible proof of that. And he was dying from the wounds he'd received during the robbery. He hadn't come right out and said that, but she had read the truth between the lines.

She pushed the envelope under the blotter on the desk. She wanted to confront Farley with what she'd discovered, but she couldn't. For one thing, he hadn't done anything wrong; it was his life, and if he wanted to go back to 1892 and throw it away in a gunfight with a pack of outlaws, that was his prerogative. No, Farley wasn't the only one with integrity; Rue had it, too, and in those moments, the quality was her greatest curse.

Rue paced. She could warn him. Maybe if she did that, he would at least avoid stumbling into that bank at the wrong moment and getting himself killed.

Finally she remembered the registry at the graveyard in Pine River, got the number from information and put a call through. After half an hour and a string of hassles that height-ened her frustration to new levels, a clerk in the church office finally unearthed an old record book and found Farley's name in it.

"Yes, he's listed here," the woman said pleasantly. "His grave would be out in the old section, under the oak tree. I hope that helps. It might be hard to find otherwise. Not every-one had a stone, you know, and a wooden marker would be long gone.''

Rue squeezed her eyes shut, almost overwhelmed by the images that were filling her mind. ''Does the record list a cause of death?'' she asked, her voice thin.

''Gunshot wound to the chest,'' the clerk replied after a pause. ''He was attended by Dr. Jonathan Fortner, a man who played quite an important part in the history of Pine River—''

''Thank you,'' Rue said, unable to bear another word, even though it meant cutting the woman off in the middle of a sentence. Her eyes were awash in tears when she hung up the receiver. Soldier came and leaned against her leg, whining in sympathy.

Rue knew it might be hours until Farley returned, and she couldn't stand to stay in the house, so she went out to the woodshed and split enough firewood to last through a second ice age. When that was done, she started up the Land Rover, Soldier happily occupying the passenger seat, and headed out over roads of glaring ice.

It took an hour to reach the hospital in the next town over from Pigeon Ridge. Leaving the dog in the Land Rover, Rue went inside and bought a card in the small gift shop, then asked to see Wilbur.

He'd spent the night and most of the day in intensive care, a nurse told her, but she supposed one visit would be all right if Rue kept her stay brief.

She found him in Room 447, and although there were three other beds, they were all empty. Wilbur looked small and forlorn, with tubes running into his nose and the veins of both his wrists.

''Hello, Wilbur.'' Rue set the card on his nightstand, then bent to kiss his forehead.

He looked surprised at his misfortune, and helpless.

Rue blinked back tears and patted his arm. ''That's all right, I know you can't talk right now. I just wanted to stop by and to say hello and tell you not to worry about Soldier. I'm taking good care of him. In fact, he's out in the car right now—it was as close as the nurses would let him get.''

Wilbur made a funny noise low in his throat that might have been a chuckle.

''I'd better go,'' Rue said. ''I know you need to rest and, besides, you won't want me hanging around when all your girlfriends come in.'' She touched his shoulder, then left the room. In a glance backward, she saw him reach awkwardly up to catch hold of the get-well card she'd brought.

For all her activity, Rue had not forgotten Farley's letter for a moment. She circled the thought the way a she wolf might move around a campfire, fascinated but afraid to get too close.

The sun was out when Rue returned to the Land Rover, and the ice seemed to be thawing, but it still took forever to get home, because there were so many accidents along the way. When she and Soldier arrived, Farley and the other men were driving several hundred head of cattle into the big pasture west of the house, where a mountain of hay and troughs of fresh water awaited.

Rue started toward Farley, fully intending to tell him about the letter she'd found in the safe, but the closer she got, the more convinced she became that it would be impossible. She could barely think of being parted from him, let alone talk about it.

She stopped at the fence, listening to the bawling of the cattle, the yelling and swearing of the cowboys, the neighs and nickers of the horses. In those moments as she stood watching Farley work, she realized how simple the solution really was.

All she had to do was destroy the necklace. Once that was done, there would be no way for Farley to return to 1892 and get himself shot.

He rode over to look down at her, his face reddened by the cold and his mustache fringed with snow. His smile practically set her back on her heels.

''Where have you been?'' he asked. He didn't sound annoyed, just curious.

"I went in to see Wilbur at the hospital. He's doing all right." The words brought an image of a wounded Farley to mind, a man dying in another time and place, close enough to touch and yet so far away that even science couldn't measure the distance.

Farley shook his head. "You've got no business driving on these roads."

Rue wanted to weep, but she smiled instead. "Are you jealous, Farley?" she teased, stepping close to Lobo and running a finger down the inside of the marshal's thigh. "Think I'm paying Wilbur too much attention?"

Farley shivered, but Rue knew it wasn't from the cold. He'd loved the game they'd played that morning, and her attempt to remind him of it had been successful. He bent down and exclaimed in a low voice, "You little wanton. I ought to haul you off to the woodshed and blister your bustle!"

"Very kinky," she said, her eyes twinkling even as tears burned at their edges. Then, before he could ask for the inevitable definition, she turned and walked toward the house.

That night, the power stayed on and the wind didn't blow. Rue and Farley curled up together on the couch in the big parlor and watched television. At least, Farley watched—Rue alternated between thinking about the necklace and about the letter hidden beneath the desk blotter.

Although they didn't make love, Farley seemed to know Rue would not be separated from him, and they shared the large bed in the master bedroom. He held her and for the time being that was enough.

Contrary to her expectations, she slept, and the next thing she knew, Farley was kissing her awake.

"Get up," he said, his breath scented with toothpaste. "Today is our wedding day."

Some words from the letter he didn't know he'd written echoed in Rue's heart. "I never meant to leave you forever, especially not on our wedding day." Unless she did something and soon, she would become Farley's wife and his widow without turning a single page of the calendar in between.

"I love you," she said, because those were the only safe words.

He kissed her lightly and quoted a mouthwash commercial they'd seen the night before. One thing about television, it had an immediate impact.

Rue got out of bed, passed into the bathroom and brushed her teeth. When she came back, Farley was gone.

Panic seized her. With another man, she would only have thought he'd left the room, or maybe the house. Farley might have left the century.

Dressed in jeans and a warm woolen shirt, she raced into the hallway and down the stairs. "Farley!"

He was in the kitchen, calmly sipping coffee, and he smiled at Rue with his eyes as he took in her furious expression. "A body would almost think you'd been left at the altar, the way you carry on when I get out of sight."

Looking up at him, Rue ached. Why did it all have to be so complicated? Other people had problems, sure, but not the kind that would have made an episode on *Tales from the Crypt.* "Farley, the necklace—"

"I know where it is," he said calmly. "The safe, behind that painting of the fruit."

Rue paled. "But you couldn't have known the combination."

He had noticed her terror by then, and he reached out with his free hand to caress her jaw. "I found it when I went through the ranch records, Rue," he said quietly. "I checked the safe to see if there were any more reports to go over."

Rue closed her eyes, swayed slightly and was steadied by Farley's firm grip. "But the necklace is still there?" she asked evenly, reasonably. "You didn't move it, did you?"

"No," he answered. "But I want your promise that you won't move it again, either. I need to know where it is, Rue. Now, for the moment, all I want you thinking about is becoming my wife." He bent his head, bewitched her with a soft kiss. "I hope you're planning to wear something pretty, though. I draw the line at a bride wearing trousers."

Rue struggled to maintain her composure; in all her travels as a reporter, she'd never faced a greater challenge than this one. "Farley," she began reasonably, "you've got to listen. If you go back to 1892, you'll die."

He touched her face. "Everybody dies, darlin'," he answered gently. "Considering that I was born in 1856, I've outlived a number of folks already."

She stepped back, raised her fingertips to her temples. It sounded as if Farley knew what was going to happen to him if he went back to 1892 and that he'd resigned himself to that fate. "You found the letter, too."

"By accident," he said. "I spilled a cup of coffee on the desk, and when I moved the blotter, I came across an envelope with my own handwriting on it. I would have put it aside if it hadn't been for that."

Rue sagged into one of the kitchen chairs. "You'd go back, knowing you were going to be shot by a bank robber and die of the wounds?"

"I have to settle my affairs, Rue. I told you that. And I'm still the marshal of Pine River, as far as I know. God knows, it wasn't a job the town council would be able to foist off on somebody else without a fight. If there's a holdup, I'll have to do whatever I can to intervene. Besides, I've been warned—I'll just be more careful than usual."

Rue felt sick. This was supposed to be one of the happiest days of her life. And she *was* happy, because she wanted the legal and spiritual bond with Farley no matter what lay ahead—or behind—but she was terrified, as well.

Apparently nothing would shake his determination to return to 1892. That left only one avenue open to his distraught bride-to-be.

"I'm going with you, then."

"Rue—"

"I mean, it, Farley," she interrupted, rising so fast that her chair toppled over backward behind her. She didn't pick it up. "I'm not marrying you so we can be apart. We belong together."

He looked at her for a long time, then sighed. "All right," he agreed reluctantly. He kissed her, then left the house without breakfast.

Rue was still inwardly frantic, but fortunately for her, she had things to do. She called the hospital for a progress report on Wilbur, who was doing well, then wired her mother, who had no doubt moved on from the spa to one of several favorite ski resorts.

Giving the credit-card number to pay for the wire took longer than dictating the telegram itself, a fact that seemed ironic to Rue.

"Mother," it read, "I'm marrying at last, so stop telling your friends I'm an old maid. His name is Farley Haynes, and I adore him. Love, Rue."

The message to Rue's father, who might have been anywhere in the world, but could be counted on to check with his answering service in New York on occasion, was even more succinct. "Dad. By the time you get this, I'll be married. Rue."

With those two tasks out of the way, Rue turned all her concentration to the upcoming wedding. She hadn't brought anything suitable for the ceremony—in fact, she didn't *own* anything suitable. But she remembered the line of trunks in the attic, filled with things from all phases of her grandmother's life. When she was younger, she'd worn those lovely, antique garments to play solitary games of dress-up during long visits.

Naturally, the room at the top of the house was dusty, and the thin winter sunlight barely found its way through the dirty panes of glass in the only window. Rue flipped the light switch and the single bulb dangling in the middle of the ceiling flared to life.

This was a friendly place, though cold and a little musty smelling, and Rue smiled as she entered. If there were ghosts here, they were merry ones come to wish the bride well on her wedding day.

After a few moments of standing still, feeling a reverence for the old times and wondering if her grandmother might not be here after all, young and pretty and just beyond the reach of Rue's senses, she approached the row of trunks.

The sturdy old chests had metal trim, tarnished to a dead-brass dullness by the passing of time, and the stickers plastered to their sides were peeling and colorless. Still, Rue could make out the names of a few places—Istanbul, Prague, Bora Bora.

She smiled. Grammie had been quite the traveler in her youth. What had it been like for such an adventurous woman to settle on a remote ranch in Montana?

Rue knelt in front of the first trunk and laid her palms on its dusty lid. She didn't remember her grandmother, though Gramps and Rue's own mother had spoken of her in only the most glowing terms.

She lifted the lid and right on top, wrapped tightly in yellowed tissue paper, was a beautiful pink satin dress. Rue took a few minutes to admire it, to hold the gown to her front and speculate as to whether or not it would fit, then carefully re-wrapped it and returned it to the chest.

Time blew past like the wind flying low over the prairies, and Rue was barely aware of its passing. Going through the things her grandmother had so carefully packed away, she found a lovely calf-length dress of ecru lace, with a modest but enticing neckline, a pearl choker, pale satin slippers that were only slightly too small and a lovely, sweeping straw picture hat with a wide rose-colored ribbon for a band and a nosegay of pink and blue flowers for decoration.

Because the chests were lined with camphor, the fragile old clothes smelled only faintly musty. Totally charmed, the threat of Aunt Verity's necklace held at bay for just a little while, Rue carried the treasures down from the attic and hung the dress on the screen porch to air.

Upstairs again, she gave herself a facial, washed her hair and then took a long, hot bath. She was back in the kitchen sipping from a cup of noodle soup, a towel wrapped around her head turban-fashion, when Farley came in.

"Are you hungry?" Rue asked, lowering her eyes. She'd said and done outrageous things in this man's arms, and it wasn't as if he hadn't seen her in considerably less than a bathrobe, but suddenly she felt shy.

"Yes," he answered with a smile in his voice. "But I'm still planning to wait until after some preacher has said the words that make it all right."

Rue blushed. "I was talking about food."

"I wasn't," Farley replied. "Are we getting hitched here, or do we have to go into town?"

She felt another stream of color rush into her cheeks, but since the previous flood probably hadn't subsided yet, it wouldn't be so obvious. She hoped.

"I arranged for a justice of the peace to come out. It was the same day we got our license."

"Where was I?" Farley hung up his hat and coat, then crossed to the refrigerator and opened the door. It was an ordinary thing, and yet Rue pressed the image into her mind like a cherished photograph. Just in case.

She smiled. "You were playing with the drinking fountain," she said.

Farley took the milk carton out, opened it and started to raise it to his mouth. He went to the cupboard for a glass when he saw Rue's warning glare. "I don't have a ring," he said worriedly, "or a fancy suit."

"You're still going to be the best-looking groom who ever said 'I do,'" Rue retorted, taking the carton from his hand.

He squeezed her bottom through the thick terry cloth of her robe when she bent over to return the milk to the fridge. "And after I've said 'I do,'" he teased huskily, "you can bet that I will."

The justice of the peace, who ran a little bait shop at Ponderosa Lake in the summertime, arrived an hour later.

By then, Farley had showered and changed into clean clothes, and Rue had put on makeup, arranged her hair in a loose Gibson-girl style and donned the lovely, gauzy lace dress and the pearl choker.

A couple of the ranch hands came in to serve as witnesses, wearing shiny, ill-fitting suits that had probably been in and out of style several times. One of the old-timers, Charlie, brought along his relic of a camera, which had a flash attachment the size of a satellite dish, fully prepared to record the event.

Rue didn't allow herself to think beyond the now; she wanted to cherish every second for its own sake.

Being a civil ceremony, the wedding itself was short. Even though Rue was trying to measure out the moments and make them last, the whole thing didn't take more than five minutes. When Farley kissed her, the hat tumbled off her head and the flash of Charlie's camera glowed red through her closed eyelids.

Rue would have been content to go right on kissing her husband, but, of course, they weren't alone, so that was impossible. Hope overflowed her heart as she looked up into Farley's tender eyes, and in those golden moments, she found it impossible to believe that time or trouble or even death could ever separate them.

The justice of the peace left as soon as he'd been paid, but the ranch hands stayed for refreshments, since festive occasions were such a rare treat. Sara Lee provided the wedding cake, which had to be thawed out in the microwave, and coffee and soda completed the menu.

When Charlie wasn't eating, he was taking pictures.

Finally, however, one of the other hands elbowed him in the ribs, then cleared his throat pointedly and suggested that they get back to the bunkhouse and change into their working duds. Some of the cowboys started to protest, then caught on and pushed back their chairs, beaming.

Time was more precious now than ever, so Rue didn't urge

the hands to stay. Despite her insistence that Farley take her with him when he went back to 1892, she hadn't forgotten that his letter said he'd gone alone—on their wedding day. She was glad when she and her new husband were finally by themselves.

She unbuttoned the top two buttons of Farley's shirt. ''No more virginal protests, Farley,'' she said, sliding her hand under the soft chambray to find and caress a taut masculine nipple. ''You're my husband now, and I demand my rights as a wife.''

He chuckled, but the sound was raw with other emotions besides amusement. No doubt he, too, was wondering how much of their destiny could be changed, if any. He swept Rue up into his arms and mastered her with a thorough kiss, then carried her to the bedroom.

''You look so beautiful in that dress,'' he said after setting her on her feet at the foot of the massive bed. ''I almost hate to take it off you.''

For Rue time no longer stretched into the past and the future, forming a tapestry with no beginning and no end. Nothing and no one existed beyond the walls of that room, and their union would be eternal.

She didn't speak, but simply began unfastening the pearl buttons at the front of her gown, her chin at a high, proud angle, her eyes locked with Farley's, challenging him to resist her.

He couldn't; sweet defeat was plain in his face, and the knowledge made her jubilant.

The dress fell over her hips, and Rue hung it over the back of a chair, then kicked off the tight slippers. She kept stripping until all that was left was the wide, pearl choker at her throat.

Farley's throat worked visibly as he swallowed, looking at her as if he'd never seen a naked woman before. When Rue lifted her arms to unclasp the choker, Farley rasped, ''No. Leave it,'' and she obeyed him.

He began taking off his own clothes, starting with his boots, setting them aside with a neatness that made Rue impatient.

She watched with brazen desire as he removed his shirt, unfastened his belt, stepped out of his jeans.

Finally, Farley stood before her wearing only his skin, and he was as incorrigibly, magnificently male as a wild stallion.

He held out a hand to Rue. "Come here, Mrs. Haynes," he said.

It wasn't the time to say she meant to hyphenate both surnames into one; in that bedroom, alone with her mate, no title suited her better than Mrs. Haynes. Rue yearned to give herself to Farley totally.

She went to him and he drew her upward into his kiss, a tall shaman working his treacherous magic. Rue trembled as she felt his hand cup her breast, and she moaned into his mouth as his fingers lightly shaped the nipple.

As Rue's body was pleasured, so was her soul. There was a joy in the depths of her being that overruled all her fears and doubts and furies. She was, while Farley loved her, in step with a dancing universe.

He continued to worship her with words and kisses and caresses while she stood with her head back, lost in glorious surrender. When he knelt to pay the most intimate homage, she gave a soft, throaty sob and burrowed her fingers in his thick hair, holding him close, stroking the back of his head.

Their lovemaking was woven of silver linings plucked from dark clouds, golden ribbons of sunset and lengths of braided rainbow, formed at once of eternity itself and the most fleeting of moments. Farley's and Rue's souls became one spirit and did not exist apart from each other, and this joining sanctified their marriage in a way an official's words could never have done.

There was no room in Rue for any emotions other than soaring happiness and the most intense pleasure, not while she and Farley were still celebrating their wedding. Finally, however, she dropped off to sleep, exhausted, perspiration cooling on her warm flesh.

Farley held Rue for a long time. He'd heard other men talk about love, but he'd never imagined it could be the way it was for him with this woman.

He kissed the top of her head, even though he knew she wasn't awake to feel the touch of his lips, and his eyes stung. Returning to 1892 wasn't really his choice, as he'd implied to Rue earlier, but it was his fate—he knew that in his bones. The letter, penned in his own handwriting, was irrefutable proof of that.

Farley grew restless. If he managed to circumvent destiny, somehow, and stay in the twentieth century with Rue, would the letter stop existing? Would his fate, or anyone's, be altered?

The room was filling with gray twilight, and Farley felt a chill. He eased himself apart from Rue and went into the bathroom, where he took a shower. Then he put on the same clothes he'd worn earlier, because he'd been married in them and because they'd borne a vague hint of Rue's scent. He stood beside the bed for a long time, memorizing the shape of her face, the meter of her breathing, knowing his heart was beating in rhythm with hers, even though he could hear neither.

"I love you," he whispered raggedly. He knew he should wake her, since any parting could be a permanent one, but he turned away. If he looked into her eyes, he would see the reflection of his own despair, and the pain would be beyond bearing.

Downstairs, Farley put on his coat, took the necklace from the safe, left the house and strode toward the barn. Most of the men were in the bunkhouse, since the day's work was over, but he found Charlie puttering around in the barn.

Farley touched the brim of his hat as he passed the man, but he didn't trust himself to speak. He needed to ride, cold as it was, and let the fresh air clear his mind. Maybe then he could figure out some way to change things.

He entered the separate part of the barn where Lobo was stabled, led the big stallion out of his stall and saddled him. The animal nickered and tossed his head, as eager for the open spaces as Farley was, and it was then that a profound, almost mystical bond took shape between the man and the horse.

Farley led Lobo outside, under a full but icy moon, and swung up into the saddle.

"Everything all right, boss?" Charlie inquired. He was leaning against the paddock fence, Soldier at his side, both of them lonely for Wilbur.

Farley looked around him at the land, the kind of land that could soak up a man's blood and sweat and still make him happy. In his mind the ranch would always be Rue's, even if he managed to keep himself from getting shot back in 1892 and found his way home to her. One day, though, the land on either side of Ribbon Creek would belong to their child, if he'd been fortunate enough to sire one, and Farley wanted to guard the place and make it grow almost as much as he wanted to stay with Rue.

He looked toward the big house, adjusted his hat and finally answered the ranch hand's question. In a way. "You'll look out for her if something happens to me?"

"Exactly what is it you're expectin' to happen to you, Mr. Haynes?"

Farley lifted a shoulder. "Maybe nothing." He reined an impatient Lobo toward the south, where the moon spread silver over the snow.

He rode until neither he nor the horse could travel any farther, until he wasn't even sure he was still within the borders of the ranch. He pulled off his gloves and reached into his coat pocket for the thin cigars he loved, but instead of the package, he felt a cold, fragile chain between his fingers.

He'd tried to forget he was carrying the necklace.

"Go on," he muttered hoarsely, glad nobody was there to hear him talking to a trinket. "Do your worst and get it over with!"

Farley held the pendant up, watched the moonlight do a twinkling dance along the length of the chain. He considered flinging it aside into the snow, but he knew now that that would do no good. A force he did not begin to understand had brought the necklace into his life, for good or evil, and that force would not be denied. He had to tie up the loose ends of his old life so that he could live the new one to the fullest.

"Rue." Her name was a ragged, broken whisper on his lips. Once again, his vision blurred, and he wasn't sure whether the necklace was working its bitter magic or if he was finally giving way to the grief dammed up inside him.

Five minutes passed, then ten, while the stallion rested and Farley waited.

When the transition occurred just as the sun came up, it was a subtle one. There was a roaring in Farley's ears, and Lobo fretted and sidestepped beneath him. The power lines and the distant gray ribbon of the highway dissolved into nothingness.

Farley knew without consulting a calendar that he and the horse were back in his own century, and it was a long way back to Pine River from the Big Sky Country.

Still, he dropped the necklace into his pocket and rode back to the place where the house should have been, where Rue should have been drinking coffee in a warm kitchen and Soldier should have been barking. There was nothing except for an abandoned cabin and a single grave marked with a wooden cross.

Farley took off his hat for a moment, his throat thick with misery, his heart full of the kind of loneliness that can drive a person to do stupid, reckless things. He lowered his head for a few moments, struggling with his emotions, and then turned Lobo west, toward his destiny.

Rue stirred in her marriage bed, dreaming. She saw Farley riding alone through a winter dawn, his horse's gleaming onyx coat contrasting starkly with the pristine snow. Knowing she could never catch up with her husband, she struggled to awaken instead.

The instant Rue opened her eyes, however, she knew the nightmare was real and she hadn't escaped it. She and Farley had said their vows and consummated them, and now he was gone.

A frantic sob tore itself from her throat and she covered her face with both hands, trying hard to get a grip on her emotions. Farley was probably downstairs, reading one of his how-to books with one eye and watching his favorite TV program with the other.

She jumped out of bed, found her robe, pulled it on and dashed downstairs.

"Farley?"

The parlor fire was out, and the TV screen was blank.

Rue hurried into the study, but she knew before she reached it that Farley wouldn't be there. His presence had a substance, an impact all its own, and she felt nothing except a rising numbness.

"Oh, God," she prayed, unable to go farther, stumbling through the darkening house to the kitchen.

No fire in the cookstove, no coffee brewing, no Farley reading at the table.

Rue was still in shock, but she could feel her emotions moving underneath the hard layer of control. Soon they would break through and panic would reign.

She continued to entreat heaven as she ran back up the stairs to shower quickly and dress. Her hair was still damp when she followed Farley's boot prints along the path that led to the barn. She nearly collided with Charlie at the gate.

"He's gone," she choked out miserably when the aging man gripped her shoulders to steady her.

"He took Lobo out hours ago," Charlie said, his craggy, ancient face looking worried in the light of the moon. "I'm going to wake the other men so we can saddle up and start lookin' for him soon as the sun's up."

"I'm going with you," Rue insisted, as if anyone had given her cause to argue. "I think we should start right now."

"Mr. Haynes made me swear to look after you," Charlie said stubbornly. "And lettin' you ride out in the dark of night over dangerous ground ain't my idea of keepin' my promise."

Rue's heart stopped for a moment, and she felt her eyes widen. "Farley asked you to take care of me?" The certainty came to her then that they weren't going to find her husband, no matter how long or how thoroughly they searched, but since the realization wasn't one Rue was ready to accept, she pushed it to the back of her mind.

"That's right," Charlie responded with a nod. "Now, you just go back in that house and mind your p's and q's until we can head out. Remember this, too—you won't be a damn bit of good to the man if you've worked yourself up into a tizzy."

Doing fierce battle with a flock of instincts that bade her to do otherwise, Rue obeyed. She walked stiff legged into the house, brewed coffee, drank a cup and then ran to the bathroom to throw up.

That ruled out the idea of breakfast—she would only have been going through the motions anyway—and her knees were too shaky for effective pacing. She took a chair at the kitchen table and laid her head on her arms.

The shrill ringing of the wall phone made her jump a good six inches off her chair, and she snatched the receiver off the hook and yelled, "Hello! Farley?" before she realized he wasn't very likely to call.

Even in the face of logic, however, Rue's disappointment was keen when an operator announced that she had a telegram for Ms. Rue Claridge.

She closed her eyes. "Read it, please," she whispered.

"'A set of sterling is on its way. What do you know about this man? Is he a fortune hunter? Have they found poor Elisabeth yet? Do write. Love, Mummy.'"

"Thanks," Rue muttered when she was certain the operator had finished. Under other circumstances, the message would have embarrassed her, but she was too distraught over Farley to feel anything so mundane.

"Will there be an answer?"

"Not one you could send over a public-communications system," Rue answered with wooden sweetness. Then she hung up the receiver. At least the annoyance of her mother's passionate disinterest had put some starch in her knees and she was able to pace for a while.

Rue even drank another cup of coffee, but that proved to be a foolish choice. She was back in the bathroom, in the midst of violent illness, when she heard the back door open and close.

Quickly, Rue rinsed her mouth and washed her face, but when she hurtled into the kitchen, Farley wasn't there. Charlie was, and he stood, hat in hand, looking worried and authoritative, obviously trying to do and say the things Wilbur would have. The crisis had made him younger and stronger, if only for a little while.

Rue didn't speak. She just put on her winter gear and followed him outside. Her mare, Buttermilk, had been saddled, and all the hands were mounted and ready to ride out.

Lobo had left a trail of hoofprints in the hard snow, and they followed it for several miles, their breaths and those of the horses making white clouds in the bitterly cold air.

The tracks led to the middle of a vast clearing, and there they stopped. Rue, who had been riding in front, alongside Charlie and a younger man called Bill, closed her eyes, absorbing the shattering reality that Farley was gone.

Without her.

Recalling the words of Farley's letter, written from his deathbed, Rue reminded herself that he had left her reluctantly. It was that damn code-of-honor thing, the need to finish all his business before he took up something new.

He was gone, and he surely had the necklace, so there was no way to follow him.

The hands were circled around the pattern of tracks in the snow, exclaiming. Naturally, they'd never seen anything like that before. One even speculated that both Farley and his horse had been abducted by aliens, and Rue wondered disconsolately if that theory was really any stranger than the truth.

Reining Buttermilk toward the house, feeling too broken inside even to cry, Rue let the animal take her home. She was aware of the men riding with her, although she didn't look at them even once.

"I'll get the sheriff out here quick as I can, Mrs. Haynes," said one. "Don't you worry. We'll find your bridegroom."

Tears glittered in Rue's eyes, but she kept her chin high.

"They won't find him," she managed to say. "Nobody could find him."

"You don't believe that crackpot idea of Buster's about the spaceship and the little green men, do you?" Bill asked.

Rue meant to laugh, but a sob came out inside. "Right now," she said when she could speak, "I don't know what I believe, but I'm sure of one thing—wherever Farley is, that's where I want to be."

The sheriff came, and he called in the state police. They summoned the FBI, and all the ruckus attracted reporters from the tabloids. A week passed, and no trace of Farley or the horse was found, and in every supermarket check-out line in the country, the front page of the *National Scoop* screamed, UFO SNATCHES MAN AND STALLION, STATE OF MONTANA ON RED ALERT.

If Rue hadn't been in mourning, she would have thought it was all a wonderful joke.

It took Farley a full week, riding hard, to reach Pine River. Having no money and no gun, he'd lived on what he could scavenge, which wasn't much, considering there was snow on the ground. Lobo, once fat from his winter confinement in the stables at Ribbon Creek, was now sleeker and leaner, the kind of horse a man could depend on.

Folks shouted from the sidewalks and waved from the windows as Farley rode through the center of town, but he not only didn't stop to talk, he didn't even acknowledge them. His whole being was focused on a single objective: getting back to Rue.

As he came abreast of Jon Fortner's office, Farley saw his friend waiting by the hitching rail out front, his arms folded, his gaze steady.

"That's a fine-looking horse, Farley," the doctor said.

The marshal drew back on the reins, dismounted and tethered the stallion to the rail. He needed to talk with Jon, but he feared to start because his emotions were so raw and sore and so close to the surface.

Jonathan came down the steps and laid a reassuring hand to Farley's shoulder. "I've been there, too, remember?" he said, keeping his voice low so the gawking townspeople wouldn't hear. "Come on inside, and I'll pour you a cup of my special medicinal coffee."

For the first time in more than a week, Farley smiled, though he knew the effort was probably somewhat on the puny side. "How about just giving me a cup of medicine with a little coffee in it?"

* * *

Rue was lying in bed one night, a month after Farley's dramatic disappearance, when the memory invaded her mind, three-dimensional and in full color.

She saw herself in Pine River, at the churchyard, talking with a dark-haired young man. Michael Blake, that was his name, and he'd said Elisabeth and Jonathan Fortner had been his great-great-grandparents.

Now her heart was pounding like some primitive engine, and the fog of pain and confusion was finally lifting. She heard the young man say cordially, *My grandmother would really like to meet you, since you're a shirttail relation and everything. She lives with my mom and dad in Seattle. Why don't you give her a call sometime?*

Rue threw back the covers and leapt out of bed. Michael had written a name and telephone number on a page from a pocket-size notebook. She squeezed her eyes shut. Where had she put that piece of paper?

At the same time she was pulling on clothes, Rue was ransacking her memory. Whenever someone handed her a business card or anything like that, she always slipped it into her pocket, and she'd been wearing a Windbreaker jacket that day....

Her stomach clenched into a painful knot as she struggled to pursue the recollection further. It was like trying to chase a rabbit through a blackberry thicket, but Rue followed tenaciously, because finding Farley and saving him from the bank robber's bullet was so critically important to her.

''My purse!'' she yelled, flipping on the overhead lights. She snatched her bag from the bureau top and upended it over the bed, sending pennies and gum wrappers, credit-card receipts and scruffy tissue all over. After a feverish search, however, she unzipped the change pocket and found the paper folded inside.

On it, Michael had written a name, Mrs. Elisabeth R. Blake, and a telephone number.

Rue reached for the bedside telephone, then caught sight of

the alarm clock and realized it was four o'clock in the morning, and just three in Seattle.

"Hell," she muttered, wondering how she could contain herself until a decent hour. Maybe Mrs. Blake was one of those old ladies who have trouble sleeping, and she was sitting up, working a crossword puzzle or watching one of the cable channels.

Rue's speculations changed nothing. Michael had said his grandmother lived with his parents, and *they* were probably sleeping, with no clue of what a mystery their existence really was.

She went downstairs and made herself a cup of tea, since she could no longer tolerate coffee, a drink she'd once loved. She felt dizzy sometimes, too, and she was cranky as a bear recovering from a root canal, but she attributed these symptoms to the stress she'd been under for nearly a month. Pregnancy was both too wonderful and too terrible a prospect to consider.

Soldier, who had been sleeping on the hooked rug in front of the cookstove, as usual, traipsed over to give Rue a friendly lick on the forearm. Idly, she patted his head and went right on sipping her tea.

Perhaps this delay was a good thing. Rue didn't have any idea what to say to Mrs. Blake once she reached her, but she knew the woman was her only link with Elisabeth and Farley, now that the necklace was gone.

Slowly, the icy gray light grew brighter at the windows. Rue fed Soldier, let him out and wandered back to the study.

The photographs taken at the wedding were there, tucked into a place of honor in a drawer of her grandfather's cherry-wood desk. Although it always did her injury to look at them, Rue could no more have ignored those pictures than she could have given up breathing or stilled the meter of her heartbeat.

She flipped through them, smiling even as tears pricked her eyes. Farley with coconut frosting all over his mouth. Herself wearing the gauzy dress from the attic. The bride and groom kissing right after the justice of the peace had pronounced them man and wife....

Rue carefully returned the photos to their envelope, then put on her coat and boots and made her way to the woodshed. She brought back an armload of pitchy pine logs, feeling better because of the effort of wielding the ax.

She made a fire and watched an early-morning news show in the study. When eight o'clock came around, Rue simply could not wait any longer. She sat down at the desk, pulled the telephone close and carefully punched out the number Michael had given her that day in the graveyard.

There were a few vague thumps on the line, then a long ring, then another.

"Blake residence," a pleasant male voice answered.

"My name is Rue Claridge-Haynes," Rue blurted. "I'd like to speak with Mrs. Blake—the senior Mrs. Blake—about some genealogy research I've been doing."

"That would be my mother," the man said. "If you'll wait just a moment...." There was a thumping sound as he laid the receiver down, and Rue chewed a fingernail while she waited.

After what seemed like a long time, though it was probably not more than a minute or two, a woman's voice came on the line, almost drowned out by the racket of an extension being hung up.

"Rue Claridge?"

Rue shoved a hand through her hair. "Yes. Mrs. Blake, I'm calling about—"

"I know what you're calling about," the old lady interrupted, crisply but not unkindly. "I've been waiting all my life for this moment."

"I beg your pardon?"

"My grandmother, Elisabeth Fortner, left something for you under the flyleaf of her Bible."

Rue's heart was hammering. This, she realized, was what she had been subconsciously hoping for. Elisabeth had found a way to reach across a hundred years, to send word about herself or Farley.

"Miss Claridge? Are you there?"

"My name is Claridge-Haynes now," Rue said. It sounded

totally inane, she knew, but she was in shock. "I'm married."
She paused, cleared her throat. "Mrs. Blake, what did my
cous—your grandmother leave for me?"

"It's an envelope," Bethie's descendant answered. "A letter, I suppose. I didn't look because Grandmother's instructions said I mustn't. No one but you is to open the packet,
and I cannot send it through the mail or by messenger. The
note on the front specifically says that you will contact me
when the time is right and that I must insist on your coming
for it in person."

Rue was practically dizzy with excitement and suspense.
"I'm in Montana, Mrs. Blake," Rue said. "But I'll be there
as soon as I can."

Mrs. Blake gave Rue an address and told her to call the
moment she arrived in Seattle, no matter what time it was.
"I'll be waiting by the phone," she finished.

Rue immediately called the nearest airport, but there were
no planes available, charter or otherwise, because of the
weather. Rue accepted that disappointment. She told Wilbur,
who was recuperating at the ranch house under the care of a
nurse, that she was leaving and he was boss until further notice, then threw her suitcases into the back of the Land Rover
and left.

The storm started out as a light, picturesque skiff of snow,
but by the time Rue reached Spokane, it had reached blizzard
proportions. She stopped there and forced down a hearty dinner while a man at a service station across the street put chains
on her rear tires.

"You shouldn't drive in this, ma'am," he said, when Rue
returned from the restaurant and was settling up the bill. "It's
a long way to Seattle, and you've gotta go over the mountains.
Snoqualmie Pass is probably closed anyway...."

Rue smiled, nodded, got behind the wheel and went right
on.

Hours later, she reached the high mountain pass that connected the eastern and western parts of Washington state. Sure
enough, traffic was backed up for miles, but the road was
closed only to people who didn't have chains on their tires.

On the other side of the mountain range, there was hardly any snow, and a warm, drizzling rain was washing that away.

Just over an hour after that, Rue pulled into the parking lot of a convenience store in the suburbs of Seattle. She called Mrs. Blake, who was awake and waiting, as promised.

After washing her face, combing her hair and brushing her teeth in the rest room, Rue bought a tall cup of hot chocolate and went on.

She found the Blake house with relative ease, but even though her exhausted state made her feel slightly bewitched, Rue wouldn't let herself attribute the fact to anything mystical. She had always had a good sense of direction.

A white-haired old woman with a sweet smile and soft blue eyes came to the door only an instant after Rue rang the bell.

"Rue," she said, and something in the very warp and woof of the woman reminded Rue of Elisabeth and filled her with an aching sense of nostalgia. Bethie's *granddaughter*—how impossible that seemed. "Come in."

"I hope I haven't awakened anyone...."

"Mercy, no," Mrs. Blake said, linking her thin, age-spotted arm with Rue's and ushering her into a large, tastefully decorated room to the left. "Phillip, my son, is a surgeon, and he's been up and gone for hours. Nadine, my daughter-in-law, is at the health club, swimming, and, of course, Michael lives in one of the dorms at the university now. I pretty much have the place to myself, except for the maid. Won't you sit down?"

Even though she felt sure she would faint any moment, Rue was so tired, she was almost painfully tense. She sat in a graceful Queen Anne chair, upholstered in a pretty blue-and-white floral pattern, and tried to keep calm.

"Would you care for some coffee?" Mrs. Blake inquired, taking a chair facing Rue's and gesturing gracefully toward the silver service on the cocktail table.

Rue shook her head. "No, thank you," she said, and then bit down hard on her lower lip to keep from demanding the envelope Elisabeth had left for her.

"Well, then, there's no sense in dragging this out, even if

it is the biggest thing to happen around here since Nadine's friend Phyllis crawled out on the roof during last year's Christmas party and made a world-class fool of herself. She sang twenty-two different show tunes before the fire department got her down, you know, and every note was off key.''

Rue smiled and nodded and tapped the arm of the chair with her fingertips.

Mrs. Blake flushed slightly. ''I'm sorry, I do get to running on.'' She pulled a battered blue vellum envelope from her bag, which was resting on the marble-topped table beside her chair, and held it out to Rue.

Rue forced herself not to snatch it out of Mrs. Blake's fingers. She must have looked calm on the outside, but inside, Rue was suffering an agony of hope. If this was nothing more than a cosmic postcard—''How are you? I am fine. Wish you were here''—the disappointment would be beyond tolerance.

Rue made herself read the faded but familiar lettering on the front of the envelope, and tears filled her eyes. Elisabeth's cryptic instructions were all there, just as Mrs. Blake had relayed them.

Finally, like a child opening a fascinating, fragile present found under the Christmas tree, Rue broke the old wax seal and pulled a single page from inside the envelope.

The necklace did not tumble to her lap, as Rue had hoped it would, but she'd mourn that oversight later. Now, she would read words that had waited a hundred years for her attention.

My Dearest Rue,

I know you probably expected to find the necklace folded inside this letter, so that you could return here to find Mr. Haynes, but, of course, once you think about it, you'll realize that I couldn't take a chance like that. You and I know only too well what magic Aunt Verity's pendant is capable of.

If you *must* find it, I can only tell you to remember that rainy afternoon when we were thirteen and we decided to make a time capsule.

I hate writing this part, knowing what an awful impact

it's going to have, but you married Farley, and I think you have a right to the truth, so you can get on with your life. Rue, Farley was shot ten days ago while stopping a robbery, and last night he died of his wounds.

Rue stopped there, fighting to hold on to consciousness while the gracious room swayed around her, then forced herself to go on reading.

"There are no words I can say to console you, except that I know Farley loved you desperately, and that his greatest wish was to return to you.

Rue, I told you where to find the necklace because I know I don't have the right to withhold a choice that rightfully belongs to you, but I beg you not to try to return. The power of that pendant is unpredictable, we know that if hardly anything else, and it's dangerous. Anything could happen.

I love you, Cousin, with my whole heart, and I'm depending on you to do your grieving, then pull yourself together and go on.

Forever, and with a new understanding of the word,

Beth

When Rue let the letter crumple to her lap, Mrs. Blake was ready with a glass of cool water.

"Here, dear, drink this. You look as waxen as a ghost."

Rue might have smiled under other circumstances. As it was, she only reached out a trembling hand for the glass and drank with desperate thirst. Once she felt a little steadier, she thanked Mrs. Blake, carefully folded Bethie's letter and tucked it into her purse.

"I can't share it," she confessed softly. "I hope you understand."

Mrs. Blake's smile was reminiscent of Elisabeth's. "I won't say I'm not curious, dear," she replied, "but I understand. There are mysteries aplenty in this life, and I've learned to accept the fact."

Rue kissed the old lady's cheek lightly. "Thank you again, Mrs. Blake. And goodbye."

Barely an hour later, Rue was back in Pine River, her eyes puffy and sore. Alone in the Land Rover, insulated from a world that couldn't have comprehended her pain, Rue had screamed in rage and grief over her husband's unfair death. Tears had left acid trails on her cheeks, and her throat was so constricted, she could barely breathe.

Instead of heading for Aunt Verity's house, Rue stopped at the churchyard. She found Farley's grave, under the old oak tree as the clerk in the church office had told her. If there had ever been a stone or a wooden marker, no trace remained.

Rue was mourning a man who'd been dead a century, and there wasn't even a monument to honor his memory.

The cemetery was cold on that grim winter day, and Rue's strength was almost gone. She turned—she would visit Elisabeth's and Aunt Verity's graves some other day—and made her way back to the muddy Land Rover.

Moving like a person in a voodoo documentary, Rue bought soup and soap and tea and other supplies at Pine River's state-of-the-art supermarket, then drove to the house where all her adventures had begun.

The mail was knee-deep in front of the slot in the door, and there were so many messages on the answering machine that the tape had run out. Rue didn't play them back. She just put away her groceries, made a bowl of tomato soup and ate without actually tasting a single spoonful.

After rinsing the bowl, she went upstairs, put fresh sheets on one of the beds, took a shower and collapsed. She slept for fourteen hours straight, got up and made herself another bowl of soup, then went back to sleep for another seven.

When she awakened, rested at last, but still numb with sorrow, Rue took Elisabeth's earlier letters from their hiding place in the rolltop desk in the parlor and read them again.

Her heart began to thump. Time did not necessarily run parallel between then and now, she remembered, with growing excitement. If she found a way back—and the whereabouts of the necklace was teasing the edges of her consciousness even then—she would probably arrive after Farley's shooting. But she could also get there before it happened.

Maybe she could intercede.

She ran to find her purse—she'd discarded it on the floor of the downstairs hallway when she first returned—pulled out the letter Mrs. Blake had kept for her and scanned it.

Her gaze snagged on one particular sentence. ''...I can only tell you to remember that rainy afternoon when we were thirteen and we decided to make a time capsule.''

Rue yelped in frustration and began to pace. Her memory wasn't good when it came to things like that, though she could reel off statistics and stock prices and phone numbers until her voice gave out.

''Time capsule, time capsule, time capsule.'' She repeated the words like a litany, hoping they would trigger some rusty catch deep down in her mind.

Suddenly, gloriously, the memory was there.

Rain on a leaky roof. The smell of dam dust and moldy hay. Two adolescent girls, herself and Elisabeth, in the barn loft, talking about the distant future. They'd wanted posterity to know about their lives, so they'd swiped a lidded plastic bowl from Aunt Verity's kitchen and put in things they considered representative of Planet Earth in the 1970s. Lip gloss. Pictures of their favorite rock group, carefully snipped from fan magazines. A candy bar with peanuts and caramel....

Rue hurried through the house and outside, crossing the dead winter grass in long strides. The barn was old and flimsy and should have been torn down years before, but safety was the last thing on Rue's mind as she went inside.

She did test the ladder leading up to the loft, but only in a quick and cursory way. The boards under her feet swayed a little when she reached the top, but that didn't stop her, either. She and Elisabeth had put their time capsule into the creaky framework where the floor and wall met with great ceremony.

''X marks the spot,'' she said breathlessly when she found the hiding place and knelt to wrench back a board. The whole loft seemed to shimmy at the intrusion, but again Rue was undaunted.

Behind the filthy, weathered board was a dirty plastic container riddled with the tooth marks of some creature that could probably qualify for top billing in a horror movie. Rue tossed the bowl aside without lifting the lid to look inside and peered into the crevice behind it.

At first, she could see nothing but darkness, dirt and spider webs, but after a few moments her vision seemed to sharpen. Well behind the place where her and Elisabeth's treasures had been hidden, a solid-looking shadow lurked in the gloom.

Rue grimaced, reached deep into the unknown and closed her hand around the object. Having found what she sought, she drew back so fast that a splinter or the tip of a nail made a long, shallow gash in her arm.

She paid no attention to the wound; all she could see was the round, rusted tin she held. Once it had held salve, and the distinct possibility that it was nothing more than a stray piece of trash raised panic into Rue's throat like bile.

"Please," she whispered, and it was at once the most sincere and the most succinct prayer she had ever said.

It was hard, and she broke a couple of fingernails, but Rue finally managed to pry off the lid of the tin. Inside, dusty and tarnished and as full of mystery as ever, lay the necklace.

Rue's eyes filled with tears of relief, and she clutched the pendant to her chest. Now, if only the magic would work again.

Nothing happened, so Rue carefully tucked the necklace into the pocket of her jacket. Only then did she notice that the bit of paper lining the salve tin had writing on it.

Carefully, Rue lifted it to the thin light coming in through one of the wide cracks in the barn wall. "I knew you wouldn't listen!" Elisabeth had scrawled.

Rue smiled, dried her eyes with the back of one hand and climbed cautiously down the ladder again.

Inside the house, she laid the necklace on the drainboard beside the kitchen sink and washed it with cotton balls, mild soap and water. When the pendant was clean, she patted it dry with a soft paper towel, draped the chain around her neck and carefully closed the clasp.

She shut her eyes, gripped the edge of the counter and waited. Hoped.

At first, nothing happened, but then a humming sound filled Rue's ears, rising steadily in pitch. The floor buckled and rolled under her feet, and it seemed that she could feel the spin of the earth itself.

Someone screamed and something crashed to the floor.

Rue opened her eyes to see Bethie's housekeeper standing there, aghast and staring, a shattered crockery bowl at her feet. Its contents covered the length of the woman's calico skirts.

"Ellen, for heaven's sake…" a familiar voice complained, and then Elisabeth appeared in the doorway leading to the main parlor. When she saw her cousin, her blue-green eyes widened and her face lit up with a dazzling smile. "Rue!"

"She just came out of nowhere, missus," Ellen blathered. "I'm telling you, I don't know about the goings-on in this house. I just don't know. And now I've got myself a sick headache."

"You'd better go and lie down," Elisabeth told her gently, but she didn't look at the housekeeper again. She gave Rue a gentle hug.

"Is he dead?" Rue whispered, unable to bear the agony of wondering for another moment.

"Who?" Bethie asked, and her look of puzzlement raised Rue's spirits considerably.

"Farley. Farley Haynes, the marshal." For the first time, the thought occurred to Rue that she might have come back not only before her husband's death, but before he knew her.

"Well, he hasn't been very happy about being separated from you," Elisabeth said with a fond smile, "but people don't usually die of a broken heart. They just *wish* they could."

Farley was alive, and he would know her. Rue's knees literally went slack with relief, and she might have collapsed if Elisabeth hadn't steadied her.

"I've got to go to him right now," she said after a few deep breaths.

"But you're shaken—you need to sit down and have a cup of tea—"

"I need to find my husband!" Rue said. "Is there a horse I can borrow?"

Elisabeth offered no further argument; she knew her cousin too well. "There's a chestnut mare in the barn. Her name is Maisie, and she prefers to be ridden bareback."

Rue hugged her cousin, bade her a good life with Jonathan and raced out the back door, nearly tripping because the steps were different from the ones she was used to. The barn that had been a teetering disaster the last time she entered it was sturdy now, and well maintained.

Quickly, Rue bridled the small mare and swung up onto its back. A woman in pants, riding astride no less, was going to come as yet another shock to the fine people of Pine River, but that could not be helped. The necklace had slipped beneath her shirt; it felt warm against her collarbone, and she was filled with a new and terrifying sense of urgency.

She'd gotten back in time, but just barely. There wasn't a second to lose.

Sure enough, Rue heard the shots just as she and Maisie hit the foot of the town's main street. Rue spurred the animal through the uproar and confusion—everybody was trying to take cover—weaving her way around wagons and buggies and other horses.

Undaunted, Rue rode hell-bent for the bank. If she had to, she would catch that outlaw's bullet herself before she let it strike Farley.

Two men ran out of the bank, their faces, except for their eyes and foreheads, covered by dirty bandannas. It was just like a scene in a John Wayne movie, except that here the bullets were real.

Rue looked frantically for Farley, which was why she was caught completely unprepared when an arm as hard as iron wrenched her off the mare's back and onto another horse. After that, everything was a dizzying blur.

Either she was dreaming, or she was sitting sidesaddle behind Farley, clutching his canvas duster with both hands. The magnificent animal carrying them both was Lobo. She felt the swift, skilled movement of the marshal's arm as he drew his .45. Then she heard two shots in rapid succession and felt the recoil in the muscles between Farley's shoulder blades, where her cheek rested. The air seemed thick with the smells of horse manure and burned powder, and Rue figured if she survived this, the first thing she was going to do was vomit.

In that moment, of all moments, she realized she was definitely pregnant.

A brief silence followed. Rue clung to Farley, soaking in the hard strength of his body in front of her. He was alive, and so was she.

He turned his head to look back at her, and although a muscle in his jaw jumped in irritation, Rue could see joy in his eyes. "That was a damn fool thing to do," he bit out. "You could have been killed."

The necklace was searing Rue's skin. She locked her hands together in front of his stomach, determined that even a brand new Big Bang wouldn't blast her loose. "I love you, too, Farley Haynes," she said.

The magic was beginning again; the air was filled with a vibrant silence so noisy that Rue could hear nothing besides her own voice and Farley's heartbeat. She threw back her head and shouted for joy, at the same time tearing the necklace from her throat and flinging it away.

They might land in heaven or in hell. Either way, the die was cast.

"Tarnation," Farley marveled when the spiritual storm subsided. The marshal, Rue and Lobo were square in the middle of the deserted parking lot at Pine River High School. It was twilight, and the wind was chilly, but to Rue, the sky had never looked brighter nor had the air felt warmer.

Farley turned, his beautiful teeth showing in a broad grin. "Well, Mrs. Haynes," he asked, just before he kissed her, "what do we do now?"

It was a long moment before Rue caught her breath. "That's easy, Mr. Haynes," she replied. "We ride off into the sunset."

INNISFIL PUBLIC LIBRARY

INNISFIL PUBLIC LIBRARY